"ST...
A...

Harding unclipped his binoculars and lifted them to his eyes. The black silhouette of the ship in the powerful lenses was visible as a dark smear on the horizonless ocean.

Harding found himself chewing his lower lip, wondering how long he dared wait before firing, how efficient the escorts' radar, how good the target's lookouts.

Harding knew that he had to be a lot closer than he was to be certain of a kill with so little data and such poor visibility . . .

H.M.S. TRIGGER

A thrilling novel of war—and love . . .

H.M.S.
TRIGGER

Antony Melville-Ross

BALLANTINE BOOKS • NEW YORK

Hardcover edition published as *Trigger* in Great Britain
Copyright © 1982 by Antony Melville-Ross

ISBN: 0-345-30163-3

This edition published by arrangement with William Collins
Sons & Co. Ltd.

Manufactured in the United States of America

First Ballantine Books Edition: November 1982

For my step-daughter Sally with love

CHAPTER I

ELLESTON STOOD VERY STILL, WATCHING THE crouching man. It was important to stay still because he was afraid. He didn't want him or anybody else to know that and if he moved he was sure they would. The man's right eye, the only one he could see, shone with a little circle of brilliant white light where the pupil should have been, giving him a supernatural appearance. Like an artist's impression of the devil, Elleston thought.

It was hot and rivulets of sweat ran down the man's bare back, darkening the waistband of his khaki shorts. Someone standing behind him reached over his shoulder and wiped his forehead with a cloth as if he were assisting a surgeon at an operation.

"Thanks," the man said, paused, then, as if it had been an afterthought, added, "Open fire." He had spoken quietly, almost as a mother would when persuading a small child to do something it wasn't interested in. Not like the devil.

"Open fire, sir," Elleston replied and was pleased with the languid sound of his voice. Mentally he replayed it to himself. Nothing happened. Nobody moved. Nobody did anything.

Two more seconds passed before the crouching figure straightened. He was a pleasant-faced man with rather pale blue eyes, indeterminate brown hair, and a shy disposition who might have been a recently qualified doctor, a young company executive, or something in the Foreign Office. In fact he was Lieutenant Peter Harding in command of His Majesty's submarine *Trigger*.

Clicking the handles of the periscope into a vertical position, he watched it sink down into its well with a subdued hiss of hydraulic power.

"Sixty feet," he said.

The first lieutenant's murmured acknowledgment came to him and he glanced round the control room. It seemed very dark to him after the brightness of the Mediterranean day above his head. Purposely he avoided looking at Elleston standing under the gun tower hatch. From his blasé tone it was clear to him that Elleston was nervous. That was natural enough. This was his first time and he'd stay nervous for all the other times to come if he had any sense. But how nervous? The question would be answered very soon now and, meanwhile, staring at the boy could only make things worse.

"Sixty feet, sir."

"Very well. Gun action. Surface."

"Blow main ballast. Full ahead..." The rest of the first lieutenant's words were lost in the roar of high pressure air blasting seawater from the tanks. It didn't matter. Everybody knew what to do.

For a moment the submarine hung where she was, the hydroplanes counteracting the increased buoyancy, then buoyancy began to win. Harding watched the planes move to the full rise position and felt the deck press against the soles of his sandals like an elevator. He turned toward the conning tower ladder and waited, listening to the first lieutenant shouting the depths, looking at the pair of hairy legs, the only visible part of Corporal Ackroyd, second Royal Marine commando, Special Boat Section.

"Forty-five feet—forty—thirty-five..."

They would open the hatches, both the conning tower and the gun tower at twenty feet with the submarine still underwater, and he pictured the momentary disorientation the men doing it would experience. The small maelstrom set up by water trying to get in and air, slightly above atmospheric pressure, trying to get out was always confusing. A little cascade of water and his eardrums popping. There they went and he followed Corporal Ackroyd up the ladder, with the Oerlikon gunner and his loader ahead of them.

Near the top of the tower the order "Shoot!" reached his

ears, followed immediately by the heavy slam of the four-inch gun. Good. Elleston was doing his stuff, not waiting for his captain, which was why he had been authorized to open fire minutes earlier.

The transition from the calm and silence of periscope depth to the bedlam of a surface engagement never ceased to surprise Harding. No matter how often he experienced it, the wind, the seasounds, the shattering explosions of propellant charges, deprived him briefly of the ability to think. Familiarity had lessened that short period of time, but the surprise was always there. Pulling himself through the upper hatch, he stepped around the forward periscope standard to the front of the bridge.

The coastal tanker was five degrees on their port bow, nearly stern on to them and only two hundred yards away. Already there were three jagged holes in the superstructure where four-inch-caliber high-explosive shells had struck home. Smoke was coming from one of them. At such short range with the sea almost smooth it was virtually impossible to miss and that had been Harding's strategy. Surprise and point-blank fire.

He looked down at the small group of near-naked men working the gun and at the blond head of his new gunnery officer standing behind them.

"Fire into the hull, Elleston," he said.

"Aye aye, sir. Steady there, Peters. Point of aim the hull."

Figures appeared on the afterdeck of the tanker, running toward the big gun mounted there.

Harding looked at the burly man beside him watching the German ship over the sights of the gas-operated Vickers machine gun he had carried up the ladder in one hand and fixed to its mounting.

"Take care of those men please, Corporal Ackroyd."

"Yessir."

The Vickers fired in a short, ripping burst, like the tearing of corrugated paper, and two of the running men fell. The rest turned and ran for cover.

A plaintive shout from behind Harding. "Oerlikon won't bear, sir."

"All right, Chivers. You can't have them all."

The voice pipe. "Radar bridge?"

"Bridge."

"Aircraft bearing 340, fifteen thousand yards, closing."

"Thank you," Harding said. Then to the port lookout, "Aircraft in your sector, Smith. Relative bearing about Red 145. Let me know when you see it." He didn't take his eyes from the enemy ship. It was turning slowly to starboard exposing its side to the long barrel of the four-inch. Eleven rounds fired if he remembered correctly. No misses as far as he could tell. Another slamming report. Another hit.

He ordered an alteration in course to stay astern of the tanker and prevent them using the two heavy guns mounted forward and immediately Able Seaman Chivers added to the uproar with the raving of his twenty-millimeter Oerlikon cannon.

More men running, not to the guns, not even to the lifeboats, but straight to the side and over. For a moment he watched, puzzled. Some dived, most jumped feetfirst, all began to swim frantically away from the ship. Then he understood and raised his voice for the first time.

"Cease fire! Clear the gundeck! Clear the bridge!"

Only vaguely aware of figures disappearing one after the other down through the two hatches, but hearing distinctly a vicious obscenity as someone trod on someone else's fingers, he saw the tanker open slowly like some exotic flower, pale flame blossoming skyward, smokeless flame. A heavy thump, felt as much as heard, then the heat reached him.

Into the voice pipe, "Dive, dive, dive," he said and the klaxon snarled twice. Plumes of spray soaring up from the opened vents in the ballast tanks, drifting down, cooling him. The bow dipping, its outline still visible under the clear water. The gun tower hatch thudding shut. The sea rising toward him, swirling around the four-inch gun. A wall of pretty, pale flame running, running, swallowing the desperate swimmers with their silently screaming mouths, coming closer, hiding the dying tanker from his sight.

Harding saw the plane for an instant as he lowered himself into the conning tower. It was about three miles away and pointing straight toward him. He pulled the hatch shut and clipped it in place, then dropped to the control room, breaking his rate of descent with practiced snatches at occasional rungs of the vertical brass ladder.

"One hundred and twenty feet. Shut off for depth charging.

Up periscope. Steer 180." A glance at his watch told him that *Trigger* had been on the surface for ninety-five seconds.

At first he thought that the periscope lens had already dipped underwater, then realized it was surrounded by fire.

"Down periscope."

A giant sledgehammer blow on the hull shook the submarine as it was passing seventy feet. It was followed by a prolonged reverberation. Then a second, followed again by its rumbling aftermath. A light shower of cork insulation fell from above their heads and two light bulbs went out.

Harding looked at the first lieutenant and smiled.

"That's his lot, Number One. They carry four bombs or two depth charges. I think those must have been depth charges."

The first lieutenant returned his smile. "I got the same impression myself, sir."

"All right. You can go to patrol routine now. Stay at a hundred and twenty feet for fifteen minutes, then go back to periscope depth."

The crew moved from their action stations to their patrol positions, or their messes. When the traffic had ceased, Harding walked to the wardroom. Elleston was there, talking excitedly to the engineer officer.

"That was well done, Guns," he said.

It was the first time Elleston had been accorded his unofficial title and he grinned.

"Sir."

"But don't forget that next time they may be firing back at you. It was thanks to Corporal Ackroyd that they didn't just now."

"Aye aye, sir."

The captain moved away, then looked back.

"Oh, there was one thing."

"Yes, sir?"

"I'd be a little wary of saying things like 'steady' to your gun layer when it isn't necessary. That was Leading Seaman Peters' ninth sinking and I haven't seen him unsteady yet."

When Harding had gone, Elleston looked at the engineer officer.

"The Old Man doesn't miss much, does he, Chief?"

"Not that I've noticed."

"I think I was really saying 'Steady Elleston.' Black mark for me."

"Yes, well don't start chewing on it," the engineer officer said. "All you got was a bit of advice and it'll probably be a long time before you hear him tell anybody something was well done, so you've got nothing to complain about."

In his tiny cabin Harding pulled down the wooden cover over the washbasin, converting it to a desk. From a drawer he took the notes on which his patrol report would be based and began to write.

"The arrival of the enemy tanker of which you forewarned me by signal (see previous para) occurred on schedule. She was intercepted and sunk by gunfire between Giglio Island and S. Stefano. The cargo appears to have been high-octane aircraft fuel. There were no survivors. The fact that this modern ship with its valuable cargo should have been permitted to proceed unescorted is yet another indication of the enemy's apparent inability to replace his heavy losses of antisubmarine vessels. . . ."

The word "vessels" was almost illegible. He crossed it out and wrote it again, but it wandered up into the line above. Carefully, as though it were something very delicate, he put his pencil down, got to his feet, and eased himself into the bunk beside him. Although he was not a particularly tall man, his head rested against one end and the soles of his sandals the other.

A few seconds later the shakes started.

He didn't fight them. Experience had taught him that it didn't help to do that. It was much better to let them have their way with him provided he was alone. They left him feeling drained, but calm again. The tiredness didn't count. It had been with him for a long time now, he had learned to live with it and it was a small price to pay for steady nerves during the intervals between the spasms.

Whether he was afraid for himself, for the seventy-seven men in his charge, of being seen to be afraid, or was simply physically and mentally exhausted he was unsure. It seemed logical to assume that it was a combination of those factors so, logically, he assumed it and it didn't help him at all. As he often did, he tried to pinpoint the moment when the flaw had first become apparent to him and to help in the search he let his mind drift back to the beginning of it all.

The summer sun sparkling on the skittish little waves of Scapa Flow and reflecting like a million diamonds from the burnished metal fittings of the majestically ponderous battleships and carriers and the sleek cruisers with their rakish lines. But the diamonds were vanishing, flicking out of time and space, as a thousand hands wielding a thousand brushes gray with paint obliterated a thousand hours of polishing.

The island of Flotta, undisturbed save for the gentle grazing of half a hundred sheep, lay to port. To starboard the Battle Fleet. Ahead, the big modern cruiser flying an admiral's flag had her anchor clear of the surface, water jetting from the hawse pipe washing it clear of mud. From the forecastle of his own ship the steady clank-clank-clank of the anchor cable coming in.

From the flagship's bridge the staccato message of a signal lamp had been startlingly blue-white in the sunshine.

"Sublieutenant Harding?"

"Sir?"

"Did you read that?"

"Yes, sir. From Flag to ships in company—'Cry havoc.'"

The tall man with the four gold rings on his sleeves had nodded, then looked at him over his shoulder.

"Can you complete the quotation, laddie?"

"Yes, sir. 'And let slip the dogs of war.' Henry the Fifth before Harfleur."

The captain had smiled and said, "There's a good lesson for you in not volunteering unasked-for information. Right author, wrong play. It was Julius Caesar before the senate." The smile had disappeared. "My compliments to the commander and I'd be obliged if he will spare me a moment of his time."

Ten minutes later an order had gone to every department—"Complete fusing of all shells, fit torpedo warheads, prepare for war." Harding had entered it in the ship's log under the date August 31, 1939.

Three days had gone by and with the five cruisers steaming in line ahead, pitching and rolling in a heavy Atlantic swell off the east coast of Iceland, a signal had been received before

Prime Minister Chamberlain spoke to the world. A young seaman, complacent in his foreknowledge, had entered the gun
room, his cap under his left arm, a copy of the signal in his
right hand. He had handed the flimsy sheet of paper to the
nearest midshipman who had passed it to Harding, and the rest
had gathered around to read what was written on it. It said
simply, "Total Germany."

The trembling was easing and Harding levered himself into
a sitting position on his bunk, forearms resting on his knees.
For the moment the need to analyze had gone, but his mind
completed the memory for him with the cheers, his own among
them, those two words had produced. There had been no fear
then, only elation, but that had been a long time ago. Now,
as a full lieutenant, he was as much the "Old Man" as the four-
striper on the cruiser's bridge had been.

The thought reminded him that his twenty-fifth birthday had
been some time during the past week.

The bicycle cart lay half on its side, one wheel in a ditch.
Giovanni Villari lay in the ditch near it. He was snoring gently,
apparently oblivious to the hot sun on his tanned face, seemingly unaware of the two German soldiers looking down at
him.

"It's the fish seller," one of them said. "You'll often find
him like this. When he's drunk he sells fish to the people who
can't get into the city and fornicates with any woman who'll
have him. When he's very drunk he falls off this machine of
his and sleeps where he lies."

The other grunted. "Fornicates, eh? That has a fine old-
fashioned ring to it. What does he do when he's sober?"

"He never is. He spends a lot of his time and all his earnings
in the dockside bars. How he manages to put so much away
and still satisfy all his women I shall never know."

In his ditch Villari thought gloomily that he didn't know
either and that whatever the answer might be it couldn't be
much longer before it ceased to apply. He was very tired and
it was a long time since the alcohol he had first employed as
additional cover had become a necessity to him. An over-
powering necessity. He wished the two krauts would go away,
not so much that he was afraid of them but because he was in

danger of falling asleep genuinely, and before they had come into sight the radio in the false bottom of his cart had been providing him with information it was important he should pass on to the British quickly.

"Why don't they put him to work properly?" the second soldier asked.

"Oh, that was tried, but it was no good. Shot in the leg by the English in North Africa and left for dead in the desert for several days. The experience broke him up and he's been a confirmed alcoholic ever since. Sad really."

"Sad? We ought to shoot him ourselves. One less mouth to feed."

"I don't know," the first speaker said. "He has his uses. Pedals that thing all over the area with his fish. Saves gas. Come on, we'll be late."

Villari watched them out of sight, then dragged his cart back on to the road and pedaled erratically away, miming drunkenness. A narrow lane led to a copse of trees and he turned onto it feeling his nerves fluttering. It was so much safer to operate in the open by day as he always tried to do, not to give any impression of attempted concealment, but he needed the trees for his aerial if he was to raise Algiers.

They answered his call sign at once and it took him only four seconds to transmit the particle of news he had intercepted on the Italian air force wavelength that a hostile submarine had been located by a reconnaissance bomber. The fact that its position was far to the south of the area for which he was responsible made no difference. Anything of interest he heard or saw he reported as a matter of course.

Replacing his equipment in the cart he began to wonder, as he sometimes did when alcoholic depression had hold of him, if what he was doing was really worthwhile. The couriers who brought him fresh batteries for his transceiver and new codes to memorize were always complimentary, but never specific. That London was pleased was all they would say. And that, he thought with some bitterness, was the British for you.

For more than two years many ships and men had died as a result of intelligence provided by Villari, but apart from occasional rumors overheard in the dock area, he had no means of knowing what had taken place beyond the horizon. He was not even able to make the connection between the sighting of the submarine about which he had just told Algiers and a transmission of his made twelve hours earlier which had condemned twenty-two men southward bound from Spezia in a German auxiliary tanker to an appalling death.

Never having heard of Harding, or any other of the executioners who carried out his sentences, Villari was very much alone.

The engineer officer and Elleston stood up when Harding came into the wardroom. The action always embarrassed him, but the first lieutenant insisted that it be done. "I'm responsible for the ship's discipline, sir," he had explained, "And as we're all lieutenants I want some differentiation in your case." Harding had let it go.

"Please sit down," he said. "Any signals for us on the last hourly routine, Chief?"

"Only one, sir," the engineer officer told him. "Usual thing. 'You were probably sighted by enemy aircraft at 1430 today.'"

"Ha—ha—ha," Elleston said. "We could have told them that. I distinctly heard the noisy bugger. You saw it, didn't you, sir?"

Harding nodded and turned toward his cabin hearing the engineer officer say, "You may find it amusing, youngster, but to me it's plain spooky. Can you tell me how they know that in Algiers?"

The extent of Algiers' knowledge had always surprised Harding too, or more accurately, as he was not without imagination, the speed with which it was acquired. That he had never heard of Giovanni Villari and his pedal cart, or of those others like him who plied their perilous trade in Italy, was not his fault. He was not supposed to have heard of them.

CHAPTER 2

HIS REMAINING FISH WERE SMELLING TOO STRONGLY now for it to be logical for him to keep them and Villari tossed them into the bushes, knowing that the residual stench would prove an effective deterrent to close examination of his cart. When he had placed the transceiver on the ground, he picked up the coil of wire which served it as an aerial with his left hand, took the weighted end in his right, and began to swing it in a circle. Long ago the routine had become second nature to him, but because he was more than a little drunk he had to concentrate on focusing his eyes on the high branch of the tree in the darkness. Sure at last that he could see it, he threw the weight upward and let the coil follow its flight. The wire did not fall down again, so he knew that it had passed over the branch.

Lowering himself to the grass, he sat looking at the luminous dial of his watch and listening to the night. Three minutes later his eyes told him that it was 0159 local time and his ears that the night was neutral. Switching on, he pressed a single earpiece to the side of his head. He never wore a headset because he needed the other ear to warn him if the night, or the day, had abandoned its neutrality.

Precisely on the hour he heard the abrupt stuttering of the Morse letters, "H," "R." Algiers was standing by and he began transmitting immediately, using the code the last courier had given him. He was very good with numbers so, drunk as he was, the signal he had imprinted on his brain transferred itself faultlessly to the fingers fluttering over the key. In nineteen

11

seconds he had signed off. In another eight his equipment was again in its mobile hiding place and he was pedaling back to the cottage where he had left the woman sleeping, hoping fervently that effective action would be taken over the most important single message he had ever sent about impending shipping movements out of Spezia.

As soon as he eased open the door of the little two-room building he knew from the sound of her heavy breathing that she was still asleep. He crossed the room silently, switched on the light beside the bed, and withdrew as quietly as he had come, then watched her through the crack of the door he had not completely closed.

The woman awoke slowly, reluctantly, narrowing her eyes in protest against the intrusion of the light from the lamp, trying to remember where she was. Gradually the room took on its familiar shape. It was her own room. Confused, she lay still for a moment, seeking a reason for the fog which seemed to be drifting inside her skull. Too much wine the night before? Possibly, but that had never left her feeling like this before. Then, quite suddenly, the fog dissipated and memory came flooding back. Giovanni had been with her. Darling Giovanni.

Smiling reminiscently, she stretched out an arm. The space beside her was empty, the sheet cold, and she knew that he had left to buy fish from the trawlers which returned to harbor at dawn before he started his daily rounds. She smiled again thinking how handsome he was, the best-looking man she had ever seen, and a hero too. Fighting the British at some places in Africa she had never heard of had won him two medals before he was wounded and given a medical discharge.

Outside the cottage someone retched and she jerked into a sitting position, pulling the sheet around her body. The movement made her head swim.

"*Caro?*" she called. "*Caro,* is that you?"

"Yes." His voice came back to her. "It's only me."

He appeared in the doorway then, rubbing his temples with the tips of his fingers, blinking in the light.

"Sorry. I felt sick."

She nodded, frowning worriedly at him. "That's strange. I feel peculiar too. Did we drink a great deal last night?"

He limped to the drainboard, picked up a nearly empty wine bottle, sniffed it, and poured the remains into the sink.

"No," he said, "but we won't drink any more of it either. It's my fault. Next time I'll be more careful what I bring."

Ten minutes later he rode off, thinking about the woman. She was pleasant enough and had always been reasonable before, but last night she had been both wakeful and demanding and he had had to drug her drink before he could get away to transmit his message to Algiers. That done, to return to her had been essential so that he could act out his pantomime of mutual sickness. Anything less might have given her ideas about him, the kind of ideas he could not afford to let anyone have.

Her bed and nearly thirty others in and around Spezia belonging to single women, women whose husbands had been killed or were prisoners of war, were the bases to which his looks gave him ready access and his bases were widely dispersed. He rarely used the same one at less than three-week intervals because of the radio direction finders.

The job he had invented for himself gave him mobility and the reputation he inevitably acquired made him more a butt for envious ridicule than an object of suspicion, so that the patrols he occasionally encountered on the country lanes at night sent him on his way with ribald encouragement.

Villari knew now that, in the course of his work for the British, alcohol and women constituted a greater threat to his continued existence than did the Germans, but alcohol was part of his cover and women his *modus operandi*. It was, he thought, a pity that the two did not go together.

"Jesus, I'm tired," he said and frightened himself, not by speaking aloud, but by doing it in English. He had not used that language more than a dozen times in two years and only then when a courier passed through his area.

CHAPTER 3

HARDING SAID, "COME IN," FINISHED THE LINE HE
had started in his patrol report notes, then looked up at the tall
figure of his first lieutenant stooping in the doorway of the
little cabin.

"Hello, Number One. What's the score?"

"Do you think you could see that defaulter now, sir? We've
been at sea for nine days and I expect he's getting worried."

"Oh damn!" Harding said. "I'd forgotten all about him. It's
Able Seaman Norris, isn't it?"

"Yes, sir."

"All right. Five minutes."

Exactly five minutes later Harding walked into the control
room and glanced automatically at the depth gauges. Both were
steady on thirty-four feet, the two men sitting facing them
barely moving the bars which operated the hydroplanes by
hydraulic power. For a moment he let his thoughts wander,
recalling that in an American submarine the gauges would read
sixty-odd feet because they employed the much more sensible
system of measuring the distance from keel to surface, not
control room to surface. Irritably he jerked his mind back to
the present, knowing that it made no difference at all where
it was measured from as long as the measurement was correct,
knowing too that he was simply delaying for a few seconds the
business he disliked so much of dealing with defaulters.

They had set up a small table near the forward periscope.
The first lieutenant and young Elleston, who had been officer
of the day when Norris had come aboard, to one side, the

15

coxswain on the other. Beyond them Able Seaman Norris standing rigidly at attention. It was odd to see them all in caps and uniform. Nobody bothered about uniform or caps at sea. It was too hot, there was insufficient fresh water to waste on laundry, and everybody knew who everybody else was anyway. But on occasions like this . . . Harding stiffened his shoulders, adjusted his own cap and stepped up to the table.

"Tenshun! Off cap!" The coxswain could have been addressing someone a hundred yards away.

Already at attention Norris shuffled his feet awkwardly and snatched the cap from his head, his eyes fixed on some point behind Harding's right shoulder.

"Able Seaman Norris, sir. Absent over leave from 2000 to 2146 on the evenin' of July twelfth, the ship bein' under sailin' orders at that time."

The last part was the clincher. An hour and three-quarters overdue would normally have merited mild punishment, but with the ship under sailing orders the charge became serious. Harding sighed silently and looked at Elleston.

"Was Norris sober when he came aboard?"

"Perfectly, sir."

"Do you have anything to say for yourself, Norris?"

"No, sir." Norris's eyes flicked to meet Harding's, then away again.

As though a blockage in his ears had cleared itself, Harding suddenly became aware of the sounds of the ship around him. The subdued hum of the big electric motors driving it slowly forward, the murmur of the ventilation system, the hiss of the periscope being raised, even the breathing of the men on watch in the control room. They were a study in disinterest, those men, but he knew that their ears were straining to catch every word spoken by the group at the table. How much better, he thought, if these procedures could be conducted in private, but there was no privacy anywhere in the near-hundred-yard length of the submarine with a man for almost every yard of it.

"Norris."

"Sir?"

"You came within fourteen minutes of missing your ship. Had you in fact missed it your action might well have been construed as desertion. Add to that that the ship was sailing for a war patrol and that desertion could have been considered desertion in the face of the enemy. Nasty things happen to men who desert in the face of the enemy, Norris."

Norris didn't speak and Harding went on, "But you didn't miss the ship, did you? You simply deprived it of your services at a crucial time. You're a member of the casing party and your job when we leave harbor is to help stow our berthing wires inside the casing, stow them in such a way that they cannot move under any circumstances. What happens if they *can* move, Norris?"

"They make a noise, sir."

"As you say, they make a noise. They make a noise that can be picked up by a destroyer's hydrophones. You may not set much store by crawling about inside the casing securing wires and if that is so I can only conclude that you have a death wish because if rattling wires are heard on a destroyer's hydrophones you are quite likely to die. That would be sad. What would be much sadder is that the whole ship's company would die with you. There are no unimportant jobs in a submarine, Norris, and no passengers."

Harding talked on and Elleston, who had never stood at the defaulters' table with this commanding officer before, thought that the quietly spoken words were much more chilling than any ranting and raving he had undergone from instructors in his cadet training ship. Norris, he noticed, had gone very pale.

A minute later Harding ended by saying, "I've explained all this to you because there is no point in punishing a man unless he understands why he is being punished. Now, for the second and last time, do you have anything to say in your own defense?"

"No, sir."

The navigating officer at the periscope said, "Ninety feet," and Harding glanced inquiringly at him.

"It's all right, sir. Just a plane heading toward us. It's miles away."

Harding nodded, turned his regard back to Norris, and started slightly at the barked words. "Permission to speak, sir?"

He looked curiously at the chief petty officer and said, "By all means, Cox'n."

"Sir, Able Seaman Norris's brother was aboard that 'ospital

ship in Algiers, sir. 'E's a pongo. I mean a soldier, sir, wounded in the left arm. They're goin' to 'ave to take it off, sir. Able Seaman Norris was attemptin' to see 'im, but 'e couldn't talk 'is way past the army doctors for some reason. Thought you might like to know, sir."

"Thank you, Cox'n. Norris, do you consider that to be an excuse of some sort?"

"No, sir."

Watching the stubborn set to the pale face in front of him, Harding could read it all. The man knew the rules, knew that he had offended against them, knew that he would be made to pay for his transgression, and was not about to plead with anybody.

"Well, I *do*," he said. "Someone who wouldn't take a risk to see his own brother before an amputation isn't the kind of person I'd want in my crew. Case dismissed."

The roar of the coxswain again. "Case dismissed on cap about turn quick march lep right lep . . . !" There were no pauses between the commands.

"Norris!"

Norris had reached the small passage between the galley and the radio room when his captain's call seemed to spin him around. He looked confused.

"Yes, sir?"

"Apart from giving you orders, have you got the remotest idea what your officers are for?"

"I—I'm not sure, sir."

Tiredly and very softly Harding said, "Oh Christ," then slightly more loudly, "Tell him, Cox'n." He went into his cabin and lay down on the bunk. The depth gauge at its foot read fifty-nine feet and sinking. The navigator would go down to ninety where there was no chance of the approaching aircraft seeing them through the clear water, then return to periscope depth.

The coxswain's voice came to him faintly. ". . . if you'd told me before 'and I'd 'ave taken you to see the first lieutenant or the skipper and you'd 'ave been given a note readin' 'Dear General, This twerp A. B. Norris wants to see 'is brother who's been 'urt. Kindly arrange,' and you'd 'ave been past those pongo officers like a dose of salts. But instead of usin' your loaf you go and pull a bloody stupid act which..."

Harding turned on his side and went to sleep.

The big German staff car drew into the side of the road and stopped within ten feet of Villari. He glanced automatically at the divisional insignia displayed on it in case it should indicate the presence of some new unit, something which might interest Algiers. It was of no interest to Algiers. The Seventy-first Infantry had been around for a long time.

The passenger in the back would, he guessed, be of enormous interest to very many people in Algiers, but not to him. He was sick of women, sick to death of them, but for all that, the legs of the chair he was sitting on outside the small bar squeaked on the pavement when he turned it to look at her more easily. The chairs of some of the sailors whose talk he had been listening to squealed in unison with his.

Not to look at her would have been unnatural for any Italian or, because she was very beautiful, for any other nationality, so he looked because he had learned always to seem to do the natural thing.

The army driver got out of the car, spoke briefly with the woman, clicked his heels, and walked toward a shop near the bar. She lay back and scanned the small group outside the bar with bored eyes, pausing briefly on each face. When she had examined them all, the eyes switched back to engage Villari's, holding his gaze until, feeling uncomfortable, he raised his glass of grappa in a half salute and looked away.

It was a relief when the driver returned carrying a package and the car moved on. He knew, without turning his head, that she was still staring at him as it did so. He did not know that her regard held his fate in its brown depths.

The control-room messenger put his head round the curtain of the petty officer's mess and said, "Skipper wants a word with you, 'swain. In his cabin."

"Right, lad."

Chief Petty Officer Ryland put his hand of cards facedown on the table, said, "No peekin', Lofty," to the chief yeoman of signals and strode aft along the passageway flanked on one side by bunks holding sleeping forms, on the other by the engine-room artificers' and officers' messes. He tapped on the door of the captain's cabin, stepped in, and slid it shut behind him.

"Sir?"

"Oh hello, Cox'n," Harding said. "You weren't asleep, were you?"

"No, sir. Practicin' cheatin' at cards."

"Good for you. I just wanted to speak to you about that Norris business. I shouldn't really have let him off, you know, so it might help to keep me out of the shit when we get back to harbor if you could falsify the records a little."

The coxswain looked thoughtful, muttered "Norris" to himself twice, then his face lit up.

"You've cleared up somethin' that's been puzzlin' me, sir. One of the pages of me punishment book got soaked with seawater and the ink run. I 'ad to tear it out. There was probably some mention of Norris on that."

Harding smiled at him. "Careless of you."

"Yes, sir. 'E's a good 'and, sir."

"I know he is," Harding told him.

Letting himself out, the coxswain paused in the doorway and said, "What? . . . Oh," then turned back to Harding. "Officer of the watch wants you, sir."

In the control room Harding waited while the first lieutenant turned the periscope through a complete circle searching the horizon for aircraft, then saw him steady it on the port beam.

"Would you take a look at this, sir? It could be a flat-roofed building near the beach, but we've been along this stretch of coast before and I don't remember seeing anything like it." He stepped back and Harding took his place, adjusting the binocular lenses to the distance apart of his own eyes.

After a moment: "Search me. Down periscope," he said, then looked thoughtfully at the first lieutenant.

"I think we'd better surface and take a clearer look, Number One."

"Aye aye, sir." The first lieutenant reached for the microphone of the tannoy public-address system, pressed the button on its stem, and spoke into it.

"D'you hear there? The ship will be surfacing for a few seconds. Pay no attention." He replaced the microphone.

Harding opened the lower conning tower hatch and said, "Binoculars, someone," took the pair handed to him, and turned to the first lieutenant. "Not too much buoyancy, Number One. I'll climb up onto the periscope standards. You use the 'search' periscope. Dive again as soon as you see my feet coming down through the upper hatch."

Trigger surfaced sluggishly, wallowed, then submerged again like a gigantic whale sounding. Dripping wet, Harding pushed his mousy hair out of his eyes and looked at the water swilling about on the control-room deck as though he couldn't understand how it got there.

The coxswain said, "Chivers, get the captain a towel. You two, swab up this lot."

"It's a bloody great floating dock, Number One." Harding sounded as puzzled as he had seemed at the sight of the water.

"Yes, sir. I got a good view of it through the periscope. Three small tugs towing it northward."

"Ah. I couldn't see them from my elevation. Could have saved myself a soaking." He took the towel Chivers was holding and said, "Thank you. Well, let's go and see if we can make it unfloat. Port fifteen, steer 075."

The submarine idled in toward the Italian shoreline, conserving battery power. There was no hurry. The three tugs with their ungainly charge appeared to be making less than three knots and it was nearly two hours later before the crew went to action stations.

"I don't know," Harding said to nobody in particular. "It was never like this on the Attack Teacher. Mostly cruisers zigzagging at thirty-four knots."

Standing by the data computer which provided torpedo firing angles and was commonly known as the "Fruit Machine," Elleston said, "Piece of cake, sir."

"I'm glad you think so, Guns. I don't know much about floating docks, but if that thing can lift a fifteen-thousand-ton ship out of the water it must have a buoyancy factor in excess of that weight. How many holes do I have to blow in how many compartments to let in that amount of water? Don't get your slide rule out. The question was rhetorical. Stand by numbers one and two tubes. Depth setting six feet."

Harding heard his order relayed and then the reply. "One and two tubes standing by. Bow caps open."

"What's the director angle?"

"Green 2, sir."

"Put me on Green 2."

The man standing behind him put his hands over Harding's on the periscope handles, looked up at the azimuth ring above his head, and turned the periscope slightly to the left. Harding's eyes remained fixed on the image of the floating dock.

"You're on Green 2, sir."

"Thank you, Bates. Do an all-around sweep with the after-periscope, Pilot. Fire one, fire two."

Two slight bumps as though the submarine had run into something soft, then a slight sense of increased pressure on the ears as the compressed air which had expelled the torpedoes vented back into the ship.

"Clear all around except for the target, sir," the navigating officer said and the sonar operator, "Both torpedoes running."

A minute and a half later Harding whispered, "Damn it. Both tracks passed right underneath." Then in his normal voice, "Stand by numbers three and four tubes. Set them to run on the surface."

"We've got magnetic warheads in five and six, sir."

"I know, Number One, but they'll explode right underneath and blow holes in the floor of the dock. The buoyancy's in the walls."

Both torpedoes of the second salvo hit. Harding watched the two columns of water soar skyward. All heard and felt the sharp double detonation. *Trigger* shuddered briefly in the shock wave. The dock itself rolled on the flat surface of the sea as if riding out an Atlantic gale. Nothing else happened.

"I'm not wasting any more fish on the thing," Harding said. "We'll have a go at the tugs. Stand by gun action."

"Captain, sir?"

"What is it, Pilot?"

At the after-periscope the navigating officer said, "I think the tugs are slipping their tow."

"Are they, by God? Yes, you're right. Belay gun action

stations. Stand by boarding party. Side arms and demolition charges. Ask the engineer officer to come here. Down periscope."

Vaguely Harding was conscious of Elleston shouting names, "Petty Officer Parr! Leading Seaman Torrance! Able Seaman Norris!" and then of two distant explosions. Those would be his first salvo of torpedoes hitting the coast, he knew.

When, water streaming from her, *Trigger* reared to the surface the three tugs were already smaller with distance. The dock, motionless but for a gentle rocking, was twenty yards away. Harding maneuvered *Trigger*'s bow to within six feet of its open end.

"Remember, Elleston, three minutes only. With those tugs yelling their heads off on the radio we can expect aircraft anytime."

"Aye aye, sir."

The bow edged to within a foot.

"Over you go," Harding called and watched the boarding party jump the narrow gap. Elleston and Norris had Webley .45 revolvers in their hands, the engineer officer a crowbar, the rest demolition charges.

Only Corporal Ackroyd was on the bridge with Harding.

"If there's any trouble, Corporal, stop it."

"Yessir," the commando said and fondled his machine gun.

It was Able Seaman Norris who found the two Italians hiding in a rusty cubbyhole, small men crouching in a corner. One crossed his forearms over his eyes and said, *"No! No! Non spari! Non spari!"* Norris didn't understand this appeal for life, but when the other stammered, *"Prego! Prego!"* he said, "Well, don't have a miscarriage on me, mate," put his gun back in its webbing holster, and grabbed them both by the hair.

Elleston found the compartment with the flooding valves in it, shouted, "Over here, Chief!" and then helped to turn the big wheels when the engineer officer had snapped the padlocked chains from them with his crowbar.

From *Trigger*'s bridge Harding watched Norris curiously, a very different Norris from the man he had looked at recently across the defaulters' table. He was striding toward a small boat lying bottom up on the dock floor not far from the submarine's bows. Two small, dark men trotted beside him, propelled by his grip on their hair. Norris half threw them at the boat, slashed the lines holding it down with his knife, and said, "Fucko offo, bloody pronto." Harding smiled and glanced at his watch. There were twenty seconds to go and the boarding party was streaming back over the bows.

"The dock turned turtle and sank twenty minutes later," Harding wrote in his patrol report notes. "I regret the waste of four torpedoes on this target, it now being apparent that the tugs would have been frightened off had I simply surfaced near them. The members of the boarding party conducted themselves well."

He put his notes aside and sat, remembering the sight through the periscope of Norris's Italians rowing furiously for the coast, away from the heavily listing dock. Perhaps, he thought, nobody having been hurt explained why there were no shakes this time, then shook his head. It wasn't that simple, and in any event, he had no feelings about killing the enemy.

Kapitan-sur-see Jurgen von Liebnitz sighed gustily and looked across the table at his Italian superior. He liked the *vice-ammiraglio* and regarded him as living proof that there *were* good officers in the services of Germany's suspect ally. His depression stemmed from the fact that having the obvious pointed out to him with forceful logic left him with no idea what he was going to tell Berlin.

"I have no idea what I am going to tell Berlin," he said and added fuel to his dejection with the unspoken acknowledgment that Berlin's dictum had become more important than either strategy, of which he knew a little, or tactics, about which he knew a great deal.

"Tell them the truth, my dear captain. It's time somebody did. With insufficient escort vessels it is not possible to provide protection for every ship that puts to sea. Surely that is not a difficult concept to grasp."

The captain stared at his hands, saying nothing, and the admiral went on. "I sometimes wonder if they have yet accepted the fact that Mussolini's *Mare Nostrum* stopped being our sea on the day we declared war. From then until now, except for the period during which our combined air forces controlled parts of it, the Mediterranean has been a British lake. Not a very comfortable lake for them, but theirs. If this is still not clear to Berlin, perhaps they should ask themselves why the great Rommel is not astride the Middle East and why the Allies landed in Sicily last week."

"What I meant, sir, was..."

"Yes, yes, Jurgen. I know. You don't want to listen to an old man's ramblings. You want specific answers to silly questions put to you by people who have no choice but to ask them although they know how stupid they are. There is but one God to whom they must bow and his name is certainly not Allah. Knowing you, I don't imagine that you will report that remark, but do so if you feel you must. I'm really past caring, because this year will see the end of my country as a fighting force."

"That, sir, I do not believe," von Liebnitz said.

"Are you inviting me to ramble on, Jurgen?"

"I've always respected your opinions, sir, and have never known you to ramble without a destination in mind."

"Very well, Captain von Liebnitz. I say to you 'know thine enemy.' Consider first the British, as they have been our main adversary in this area. A devious people, deeply steeped over the centuries in a maritime tradition on which their strategy has been based. Accustomed to fighting protracted wars against numerically superior European powers since first they became truly one nation. Accustomed to winning them too. Then there is their colonization of half the globe. A formidable opponent, and now the Americans are with them there is..." The admiral shrugged and left the sentence unfinished.

"Surely you wouldn't describe the Americans as formidable too, sir."

"No, I think I'd choose the word 'invincible.'"

Jurgen von Liebnitz watched the older man curiously for several seconds before saying, "I didn't notice anything particularly invincible about their performance in North Africa. Why, it only took..."

"Oh, Jurgen, Jurgen, Jurgen. You mustn't let your thinking be clouded by a minor incident in which some of Germany's most battle-hardened troops turn for a moment from the British to maul a collection of green young men from Nebraska or wherever they came from. The Americans learn very fast. They always have and now they're in Sicily which they will overrun without undue trouble. You'll see."

The admiral sighed, not gustily as the German had done, but with quiet resignation. "Then, with their colossal reserves, they and the British will invade us as a stepping stone to the Balkans, or smash their way through your Atlantic Wall. There'll be no stopping them now." For a moment he rolled a pencil aimlessly about on the table, then went on. "The Japanese Admiral Isoroku Yamamoto used prophetic words to subdue the elation of his officers after the victory at Pearl Harbor. I do not remember them exactly, but in effect he said, 'We have kicked a sleeping giant. There is no telling what the outcome may be.'"

"So you think the war is lost, sir?"

"Lost? Of course it's lost! It began to slip away in the skies over England. It was finally and irrevocably lost at Stalingrad and Alamein."

The admiral's tone changed abruptly when he said, "But enough of that. We still have to fight it and Berlin wants to know why we have lost eleven vessels in four days between La Spezia and the Sicilian front. Well, you know the answers and all I can offer is advice. Don't let them waste your time filling forms in triplicate for each incident. The inquiry probably originated with some fat-headed *Kriegsmarine* clerk anyway. Tell them that nine ships were sunk in convoy by enemy air and submarine action near Sicily which is more than we anticipated, but less than might have been the case. That takes care of nine of the eleven. All right so far?"

"You're ruining my chances of promotion, sir," von Liebnitz said and smiled.

"Promotion to what? You don't have enough surface ships left for you to hoist your admiral's flag, and even if you did, there are a lot of officers ahead of you in the captains' list. Now for the two incidents I suspect they are really seeking a scapegoat for. Both vessels sailed without escort on my orders and you are free to say so. The reason lies out there."

As though drawn by the same field of magnetic force, the two men rose from their chairs and walked to the window overlooking the port. A large crane was lowering a tank into a hold of one of the freighters. The others appeared to have finished loading. Smoke was rising from the funnels of all four of them as well as from other ships riding at anchor away from the wharves.

"The last chance for Sicily," von Liebnitz said.

"As you say and you can tell Berlin that too. Every seaworthy escort still available to me goes with them. They may even get there because we know that the British submarine flotillas are very short of torpedoes. That is why there was no protection for the coastal tanker and the floating dock. I gambled that they would not waste torpedoes on either target and I was very nearly right. What I had not anticipated was the enemy's foolhardiness."

Turning from the window, the admiral returned to his chair. The German officer remained where he was, staring at the ships.

"You might, Jurgen, care to rub Berlin's nose in the fact that the tanker was a heavily armed German naval auxiliary, virtually a warship, and that, according to the air force, it was sunk in a gun action with a submarine with a third of its firepower. Perhaps they would like to court-martial the captain posthumously, as I can only assume that he did not have his guns manned. As to the second case, the action of the submarine commander was equally rash and unpredictable. To remain stopped on the surface and put a party of men aboard the dock within sight of Civitavecchia is beyond all reason. I suspect that some young man is going to get his knuckles rapped when he returns to his base."

"He sank it, for all that," von Liebnitz said, then asked, "Why was there no air cover, sir? One plane would have done."

"There was to have been. It arrived on station to find it had only the towing party of two in a rowboat to cover. An error in timing for which I am trying to apportion the blame between the air force and the senior tug master. Rather an unrewarding exercise. I have summoned a meeting of the masters and commanding officers of the Sicily convoy for one hour's time in an effort to obviate any chance of similar 'administrative' errors. The air force will be represented too. I'd be glad if you would attend."

For a moment longer von Liebnitz kept his eyes fixed on the scene in the harbor, then left the window abruptly, faced his superior, and clicked his heels.

The admiral looked up at him, not quite smiling.

"Whatever it is, Jurgen, I decline to listen until you sit down. I've never liked formality between senior officers. Ah, that's better. Now, you were about to remind me that you are an antisubmarine specialist. In fact an ex-instructor. Therefore you want to sail with the convoy escort."

"I could be useful, sir. I was in U-boats too before that, so I know what their tactics are likely to be."

"I know you could," the admiral told him, "and you have just saved me the trouble of asking you to go, but before you do, be a good chap and get that report off to Berlin. If you leave it to me I'll be bound to say something tactless."

CHAPTER 4

IT WAS THE SAME NIGHT ON WHICH HE HAD MADE the transmission about the convoy that they smashed Villari's door in with a rifle butt. He had been about averagely drunk when he fell asleep on the two old mattresses he used as a bed, and when the crash woke him and he saw them standing there in the early-morning light he realized thankfully that he still was because he wasn't particularly afraid.

"What did you do that for?" he asked. "It wasn't locked. In fact there isn't a lock."

He had asked the landlord to install a lock once. The man had laughed at him and said there was no point because he spent most of his nights in other people's bedrooms. "Install one yourself if you're worried about some woman following you home," he had added and laughed again, but Villari hadn't bothered.

"*Sprechen Sie deutsch?*"

Hands upturned, mouth stretched, shoulders lifted toward his ears as he had seen his father do so often. He spoke fair German and understood most of it, but only he and the British knew that, because it was one of the things they had taught him.

The *Wehrmacht* officer frowned, turned toward the door and shouted, "Gruenther!"

A fourth soldier joined the three already in the single room which was Villari's home.

"*Herr Oberst?*"

29

The new arrival listened to the colonel, then addressed Villari in bad Italian.

"Your papers."

Villari fumbled in the hip pocket of the trousers he hadn't bothered to take off and handed over some dog-eared documents.

"Your name?"

"It's written on the papers."

"Your address?"

"You're at it."

The soldier seemed to be flustered by the abrupt replies and overcompensated for the condition by shouting.

"You sell fish!" He made it sound like a crime.

"I sell fish."

"Where is your fish cart?"

Sudden coldness in the stomach and the alcohol dissipating in his veins, but his voice was steady when he spoke.

"I keep it in a shed at the back. It's too big to bring up the stairs."

"Insolence will not help you. Why are you not fighting?"

"Look," Villari said, "if you can't read, give those papers to the officer. There's a medical discharge there. I was fighting in Africa before you left school, that is, if you ever went to one."

The man scowled, then began to read the papers as if to prove that he had been to school and Villari's attention moved to the colonel standing by the small unpainted chest of drawers. He was looking down at the two Italian medals the British had provided lying on the palm of his hand.

The hand stretched out toward the soldier wearing the insignia of a sergeant and Villari listened to the colonel saying, "Look at these, Muller. Issued to commemorate their glorious defeats in North Africa. They struck another one when their naval squadron was destroyed by the English off Cape Matapan."

"Peculiar allies we have, *Herr Oberst*."

Strange, Villari thought, how the Germans nearly always talked of the English, not the British. Perhaps they disliked them more than the Scots, Welsh, and Irish. Possibly he had something in common with them after all, he told himself, but couldn't be sure because he was pretty vague about the different races making up the British Isles.

The realization that he was handling this all wrong came to him like a jolt of electric current. Levering himself upright, he took the four paces separating him from the colonel and snatched the medals from his hand.

"Leave my things alone and get out of here!" he said. "You're not the police and you have no right breaking into the room of one of your allies. Go on, get out and take these men with you or I'll report this to the area commander!"

The colonel looked at Gruenther and asked mildly, "What's he saying?"

Gruenther translated for him.

"Ah, the fish seller wishes the *Wehrmacht* to withdraw. So be it. Tell him he'll be hearing from us again."

From his window Villari watched all four get into an army car and drive away. None had gone to the back of the building to look at his fish cart.

He sat down on his double layer of mattress, took a liter bottle of wine from between it and the wall and drank half of it in long gulps. It was then that he remembered that he had forgotten to ask for his papers back. He drank the rest of the wine. Ten minutes later he was on the ground floor in the house's only lavatory bringing it all up again, but his stomach seemed to have absorbed enough alcohol to steady him.

Back in his own room he walked up and down trying to understand what was going on. His radio transmission had been much longer than usual, about three times longer than he liked, but his message was important. The convoy he had heard the sailors talking about and then watched assemble was a big one by Spezia standards. Four large freighters, a troopship, and a tanker had sailed at dusk. The escort of destroyers and other antisubmarine vessels which followed it out of harbor had equaled it in numbers. Algiers had had to know.

Had the radio direction finders got a fix on him? Had he then been spotted by a patrol and followed home? If so, why hadn't the soldiers arrested him instead of going meekly off when he told them to without even searching the room properly and examining his pedal cart? It didn't make any sense. And why had they taken his papers with them? Forgetfulness? He doubted that very much. "You'll be hearing from us again," they had told him.

More nervous than he had been at any time since the first anxious weeks in Italy, Villari opened another bottle of wine, but his stomach churned at the first mouthful and he drank no more until he had breakfasted on a stale roll and piece of salami.

It was midday before he left his room, too late by then to collect any fish from the trawlers, too worried to think about anything but to whom to apply to get his documents back. He was sitting outside one of the bars he frequented near the docks when he saw the soldier called Gruenther walking slowly in his direction, peering into other bars and at the drinkers outside of them. Villari got up and went to meet him.

"Ah, there you are, fish seller. I was looking for you."

"Well, you've found me and I want my papers."

"You may collect them from the Palazzo Millefiori at ten o'clock tonight," the German said, handed him a pass, and turned away.

"The officer of the watch says it's beginning to get light, sir."

"All right, Smith," Harding said. "See if there's a cup of coffee going spare, would you?"

"Got one for you here, sir."

"So you have. Thanks."

Harding sat on the side of his bunk, balancing himself against the violent motion of the ship, nursing the coffee between his hands. Twice he sipped at it, but it was too hot to drink and he poured it into the washbasin.

The control room wore its nighttime Aladdin's cave look, red lighting reflecting dully from steel fittings, painting the columns of the periscopes and radar mast with pink like the trunks of trees touched by the setting sun. Dimly seen figures sitting, one at the steering wheel fighting the sea, others motionless by the diving panel, waiting, ready to send the ship sliding under the surface at the first word of the thrice-repeated order "Dive."

In the conning tower he fought the usual battle against the downdraft of air feeding the big diesels and pulled himself onto the bridge with his hair flattened around his face. There the wind caught it and tossed it about before he could push it out of his eyes. The sudden change in the weather from the almost glassy calm of the past few days had come at the same time that the signal from Algiers about the convoy had reached him. Now *Trigger* was thrusting northwest into a short steep sea, her long narrow shape lifting to a wave, then smashing down onto and under the next six. There seemed to be water everywhere. At one moment it poured over the bridge in a solid stream, at the next spray slashed across his face like knotted string. Harding was soaked before he had eased his way past the port forward lookout to join the first lieutenant.

"Morning, Number One."

"Good morning, sir. Pianosa Island should be fine on the port bow and . . ." They both ducked as a wave cascaded about them, then stood upright again. ". . . and Elba ahead, but we haven't sighted either yet. Too dark and too much ocean flying around. These are useless in this muck."

Out of the corner of his eye Harding caught the movement of half-lifted binoculars immediately dropped to dangle from their strap.

"Quite," he said.

Despite the red lighting inside the ship his eyes had yet to adjust fully to the darkness, but away to the east he thought he could make out the beginning of day. In every other direction was a black nothingness.

"Do you want to risk a radar fix, sir?"

The first lieutenant's question was unanswered for so long that he was wondering if he should repeat it when Harding spoke.

"I'd dearly love to know exactly where we are, but I don't dare chance it. They may be getting better than we think at picking up radar transmissions and I want them to believe that we're still messing about off Civitavecchia. Let's wait. We're either where we hope we are, or we aren't. Another ten or fifteen minutes should tell us."

Dawn took its time penetrating the scudding overcast and its arrival showed them nothing but gray-green tossing waves, their tops torn into white streamers by the wind.

"Christ!" Harding said. "This must have slowed us down a lot more than I calculated." He paused before adding, "All right, Number One, start zigzagging. I'm staying on the surface."

From behind him he heard a voice say, "Cor, fuck it!" He didn't turn around.

"Do you have some objection, Jameson?"

"Who, sir? Me, sir? No, sir. I like it up here. I thought it was starting to rain, but it's only seawater."

Except for the larger waves the two officers and four lookouts had given up ducking. There was no point to it. Harding watched *Trigger*'s bow soar skyward, then drop sickeningly until there was nothing to be seen forward of the bridge except the four-inch gun with the sea boiling round it. It seemed a very long time before the casing and pressure hull emerged again, tons of water spilling from them, then the process repeated itself, the ship whipping along its full length at each impact.

"Bridge?"

Harding bent to the voice pipe. "Bridge here. Captain speaking."

"Request permission to reduce speed, sir." It was the engineer officer's voice. "We're having trouble with the starboard vertical drive. I'm afraid I'm going to have to strip it down."

"How long do you give it, Chief?"

"Half an hour at the outside, sir. We've been nursing it all night, but I've got to stop that engine."

"Try to give me that half hour, Chief. I need every mile we can log. Sacrifice an engine-room artificer to the damned thing if you have to."

Tiredly the voice pipe said, "I can't stand the sight of blood, sir. I'll see what prayer can do."

As Harding straightened up, the first lieutenant reached out a hand and touched him on the shoulder.

"Would you look where I'm looking, sir? Can't give you a bearing because I don't dare take my eyes off it, but I think it's land."

Moving one step to the compass binnacle, Harding took a bearing in the direction the first lieutenant's binoculars were pointing.

"A little south of west."

He wiped his own binoculars with a wad of tissue, pressed

them to his stomach, and crouched to protect them from another flood of green water, then looked for himself. Nothing but racing waves, or was there a dark patch on the horizon just abaft the port beam? *Trigger* lifted to the next rolling swell and he saw it clearly. "You're right, Number One. That's Pianosa Island. Now, in that case we should be able to see..."

"Land bearing Green 15, sir."

"Elba." Harding finished, then added, "Good for you, Jameson. That must *be* Elba. Now you can get below before it starts to rain. Clear the bridge. Press the klaxon button on your way down, Number One."

The slither of feet on the wet deck, then the double squawking snarl of the klaxon registered in his mind. Alone on the bridge he watched, without seeing the forward hydroplanes turning ponderously out like the steel wings of some gigantic mechanical butterfly. He was hoping that he had guessed right, that the convoy commander would choose the Elba-Pianosa passage and not risk his charges in the confined waters between Elba and the Italian mainland.

If there was spray rising from the main vents, it was unnoticeable in such weather, but Harding knew that they had been opened because *Trigger* wasn't rising to the waves any longer. Her bow had dipped beneath the surface and stayed there. He pushed the heavy handles of the voice pipe cocks shut, lowered himself into the conning tower, and closed and clipped the hatch above him. Then he clambered slowly down the ladder.

"Thirty-two feet," he said.

It was quiet and still in the control room, the fury of the gale cut off as though it had never been. The deck barely moved under his feet and only the tick of the gyro repeater, the quietly spoken orders of the first lieutenant, and the steady patter of water dripping from sodden clothing broke the silence.

In answer to his hand signal the search periscope slid upward and immediately the storm was back, buffeting across the face of the world, but silently as though the sound track had been cut. Spume misted the periscope's upper lens, wind cleared it again, waves rolled right over it, and he could see only the shimmer of their undersides.

"Bring her up to thirty feet."

He could see better then for periods between the larger waves and turned slowly through a full circle, scanning the heaving horizon. Nothing except the dark bulks of Pianosa and Elba, clearer now that the low overcast had lifted with the coming of day. Not that he expected anything yet. *Trigger* was where he wanted her, positioned so that he could intercept the convoy whether it passed between the two islands or to the west of Pianosa. As long as it didn't pass too far to the west. Harding frowned, then shrugged. His choice had been made and he couldn't be in more than one place at a time.

"Take over the watch, Pilot," he said. "Come on, Number One. Let's get out of these wet clothes."

The commander of the Italian destroyer said, "With your approval, sir, I propose to proceed in a straight line from here to the west point of Elba, cut through the Elba-Pianosa channel, thence directly to Sicily across the Tyrrhenian Sea."

"Why?"

"Because, sir, enemy submarine activity is concentrated mainly along the coast. The last two reported sinkings north of Rome were one between Giglio Island and the mainland and the other very close to Civitavecchia. They don't have the numbers to patrol the open sea."

"That makes excellent sense to me," von Liebnitz told him, "but let us get one thing absolutely clear between us."

"Sir?"

"That word for a start. I think you would be wise to address me as von Liebnitz. You're the captain of this ship. You are also the senior officer of the convoy escort. I know I outrank you, but I am here as an adviser, should you require advice, on antisubmarine warfare and nothing else. There cannot be two commanding officers."

The expression, part offended, part hostile, which the Italian's face had worn from the moment von Liebnitz had arrived on board, changed to surprise, then softened to contentment.

"In that case," he said, "in the event of submarine attack, I shall be most grateful if you will be so good as to control the countermeasures of the escort group. I have been informed of your experience in this connection and there is no sense in wasting time while you make suggestions to me. At all other times command remains in my hands."

"So be it."

"I will, of course, intervene if I consider that the safety of my ship is in doubt."

"Naturally," von Liebnitz said gravely. He thought that the Italians, particularly the younger ones, were very peculiar people. So easily offended by some imagined slight, so quick to make pompous remarks when they recognized that a concession had been made to them. It didn't matter. He had removed the younger man's transparent resentment at his presence and thereby made an efficient working relationship more probable.

Leaving the chart room he walked to the port wing of the bridge, grasping occasionally for support as the destroyer wallowed awkwardly in the following sea. He was glad that there was a storm brewing. It would, he admitted to himself, make it difficult to spot a periscope, but it would also make observation and depth keeping very difficult for a submarine.

The dark shapes of another destroyer and one of the freighters were just visible, but the rest of the convoy and escorts were lost against the black backdrop of the land. For a moment he stood listening to the steady pinging of the sonar transmissions, then made his way down the ladder toward the cabin allotted to him.

Although he did not know it, he had looked at that particular freighter for the last time.

CHAPTER 5

ABLE SEAMAN WILLS ON SONAR WATCH DE-tected it first.

"Hydrophone effect almost dead ahead, sir. Sounds like a slow reciprocating engine. Not sure yet though."

"Up periscope," Elleston said.

He searched all around as he had been taught to do before concentrating on the forward sector.

"Nothing in sight, but ask the captain to come here, please."

It was nearly half an hour later before Harding caught his first glimpse above the wave tops of the masts and tall upright funnel of an old-fashioned merchantman. It was rolling violently and he guessed that it was in ballast.

"The bearing is that," Harding said and the man behind him watching the azimuth ring added, "Green 17."

"I'm ten degrees on his starboard bow. What's his course?"

Elleston jumped toward the "Fruit Machine" and wound two handles.

"Enemy's course 115 degrees, sir. Shall I close up the attack team?"

For several seconds Harding didn't reply, then Elleston saw him grin and shake his head.

"No thank you, Guns. We'll let him go. It's a 'come-on.' I can see men sitting in the lifeboats now, the silly asses. What do they want to give the game away like that for?"

Harding stepped back from the periscope, watched it begin to sink into its well, then caught the bemused expression on Elleston's face.

39

"Wake up, Guns," he said. "If we torpedo that broken-down old scow the convoy will do a smart about-face and leave us stranded in the outfield. They *want* us to attack it. Go deep if it zigs toward us and let me know when it's gone by."

Kapitan von Liebnitz returned to the bridge at dawn to find the destroyer steaming slowly in a circle. The convoy was widely scattered, two of the ships out of sight altogether, hidden, he imagined, by the curtain of night still hanging on the western horizon. One of the missing vessels was a destroyer.

He wished the commander a good morning, then asked, "Usual trouble?"

The man turned a tired, darkly stubbled face toward him and nodded.

"Yes. Damned civilians. A bit of a storm in the dark and you'd have to rivet them together to make them keep station. I'm waiting for this lot to re-form and I've detached *Falcone* to stand by *Imperatore* who developed engine trouble during the night. They've cured it now, but it'll take them some time to rejoin. She's the big freighter which was leading the column on our port beam last night."

"I remember."

It amused von Liebnitz slightly that the Italian commander, denied the right to address him as "sir," had decided to call him nothing rather than use his name.

"What particularly infuriates me," the man said, "is that it would have been a great deal easier to have moved all this by rail or road. Much safer too."

Amusement was replaced by irritation, but von Liebnitz suppressed it.

"That isn't the way the staff saw it, Commander."

"Oh? Why not?"

The German glanced at him then away again, wondering if an explanation would serve any useful purpose. Probably not, he thought, but he had nothing to do at the moment, so he might as well provide one.

"The road and rail systems south of Rome are jammed by troops moving to the Sicilian front," he said. "They are also coming under increasing air attack. I understand that there is a great deal of confusion. Probably you are unaware of what is entailed in moving, say, a single infantry division on land. Why should you know? It has never been your responsibility."

"Tell me."

The words were spoken with an indifference which clearly implied the additional unspoken sentence "You're going to anyway."

"Very well. To transport it by rail, something considerably in excess of one thousand ten-ton trucks would be required. By road, double that number of transport vehicles and those vehicles, properly spaced to minimize the dangers of strafing from the air, would cover about one hundred and fifty kilometers of roadway."

The Italian's eyebrows shot up, then he frowned and said pettishly, "We're not transporting an infantry division."

"No," von Liebnitz agreed. "We are not. We are transporting something much more powerful than that. Tanks, ammunition, fuel, and men for the Hermann Goering Division which is understrength, replacements for the Fifteenth Panzer Grenadiers, and ammunition and supplies of all sorts for the close to two hundred thousand men you have in Sicily. Don't underestimate the importance of this convoy, Commander. It just might deprive the Allies of their toehold on European soil. Now I think I'll go to breakfast while you get it back into some sort of order."

He left the bridge angry with himself at having let slip the criticism implicit in his last remark. At the foot of the ladder he hesitated, remembering that he had forgotten to ask if there had been any word from the old decoy ship steaming far ahead of the convoy, then walked on. Stupid! That would have been the first thing the commander would have told him about.

It was nearly two hours before the destroyer's idling engines took on a more purposeful note, and when he looked out of the scuttle he could see from the position of the watery sun that the course was southerly again. Four other ships, in close formation, were visible through the small aperture. Presumably the convoy had reassembled. Reluctant to seem to be interfering, but anxious to know the situation, he made his way back to the bridge.

The commander was still there, still unshaven, and both facts annoyed von Liebnitz. He had no time for anyone without the confidence to delegate authority for long enough to rest and make himself presentable.

"I see we're on our way again," he said and annoyed himself the more for making a patently obvious remark with its undertone of sarcasm.

The Italian appeared not to notice. "Yes. All ships are now back on station except for *Imperatore* and *Falcone*. They're making fourteen knots so they'll be with us in an hour or two as our speed of advance is only eight. That's the fault of that damned tanker."

Nodding, von Liebnitz turned away and surveyed the assembled company of ships. The "damned" tanker, which he apparently alone realized contained the lifeblood of the entire operation, was very low in the water and less affected by the following sea than the rest. The escorts, including the one he was in, had the worst of it, wallowing and corkscrewing uncomfortably.

"I think that's Elba on the port bow at last," the commander said.

Able Seaman Wills had completed his watch, eaten, and slept. Now he was back in front of the sonar set again and said nearly exactly what he had earlier in the day.

"Hydrophone effect almost dead ahead, sir. Not sure what it is yet though."

When the control-room messenger told Harding, he said, "Very well. Ask the officer of the watch to keep an eye on the bearing. I'll be along shortly." Then he let his body go slack and the shakes have their way with him. They had struck him ten minutes earlier out of nowhere and for no reason, and that worried him intensely because previously he had always been able to relate them to some incident. Had that been coincidence? Had he been rationalizing? He didn't know the answer to either question and that worried him the more. It also made his trembling worse but, miraculously, brought it to an end more quickly than he was used to.

Puzzled, but deeply thankful, he rolled off his bunk onto the deck and wiped the sweat off his face and body with a towel. Then he walked into the control room.

"What's the situation, Pilot?"

The navigating officer said, "Faint hydrophone effect between Red 5 and Green 7, sir. Can't identify it yet, it's a long way off, but from the spread I imagine it's the convoy."

"So do I," Harding told him and looked thoughtfully in the direction of the engine room. A few strides carried him to it and through the oval watertight doorway into the longest compartment of the ship, housing the huge diesels to either side, with the electric motors beyond them. It was cathedral-like in its silence, a complete contrast to the racketing bedlam of its surface condition when orders were shouted if they were to be heard and obeyed.

"How's it going, Chief?"

The three men crouching on the steel deck turned their faces up to him. The engineer officer's looked gray, drawn, with dark circles under the eyes.

"All right, sir." He gestured toward a collection of bits and pieces which Harding assumed made up the defective vertical drive. "We machined some new parts while we were dived yesterday. That kept it going through the night and we finished the rest today. It's just a matter of putting it back together now."

About thirty hours, Harding thought, and looked at the senior of the two engine-room artificers.

"You two had any sleep?"

"Yes, sir. We've been alternating with Greenway and Beckett."

Harding raised his eyebrows questioningly and jerked his head in the direction of the engineer officer. The artificer gave a tiny shake of his own head.

"Go to bed, Chief."

"But sir, I..."

Turning abruptly, Harding left the engine room. Perhaps because the engineer officer was several years older than he made him dislike giving him orders, but whatever the reason, he wasn't going to be put in the position of repeating them.

The engineer officer watched Harding's retreating form, then turned back to the man who had spoken.

"The next time you exchange signals with the captain, you'd better not let me catch you at it, Chisholm!"

"Yes, sir. Now why don't you do like the skipper says? You're wiped out."

The engineer officer stood slowly upright.

"Christ!" he said. "I haven't been sent to bed since I was about ten. Do you two know which piece is which?"

"If we get in a muddle we'll ask the cook or the wardroom steward, sir."

As he left the engine room he heard Chisholm say, "Gimme that left-handed hammer, Harry."

He smiled and suddenly the desire for his bunk was irresistible.

The control-room depth gauges showed seventy-three feet and the inclinometer a bow-down angle of eight degrees.

"Aircraft?" Harding asked. It was an unnecessary question. Had it been anything else he would have been told.

"Yes, sir."

"Did you get the type?"

"Savoia-Marchetti medium bomber, I think. It was heading almost directly toward us, so I'm not certain."

"I see. What have you got, Wills?"

The sonar operator, with earphones on his head, didn't hear him and Harding walked to his side.

"Anything new, Wills?"

"Not much, sir. The angle's widening and I believe I've isolated turbines, but it's still pretty mushy."

In the wardroom Harding glanced at the drawn curtains of the engineer officer's bunk. Rumbling snores were coming from behind them, and Harding guessed the occupant couldn't have been there for more than thirty seconds. He picked up a copy of *Good Morning*, the newless newspaper printed specially for the Submarine Service by the *Daily Mirror* which the coxswain issued in numerical order each day. In the comics section he saw that "Jane" was down to her bra and pants for the second time that week.

Somewhat to his surprise he found himself wondering if he would ever see a woman again, if any man aboard *Trigger* would. There was no premonition in his thoughts. More a possibility to be considered. Not fear of death. That was always there, no matter how much he pretended it was not. Just the crying waste of not being able to look at another girl before it caught up with him.

Almost immediately surprise became suspicion and he examined himself for any sign of the return of the shakes. There was none and he concluded that he was subconsciously shying away from the ghostlike whisper of water-borne sound betraying the slow advance of a wall of steel, such a wall as he had never encountered before. Six big merchantmen and six anti-submarine vessels, four of them destroyers, the signal had said. The ratio was, he knew, exceptional. In the Atlantic, Anglo-American convoys of vastly greater size would consider themselves fortunate to have so many escorts.

Tactics? Standard submerged attack. Pierce the screen of warships, sink as many of the merchantmen as possible, surface after dark, night radar stalk working around ahead of the survivors, dive before dawn and knock off the rest. No problem. A piece of cake, Elleston would call it.

Harding smiled wryly and looked again at the pictures of the dizzy blond whose uncanny affinity for brambles and barbed wire invariably deprived her of her dress.

Aboard the Italian destroyer *Aquila*, "Any sign of *Imperatore* and *Falcone* yet?" von Liebnitz asked.

"The masthead lookout reports smoke astern. That'll be them."

The German officer wanted to point out two things. The first that it was unforgivable for the ships to be making enough smoke to be visible in weather which should dissipate any reasonable amount before it became a target for the English. The second that the speed of the convoy should be reduced to enable them to rejoin. Having been at pains to lay down his own terms of reference he made neither point and that was to prove unfortunate.

He stood for a moment, vaguely aware of some change in the situation he was unable to identify. Something was happening which hadn't been going on before. Or perhaps something wasn't happening which had. Then he got it.

"The sonar transmissions have stopped, Commander."

"I know," the Italian said. "I've instructed the escorts to maintain sonar silence."

"You've done *what?*"

"I imagine you heard me. There is no point in advertising our whereabouts. Sonar is audible for miles."

There was incredulity in von Liebnitz's voice when he asked, "Do you imagine that the engine and propeller sounds of all these ships are not?" Without waiting for a reply, he added, "I must insist that you countermand your order."

"And I must decline to do so. I have authority from you to act as I see fit until we are under submarine attack."

Very quietly von Liebnitz said, "Without sonar you will never know whether you are under submarine attack or not until it is too late. Do you really expect to sight a periscope in this gale? Don't you know that the English are perfectly capable of firing an accurate salvo of torpedoes at a much smaller target than this by sound alone?"

It was a relief to him to hear the other say, "Signalman, make to all escorts resume standard sonar sweep," but the indifference with which the order was given worried him deeply. Unprofessionalism was something he didn't understand, something his training made it impossible for him to understand.

Harding sighted the masts of the convoy first. He had come to the control room on being told of the sonar transmissions, almost relieved by their existence because the lack of them had puzzled him. His first periscope observation had shown him nothing but heaving sea. At the second there they were, a young forest of masts and, in two cases, the tops of funnels were visible. The sudden appearance came as no surprise to him. With the periscope lens only three feet above the surface the horizon wasn't very far away.

At his order men went quickly, almost silently, to their action stations; then, "Start the attack," he said. "Target is a column of three ships. Two ten-thousand-ton freighters, one fifteen-thousand-ton tanker. I am fifteen degrees on the port bow of the leading ship."

Bearings and ranges followed. Elleston wound the handles of the "Fruit Machine" industriously, the navigating officer worked with pencil and ruler on the chart, hardly anybody else moved at all. The silence was expectant rather than oppressive.

"Give me a course for an eighty track."

"One hundred eighty-three degrees, sir."

"Steer 183. Sixty feet. Group up. Full ahead together."

Trigger began to vibrate and the hiss of water displaced by her hull became clearly audible. The position was perfect, Harding thought, depending on the destroyers. Always depending on the destroyers. He hoped very much that they were manned by Italians, not Germans.

There was a petty officer at the sonar set now, headphones off because the disturbance caused by the submarine's speed obliterated other sounds. Harding turned to him.

"McIntyre, there was a destroyer about five degrees on the port bow and another on the starboard beam. When you can hear again, try to pick them up. The bearings should be roughly..."

"Aye aye, sir. I've made allowance for our course change. I had them both before we speeded up. Fast turbine."

"Fast? How fast?"

"Buzzing around like blue-arsed flies, sir. I reckon something over twenty knots."

"Good," Harding said. "They won't hear much at that speed."

Three minutes later he was back at periscope depth. The ships were in full view, their sides visible right down to the broken waterline, but it was still a long torpedo shot. None of the escorts was particularly close and he saw, as McIntyre had suggested, that they were moving fast, weaving back and forth ahead and at the sides of the convoy. Rapidly he gave new bearings and ranges, then sent *Trigger* deep and fast again.

"Plot suggests enemy course and speed 095 degrees at seven and a half knots," the navigating officer said.

"Use those figures."

Elleston adjusted the settings on the "Fruit Machine" and Harding went on. "I shall be firing six fish initially, two at each ship in the column. As soon as we slow down stand by numbers one, two, three, four, five, and six tubes. Incidentally, make a note that I think there are only two ships in the second column, not three." He turned toward the chart table and added, "I caught a brief glimpse of your Savoia-Marchetti, Pilot. It's been joined by a Cant seaplane now."

Harding had the thinner-topped "attack" periscope up before the submarine had risen to forty feet, waiting for the upper lens to break surface. When it did, at first he could see only waves and used the time to turn through a full circle searching for the two aircraft. There was no sign of them.

"Six internal bow tubes standing by, sir. Bow caps open."

"Thank you."

He settled on the bearing of the convoy and those watching him saw his shoulders slump.

It was several seconds before, in a flat voice, he said, "They've turned ninety degrees to starboard, Number One. I'm practically astern of them."

"A zig, sir?"

"Afraid not. They've altered course for Sicily. Never dreamed they'd pass that close to Pianosa Island. I hope they run into the bloody thing. Oh well. We'll give them time to get out of sight, then surface and track at long range until dark. Shut bow caps."

Petty Officer McIntyre said, "Loud hydrophone effect bearing Green 115, sir. Sounds like turbine and reciprocating."

Harding swung the periscope around and, for him, his voice was loud when he spoke.

"Belay the last order. Bow caps to remain open. Shift target. Starboard thirty. Full ahead together. Bearing is that. Range is that. I am forty degrees on the port bow. Give me a course for a one-twenty track. It must be the sixth ship trying to catch up with the convoy, so set a target speed of...Oh hell, I dunno. Say fifteen knots."

The man behind him called out the bearing and range and Elleston fed them to the "Fruit Machine."

"Course 250 degrees, sir."

"Steer it."

The illuminated red figures of the gyro repeater tape clicked slowly, agonizingly slowly, across the glass screen in front of the helmsman: 198—199—200—201.

"Come on! Come on!" Harding whispered.

"Angle the fish, sir?"

"No, I don't think so, Number One. There's just time for a straight shot—I hope."

215—216—217. *Trigger* was swinging faster now.

"She's another ten-thousand-tonner," Harding said. "I'll be firing four fish."

239—240—241, the gyro repeater read.

"Would you get rid of five and six, sir? We've still got reloads for them and they'll be in the way if we have to pull flooded fish back for routining."

"Well done, Guns. Three, four, five, and six it is. What's the director angle?"

"Green 12, sir."

"Up periscope."

"Course 250, sir," the helmsman said.

"Dammit, Number One, I must see! I'm looking at a lot of bloody water. Give me another three feet at least. Speed up if you have to. Ah, that's better."

For two seconds Harding stood as though frozen, then pushed the periscope through a complete circle. He noted that the convoy with two planes above it was already some distance away.

"Put me on Green 12. Stand by. Stand by. Fire three... fire four... fire five... fire six. Down periscope."

Four slight jolts. Four increases of pressure on the eardrums. Harding ordered a sharp alteration of course to carry them clear of their firing position.

"All torpedoes running, sir."

"Thank you, McIntyre. By the way, you were right about there being turbine as well as reciprocating engines. While I was firing, a destroyer's bows appeared beyond the target. I expect he'll be after us soon, so listen out for any increase in revolutions."

Even at forty-five knots it would, Harding knew, take the torpedoes over two and a half minutes to cover the distance to the freighter. He wanted to walk up and down for something to do, anything to ease the anxiety he felt. But that wouldn't do because it would reveal his anxiety to those around him, so he stood where he was, legs astride, hands behind his back, trying to look pensive. It had all happened so quickly, the shift of target from the convoy to the lone merchantman. There had been no time to plot course and speed and he had had to guess what they were. His whole being was consumed with the hope that he had guessed right, the fear that he had not.

He hadn't guessed right. Not exactly right.

"Five seconds to impact, sir."

"Thank you."

The periscope rose in response to the gesture of his hand. Nothing had changed except that the whole length of the destroyer was now visible beyond the freighter. It wasn't until later, when he had the time to work it out, that Harding realized that it was the third torpedo he had fired which cut twenty feet of the bow off the big ship as neatly as if it had been slashed by a knife and the fourth exploded under her bridge. *Imperatore* died gracefully, the stern lifting skyward in a great arc until it was vertically above the sea, hesitating then slipping downward until there was nothing left, nothing to mark her passing in the already troubled water.

Harding's mistake had been slightly to overestimate the speed of his target and his first two torpedoes had passed ahead of it. As they had farther to run, it took them longer to reach the destroyer.

Falcone died in a fury of flame, smoke and the subsidiary explosions of the ammunition on her decks, a fury subdued only when a main magazine blew up. The wind tore the black pall marking the grave into tatters and threw it away.

CHAPTER 6

"WHAT WAS THAT? I THOUGHT I HEARD AN EXPLO-
sion." The words came out jerkily because von Liebnitz had
taken the ladder to the bridge three rungs at a time and he was
no longer a young man.

"I've no idea," the Italian commander told him, "but there's
a lamp signal coming through from *Vesuvio* astern of the convoy
now. What's it say, signalman?"

The signalman continued to watch the distant flashing light
for a moment, then his own lamp clattered an acknowledgment
before he replied.

"*Imperatore* and *Falcone* sunk three miles to the north of
Pianosa. Presume submarine. Investigating."

Quietly von Liebnitz said, "I'll take over now, Commander.
Hard a 'starboard. Revolutions for thirty-five knots. Steer
north. Close up depth-charge crews. Signal the convoy to make
all possible speed and *Stromboli* to take station ahead with the
submarine chasers on either beam."

Aquila rolled heavily as she turned across the sea and then,
with her speed increasing rapidly, smashed directly into it, the
whipping of the hull almost constant, the waves exploding
under the stem hurling spray mast-high. It was too much for
the Italian commander.

"I must ask you to reduce speed. This comes under the
heading of hazarding my ship."

Sparing him only the briefest glance, von Liebnitz said,
"We have just lost a sixth of our force. Unless we can sink or
cripple that submarine we are very likely to lose more. She's

51

a lot faster than your convoy and could be back in position to attack again before dawn."

"But . . ."

"No 'buts,' please. I'm sure you would not wish me to subscribe to the fiction that your ships were designed to move so quickly for the sole purpose of enabling them to run away from the English."

The German chided himself for the remark, but only gently. He was really past caring and went on, "I intend to get to the scene of the sinkings before the submarine has had time to alter its position radically. Now please stop bothering me."

He swung around and looked at the destroyer's boiling wake, at the convoy, the nearest ship already a mile away, at the depth-charge crews, oilskins streaming, huddled for protection against the after-guns. When he faced forward again he caught the distant flickering of a lamp.

"From *Vesuvio:* in contact. Attacking," the signalman said.

The gleaming giant pencil shape of the reload torpedo for number-five tube, twenty-one inches in diameter and stretching almost the whole length of the torpedo stowage compartment, seemed reluctant to move.

Straining on a rope's end, while three other men did the same with their own blocks and tackles, "Shift, you great steaming cow!" Able Seaman Norris told it.

"Be nice to it, Norris," Elleston said. "It's only a poor dumb beast."

"Aye aye, sir. Shift, you poor fucking dumb beast!"

The torpedo slid obediently forward, and when it was housed in its tube, Norris addressed the small group of sweating, panting men.

"I always say it takes an officer to handle a tricky situation like that. Now, if . . ."

He stopped talking at the buzz of the bulkhead telephone. Elleston answered it.

"No. Only the first, Number One. Still another to be loaded . . . oh, I see . . . yes, of course."

Elleston clipped the receiver back in place and turned to the loading party.

"Silent routine, chaps. We have company."

The men glanced at each other, then bent down and began to take off their shoes.

When Elleston reached the control room Petty Officer McIntyre was saying, "Confirmed fast turbine, sir. A destroyer for my money. Sonar transmissions too, but she's not sweeping. It's as if she's got a contact, but it certainly isn't us. She's passing right down our starboard side, sir."

Harding nodded. "They're probably getting echoes off the freighter. Wrecks often hang suspended not far down for a time."

The noise of the pattern of fourteen depth charges detonating was thunderous, much noisier than the results of the torpedo attack, but it was distant and had no more effect on *Trigger* than to wake the engineer officer. He stumbled into the control room, rubbing his eyes with the backs of his hands.

"What the hell's going on?"

The first lieutenant looked at him. "The natives are getting restless, Chief. We've just sunk two of their war canoes."

"Well, thanks very much for letting me know. It's nice to feel needed."

"Nothing you could have done at the time, Chief. Sorry they woke you up."

The engineer officer said, "Tchah!" and walked away in the direction of the engine room. The first lieutenant watched him go, then turned to his captain.

"You know, sir, I've seen that exclamation printed often enough, but I never heard anyone use it before."

Harding laughed. "He'll get over it, Number One. At least he had ninety minutes sleep and that's the important thing."

It was to be long hours before anybody aboard *Trigger* would laugh or sleep again.

It had taken von Liebnitz less than twenty minutes to introduce method into the hunt for the submarine and now both destroyers were steaming slowly south on parallel courses, their sonar sets probing ahead and to either side.

He listened impatiently to the Italian commander's argument that, after such a successful attack, an enemy with his wits about him would break off the action and retire northward, then replied with nothing more than a curt shake of the head. No antagonist worthy of the name would deliberately put distance between himself and a target as valuable as the remaining ships in the convoy. He had manned the sonar set personally and tried to explain to the operator the difference between contact with a moving submarine and any other underwater object. The man seemed never to have heard of Dopler effect, which made it difficult. He had denied the excited claim of the captain of *Vesuvio* already to have disposed of the enemy and painstakingly signaled the means by which the two ships would work in tandem. That had taken the longest time of all. It hadn't occurred to him that they could be so ignorant of basic procedure.

To his surprise *Vesuvio* made the first contact and it proved to be good.

"They're both in contact, sir," McIntyre said. "Moving dead slow. One astern and one on the port beam."

"Very good," Harding replied and immediately wondered why he had used that particular stock phrase for acknowledging the receipt of information. There was nothing very good about it because somebody up there, two hundred and fifty feet above his head, knew what he was doing. These were the tactics the hunter-killer groups used against the U-boats in the Atlantic. One or more holding the target, the others free to attack it without having to worry about the inevitable loss of contact when the range shortened. A far cry from the haphazard, hope-for-the-best, high-speed runs employed by the majority of Italian escorts.

He could hear the sonar transmissions without the use of earphones now, the faintest bat squeaks of sound on the hull, as though an elf were seeking admittance. The skin on his stomach crawled and he scratched at it to dispel the sensation.

"Revolutions increasing astern, sir. Maintaining contact. Bearing steady. Attacking, sir."

The vibration of the hull and the hiss of water as *Trigger*, wheel hard over, worked up to full speed, was not enough to drown the sound of the destroyer's racing propellers. They seemed to pass directly overhead, then the waiting began for the charges to sink through nearly a hundred yards of water.

Harding looked around him. Elleston, shoulders raised high, had his eyes screwed tightly shut. Another man was covering his ears with his hands.

He was lying on the deck, feeling it rolling under him as if the ship was surfaced in a heavy swell. His head was hurting and he couldn't remember hearing the depth charges explode. Concussion resulting in retroactive amnesia he supposed. There was broken glass all around him and he saw that the emergency lighting was on.

"Guns! Pilot! Help the captain! All compartments report damage!" The first lieutenant's voice. Hands helping him to his feet.

"You all right, sir?"

"Yes, I think so, Pilot. Can't focus too well yet. What's the depth?"

"Forty-five feet, sir. Blew us right up, but it looks as though Number One has caught her just below the surface. Hold on to the chart table while I get something for your forehead. You're bleeding a bit."

"And somebody bring a chair," the first lieutenant said.

Harding subsided onto it, frightened that his vision might be permanently damaged, unaware that blood was running down into his eyes.

"You have command, Number One. At least until I can see. Just let me know the score when you can."

"Aye aye, sir. We're on our way down again passing seventy feet. Angle of dive twenty-five degrees. Don't want to hang about up here. Enemy has lost contact in the turbulence caused by the depth charges. We . . . Just a minute, sir. Repeat that, please . . . Right. Get the engineer officer onto it and keep me informed about the motor room."

The smell of burning mixed with antiseptic. A damp cloth on his face, wiping gently at his eyes, fingers fixing a plaster somewhere above them. He could see again, not completely clearly, but he could see.

"There you are, sir. Should have an interesting little scar there. The girls will go for that."

"Thank you, Pilot. Thank you very much indeed." Explain that he meant for his sight, not for the scar the girls would like? Oh, forget it.

"Damage not too bad, sir," the first lieutenant said. "No power to the after hydroplanes, so they're being worked by hand. Small fire in the motor room, but that's out now. You can probably smell burning. The welding on the port main motor switchboard sheared, but they've lashed it in place temporarily and it's operational. Slow leak from one of the high-pressure air bottles. The chief's working on that, but we have three inches of pressure in the boat, so you had better have somebody hanging on to your legs when we surface."

The hull was shuddering with the ship's speed.

"Hadn't you better slow down, Number One? We must be making an awful racket."

"No, sir. They dropped a twenty-five-charge pattern on us, as near as we could count. It'll be some time yet before the water settles down enough for them to hear anything."

"Did they, by God? Then you're quite right. Keep going."

"Yes, sir. I'm going to three hundred and fifty feet, then we'll run silent again."

"Good," Harding said. He was very pleased with his first lieutenant. No queries, no hesitation, no backing down on his decisions. The ship was in excellent hands.

"What about casualties?" he asked.

"Petty Officer Murchison got burnt on the hands and face in the motor-room fire. Not too badly. He did very well. Propped up the switchboard while it was arcing all over the place. Leading Seaman Gerrard has a broken wrist, Able Seaman Bremner has a gashed cheek and you sort of levitated and gave your head a hell of a crack. Apart from that, and Lieutenant Elleston putting in a request for immediate compassionate leave, we're okay, sir."

Harding squinted at Elleston, his focus still faulty.

"Worried about your aunt in Dulwich again, Guns?"

"No, sir. She's fine. It's the other one in Bristol. Seventy's a bit old to be pregnant," Elleston said and grinned.

Strange, Harding thought, how a frightened kid could grow up in a week, and smiled back at him.

The first lieutenant was speaking into the tannoy microphone.

"... and any man not actively engaged in the handling of

the ship is to lie down. If you can't find anywhere else, lie on the deck. That is all."

And that was right too. The time since diving that morning was not yet excessive, not even normal so far because there was quite a lot of daylight left up there, but there were other factors to be considered and Harding, his head aching savagely, considered them.

The physical exertion of loading even one torpedo would have consumed some oxygen and operating the after-hydroplanes by hand some more. The small fire in the motor room and the foul air, meant not for breathing but for blowing ballast water out of the tanks, leaking out of the high-pressure bottle wouldn't have helped either. Then there was the question of how much longer the enemy could force them to stay submerged. If they could do it for long enough . . . "Quite," he told himself. All oxygen consuming movements had to be restricted to a minimum.

"After hydroplanes back in operation. Ship running silent at three hundred and fifty feet, sir."

"Thank you, Number One."

Four minutes later Petty Officer McIntyre said, "Sonar transmissions bearing Green 135. In contact, sir."

The second attack was less accurate than the first, but still close enough to throw the fragments of glass and shattered crockery littering the decks a foot into the air. The few light bulbs the first lieutenant had permitted to be replaced broke again. As if as an afterthought the glass of a depth gauge cracked and fell out over the hands of the man operating the hydroplane control below it.

"Kiss me, 'Ardy," Chief Petty Officer Ryland said.

"You wounded, Cox'n?"

Without looking round at the first lieutenant standing behind him, the coxswain raised his right hand for inspection. There was a small spot of blood on one finger.

"Yes, sir, but don't give up the ship."

"You're getting your battles a little mixed, aren't you?"

"Oh! Am I, sir? 'Ow many charges do you reckon that lot was?"

"Fifteen, I think."

"Me too," the coxswain said, took a piece of chalk from

his pocket, and added another fifteen marks to those already stretching three-quarters of the way around the circular rim of the broken depth gauge. There had been, Harding knew, over two hundred chalk lines there before this day had begun. It was while he was idly counting them again that he realized that his vision was perfectly normal. He sighed contentedly and stood up.

"Thanks for minding the ship, Number One. My eyes have popped back into place, so I'll take her now."

"Good for you, sir."

"Both ships in contact, sir, bearing Green 50 and Red 40."

"I'm beginning to develop a curious dislike for you, Mc-Intyre," Harding said. "All right. We'll try something else this time."

"I've lost contact, sir," *Aquila*'s sonar operator reported. "Or rather I'm getting echoes over about fifteen to twenty degrees."

"Let me hear that."

The operator surrendered his earphones to von Liebnitz, watched his eyes narrow in concentration, then heard him say, "Break off the attack."

"What's the trouble?"

Over his shoulder von Liebnitz said, "From what I can tell, my dear commander, the trouble is that the submarine turned broadside onto both *Vesuvio* and ourselves, presenting us with a perfect target. It then went full astern leaving a long streak of turbulence off which we are getting echoes. No doubt it is now going ahead again, creeping away behind the sonar barrier it has created. I used the trick myself once or twice in the early days. We'll be back in contact shortly, given any luck."

It took them twenty-five minutes to find the submarine and von Liebnitz had been on the point of abandoning the hunt when *Aquila* obtained an echo. He directed *Vesuvio* onto the bearing and watched through binoculars as she made her run. The wind had dropped and the sea with it, leaving only a long swell, so he had a clear view of the sequence of events after the dropping of the pattern of depth charges. The sight had always intrigued him.

At the moment of detonation of each charge the surface of the sea above it seemed to quiver in anticipation, settle again, then build itself slowly into a low dome. A disappointing phenomenon until the dome, with no further warning, was obliterated by a soaring column of water thicker than any tree, a column which lived for long seconds, then subsided, tumbling into nothingness.

Nine such columns he counted and that was the number he had insisted on now as the maximum for each attack because there was still a very long way to go to Sicily. Quite well spaced they were too, but he thought he could do better with *Aquila*. It was important to finish this quickly because the Italian would soon insist on rejoining the convoy and it would not be possible to argue against that.

His command of the Italian language was very good, but he took particular pains this time to ensure that there was no possibility of their misunderstanding his orders.

Harding listened to the sound of his own breathing, slow, deep, unsatisfying breaths drawn in and released through the mouth. Everybody in the control room was, he saw, inhaling and exhaling in the same labored fashion. The motor-room fire worse than he had assumed? Probably. Oxygen consumption greater than usual because the fear of the entire crew had called upon it to meet increased pulse rates? Certainly.

The main battery low, very low, after a day submerged with too many bursts of speed, first when attacking the convoy and then in taking evasive action. Now, either the third or fourth attack had cracked some proportion of the three hundred thirty-six huge cells which provided *Trigger* with power, because there was battery acid in the sumps.

"Add seawater to taste and produce delicious chlorine gas," Harding said, but he said it to himself.

The thought of gas reminded him of the air again. He could no longer smell it, not even the tang of fright-sweat or taint of burst rubber, but it tasted bad, bitterness in his saliva, a sharpness at the back of the throat. Temperature and humidity high too. The deck itself at about 125 degrees Fahrenheit, from the heavy discharge of the batteries, heating the air above it. The air itself static and saturated with the ventilation system and dehumidifier stopped. The last two factors at least he could ignore because if he allowed the present situation to continue nobody would live long enough to get heatstroke.

"Number One, come over here and look at this chart," he said.

The first lieutenant, his body slick with moisture, heaved himself upright from a squatting position on the deck.

"Yes, sir?"

Harding, pencil in hand, leaned over the chart and began to sketch the outlines of a female figure. He talked fast and very softly.

"Listen to me, Number One, and don't interrupt. Whoever it is up there is bloody good. I once went through nineteen hours of almost continuous depth charging and the damage was nowhere near what he's achieved in only four attacks. If we're going to get out of this we've got to do something unusual."

Something about the figure on the chart was wrong. He erased one arm and drew it in again at a different angle.

"Now, I'm going to tell you a very short story, cutting out nearly all the detail. When you do your command course, they shut you in an airtight tank with a doctor and make you lift weights until the oxygen supply is depleted. The lights go out and he tests your night vision with a luminous clock face with a dimmer attachment. Result abysmal. Next thing, he tells you to add two and five. Easy. Add forty-five and sixty-eight? You can't do it. Lot of other things, but never mind. Message is simple. Don't try anything smart at the end of a long day's dive because your brain isn't functioning properly. The danger isn't carbon dioxide poisoning, it's oxygen deprivation."

The pencil seemed to hurry as though trying to keep pace with his words.

"I want to go deeper, Number One, to look for a temperature layer that will block his sonar. Possibly as much as two hundred feet deeper and we're already at our tested diving depth. If we do, the pumps won't work, blowing main ballast may get rid of a couple of pints of water at the pressure we'll be under down there and the only thing that will pull us out, if the hull doesn't collapse first, will be the motors, assuming there are enough amps left in the box to produce power."

Eyes too far apart. He rubbed them out and drew them in again closer together.

"Okay. I'm suffering from oxygen deprivation, the whole crew is suffering from oxygen deprivation, and that includes you. But you have the advantage over me of not having cracked your head. I may also be suffering from concussion. What do you think?"

The first lieutenant said, "Five hundred and fifty feet, Cox'n," listened to the unquestioning acknowledgment, "Five 'undred and fifty feet, sir," then pointed at the chart. "That's jolly good. I've never seen 'Jane' without any clothes on at all and I didn't know you could draw."

"It helps to pass the time," Harding told him.

The bathythermograph recorded a sharp change in water temperature as *Trigger* was passing five hundred and ten feet. Twenty feet below that she leveled off.

"I thought they'd regained contact a moment ago, sir, but they've lost it again."

Harding looked at the petty officer. "On second thought, McIntyre, you're really quite likable."

He stood for a moment, leaning against the chart table, listening to the hull groaning in protest at the titanic water pressure he was asking it to withstand, not yet ready to bless the much-maligned dockyard workmen who had built it, strange clicks and snapping sounds making his nerves jump.

One, two, three, seven, nine cracking explosions making the deck hum like a tuning fork. A long way off.

"Really quite likable," he repeated, then to the first lieutenant, "I'm going to walk through the ship, Number One."

"Aye aye, sir."

The shambles in the control room was something he had grown accustomed to and it did nothing to prepare him for the seeming havoc elsewhere. That it was superficial he knew, but the knowledge failed to lessen the visual impact. Bunks torn from their fastenings, cupboards that had burst open spewing out their contents, a framed photograph of Rita Hayworth hanging upside down because its top fastening had been carried away, smashed gauges, and in one place, a square section of decking had sprung from its fastenings, showing the tops of the battery cells underneath. The dim emergency lighting only added to the appearance of desolation.

There were some twenty men in the torpedo stowage compartment, two of them lying along the length of the one remaining reload torpedo, others on the deck, a few in hammocks. One was squatting on a bucket. The smell was very bad.

The man on the bucket made an embarrassed attempt to rise.

"It's all right, Mitchell. This isn't 'Captain's Rounds.' The head's full?"

"Yes, sir."

"Use the officers' until further notice. There's fewer of us. You all right, Norris?"

"Can't complain, sir."

"Brockway?"

"Permission to go ashore, sir?"

"Sorry. Lieutenant Elleston beat you to it. We gave him an escape set and let him out through the gun tower. He'll be nearing Malta by now."

"That's not fair, sir. He hasn't done one patrol yet. We've done five."

"Well, you know how it is. Officers first. Now, belt up everybody and save what's humorously known as air. I hope to be going back to periscope depth shortly and I'll let you know as soon as it's safe for you to blow the heads."

On his way aft another smell came to Harding's nostrils. He sniffed experimentally, trying to establish its source, then peered down into the darkened pit of the forward machinery space. Dimly he could see a figure crouched by the ballast pump and the faint glow of a shielded cigarette.

"Come up here, that man," he said.

Three minutes later, Able Seaman Edgecombe stood in the watertight doorway to the torpedo stowage compartment. He was white-faced and trembling visibly, his voice a near shout.

"He's fucking mad, setting up the defaulters' table at a time like this!"

"What are you going on about, Edgecombe?"

"That medal-crazy bastard Lieutenant fucking Harding! He's going to have me court-martialed when we get back to Algiers!"

Norris rolled slowly off the torpedo, stood up, and hit Edgecombe hard in the face. Then he lay down again.

"Now, now, Norris boy," somebody said. "No unnecessary exertion."

"It was necessary."

"What do you suppose he done?"

"I dunno," Norris replied, "but if the Old Man's fixing a court for him it's for more than just being fucking stupid take my word. Anyway, that's their problem. It's his manners I object to."

Nobody moved to help Edgecombe, slumped in a corner with the blood pouring from his broken nose.

"Silent all around, sir. Two sets of turbine last heard receding in a southerly direction at high speed."

"Thank you, McIntyre. Periscope depth, Number One. Who's the heaviest man in the crew?"

"Umm. Corporal Ackroyd?"

"Of course. Send for him, will you? Oh, you're there, Corporal. Listen, we've got nearly four inches above atmospheric pressure in the boat, and when I open the hatch it'll be like being in a wind tunnel until it's equalized. We haven't got the time or the power left to reduce it with the compressors, so I'm going to need you hanging on to my legs and for Pete's sake hang on tight or I'll go out like a champagne cork. Okay?"

The commando shook his big arms like an ape and said, "You won't be going nowhere, sir," and it occurred to Harding that that was the first time he had heard him say anything but "Yessir."

It was bad in the conning tower when he unclipped the heavy hatch and had it snatched from his hand as if it were paper. Worse than he had ever experienced. Disorientation was almost total as the hurricane tore upward around him, but he had expected that. He had expected the pain in his ears too, but not its intensity. It stopped in seconds, the hurricane, but not the pain. He felt his legs released and staggered up onto the bridge, pressing his hands to the sides of his head, shaking it.

A strong smell of ammonia. That always happened during the transition from stale to fresh air and he had never understood why, although they had demonstrated the effect to him by making him breathe into a paper bag for a minute when first he joined the Submarine Service. Then the dizziness hit him as unaccustomed amounts of oxygen flooded his system and he grasped the side of the bridge for support.

"Careful! Careful! Look for the bloody destroyers," he said aloud and heard the words booming inside his skull. There had been no sign of them through the periscope. Up here there might well be. Eventually he saw them in the evening light. Two hair-thin masts piercing the southern horizon. The tension ran out of him and first one and then the other of his ears cleared themselves. The pain vanished.

At his commands men joined him on the bridge, the ship began to come to full buoyancy, and the diesel exhausts coughed and broke into a burbling rumble of power.

Harding felt almost content and thought he would have been completely so but for the criminal idiocy of the man Edgecombe. Even to think of the solemn ritual of the court-martial, its inevitable verdict and severe sentence distressed him and he sighed heavily.

"Up spirits, sir?" the voice pipe asked.

Good Lord, he'd forgotten all about that. The thing dearest to the men's hearts. Their daily ration of rum, rum they would have had at eleven that morning had they not been otherwise engaged.

"Up spirits, by all means," he said. "Then let's get this garbage heap looking like a warship again."

Trigger's bow steadied on south and she slid across the flattening sea in pursuit of the distant convoy.

CHAPTER 7

WHEN ITALY INVADED FRANCE IT HAD BEEN THE last straw for John Villar, professor of advanced mathematics at the Massachusetts Institute of Technology. He loved the country his parents had adopted and in which he had been born. He liked most of the people he met, it was a pleasant place to live, and it provided him with the opportunity to exercise his undoubted mathematical talent to a degree he would never have achieved in Italy. But he was very fond of Italy too, and hated what was happening to it, loathing Mussolini together with everything he stood for, detesting the role of jackal to the German lion the country had cast itself in.

It was obvious to him that before Italy could be returned to its senses and its people the Fascist military machine which controlled it would have to be destroyed. He knew that he had to provide whatever assistance he could in achieving that destruction. Resigning his job and putting mathematics out of his mind, John Villar went to Canada, as many Americans were doing, and tried to enlist in the Royal Canadian Air Force.

The Canadians were polite, but regretful. "Your eyesight is substandard" they told him, and never having felt the need for glasses, he returned angrily to the States and made his way to Washington D.C., his objective the British Embassy.

Villar didn't know much about the British except that they were reputed to be a supercilious and arrogant race, but they did seem to be the only people who were still doing anything about anything in this new European war against the Berlin-Rome axis. He thought that he'd go right to the top and seek an interview with the ambassador, but the ambassador was away and the chargé d'affaires not sufficiently interested in his importunities to see him.

It was pure chance that led him into a conversation with one of the British Embassy's second secretaries at a cocktail party, a second secretary whose duties included more than simple diplomacy, but even that contact began inauspiciously.

"The embassy isn't a recruiting center, Mr. Villar."

"You could have fooled me," Villar said. "I get the impression that your chief preoccupation is recruiting the entire armed force of the United States."

"Well now, that certainly would be a help to us," the man agreed. "If you have any influence with Congress, perhaps you'll put in a word for us. Excuse me, will you?"

The Britisher turned to go, but Villar detained him with a hand on his arm.

"I could be a help to you too, Mr. Harrington."

Harrington started to frown, then smiled in resignation and asked him why he thought so.

The idea only came to Villar at that moment. He glanced around the crowded room and began to develop it in a voice even lower than the one he had been using, but he had spoken only ten words before Harrington said, "That's enough. How long will you be in Washington?"

"As long as it takes to persuade you guys to let me give a hand."

"Where are you staying?"

When he had been told, Harrington nodded and walked away without saying anything. Villar was satisfied, but it was three days before he was contacted.

"Harrington," Harrington's voice said from the telephone receiver. "There's somebody here who wants a word with you. Hold on."

"Parla l'Italiano?" the next voice asked.

"Si," Villar replied and continued to answer questions in rapid Italian for almost a quarter of an hour. The questions were about his parents, his friends, his work, his hobbies, and from the way they were put to him he realized that most of the answers were already known, that they hadn't wasted the three days.

When it was over, Harrington came on the line again.

"I'm told that you're pretty fluent."

"Don't give me that British understatement crap," Villar said. "I'm bilingual and your Italian buddy knows it."

"Well good for you. In that case perhaps you'd better come round here for a chat."

"When?"

"Now, if it's not too much bother," Harrington said and cut the connection.

Arrogant and supercilious they definitely seemed to be, Villar decided, left his hotel room, and took a cab to the British Embassy. A few days later, when they had flown him to England via Iceland and Scotland, he discovered that they were also bastards.

Six weeks passed in a blur of tiredness, frustration, and fury. They seemed to have got it into their heads that he was a cross between a common criminal and a spy. Questioned all day, he was frequently dragged out of his canvas cot at night and questioned again. One of his interrogators angered him particularly with his habitual greeting: "How's our pretty wop today?"

Finally fed up, "As you seem convinced teeth are going out of fashion, maybe I can get you back in vogue," Villar said and struck savagely at the sneering mouth in front of him. The man brushed the blow aside and threw him across the room, then stood, watching him curiously.

Looking up from the floor, Villar heard him mutter, "Well, I don't know," then more loudly, "Either you're much brighter than you pretend to be, or you're genuine. Not even an *Eyetie* agent could be as bloody helpless as you."

He was surprised when the man reached out a hand and pulled him to his feet, surprised again to hear him say, "Listen, if you want to stay alive in this game, don't make speeches about what you're going to do. Just do it. All right?"

"Sure. Thanks," Villar said and received his first smile in England.

Things got better after that. He was allowed to sleep at night; interrogation became discussion, and suspicion guarded friendliness. When the British routed the Italian armies in North Africa with contemptuous ease, he was given newspapers to read. The battle was won as he would have wished, with low casualties and prisoners taken in tens of thousands. Unable to conceal his delight, he walked up and down his room smiling. That helped him too because his reactions were being observed through a spy hole.

The day came when he was taken to a room he had not been in before and an army officer got up from behind a desk and shook him by the hand.

"Whiskey, Mr. Villar?"

"Why not?" It was to be his first alcoholic drink in two months.

"Like gold, this stuff," the major said. "Exporting most of it to you people in the States."

"Uh-uh."

"Well, sit down. We've decided we can trust you."

"Dandy. What took you so long?"

"Don't be naive, Mr. Villar. To coin a phrase, there's a war on."

"Yeah, I'm sorry. And thanks. I'm very glad."

The major looked at him for a long time before saying, "I hope you'll still be glad when you've heard what I'm going to suggest to you."

"Try me."

For ten minutes he listened while the major talked quietly, ending by saying, "I recommend that you go away and think about it for twenty-four hours, then let me have your decision."

Villar shook his head. "If I think about it for twenty-four hours, I'll chicken out. Have them get on with it, will you?"

"You realize that you'll be like it for life."

"If I live that long," Villar said.

They had given him an anesthetic and shot him through the right lower leg with a heavy-caliber bullet which smashed the tibia, but left the calf muscles intact. Then they gave him an honorable discharge from the Italian army, signed with the forged signature of one of Marshal Graziani's generals known to be dead, and two medals for gallantry during the retreat from Egypt. They also gave him a totally new life to memorize while he was recuperating and intensive lessons in radio maintenance and the Morse code.

When he could limp along without pain on his shortened

leg they taught him a lot of other things, then put him ashore on the Italian coast by submarine.

Now, over two years later and using the Italianized version of his name, he was limping up the hill to the Palazzo Millefiori to recover his identity documents. He had left his pedal cart behind because to take it and its hidden contents into the Area GHQ of the German army seemed a little rash. That he was nervous there was no question at all, his mathematical mind balking at a development with no logic to it. If he was "blown," he would have expected attention from the *Gestapo*, not the *Wehrmacht*. Shaking his shoulders to rid himself of the sensation of cold fingers probing his alcohol-sustained defenses, he limped on.

Villari handed the piece of paper the soldier called Gruenther had given him to the sentry at the main gate of the Palazzo and watched through the window of the guardhouse while the man talked into a telephone.

When he came out again the sentry gestured him toward a bench.

He waited for an hour and ten minutes before they let him through.

"Rechts fahren und . . ."

"I'm sorry. I don't understand German."

"No matter. Keep to your right and report to the *Leutnant* at the top of the steps to the patio."

"Thank you."

The *Leutnant* was standing beside a door several paces along the patio. He said, *"Halt!"* and Villari stopped, as there was no point in pretending he didn't understand that.

The officer turned, knocked on the door, opened it, and motioned Villari inside with a jerk of his thumb.

"My God, you're dirty," she said. "Go through there and have a bath."

She was even more beautiful than his memory of her, staring with cold arrogance from the backseat of the open army staff car and he could not possibly have cared less.

"I don't feel like having a bath at the moment."

"Don't you indeed? Well, you're certainly not going to sleep with me in that state."

"I don't feel like sleeping with you either."

He disliked her a little less when she laughed openly.

"Oh yes you do. Everybody does, and you particularly. It's the price you have to pay for your papers. You'll get them back when I'm tired of you."

"I had actually guessed that that was the idea," he told her and looked around him at the lavishly appointed room before adding, "and I imagine I don't have much choice. An appeal to higher authority wouldn't seem likely to succeed against anyone who lives in this style and can send a colonel and three men to do their pimping for them."

She laughed again. "You're quick as well as good-looking. Nobody in their right mind refuses a field marshal's mistress when he has given orders that she is to have anything she wants while he's away."

Lying in the bath, Villari's brain was working on the problem of how best to extract useful intelligence information from the mistress of a very senior German officer to offset the loss imposed on him by an indefinite restriction of his movements. He was not consciously aware of just how professional the British and his own experience had made him. It was enough to know that the return of even a bizarre form of logic to the situation had restored his ability to think constructively.

CHAPTER 8

THE FLOTILLA CAPTAIN WAS THE GUEST OF THE depot ship officers at dinner when *Trigger*'s signal was received. Sitting on the right of the president of the wardroom mess, a place he never entered except when invited by his subordinates to leave the lonely quarters to which his seniority condemned him, he glanced down the length of the gleaming mahogany table. The noise level, particularly from a group from the two submarines in harbor, was increasing. There would, he knew, be bruises and smashed furniture later that night when the submariners had succeeded in goading the depot ship staff into battle. He smiled reminiscently. It was good for them to let off steam and the depot ship people would put up with it all with good-natured resignation.

A marine corporal, envelope in hand, moved quickly down the length of the long room and whispered something to the mess president.

"The lieutenant commander with the red hair nine or ten places along on that side."

"Thank you, sir."

The captain watched his operations staff officer take the envelope from the marine, slit it open and read the contents, then look at him with raised eyebrows and an interrogative jerk of his head toward the door. He turned to his host.

"Sorry, George, but Donaldson and I have to go. Will you excuse us please?"

"Of course, sir. What rotten luck," the mess president said and reached for his gavel.

"No, don't bang that thing," the captain told him. "We'll just slip out quietly."

As they left the mess, *"Trigger,* sir," Lieutenant Commander Donaldson said. "She wants permission to leave her patrol area to chase that Spezia convoy. She's knocked off part of it already."

"I see."

The captain strode toward the operations room, nodding absently to men who sprang to attention at the sight of the four gold stripes on his shoulders. Inside he stood, hands behind his back, looking at the big wall chart of the Tyrrhenian Sea.

"Read it to me, Ginger."

"Yes, sir. 'Firstly, your 147. German auxiliary tanker sunk by gunfire in Giglio Island passage. Secondly, large floating dock boarded and sunk off Civitavecchia. Presumed being towed north to escape air attacks. Thirdly, your 173. Convoy intercepted north of Pianosa. Attempted attack on main body failed but ten-thousand-ton straggler and escorting *Aquila*-class destroyer sunk by torpedo. Forced deep by accurate counterattack until sunset. No significant damage. Enemy last seen steaming due south at seven to eight knots as if passing west of Monte Cristo. Request approval proceed south of latitude forty-two degrees north to resume attack. Six bow and three stern torpedoes remaining. Old merchantman in ballast preceeding convoy as trip-wire.'"

Donaldson stopped reading and looked at the stocky figure in front of the wall chart, one hand still behind its back, the other, thumb and forefinger spread, measuring approximate distances in nautical miles to the south and east of Monte Cristo Island.

"That's all, sir."

The captain made slow affirmative motions with his head, then began talking softly as if thinking aloud.

"Battery'll be flat after two attacks and evasive action. That means, say, four hours on one engine with a full charge on the other. Won't do much more than match the convoy's speed. Brings us to midnight or thereabouts. From then on he can go balls out after them. Yes, he can be back in contact by dawn, Ginger. Write this down. 'For *Trigger,* repeated *Tarantula, Tiger Shark,* C-in-C Mediterranean Fleet, Allied air forces, so on. Well done. Request approved but you are not to pass south of latitude thirty-nine north due risk clash with friendly submarines. Good luck.' All right?"

"Yes, sir."

"Okay. Get that off, put *Tiger Shark* and *Tarantula* in the picture and order them to cover the approaches to Palermo and the Straits of Messina respectively. Any comments?"

"A couple," Donaldson said. *"Tiger Shark* has only four fish. The rest of her tubes and reload space were filled with arms for the partisans."

"Then Philpotts had better aim them straight. Next?"

"You're leaving Naples uncovered by diverting *Tarantula*, sir. If Harding stirs them up enough to make them run for cover, the place will be wide open."

"Oh, I don't mind about that," the captain said. "As long as it isn't to Sicily, I don't give a damn where they go."

The regular changing of the watch keepers marked the passing of the hours for Harding as he leaned against the side of the bridge wearing grease-stained khaki slacks and an old pair of sneakers without laces. At sea he never wore anything with laces on his feet because it wasted seconds when the cry for him to come to the bridge caught him in his bunk. The storm had gone as quickly as it had come, leaving only the overcast behind. It was very dark.

His neck was sore from the chafing of the leather strap from which the heavy Barr and Stroud binoculars hung. He rubbed it, then, for the hundreth time, raised the binoculars to his eyes. Ahead—nothing. On either beam—nothing. Not even a suggestion of horizon separating sea and sky. Above, where the stars should have been, was a vast expanse of nothing. Apart from the soft hissing surge of water along the ballast tanks, there was little sensation of movement. Even the wind had matched its pace and direction to the submarine's and hung heavy with the sickening stench of diesel fumes. Only astern, where the ship drew a phosphorescent wake after her like a bride's train, was there any reference point in space, but time presented no such elusive problem. It was closing in like the Iron Maiden.

"Control room?"

"Control room, sir," the voice-pipe answered.

He had been going to ask the helmsman for another time check and the first lieutenant for a report on the state of the main battery. Pointless. The time was six and a half hours to dawn and the battery would be adequately charged when it was and not a minute sooner.

"Ask somebody to bring me up a shirt, will you? There's one hanging on the hook in my cabin."

"Aye aye, sir. We got some soup on. Would you like a cup?"

"Yes please," Harding said.

He went back to worrying about the time factor, the course and speed of the convoy, the fact that Algiers had given him virtual *carte blanche* which, to his mind, meant that he could not permit himself to fail. His head was aching again and that made him wonder if he'd worked everything out right.

"Permission to come on the bridge with the captain's shirt?"

"Yes."

His neck felt better with the material protecting it from the binocular strap and that, and the action of sipping the hot soup, dispelled his worries. On the basis of the data available to him, he had worked it out correctly and would be in position before first light. The door of the Iron Maiden stopped its inward movement.

"Bridge. First lieutenant here. The captain please."

"Speaking, Number One."

"We have enough amps in the box, sir."

"Good," Harding said. "Stop starboard. In starboard tail clutch. Tell the chief to work up to normal maximum revs on both engines as soon as he can."

He listened to his orders being relayed and, moments later, felt his ship begin to surge more purposefully ahead, leaving its cloud of combustion products astern. It was good to have the breeze in his face again, a breeze which strengthened as the speed increased. The wolf was running now.

The signalman put down his lamp and turned to the commander.

"For *Aquila* from *San Benedetto*—Ready to proceed, sir."

The commander grunted, then said unnecessarily, "So I

should hope. Nearly two hours lost already. Can't any of them maintain their engines properly?"

If he had an answer the signalman didn't provide it. He stood mute, waiting, until the commander added, "Prepare all ships; resume previous course and speed. And you, messenger, go and tell the German captain that we're on our way."

The inside of the submarine looked as it normally did. Broken glass and other debris swept from the decks, bunks secured in place again, cupboards restowed, the heads blown clear. Even Rita Hayworth was the right way up. Only the glassless faces of gauges acted as a reminder of what had happened.

Petty Officer Murchison, face and hands bandaged, lay in a drugged sleep. Harding moved quietly away and went in search of Leading Seaman Gerrard. He found him playing cards one-handed.

"How's the wrist, Gerrard?"

"Bloody 'orrible, sir."

"Seriously?"

"Well, it 'urts. I mean it would, wouldn't it? The cox'n, 'im and 'is first-aid course, 'e's a right butcher. Ought to be thrown overboard!"

"I'll write to *The Lancet* about him," Harding said and moved on.

"Join the club," he said to Able Seaman Bremner, tilting his head sideways with a forefinger to examine his torn cheek. There was only a strip of plaster to look at, no inflammation. "I'm told we'll go down well with the girls. We can say we were at school in Heidelberg."

"Where's that then, sir?"

"Oh, it's a..."

Harding spun on his feet and ran for the control room, the words "Cap'n on the bridge!" reaching his ears through half the length of the ship because, above all else, that was what they were attuned to. He was out of breath when he had completed his rapid climb up the conning tower ladder.

"What is it?"

"Ship bearing Red 15, sir," the navigating officer told him. "I can't see it, but Chivers can so I'm turning toward it."

"Sound the alarm. Slow ahead together." Harding's reaction

was instantaneous because Able Seaman Chivers had the best eyes in the ship and nobody doubted his sightings.

For a second he listened to the ululation of the alarm coming up the voice pipe, a sound close to the ultrasonic guaranteed to wake any sleeper, then asked, "What's it look like, Chivers?"

"Dark blotch, sir, dead ahead now. Can't tell you nothing else."

"All right. Stay on it. Pilot, you sweep the rest of Chivers' sector. Control room, warm up the radar and ask the first lieutenant to speak to me."

"First lieutenant, sir?"

"Chivers has seen something, Number One. I don't know if it's a lone ship or part of the convoy. As soon as the radar's warm, use it for five seconds or less if possible and tell me what it shows."

"Aye aye, sir."

It was a full two minutes before he thought he could make it out himself, the merest trace of greater darkness.

"Anything new, Chivers?"

"It's a ship, sir. I'll bet on that, but I can't figure out if it's a little'n close to or big'un far off. Seems to be staying at the same range now we've slowed down."

With the reduction in speed, the diesel fumes were back, enveloping them with their stench. Harding ran his tongue around inside his mouth, trying to rid himself of the taste, then he looked astern. The bride's train was still sliding after them.

"I think it's a big one at long range. If it was close we'd be able to see the phosphorescence."

"Oh. Hadn't thought of that, sir. Makes sense to me."

Engine exhausts burbling idly, deck vibration almost nil, sea sounds subdued. It was so quiet on the bridge that Harding could hear the faint rasp of material as the lookouts raised and lowered their binoculars.

"First lieutenant to captain." The words from the voice pipe were loud enough to make him jump.

"Yes, Number One?"

"It's the convoy, sir. Must have been hove to for a couple of hours. The ship you're looking at is the last merchantman in the starboard column. She's nearly a mile astern of the next ahead. I've got radar ranges and bearings of the whole lot, sir.

Would you like to send the pilot down to stick them on the chart? I'll send Guns up to relieve him."

Harding tapped the navigating officer on the shoulder and said, "Down you go," then into the voice pipe, "He's on his way, but keep Elleston there too. I may want him on the 'Fruit Machine.' Now, can you give me the rough layout?"

"Yes, sir. Five big 'blips.' Two in the port column, three in the starboard. Range to the nearest, the one you can see, is forty-one hundred yards. From the size of the remaining 'blips' I think the three destroyers are in an arc ahead of the convoy with the two antisubmarine chasers on either flank. They don't seem to be anticipating an attack from astern, sir."

"You're reading my mind, Number One. What's the range to the nearest escort?"

"Eight thousand yards to the port flanker, bearing Red 15."

"Start the attack," Harding said.

Trigger's bow knifing through the lazy, almost flat swell. Vibration strong, too strong to let him see anything with his binoculars clipped to the torpedo night-sight. He unclipped them and lifted them to his eyes. Big now, the black silhouette of the ship in the powerful lenses, visible as a dark smear on the horizonless ocean even without them. Harding found himself chewing his lower lip, wondering how long he dared wait before firing, how efficient the escorts' radar, how good the target's lookouts. The engineer officer's exclamation came to him and he said "Tchah!" to himself because he knew that he had to be a lot closer than he was to be certain of a kill with so little data and such poor visibility. He let the binoculars dangle from their strap and glanced around him.

"Clarke!"

"Sir?"

"If I catch you again looking anywhere except in your own sector, you're in for it. What the target is doing is nothing whatsoever to do with you."

"Sorry, sir."

"Yes, and you'd be sorrier still if you let a destroyer crawl up our arse."

It was, he recognized, asking the near impossible of the men not to try to snatch glimpses of an enemy they were about to attack, but it was vital that they kept the areas to which they

had been assigned under constant surveillance. Chivers understood, and excellent eyes or not, that was what made him such
a good lookout because he never stopped looking where he had
been told to. He bent to the voice pipe.

"Number One, I want another quick radar scan. General
picture and target course and speed from the plot."

"Aye aye, sir."

Christ but it looked big! Was it possible that they couldn't
see him? Apparently it was. He conjured up a picture of the
scene on the freighter's bridge. Four men, one on each wing,
an officer and the helmsman in the wheelhouse. Bored, only
half-awake, staring forward because that was where the destroyers were and where an attack could be expected to come
from. Probably they were smoking, ruining their night vision
every time they looked at a burning cigarette. Harding scowled
suddenly in self-rebuke. And just as probably none of those
things was true. Careful. Careful. Stop rationalizing.

"Captain, sir, general picture unchanged. Target steering
155. Speed eight and a quarter knots. Range twenty-three
hundred yards."

"Thank you. Stand by seven and eight tubes and give me
a course for a one-thirty track."

Harding was given it, *Trigger*'s bows swung to starboard.
Steadied.

"Seven and eight tubes standing by, sir. Bow caps open."

"What's the director angle?"

"Green 5, sir."

He cranked the bearing onto the night-sight, stared along
it, ignoring his binoculars because of the vibration, using the
naked eye. Tearing in toward the enemy ship. Range closing
rapidly. Target looming. Wait for it. Wait. A few more seconds
and it wouldn't matter if he *was* sighted. There would be no
time for the cumbersome ship to do anything.

Wait. Wait. Now!

"Fire seven. Fire eight."

Harding saw the glint of the two torpedoes as they leaped
forward from the topmost pair of tubes like gigantic salmon,
saw the splash as they hit the surface of the water, saw briefly
the glowing trail of their passage arrowing toward the enemy.

"Starboard thirty," he said, "and tell the engineer officer I want to go like the devil."

"Your conception of antisubmarine measures seems to be of the *post factum* variety," von Liebnitz said. "I implore you to close that particular stable door before we lose some more horses."

"At least it is not based on clichés," the Italian commander replied sharply. Then, in a more reasonable voice, added, "Since the loss of *Falcone* I no longer have sufficient ships to provide a rear escort. Consequently I have so disposed my forces as to provide the maximum protection in the area of greatest danger. You must agree that that is between the convoy and its destination. That is where the British will be massing."

"*Massing?* Why, they have barely enough...Oh, never mind. Just let me tell you this. They have efficient radar, which you have not, and the area of greatest danger will be where they locate a gap in your screen. That gap must be filled. You do not need three destroyers ahead of two columns of ships."

"You are misinformed. We have excellent radar."

"Please," von Liebnitz said, "do not be deliberately obtuse. You have reasonable aircraft detection radar. Your surface-to-surface equipment is embryonic and you can't even detect hostile transmissions."

"Indeed we can. We detected them twice in the last fifteen minutes."

"Did you, by God? On what bearing?"

"I don't know," the Italian said. "They didn't last long enough for us to *get* a bearing." He sounded plaintive.

The following breeze carried the double detonation clearly to their ears.

San Benedetto died slowly, listing further and further until, half an hour after the torpedoes had struck, she lay on her side and the sea began pouring in through the huge aperture of her funnel.

Five miles to the west of the convoy, *Trigger* raced on through the darkness. Once a destroyer had passed close, but Harding had turned stern-on and had not been seen. Now he was sitting in the wardroom, drinking coffee, resting his legs, hoping that the trembling in them was fatigue from his hours on the bridge, not the onset of the shakes. Although the red lighting was on, he was wearing red goggles as an additional safeguard for his night vision.

"Three down, nine to go, and only seven fish left," he said. "I could kill myself for wasting four torpedoes on that blasted floating dock!"

"Come off it, sir. How were you to know? Anyway, nobody expects you to knock off the escorts. The convoy's the thing; you've sunk a third of it and seven fish for the remaining four merchantmen sounds like better odds to me. You aren't likely to get them all, of course, but unless they've divided the cargoes equally between the freighters, which I doubt, if you only sink one more, they'll probably pack it in. What would be the point in their pressing on to Sicily with the whole load of tanks and no ammunition for them, or vice versa?"

"Long speech for you, Number One. Making noises like a staff officer. Still, you're absolutely right. I think . . . Oh, hello, Guns. Got the radar report?"

"Yes, sir," Elleston said. "The target 'blip' has disappeared from the screen, so I suppose she's gone down. The little 'blip' which is probably a submarine chaser is still in that general vicinity. Could be picking up survivors. The . . ."

"How far is the chaser behind now?"

"Seven miles, give or take, sir."

"All right, go on."

"The rest of them have stopped milling about and are back in formation. Two columns of two ships, two destroyers ahead and one astern. The remaining chaser is on the far flank of the convoy."

"Good," Harding said. "I hoped they'd think that."

"Think what, sir?"

"That we're to the east of them. That's where the torpedoes came from and why I came across to this side in such a hurry. What's the relative bearing?"

"A few degrees abaft our beam, sir."

Harding stood up. "You'd better send the crew to diving stations, Number One. I'm going in before that second chaser rejoins and completes the circle."

It was von Liebnitz who first sighted the long, low shape

of *Trigger* gliding in toward the ships in his charge. He had assumed full control and placed *Aquila* in the stern escort position as the best place from which to start a counterattack. He took rapid action, but was already too late. The double column of ships had presented an unbroken line to Harding. Those in the more distant column both filling the gap in the nearer and seeming to extend it. Such a target required no accuracy of him and his last bow salvo of four torpedoes was already on its way. The ripple of gun flashes from the destroyer was a puny prelude to the Wagnerian extravaganza which was to follow.

Pressed into a corner of the bridge, Harding felt as though he had always been there and would have ridiculed any suggestion that it had been less than twenty minutes. His lower lip was raw from the attention of his teeth. Unknowingly he had been chewing at it for the last ten of those minutes. Expecting to be sighted, wondering why he was not, his mind sidestepping to make a mental note for his patrol report that the enemy's lookouts appeared to be substandard and his radar ineffective, but not really believing it. All those ships like a darker frieze on a dark wall and none of them knowing that he was there. Incredible. The simple explanation that he knew where they were while they thought he was somewhere else, although he had planned it that way, escaped him because he could no longer envisage them neglecting any possibility.

When the last torpedo had left its tube, "You'd better come down now, Chivers," he said.

Chivers, above and behind him, on top of the forward periscope standard to give him a clear field of view across a wide arc, replied, "Aye aye, sir. Silhouette of the destroyer on the port beam shortening. Turning toward us I reckon, sir."

That was when the gunfire started and, almost incongruously, Harding added another mental note to his report. "The enemy has not yet developed flashless cordite."

The shells rumbled overhead, but he didn't turn to watch where they fell. There were other sounds to think about. The deep bellow of the big ships' sirens, the much higher whoop—whoop—whoop of the destroyers', the beating of his own heart. No, the last had to be imagination.

What he had thought of as a continuous frieze was beginning to break up as the line of ships started to turn slowly, ponderously, away. One, close enough to be recognized as a heavy-laden tanker, wasn't going to make it.

"Never in a million years."

"What, sir?"

"Nothing, Chivers. Talking to myself."

"That destroyer's shooting again, sir, and there's another coming toward us from the head of the convoy."

"Good. With any luck they'll blow each other out of the water," Harding said, and as if in confirmation of the thought a signal lamp stuttered angrily from the bridge of the first.

The passage of the shells above them was louder this time, but again Harding ignored them. He had just seen two faint lights glow, lights that were instantly extinguished, below the tanker's waterline.

"Second destroyer's turning away, sir."

"Thank you, Chivers."

"Captain, sir?"

Harding bent to the voice pipe. "Yes, Number One?"

"Two sharp explosions. Sounded like torpedoes."

"Yes, we've hit the tanker. I don't know where the other two fish went. Stand by nine, ten, and eleven tubes."

He had never fired a stern shot before and he looked half-fearfully over his shoulder toward the glowing wake, thinking about what he was going to do, hoping he would get it right.

The destroyer was getting uncomfortably close, not much more than a mile away, but the tanker, lying dead in the water, was much closer. So were the two other big ships, and for that reason he thought that the next salvo from the destroyer would be the last for the time being because, after that, there would be the risk of hitting their own people.

It *was* to be the last. It was also very nearly to be the last of *Trigger*. The nearest of the shells plunged into the sea ten feet in front of her bows and she sailed straight through the column of water it threw up. Harding wiped the water from his face with the sleeve of his shirt and from the binocular lenses with a wad of tissue from his pocket, watching the tanker he proposed to use as a shield for the very few minutes he needed and hoped would be given him.

"Steer ten degrees to starboard."

"Ten degrees to starboard it is, sir." The coxswain's voice

coming from the metal pipe sounding of nothing but cheerful acceptance. Grateful for it as he was, such trustingness from men imprisoned in a speeding steel tube with no clear knowledge of or control over the naval battle into which he had led them always frightened him a little with its reminder of the responsibility he bore.

"Ask the first lieutenant to have constant radar watch set, please. I'll be asking for ranges in a minute."

"Set constant radar watch. Aye aye, sir. Ship steady on 045 degrees."

Trigger's new course would carry her close under the bows of the stationary tanker, less distinct now with heavy coils of smoke beginning to eddy from three separate sources, flattening, obscuring the outline. The smell of oil was strong on the night air. Harding looked up at the ship as he passed, trying to read the name on the bows, but could not distinguish it, and turned his attention to the freighter stern on to him and a third of a mile distant.

"There's a little'n close by the ship ahead, sir," Chivers said. "Coming this way I reckon. Think I can see her bow wave. Chaser probably."

If his mind had needed making up on the time factor, that did it for Harding. With a destroyer due to appear within minutes from the other side of the tanker behind him, a submarine chaser approaching fast from ahead, and other escort vessels in the vicinity, there was far greater immediacy about the closing of the Iron Maiden's door than had been the case earlier.

He ordered the rudder put hard over. *Trigger* curved in a graceful arc until, with her bows pointing back toward the tanker and her stern aimed at the fleeing freighter, the last three torpedoes were launched on their journey.

Aquila died by accident. Somewhere in an armaments factory in Britain, in the maintenance shops of the depot ship in Algiers, or in *Trigger*'s own torpedo stowage compartment, somebody had made a mistake. Of the four torpedoes Harding had used against the huddled ships, two had hit the tanker, one had found no target and had sped on eventually to sink at the end of its six-and-a-half-mile range. The fourth had a defective gyro and ran in a circle. At a point on the circumference of that circle torpedo and warship intercepted each other.

In her death *Aquila* emulated the fury of her sister ship *Falcone*, but now there was no storm to tear the pall to pieces. It lay flat over the surface of the sea, spreading slowly to blend with the smoke from the burning tanker.

Harding sighed softly and then turned to look back at his final target. There had not yet been time for the three stern torpedoes to reach it, but the submarine chaser was overtaking him rapidly. It was none too soon to dive.

"Clear the bridge," he said.

Trigger's conning tower was still above the surface when the world blew up.

Above the crash of falling objects a persistent wailing scream from the direction of the engine room. A man cannoned off Harding, cursing, slithering forward, unable to maintain his footing in the extreme bow-down angle. Harding hung grimly on to the periscope wire, waiting for the emergency lighting to switch itself on. Within a second or two it did so, flickering at first as though reluctant to reveal the shambles that had once been a ship.

"What's the deep gauge read, Number One? The shallow diving gauges seem to be out of action."

"I think they all are, sir."

The first lieutenant had his arms and legs locked around the control-room ladder. The men at the hydroplane controls were operating them with one hand, clinging to whatever they could with the other. Against the back of the helmsman's chair, a figure in a blue overall with the insignia of a petty officer on the sleeve lay facedown. From the unnatural posture of the head Harding knew that the neck was broken.

"Emergency full astern together," he said.

A pause, then a voice saying, "Port propeller shaft jammed, sir, and we've another fire in the motor room."

"I see. Blow main ballast. Stand by to abandon ship."

There were other orders he wanted to give, but there was nothing he could do about that until the roar of high-pressure air stopped. He stood, his body at thirty degrees to the deck, clinging to his wire, waiting for the angle to come off, wondering bleakly if they were already too deep for the air to expel the ballast water.

It came off slowly, the angle, then became bow up and there

was the elevatorlike pressure of the deck on the soles of their feet. The blowing stopped.

"When we're on the surface I want all hatches opened, Number One. The crew will assemble on the casing wearing life jackets. Help the injured and leave the dead. As soon as you're sure that there's an escort vessel to pick them up, order everybody over the side. They're to swim away from the ship and you're to tell me when they're clear, then go after them. Understood?"

"Understood, sir," the first lieutenant said and began talking into the tannoy microphone.

Harding gestured for the periscope to be raised, but the operator shook his head at him. "Won't move, sir. Neither of 'em."

"All right."

Trigger surfaced blind and very fast, her forward section clear of the water for over half its length. Then it crashed down onto the surface and the submarine lay stopped, wallowing, in the gentle swell.

"Up you go, Number One."

There were more men in the control room than Harding could ever remember seeing at one time. There would, he knew, be similar groups waiting below the other hatches. He stood to one side watching a seemingly endless succession of legs disappear up into the conning tower until at last the control room was empty and he moved to the voice pipe to wait for the first lieutenant to tell him that the crew had left the ship.

A slight sound behind him made him turn his head.

"What the hell are you doing here, Corporal Ackroyd?"

The big commando stood, legs astride, huge arms dangling, watching him thoughtfully.

"First lieutenant's orders, sir."

"What orders?"

"Well, it's like this, sir. He thinks you may have been reading some of them books with sea stories in 'em. So, when you've pulled them main-vent levers to scuttle the ship, unless you hop up that ladder a bit bloody sharpish, I'm to hang one on your chin and get you over the side meself. Begging your pardon of course, sir."

Harding smiled, frowned, smiled again, and said, "Well, well, well."

"Yessir."

"All right, Ackroyd. I'm very grateful to both you and the first lieutenant, but I haven't the slightest intention of going down with my ship. You get up top now and swim well away from her. The suction will be pretty strong when she goes down."

Ackroyd nodded, but made no move to go.

"That's something else the first lieutenant mentioned, sir. Your swimming, that is."

"What about my swimming?"

"Not your strong point, sir, he tells me. He reckons I could tow you out of the way a lot faster than you could make it alone, so I'll stay here like he told me to."

Both touched and annoyed, but too tired to register either emotion, Harding turned back to the voice pipe just as it said, "Captain sir, I'm sending a party of men down the engine-room hatch to make sure that armature fire's out. There's just a chance we'll get away with this."

"What are you talking about, Number One? The whole place is lousy with escorts." It irritated him that he had asked "what" four times in the last minute.

"Not now it isn't, sir," the first lieutenant told him. "I think you'd better come and look. It's rather eerie."

"Come on, Ackroyd," Harding said and leaped for the ladder.

Men made way for him on the crowded bridge, watching him curiously as though he were someone they hadn't seen before. Behind him Ackroyd's voice saying, "Fuck me! Did we do all that?"

Red. Everything red. Even the men's faces washed by the light from the burning tanker on the starboard bow, flames roaring along its entire length, a towering holocaust of fire licking at the overcast. Almost ahead a patch of sea, small flames flickering and dying, flickering and dying again, marked the point the destroyer had reached when its magazine exploded because a torpedo had run wild. Astern, a submarine chaser listing, burning, hurling sparks skyward, because she had been too close when an ammunition ship had been blown to pieces by his last salvo. *Trigger* had been too close as well.

"Looks like Dante's Inferno, doesn't it, sir?"

"Maybe it does, Number One, but there are still two destroyers and another chaser to worry about, plus two merchantmen. Where on earth are they?"

"When we surfaced I thought I got a glimpse of them making off to the east." He gestured vaguely before adding, "If that is the east. The gyrocompass is on the blink, but Naples is over there somewhere. Probably they've had enough."

"Not fuckin' surprised," somebody said.

"Shut up, that man! The captain's trying to think!"

Harding tried to do that, but first it took an enormous effort of will to turn his thoughts away from the imminent probability of drowning, or life in a prisoner-of-war camp, and toward the possibility of getting his ship back to Algiers. It seemed a long time to him, but it was only seconds before he spoke.

"Get the petty officers and leading hands below with the pilot and Guns. They're to place themselves at the engineer officer's disposal and go through the boat, finding out what works and what doesn't. Everyone else to stay where they are, out of the way. I need to know first if we can move at all and second if we can dive. And hurry. They'll have planes out here by first light."

"I'll take charge below myself, sir."

"You'll do what I tell . . ."

"The chief's dead, sir."

"Oh. Then carry on, Number One."

The black and red patterns on the sea constantly shifting. Debris bobbing lethargically. A capsized boat. Bodies drifting facedown. Not far away one man swimming with slow, labored strokes.

There were fewer men on deck now that the first lieutenant had taken his party below and Harding could look around at his own ship. The four-inch gun had jumped from its ring of roller bearings and the long barrel was pointing over the port bow, not directly forward as it should have done. The Oerlikon cannon was missing altogether, torn from its mounting at the back of the bridge by the blast from the ammunition ship. Both periscope standards were out of true and the radar antenna had gone. So had the wireless aerial.

"Englander!"

Puzzled, Harding turned to search for the source of the shout, then remembered the lone swimmer.

"He's a four-stripe captain, sir," Chivers said.

"Is he, by God? The Intelligence boys would like to talk to *him*. Corporal Ackroyd?"

"Yessir?"

"You like towing people about. Fetch me that German officer, will you?"

"Yessir."

"Chivers, bring me my cap from my cabin, please, and try to find a heaving line."

"Aye aye, sir."

The commando had wrenched his shoes off without bothering to untie the laces and was balancing on the side of the bridge. His dive carried him well clear of the ballast tanks into the black and red sea. Harding turned in a circle, searching where he thought the horizon should be, but could see nothing beyond the area illuminated by the tanker. The submarine chaser had sunk.

He took his uniform cap from Chivers and put it on his head, looked at the coiled heaving line and said, "Give that to Norris on the fore casing," then watched as Ackroyd, swimming powerfully, brought the German alongside, catching the line Norris threw to him.

"Herr Kapitanleutnant? That is your rank, *ja?"*

The elderly German had seen the only figure wearing a cap and was addressing himself to Harding who had no idea what his equivalent rank in the German navy was.

"I'm the captain, sir," he said. "Who are you?"

"Kapitan-sur-see Jurgen von Liebnitz."

"Then come aboard, sir. My men will help you."

"Danke, but is no use. I am only for dying, but I wish a question first. How many undersea boats attack me since yesterday at—at—*der Mittag?* At middle day?"

"Four."

"A lie. *Ja,* I sink so. Is a lie. Why lie to a man dying?"

To Ackroyd, treading water patiently, Harding said, "Is he hurt, Corporal?"

"Yessir. Bad. I seen his guts when I was pulling him back."

Harding looked at von Liebnitz again. "Only this one, sir. I attacked you off Pianosa first. You gave us a bad time after that."

The light from the tanker was less intense now, but the look of satisfaction on the German's face was clear.

"Is good. They say you are a wolf pack. I say no, one only. You make good war, *Herr Kapitanleutnant.*"

"Control room—bridge. Give me the captain, please."

"I'm here, Number One."

"The steering's okay and you can go ahead gently on the starboard engine, sir."

"Thank you," Harding said, raised his voice, and added, "Everybody except Norris and Chivers down below. Close the hatches after you." He turned back to the German.

"We have to go now, sir. Can I give you a life belt or anything?"

"A bullet, *Englander.* You can spare one bullet after all this."

Harding saw an all-encompassing movement of von Liebnitz's arm, then, involuntarily, his head drooped forward just as Ackroyd's hand slashed at the German's neck.

Trigger was limping slowly toward the comparative safety of the darkness beyond the range of the fire when the dripping commando and Norris clambered on to the bridge.

"Ackroyd."

"Yessir?"

"Thank you. I don't think I could have shot him. Even as a kindness."

"S'all right, sir. That's what I'm for. Anyway, I reckon you done *your* bit."

Leaning back against the bent periscope standard, it occurred to Harding that he felt quite remarkably tired.

CHAPTER 9

THE AMERICAN EMBASSY DRIVER HAD TO STOP HIS car fifty yards short of Thayer Street because of the barrier across the road with a sign on it reading "Danger—Unexploded Bomb."

"Okay, I'll walk the rest. You wait here," his passenger said.

The driver nodded and lit a cigarette.

At the barrier the American was stopped by an unshaven soldier with red-rimmed eyes.

"You can't come in 'ere, mate."

"I don't much want to come in there, but I have to."

The soldier looked up at the tall civilian. "You a Yank or somethin'?"

"Yeah, I'm a Yank or something. Let me speak with your officer."

"Not likely. My officer's down a bloody great 'ole tryin' to fillet a bloody great bomb. 'E ain't got no time to talk to civvies."

Quietly the American said, "Oh Jesus. This is all I need," and looked around him. A few paces away a policeman was talking to a steel-helmeted air-raid warden. He was uncertain about British police insignia, but the officer with his back to him had silver on his shoulders. He decided to play it safe.

"Pardon me, Superintendent."

The man turned to face him. "Just Inspector, sir. Can I help you?"

"I surely hope so, Inspector. It's important that I get to that building there."

The police officer followed the direction of his pointing finger, then, without looking at him, asked, "May I see your identification papers, sir?"

He took the celluloid-covered card held out to him, read what was printed on it, and compared the photograph with its owner's face.

"You'd better come with me, sir."

As they ducked under the rope barrier the soldier said, "'Ere, where do you think . . . ?"

"It's all right," the inspector told him. "This is government business. I'll take full responsibility."

The soldier shrugged and lost interest.

There were two armed soldiers inside the heavily sand-bagged door of the building which housed that branch of the Secret Service known in official circles as the Department. The police officer handed the American over to them, saluted, and left. One of them led him to a man sitting in a cubicle where the foyer turned to the left out of sight of the street.

"You want to see the director you say? Now I wonder who that might be."

"I don't know who it might be," the American said, "but I do know who it is. It's Professor Morris."

"Ah, that's right. Slipped my mind for a moment." The man picked up a telephone. "Mr. Harkness is here. The director's expecting him. Send an escort down, will you?"

Professor Morris was a slender man of about fifty with a gentle face and a strangely multicolored beard which resembled the fur of a tabby cat. He got up and walked around his desk, hand outstretched, when the American was shown in.

"It's a pleasure to meet you, Mr. Harkness."

"My privilege, sir."

"Well, sit down, help yourself to a cigarette, and tell me what I can do for you."

Harkness sat down, waved the proffered box of cigarettes away, and said, "It's about a man named John Villar, an American citizen we've lost track of, but who we believe to have come to Britain in 1940 to get into the war. There are seventeen John Villars in your armed forces, fifteen of them British and two Irish. The trail stops there."

"Yes?"

"He's a brilliant man, Professor, and bilingual in English and Italian. It occurred to us that he might have come to you and been given a clandestine mission in Italy."

"Oh," Professor Morris said, "you want to talk to the special operations executive, not me."

"I've been to SOE, sir. They sent me to you."

"How very tiresome of them. Always sending people to dangerous places and now they've landed you next to an unexploded bomb. Quite thoughtless. Quite, quite thoughtless."

"You don't seem particularly worried about the bomb, Professor."

"Me? Heavens no. I was only teasing. It's two hundred yards from here. The authorities are simply being careful, and so they should."

Harkness suppressed a sigh of impatience before saying, "May we talk a little more about John Villar?"

"By all means, my dear fellow. Chat away, but never having heard of the man, I'm afraid I shan't be able to contribute much to the conversation."

The American sighed openly, took a sealed envelope from a pocket, and pushed it across the desk.

"For me?"

"It's addressed to you."

"So it is."

Morris slit the envelope, took out a single sheet of paper, and read aloud, "Mr. George G. Harkness of the Office of Strategic Service is to be given your utmost cooperation." Then, "Signed by *him* too, eh? Why didn't you show me this in the first place?"

"Because I dislike going around waving bits of paper which override other people's authority. We're pretty sure you've got Villar and hoped you'd give him back to us without our having to invoke the prime minister's name."

"Very nice of you to put it that way."

"Have you or have you not got Villar, Professor?"

"Oh, we've got him all right and I'm going to fight you for him, prime minister or no prime minister. He's one of the most consistently successful agents we've ever had. Carries entire numerical code sequences in his head as though they were the multiplication table. Pages of 'em, and the services tell me the information he has provided has been beyond value. Why don't you find yourself a fluent Italian speaker somewhere else? There must be thousands of them. I can't imagine what the PM's thinking of."

Harkness shuffled his feet as though in embarrassment before saying, "We're not interested in his languages. He has other talents of far greater importance to both our countries."

"Aha! Got you! Chair of advanced mathematics at MIT. You want him for the Manhattan Project. Wouldn't be making all this fuss otherwise." Morris sounded like a boy who had just made a telling point at the school debating society.

"I don't know what you're talking about, sir. What project did you say?"

"Come now, Harkness," Morris said. "Don't be coy. I know exactly who you are, what your responsibilities are, and what your security clearance is. If I didn't, you wouldn't be in this room. This OSS stuff is just cover. And another thing, people of your prestige and seniority aren't given messenger-boy jobs. If you want Villar for the Manhattan Project, say so and I'll see what I can do. If you want him for anything else, I'll fight you as I've said."

"I'm not cleared to discuss any . . ."

"Then let me make it easy for you. Easy for me too because I don't relish the thought of a scrap with the PM. The thing really started here when Lord Rutherford demonstrated how the atom could be split in 1924 or thereabouts at the Cavendish Laboratory at Cambridge University. Since then a lot of work has been done and the latest results passed to your people to escape the bombing. You are far ahead of us now, but I would remind you of two things."

Morris held up one finger and wagged it.

"We have just pulled Niels Bohr, who probably knows more about the nuts and bolts than Einstein, out of Denmark for you."

A second finger joined the first.

"There are British scientists working alongside your own at Los Alamos. At our level there is no secret about it."

The American nodded, smiled, and stood up.

"You know something, Professor?" he said. "Security on the damned thing is so tight that, with that particular code name, I come close to fainting if anybody mentions the Empire State Building. So I can have Villar for New Mexico?"

"Do I have the word of the United States government that that is what he's wanted for?"

"You do, sir."

"Very well," Professor Morris said. "In that case the answer is yes. *If* I can get him out of Italy."

CHAPTER 10

ONLY THE WARDROOM DEPTH GAUGE HAD SUR-
vived the blast from the ammunition ship and the subsequent
pressure the submarine had been subjected to. It had done so
because the small-bore pipe leading to it had fractured, soaking
the wardroom with a needlelike jet of water. The pipe was
repaired now and the gauge functioning. Elleston sat watching
it, calling out every time it gave a reading in excess of the five-
foot limit either side of the ninety mark the captain had ordered.

In his cabin Harding lay on the bunk listening to Elleston's
voice, the acknowledgments of the officer of the watch in the
control room, and the instructions to the planesmen or the
ballast pump operator. He thought that they had been extremely
fortunate and was shaking jerkily. When the door slid open,
he froze the spasms of his muscles and jerked his head to face
it.

"It's customary to knock!"

The first lieutenant ducked his head, stepped through the
opening, and shut the door behind him.

"Bad one, sir?"

"What the hell are you talking about, Number One?"

"These turns you have, sir. I was wondering if today was
worse than usual and if you'd—well, like to talk about it."

Harding let his body relax slowly and found that the trembling had left him, but he felt no relief.

"Oh dear," he said. "Do they all know?"

The other shook his head. "Nobody but me. I'm quite positive about that. They think you're a sort of amiable icicle."

97

"Hmm. Then what put *you* on to it?"

"Observation. You know how we both watch everybody for signs of strain, how it becomes automatic. I've seen it in your face several times just before you've left the wardroom rather abruptly and come in here. When you've come out you've been okay again."

"Anything else?"

"Not sure how relevant it is, sir, but your dislike of any kind of public occasion started me wondering too. Most of the time I have to nag you to see defaulters and last night's funeral service seemed to take more out of you than chewing up that convoy. As an extrovert you're a nonstarter. They breeze through things like that."

"I don't want to be an extrovert," Harding said, "and if you think a funeral is an occasion for . . ."

He stopped talking, his eyes fixed on the curve of the pressure hull above his bunk, but seeing the four canvas-wrapped figures lying on the casing above that. Each pair had had to share a White Ensign* between them because there were only two on board. They wouldn't have minded. The officer and the petty officer. The leading seaman and the able seaman. A cross section of the navy's structure. But his second-in-command was right, he thought, although he probably hadn't meant it that way. Or had he? For the few moments he had stood on the casing in the predawn blackness the, to him, awful necessity of reciting from memory and with no mistakes the words for burials at sea had completely obliterated his sadness. There *was* something wrong with him.

He looked at the first lieutenant again.

"All right, John. If you're going to psychoanalyze me you'd better sit down. Trick cyclists don't loom over patients on the couch."

The first lieutenant folded himself into the only chair, trying to remember if his commanding officer had ever before called him by his christian name. He didn't think he had.

There was a long silence before Harding asked, "Do you think I should hand over command to you?"

"No, sir, I do not. If I'd thought that you'd make any such

*The British naval flag.

suggestion, I would never have raised the matter. It's just that—it's just that I hate sitting in the wardroom knowing that you're having the heebie-jeebies in here. I should have minded my own business."

Harding shook his head.

"It is your business. It's your life and the life of everyone aboard."

"I don't see it that way, sir. It never happens in action. It never happens when you're handling the ship in confined spaces or strong currents. It never happens when you're planning a tricky interception or something like that. In fact it never happens when it matters."

"No, it doesn't," Harding said. "But it might."

"Yes, and you might fall down the periscope well, have somebody lower the periscope, and reduce you to raspberry jam. The likelihood is about the same."

"Hmm."

The silence came back and they both listened to it and were grateful because it was their shield. *Trigger* had dived a few minutes after the ripples made by the four weighted bodies on the flat water had died away. Thirty seconds later Harding, regretting the waste of power and compressed air, had given the order to surface to establish the cause of the desultory clanging over their heads. The strip of torn metal hanging from what was left of the Oerlikon platform had been located and thrown over the side and they had dived again.

"You're up to eighty-five feet." Elleston's voice. The control room's acknowledgment.

The first lieutenant moved uncomfortably in his chair and said, "You know, sir, you may have brought this on yourself."

"Oh?"

"Yes. I doubt you've been ashore more than four times since we left England eight months ago. You don't go to the rest camp, which is a terrific place. You duck out of the depot ship cocktail parties and guest nights. You don't swim, or sail, or ride. I've never seen you more than mildly pissed in the mess and—and I've overheard this myself at least three times— whenever one of the other captains says he's lined up a couple of lady officers for the evening, you have something desperately important to do aboard *Trigger*. Well, I know that's nonsense because, thank God, you have never interfered with my running of the ship in harbor."

There was the faintest trace of irritation in Harding's voice when he spoke.

"You seem to be remarkably well informed on what I don't do. What *do* I do?"

"Well, I don't actually follow you around, sir, but if I come to see you about anything in harbor, the chances are better than even that you're reading through a bloody great pile of the other boats' patrol reports, Intelligence info, and other classified material I'm not allowed to see. I don't believe you think about anything but the war. It's as though its outcome is your personal responsibility and you've given up everything else for the duration. Particularly people. Except us that is."

"Hermit in a cave, am I?"

"Sort of. And I think it's catching up with you."

"You're probably right," Harding said and pursed his lips. The lower one was still sore. "I'll go and see the quack when we get back to Algiers. Perhaps he'll be able to do something."

"They'll give you the push if you do that, sir. If I were you, I'd try and fix it for myself and leave the doctors alone."

"Well you're not me!" Harding told him sharply, then added, "I'm sorry. It must have been difficult coming to see me about this and I'm very grateful to you. I'll think about it on the way home. God knows that'll give me time enough at the speed we're making."

When the first lieutenant had gone, Harding got off his bunk, sat at his combination washbasin and desk, and read again the list of major defects which had been prepared for him.

The port propeller shaft was so badly distorted that nothing could be done about it without dockyard facilities. The starboard shaft was fractionally out of true and could only be operated at low revolutions above which the main bearings would overheat, destroy themselves, and cripple the ship completely and finally. Five knots appeared to be their maximum surface speed. Dived they could make barely two because of the state the main battery was in.

Of the 336 giant cells, as high as a man's chest and about two feet square, it had been estimated that more than a hundred had been cracked, the acid they held seeping down into the crankcases. It would be vital to get rid of as much of the acid as possible during the coming night. If saltwater should find its way into the battery tanks . . . For a moment Harding smelled chlorine gas, then trod firmly on his imagination.

Fire had done enough damage to the armature of the port main motor to prevent its use as a dynamo, so they were totally dependent on the starboard diesel both for propulsion and charging what remained of the battery. That, he knew, would further reduce their surface speed and Algiers suddenly seemed unbelievably remote.

Then there was the loss of the Oerlikon cannon and the damage to the four-inch gun. He didn't care about them as he was in no condition to fight anyone anyway. The radar he cared about even less. Its use would have acted only as a magnet to draw the enemy to him. The wireless aerial could be replaced and that would be done as soon as the ship surfaced for the night. A signal was already ciphered and awaiting transmission. It would be sent in a number of short bursts to lessen the chances of an accurate radio fix being made on them.

What worried Harding most was the freshwater situation. One storage tank was polluted with salt and he did not yet know how that had happened. Strict rationing of water had been imposed and washing forbidden. What was left was to be used for drinking, cooking, and nothing else.

Was there anything more of significance in the long list? He thought not, except of course for the smashed periscopes. They were not something he was prepared to worry about for the simple reason that there was absolutely nothing he could do about it. *Trigger* was blind and that was that, but with the sonar still functioning, she was far from deaf in her own element. The risks of surfacing by chance close to an enemy vessel were small because the sound of the propellers would be clearly audible to them. Aircraft were a different question. No hydrophone could hear them, but he intended to remain submerged until darkness came if the reduced capacity of the batteries permitted him to do so. *If . . .*

Harding shrugged, put the damage report down, and left his cabin to visit the fourteen injured men in the makeshift hospital in the torpedo stowage compartment.

The flotilla captain was dining alone when Lieutenant Commander Donaldson knocked on the door of his quarters.

"Come in. Oh, hello Ginger."

Donaldson had followed his knock into the day cabin without pausing.

"*Trigger,* sir. She's mauled that Sicily convoy pretty severely, but she seems to be in a mess herself."

The captain started to get to his feet, but sank back in his chair at a wave of his staff officer's hand.

"Finish your dinner, sir. Harding's transmitting in short spells for obvious reasons. There's more to come and not enough for you to act on so far."

"All right. Have you eaten?"

"Not yet, sir."

"Then get yourself a plate from the pantry and eat some of whatever this is supposed to be. Sorry my steward isn't here. I sent him on an errand."

When Donaldson had begun to eat, "Tell me about it," the captain said.

Donaldson nodded, swallowed the food he was chewing, and began to talk.

"After Harding had knocked off that straggler and its escorting destroyer, he overtook the convoy two hours sooner than he expected. Thinks they must have been hove to. Anyway, he attacked from astern and sank another freighter, then from the beam and hit a tanker which burned out, torpedoed another destroyer, by mistake he says, then fired his three stern fish at a merchantman at a range of about seven hundred yards. That turned out to be an ammunition ship."

He stopped talking, took a flimsy sheet of pink paper from a pocket, and read aloud from it, "Blast sank nearby escort vessel and damaged *Trigger.* Remainder of convoy may be making for Naples. Present position forty degrees twenty-five minutes north ten degrees fifty minutes east course south magnetic, speed surfaced four, dived one and a half. No periscopes. Parts two and three this signal follow."

"You've copied that to C-in-C Med of course."

"Yes, sir. It's being dispatched now. Your requests and recommendations to follow when we have more of the picture."

The captain nodded in his turn and Donaldson put some more food in his mouth.

"So he probably has propeller-shaft trouble and a wrecked battery as well. Gyrocompass gone too or he wouldn't have referred to south magnetic."

"That's about it, sir. He may spell it out for us in the next two sections."

Over the next hour and a half, Harding spelt it out for them. Transmission strength was poor from his jury-rigged aerial, but after two requests for parts to be repeated, they had it all. So did the Commander-in-Chief Mediterranean Fleet. In Sicily the army commanders of the British, American, and Canadian forces were told what they needed to know and, in view of the scores of Tiger tanks and the many thousands of eighty-eight-millimeter shells their troops would no longer have to face, amended their tactics accordingly. In Malta four long-range Spitfires of the Royal Air Force's Photographic Reconnaissance Unit were alerted for a predawn takeoff to locate the whereabouts of the remnants of what became known as "Harding's convoy." At an airfield near Bizerta the colonel commanding a United States medium-bomber group said that he would be glad to provide daylight air cover for a crippled British submarine in the Tyrrhenian Sea and added that his aircrews were standing by to take out whatever the submarine hadn't gotten around to sinking as soon as the Spitfires found it. Off the south coast of Sicily the Royal Navy destroyer *Cutlass* turned her stem to the west and north, her bow wave building into twin hills of white water to either side. Sixty miles further east her sister ship *Claymore* emulated her. *Trigger* was coming home if the flotilla captain had anything to say about it and the C-in-C ensured that he did.

Into the microphone of the tannoy public-address system, Harding said, "This is the captain speaking. I have good news for all of us. A signal received from Algiers states that American aircraft will be overhead at first light, that's in about three hours from now, and will remain for as long as necessary. We shall, therefore, be staying on the surface. Later in the day we shall be joined by two of our own destroyers. Those of you who are injured will be transferred to one or both of them so that you can have proper medical treatment. I'm sure you and the Cox'n will be delighted to hear that. I may transfer some of the rest of you too, but we'll see about that when the time comes."

He cleared his throat before going on. "I'll read you the last part of the signal. It says: 'The Commander-in-Chief Mediterranean Fleet wishes to be associated with our congratulations to all of you on your sustained aggression throughout a highly successful patrol.' That's it. The Yanks are coming and so are our lot. You can go back to sleep now."

The first of a succession of American bombers approached from the south shortly before the sun topped the eastern horizon. Harding caught the sound of its engines, faint above the slow rumble of the starboard diesel. He ordered the diesel stopped and the main vents opened until *Trigger* was near to submerging. Then he had them closed again and waited, water lapping almost at the top of the casing.

The first rays of sunlight glinting on silver.

He snatched up the Aldis lamp, aimed it, and flashed the Morse letters AFG. There was a pause long enough to tighten his muscles before QJK came back to him from the aircraft. Challenge and reply correct, muscles relaxing slowly, but not completely because identification codes for the day could be compromised. Then the plane banked, showing the configuration of a Lockheed twin-engined bomber with the United States insignia on its wings.

"Control room. Start the blower and bring the ship to full buoyancy. Slow ahead starboard engine. The U.S. Cavalry's here."

"Start the blower and slow ahead starboard. Aye aye, sir."

Moving fast now across his bows near to sea level half a mile ahead of him, wings wagging, a lamp blinking.

"Hi. Looks like they rearranged you some. How you doing?"

Harding's Aldis lamp clattering, swinging to keep its bearing on the speeding aircraft.

"Better for seeing you. Thanks for coming."

"You're welcome. Take it easy, you hear?"

"Will do."

He put the Aldis back on its bracket, watched the bomber climb and start to circle counter-clockwise around them at a range of about four miles. Then he turned to the navigating officer.

"I'm going below, Pilot. Dive if you or the plane sight a submarine or enemy aircraft. Anything else, call me."

"Aye aye, sir."

In the control room the chief yeoman of signals was sitting on a toolbox, a black flag with a white skull and crossbones at its center draped across his knees. He was cutting a piece of red material into narrow oblongs.

Harding was fortunate, he knew, to have such a senior petty officer in charge of visual signals. The man rightly belonged in a cruiser or a larger ship than that but had stubbornly resisted any attempt to move him out of submarines. He walked across to him and looked down at the pirate's flag emblazoned with the record of his ship's sinkings. Nine white strips in a vertical column denoting merchantmen sunk by torpedo, a pair of crossed guns recalling the first successful gun action and the stars around it subsequent ones, a lone dagger for their single commando operation. A new emblem puzzled him.

"What's that thing, Yarrow? Battersea power station?"

The chief yeoman grinned.

"Actually no, sir. It's meant to be a floating dock, but from the number of comic remarks I've been getting, I don't think I've got it quite right. I can't add it to the torpedo or gun score, sir, so I thought I'd make a shape for it."

"I'll draw it for you," Harding said. "Why these three red strips you've cut out?"

"Warships, sir. It's customary to use red on the Jolly Roger to indicate warship sinkings."

"Dammit, I know that for God's sake! I'm asking you why three."

"Two destroyers and a sub chaser, sir. Our first warships, as you wouldn't let us count that armed auxiliary tanker as one."

Harding frowned.

"I don't really think we can claim to have sunk the submarine chaser and I'm not too sure about the second destroyer. They just sort of happened."

"If you say so, sir, but a lot of things just sort of happened to that convoy and I don't think the lads would be too happy if the tally isn't kept right. Anyway, if you didn't sink 'em, I'd be interested to hear who did."

"Oh, very well," Harding said irritably and turned away, angry with himself at arguing a trivial point of detail. Yarrow had been quite right. However fortuitously it had occurred, the warships had been sunk, and however much he disliked it, it was no part of his duty to interfere with the petty conceit of the Submarine Service which had led to its ships flying the black flag on entering harbor from patrol.

In his cabin he took out his patrol report notes, read the last page, then began to write.

"Lieutenant (E) K. B. Menzies was electrocuted when he was thrown against the port main motor switchboard. Petty Officer J. R. Selby suffered a broken neck when his head struck the forward periscope-hoist wheel. The reason for Leading Seaman F. Barr's death is uncertain. He was found doubled forward as though his stomach had come into violent contact with some obstruction (? ruptured spleen). Able Seaman T. L. A. Carpenter died of a fractured skull. Again, this death was not witnessed.

"Of those injured the most serious case appears to be that of Engine-Room Artificer C. Beckett. He has a compound fracture of the left femur, and due to his high temperature and the extreme difficulty he is experiencing in passing water, a crushed pelvis is suspected. Urgent medical attention is required in this case."

Crossing out the last sentence for the pointless observation it was, Harding put down his pencil and left his cabin to talk to Beckett and the rest.

The morning passed slowly. At slightly more than hourly intervals one American bomber was replaced by another. Twice the starboard engine had to be stopped and *Trigger* lay dead in the water until the metal of the bearings had cooled enough to allow her to proceed. Engine Room Artificer Beckett sank into a coma. Nothing else happened.

Harding was eating lunch when Able Seaman Norris passed the gap in the wardroom curtains on his way forward.

"Norris!"

"Sir?"

"Come in here and show me your hands."

Norris held out his hands, hands that were suspiciously, pinkly clean.

"Can it be, Norris, that out of the entire crew you are the only one not to have been informed about the restrictions on the use of fresh water?"

"What, sir? Oh!" Norris said. "I haven't been washing my hands, sir. I've been helping the cook mix the dough."

The laughter which burst out of Harding was of the wrong kind and he cut it short by holding his breath.

When he trusted himself to speak: "Go away, Norris. You're ruining my lunch."

"Yes, sir. Horrible thought now I think of it," Norris said, smiled, and left the wardroom.

At 1435 the officer of the watch reported that the escorting American bomber was flying off in a southerly direction. Harding went to the bridge. Ten minutes later the plane returned, its signal lamp flashing.

"British destroyer bearing 175 from you, distance forty miles, closing at knots thirty plus."

Harding bent to the voice pipe.

"Tell the cox'n a doctor will be coming aboard in a little over an hour. I want him to have Beckett ready for immediate transfer to a destroyer. The rest of the injured to follow in the order the doctor decides. Got that?"

"Yes, sir. I've got it," the voice pipe said.

Much lower in the water as she was, it was natural that the people on *Trigger*'s bridge should sight the destroyer before *Trigger* herself was seen, and for the second time that day, Harding made the challenge AFG. The reply QJK came back promptly, followed by a spate of very fast Morse.

The first lieutenant had taken over as officer of the watch and Harding looked at him.

"Did you read that, Number One?"

"No, sir. Too fast for me. Intend to something, then I lost it."

"Me too. Let's have the chief yeoman up here."

When Yarrow arrived on the bridge, "Ask him for a repeat, will you?" Harding said. "It's the real navy and they're out of my class."

Seconds later, "'Intend to set up zigzag pattern three cables ahead of you immediately on arrival. Mean course 195. Advise your best possible speed.' End of message, sir."

"Make to him, 'Speeds variable. Slow, very slow, and stop. Doctor required urgently.'"

Beside Harding the Aldis lamp clattered furiously, paused, then acknowledged another message. He heard Yarrow's breath hiss between his teeth and looked at him inquiringly.

"Message reads, 'Consider transfer of personnel inadvisable by daylight in these waters. Advise symptoms of patient and doctor will recommend treatment.'"

Yarrow had spoken coldly, but the first lieutenant thought that the words were warm in comparison with his captain's.

"Make as I speak, Yarrow."

"Ready, sir."

"There are fourteen casualties on board.... One has suspected crushed pelvis... other injuries... temperature 104 and is unconscious.... Another believed to be bleeding internally. ... Remainder less serious but require immediate attention... for assorted cuts and fractures.... I have already buried four men at sea... and it is no part of my plan to bury more.... End of message."

The Aldis clacked into silence.

The destroyer was closing very fast, growing in size as they watched, its signal lamp a brilliant violet.

"From destroyer, sir, 'Heave to. Doctor to you by sea boat, but I adjure you to be very careful with the tone of your signals in future.'"

Into the voice pipe Harding said, "Stop starboard. Open the fore hatch. Norris and two hands onto the casing to help the doctor aboard. Inform the cox'n." Then to Yarrow, "Make to the destroyer, 'Thank you and please accept my apologies.'"

Bow wave subsiding, the destroyer passed down their starboard side, then heeling over in a tight half circle slowed to a stop fifty yards away, water boiling along her waterline from aft to forward as the screws took the way off her. *Trigger* rolled gently in the wake of her passage.

Harding stood looking at her and listening to the roar of the forced-draft fans feeding air to the big boilers, listening too to the metallic voice of the public-address system. "Away sea boat's crew—away sea boat's crew.... Surgeon Lieutenant Mc-

Kinnon report to the captain on the bridge please—Surgeon Lieutenant McKinnon to the bridge. . . . Able Seaman Connor report to the Regulating Office at the double—Able Seaman Connor report . . ." It went on and on, each announcement preceded by the squeal of a bosun's pipe and all the time men moving purposefully about on the decks and up and down ladders.

"I don't think I could stand it, Number One," Harding said. "What do you suppose they're all doing?"

"I don't know, sir. They do seem to make everything look and sound awfully important, don't they?"

"TRIGGER!"

The bullhorn thundered across the short expanse of sea at them and Harding looked up at the man with the gold leaves on the peak of his cap.

"Yes, sir?"

"WHERE SHALL MY BOAT COME ALONGSIDE YOU?"

"Right at the stem, sir. There are foot- and handholds. . . ."

The public-address system drowned out his words. "Damage control parties will be exercised at 1715—damage control parties will . . ."

"I CAN'T HEAR YOU."

"You could if you switched that fucking thing off for thirty seconds," Harding said, then cupped his hands to his mouth. "Right at the stem, sir. There are foot- and handholds there near the torpedo-tube bow caps. Warn your boat to keep clear of our main ballast tanks. It could capsize on them."

He got a wave of an arm in acknowledgment.

"Sir?"

"Yes, Yarrow?"

"Signal from the American aircraft, sir. I'm not sure I got it right. 'You want we should keep riding shotgun. Interrogative.' Does that make sense, sir?"

"Yes, it does. Make to him, 'Glad if you would, but destroyer is senior. Better check with it.'"

The sea boat was in the water now, casting off and moving toward them. Immediately the destroyer began to move ahead, gathering speed.

"From the aircraft, sir, 'Don't know nothing about no destroyer. Have orders to ride herd on a damaged submarine. You look like a damaged submarine.'"

Harding smiled before saying, "He's probably from New Mexico or somewhere, but just make, 'Thanks Tex.' I expect he'll forgive me if I've got it wrong."

Surgeon Lieutenant McKinnon clambered up the stem, grasped Norris's down-stretched hand, and was lifted bodily onto the casing. Somebody passed his bag up after him and he followed Norris down the fore hatch ladder without so much as a glance in the direction of the conning tower. Twelve minutes later his head appeared through the upper conning tower hatch and he looked round him at the six men standing on the bridge, six men bare to the waist, unshaven, rather dirty, capless, unidentifiable. He said, "Sir?" experimentally.

"Hello, doc," Harding said. "How are they?"

McKinnon pulled himself up out of the hatch and faced Harding.

"We've got to be very quick, sir. Can you get *Cutlass* back here at once?"

Harding gestured toward Yarrow. "My chief yeoman. Tell him what you want to say. It'll come better from you."

He stood listening to the medical officer's words and the accompanying clatter of Yarrow's lamp. *Cutlass,* circling them at a distance of a mile, turned around and increased speed. It was, he thought, useful to know the name of his escort. She was, of course, showing no distinguishing marks and the signal he had received had not specified whether *Cutlass* or *Claymore* would arrive first.

The doctor turned to go below and rejoin his patients.

"Doc?"

"Yes, sir?"

"What chance has Beckett got? That's the unconscious chap."

"Quite a good one, sir, as long as I operate quickly. I've got to perform a cystostomy. Well, you probably wouldn't know about that, but it involves cutting through to the bladder and releasing the pressure of urine. That's the urgent thing. Oh, he's conscious again by the way, if you want to talk to him."

"I'll see him over the side," Harding said. "How many of the rest are you taking?"

"All of 'em, if that's all right by you. It really is a mess down below and I don't see how you can hope to look after them properly."

"It's very much all right by me."

McKinnon nodded, lowered himself through the hatch, then looked up at Harding and grinned.

"My captain's going to be absolutely livid, sir," he said. "He was working on a right royal rocket for you if you'd been crying wolf. He'll hate wasting it." He grinned again and disappeared from sight.

Standing by the fore hatch, Harding watched his injured men being brought up, six of them in stretchers. Able Seaman Norris and Corporal Ackroyd had put themselves in charge of the transfer to the boat, pushing the destroyer's men gently aside.

"Take care of yourself, Beckett. The doctor says the only thing wrong with you is that you're full of piss."

"I know, sir. The lads have been telling me that for years."

"'Bye, Johnson. Stay out of trouble."

"Aye aye, sir. What's all that going on on the P.A. over there?"

"I think it's their version of 'Workers' Playtime.'"

"See you in Algiers, Carmichael."

"Yes, sir. Good luck, sir."

He spoke to all of them, then, when the sea boat left on its fourth trip, went back to the bridge.

"Shut the fore hatch. Slow ahead starboard. Steer south-southwest," he said. The course sounded strangely old-fashioned to his ears, but the magnetic compass was all that he had left to guide him.

CHAPTER 11

IF GIOVANNI VILLARI, WHICH AFTER SO LONG WAS how John Villar thought of himself, had overheard the conversation in Algiers between an RAF squadron leader who was a civilian and a civilian who was not, it was unlikely to have meant anything to him.

"No, we haven't been able to raise Conrad yet," the RAF civilian had said.

"Isn't that unusual?" the other had asked.

"Not particularly. You can't operate over there on a punching-a-time-clock principle. You know that. When he's having a clear run he's most punctilious, but if there are problems he can go silent for a week or more."

"Well, I could wish that he hadn't chosen this particular week. The pressure is really on from Thayer Street to pull him out."

The man in the light-blue uniform had said, "My dear old pal and Major General sir, Thayer Street's agonies are my agonies, but there is precious little I can do to assuage their or my anguish until I'm in contact with Conrad again."

The exchange would have been of small interest to Giovanni Villari because he had never heard of Thayer Street and because, of the seven people who knew him by the code name "Conrad," he was not one.

On the other hand, the exchange taking place between the woman and the colonel on the patio of the Palazzo Millefiori interested him very much. They were speaking German, for

113

the colonel was the one who had taken his papers from him and he spoke no Italian.

"The fish seller wants a pass to go into the town," she said. "See to it." She had never called him by his name, even to his face.

There was a long pause before the reply came.

"Forgive me, but I don't think that would be very prudent."

"Don't you indeed? May I ask what would be imprudent about it? All he wants is to buy some clothes and he most certainly needs them. I've never seen such disgusting rags as the things he arrived in."

"Then I'll see that some are obtained for him."

"Answer my question. Why are you against his going into the town?"

"Because, being a peasant, he would brag about his association with you and that would be an embarrassment to the field marshal."

Villari heard her laugh before she said, "You know perfectly well that it amuses the field marshal to let me do as I please. He gets vicarious kicks out of my association with other men. There's no question of embarrassment."

"There is to the *Wehrmacht.*" Stubbornness in the voice. "When you have . . . when he has finished here I intend to remove the man to Germany."

"You can shoot him if you wish when the time comes. At the moment I only want him to go as far as the town and unless you are anxious to serve on the Russian front I should stop being so obstructive. Like your führer, my patience is exhausted."

Resignation and disgust replaced stubbornness.

"Very well, I'll send Sergeant Muller with him to make sure he comes back," the colonel said, and by adding the last six unnecessary words saved, at least for that night, the woman's life.

She flared at him.

"Are you implying that he wouldn't return to me? *To me?*"

"No."

"Then let him go alone, and if he tells me that he was followed you'll regret it!"

The snap of heels clicking together. The unseen but certain

abrupt inclination of the head. The sound of army boots receding. Villari let his body relax slowly as he turned away from the living-room door and lay down on the bed.

The British had taught him a number of ways of killing swiftly and silently with his hands. "There are several more, old boy, but no point in overcomplicating the issue." He could hear the very intonation of his instructor's voice. Mentally he had rehearsed each of them and selected what he considered to be the most easily accomplished in his unpracticed state. After that he had found it difficult to avoid looking at her throat and clenching his fist so that the middle knuckle protruded, wedged in place by its fellows and his thumb.

Now that the obstinacy of conceit had got her her way and, therefore, he his, there was no need for such action. But if the occasion should ever arise, he was ready, and if he had ever had any scruples about it her words, "You can shoot him if you wish," had removed them.

When she came into the bedroom, "What was all that about?" he asked.

"Some nonsense about security. They don't like civilians coming and going at army HQ. Understandable I suppose, but I convinced the man that you're quite harmless."

Unwittingly, Villari knew, she had put her finger on it. It *was* security the colonel was worried about, not the honor of the *Wehrmacht*, and that meant that he would be kept under surveillance regardless of her threats. It also meant, although he had learned nothing from her so far, that she was a potential source of information. The knowledge did nothing to compensate him for the emasculating effect her whim had had on his personal crusade and showed every sign of producing in him physically. Ironically, the latter point had become a matter of life or death for both of them.

"I'm grateful," he said.

"I'm not interested in your gratitude," she told him. "I'm just tired of the smell."

He watched her undressing, no longer finding her beautiful, wondering at himself for having thought her so. Subjectivity? Eye of the beholder? Vision now clouded by the realization of her total lack of humanity? No, he was being perfectly objective. He had been drunk the first two times he had seen her and she was better-looking than the country women he had been associating with, but not beautiful in any way.

"I'll go to the town in the morning," he said, but it was several minutes past noon before he walked up to the guard-house and asked for his pass. It had been essential to wait until the servant who cleaned the woman's quarters had come and gone.

"One pass for a good boy," the sergeant who gave it to him said and winked at the sentry.

He had taken it, grinned sheepishly and limped away, forcing himself not to hurry, immediately aware of the man who had to be *Gestapo* following him, following him much too closely. They were so obvious, the *Gestapo*, even in civilian clothes. It seemed necessary to them to maintain their sinister aspect if only by the way they wore their hats.

When Villari reached the outskirts of Spezia, he made his way to a street he knew with blind alleys leading off it to the right. They were usually deserted at this time of day. Turning sharply into one, he took ten paces, spun round, and tiptoed back the way he had come, listening to the quickened footsteps of his follower, feeling his stomach knot with tension and the prickling of the hairs at the base of his neck.

The man from the *Gestapo* was almost running as he rounded the corner and Villari killed him exactly as he had killed the woman after breakfast that morning. He stood for a moment massaging his knuckle, looking down at the body with the smashed larynx, then dragged it into a doorway, propping it in a sitting position. Half a mile away and eight minutes later, the renewed amazement at how little it took to end a human life was still in him.

It had been a bad night. She arrogant and joylessly insatiable. He flagging and increasingly nervous, which made him flag the more in a downward spiral of defeat. There could, he was sure, be no more effective course of aversion therapy than the life he had led since his arrival in Italy, and with this its culmination, he never wanted to sleep with a woman again.

After they had breakfasted in silence, "I'll go to the shops now," he had said and been told that he wasn't going anywhere in the foreseeable future, if at all. She had gathered his clothes into a bundle and was walking past him to throw them away when he killed her, feeling nothing but surprise at the ease of it. He had drunk a lot then, his first unsupervised drinking in three days, and experienced only mild tension while the servant tidied the room with the body hidden under the bed.

It was an hour after sunset in Algiers when the squadron leader who was a civilian telephoned the civilian who was a major general.

"Contact. Shall I come to you, or will you come here?"

"I'll come there."

He put the receiver down on its rest and waited for eight minutes, doing nothing but twiddle a pencil until the other arrived.

"Marvelous news," the major general said. "What's the form?"

"It isn't marvelous news and the form's lousy."

"Oh dear."

"Yes. 'Oh dear' it is. Conrad came through half an hour ago. His message was quote, blown but operational from hiding, unquote. So I gave him the picture in the form we agreed and told him to listen out for instruction on a submarine pickup and got a flat negative in reply. Naturally I increased the pressure, U.S. government orders etcetera, etcetera, and was told in precise anatomical detail what they could do to themselves. It's incredible what that man can put into code straight out of his head."

The major general nodded absently before saying, "We can't get a courier to him if he's in hiding."

"Right."

"Have you told Thayer Street?"

"No," the bogus squadron leader said. "I thought you'd like to do that."

CHAPTER 12

FOUR THINGS OF INTEREST HAD HAPPENED IN THE twenty-four hours since the injured men had been transferred to *Cutlass*. Her sister ship *Claymore* had arrived, the American aircraft had departed, Beckett had been successfully operated on, and *Trigger* had crossed seventy-eight miles of sea. It was a pathetically slow rate of advance, but the engine-room staff were satisfied that they could maintain it indefinitely and it had carried them well to the south of Cape Spartivento, the southernmost tip of Sardinia.

Visibility had been perfect the previous night, just as good at dawn, and both the navigating officer and Harding had obtained excellent star sights. They knew exactly where they were.

"I don't understand it," Harding said. "Do you imagine he's heading for Bizerta, Number One?"

"It looks very much like it, sir."

"Well, I must say it's bloody nice of him to tell us. I don't happen to want to go to Bizerta. Still, better find out for certain. Yarrow. Make to *Cutlass*, 'Request intentions.'"

He watched the destroyer ahead of them broodingly while the lamps spoke to each other.

"From *Cutlass*, 'To escort you to Bizerta,' sir."

Harding frowned, said, "I see," and bent to the voice pipe. "Control room, ask the cox'n to come and see me, please."

"Cox'n. Aye aye, sir."

Still frowning, he straightened, hearing the voice of the helmsman down below say, "'Swain! Now where's he gone?

119

Bert, the Skipper wants the cox'n. He must have gone for'ard. Go and tell him, will you?"

Chief Petty Officer Ryland heaved himself on to the bridge thirty seconds later.

"Sir?"

"Hello, cox'n. Now listen carefully. You too, Number One. And you, Yarrow." He glanced around at the four lookouts, binoculars firmly to their eyes. "You chaps as well. Not that you wouldn't anyway, but keep looking while you do it. All right?"

Somebody said, "Aye aye, sir." The rest murmured their agreement.

"Very well. The position is this. *Cutlass* wants to escort us to Bizerta. From their point of view it's the logical place because it's the nearest. From our angle it's useless. Bizerta was in a battle zone not so long ago and I have no idea what facilities are left standing. Anyway, there won't be any periscopes or submarine battery cells and there's no guarantee that they're equipped to repair the port main motor and propeller shaft."

For a moment Harding fell silent, collecting his thoughts, conscious of the eyes of the first lieutenant and the two chief petty officers watching his face, of the lookouts scanning their ninety-degree sectors.

"If we go there," he said, "we'll be placing ourselves in balk. At best it'll mean waiting around, probably for weeks, until somebody can spare a tug to tow us somewhere because you can bet your boots once we're in, they won't let us out again in this state. At worst they'll disband us and leave *Trigger* to rust on a mud bank."

He paused again before going on, "Well, that's probably overstating the case. She's too valuable to be left to rust, but it would be the end of us as a unit. What I want to do is take her back to Algiers. It's a long way, but they'll look after us there, and if that means towing us to Gibraltar for dry docking, they'll do that too. Cox'n?"

"Sir?"

"I want you to go below and ask for volunteers to get the ship back to base. You're to explain that we may be unescorted, because I don't think *Cutlass* will play. You're to point out the fact that the starboard engine, or motor, or propeller shaft could fail and that we're very short of fresh water. In other words the job will be both dangerous and uncomfortable. There's to be no coercion and all those who would prefer it will be transferred to one of the destroyers after nightfall. Understood?"

"Not really, sir. Engine-room and motor-room staff say they can keep us goin', sir, and we can get by on the fresh water now there's less of us."

"Thank you, Cox'n. I'm well aware of those points, but if we have more main propulsion problems than we already do, we automatically increase the water shortage. That's one risk element, and there's another. I don't anticipate any trouble from enemy air or surface forces in this area, but at the speed we'll be making surfaced at night, we'll be sitting ducks for a U-boat. Now buzz off and see if we have a crew."

Ryland nodded, turned toward the conning tower hatch, then back again.

"Sir?"

"What now, Cox'n?"

"It's embarrassin', sir. You're tellin' me to do somethin' daft. If you want volunteers to go aboard that destroyer, I'll ask, but you won't get none. The lads want to see the ship 'ome, sir. You don't need no volunteers for that."

Harding knew that the coxswain was better informed on the mood of the ship's company than either the first lieutenant or himself and what the man had just said affected him deeply. That, he supposed, explained the pompousness with which he spoke.

"Let us," he said, "at least do them the courtesy of allowing them to speak for themselves."

Six minutes later he was told that nobody wanted to leave the ship. Not even Edgecombe with a court-martial awaiting him on return to harbor.

"Yarrow, make to *Cutlass*, 'My destination Algiers.'"

With his back to *Cutlass* half a mile ahead of them, he waited, looking up at the bent periscope standards swaying with the gentle motion of the ship against a perfect blue sky, looking down at what had once been the platform for the Oerlikon cannon and, beyond it, at the short-lived wake on the calm water which was all that their idling progress could produce. They had been through a lot together, he and *Trigger*, since the day he had arrived at the builder's yard to watch her slide down the slipway into the element for which she was designed. He was wondering if what might happen in the next few minutes could lead to the parting of the ways for them.

Taking their time to react to his signal. The captain not on the bridge probably. "The lads want to see the ship 'ome, sir." Why did the crew invariably refer to themselves collectively as "the lads"? Funny. Yarrow's lamp clacking beside him.

"From *Cutlass*, sir. 'Your destination is what I say it is.'"

"I was afraid of that," Harding said. "All right. We'll keep trying. Make this. 'Submit following points for your consideration . . .'"

He spoke evenly, repeating the reasons he had expressed to his own people for their going to Algiers, but he was less than half of the way through them when Yarrow said, "He's told me to stop sending, sir. Calling us now. Message reads 'Carry out your orders,' sir."

"All right," Harding said for the second time in three minutes. "I'll do just that." Then he grinned wolfishly, and watching him, the first lieutenant knew from this rarely seen expression on a normally rather diffident face that his captain was blazingly angry.

"Clear the bridge. Yarrow, stay with me. Make to *Cutlass*, 'Thank you for looking after my invalids. Am now proceeding independently to Algiers.' Don't let him interrupt and go below as soon as he's acknowledged."

"Message acknowledged, sir," Yarrow said and followed the others down the hatch, taking the Aldis lamp with him.

Harding spoke into the voice pipe, heard the diesel die into silence and the hissing roar of air released by the opening of the main vents. Rainbows danced in the plumes of water soaring from them. On his port the long shape of *Claymore*. Ahead and to starboard *Cutlass*, her signal lamp flashing persistently. He ignored it and lowered himself into the conning tower, pulled the hatch shut, and secured the two heavy clips.

In the control room, "Go down to ninety feet, Number One. Starboard fifteen. Steer west. McIntyre, they'll be in sonar contact in a minute and will almost certainly call us on it. You can't hear a thing. Understood?"

"Deaf as a post, sir."

For a moment Harding stood staring thoughtfully at the deck as though weighing the chief sonar operator's reply, then he said, "Good," in an absentminded voice, nodded to the first lieutenant, and walked to his cabin.

"Oh, bloody hell! Here, let me read it for myself."

Lieutenant Commander Donaldson handed the signal to the flotilla captain and watched him read it through twice.

"Pretty strong stuff. Insolence, undisciplined behavior, refusal to obey a lawful command. It doesn't sound like Peter Harding to me."

"Nor to me, sir," Donaldson said. "Actually, I think it's a most ill-advised signal."

The flotilla captain looked up at him.

"Go on."

"All it tells us of any consequence is that *Trigger* has elected to proceed independently to base. The rest is a long harangue against Harding with nothing specific in it at all. What lawful command? What insolence? In what way is Harding supposed to have been undisciplined? Not a clue in the whole thing. So why send it? Apart from *Trigger's* intentions that is."

"You're quite right, Ginger. When I'm cross I obviously need you around to do my thinking for me."

"There's something else, sir. All that lot was sent in one transmission, most of it isn't worth breaking radio silence for, and it's quite long enough to have given the enemy a fix to home a U-boat onto."

"Christ. The man must be out of his mind. Who is he?"

"The captain of *Cutlass*, sir? Commander L. H. Fletcher."

"Know him?"

"Yes, sir," Donaldson said. "He's a year senior to me and we served together in *Warspite.*"

"What's he like?"

"Well, I suppose he's okay."

"Come on, Ginger. Don't go coy on me just because he's got a brass hat. Anything I can use to protect one of my commanding officers I want to hear about."

Donaldson relaxed, smiled and said, "He's a 'Gunnery Jack,' sir. Spit, polish, and everything done by numbers. Not much imagination. I'm not a submariner as you know, but I've come to know them pretty well here and I'd say he's just the type to get right up their noses."

"Hmm. In that case I hope Harding hasn't been foolish enough to let him get up his and then said something stupid."

At the sound of a knock both glanced in the direction of the door, Donaldson went to answer it, and the flotilla captain went on, "I wish the Battle Fleet wasn't at sea. I'd like a private word with the C-in-C on the blower about this. Fletcher's repeated this blasted signal to him."

Returning from the doorway with a piece of paper in his hand, Donaldson said, "The C-in-C seems to have anticipated you, sir. This is from him to Captain (D) repeated you. *Cutlass* to go back to her Sicily station and submit a written report on return to harbor. *Claymore* to escort *Trigger* to Algiers."

"Thank God for a wise admiral. That's defused whatever it is for the time being."

"Yes, sir. Is there anything you want to send to *Trigger*?"

"No," the flotilla captain said. "Harding's got enough on his plate."

"What's the situation, McIntyre?"

"One destroyer in contact on the starboard beam, sir. He's sweeping all the time, but he checks on us every couple of minutes."

"And the other's definitely gone?"

"Unless he's stopped, sir. But I don't think he's done that. Hydrophone effect faded right out on the port quarter nearly three hours ago. Going very fast then he was."

"Thank you," Harding said.

He had felt perfectly calm since his fury against *Cutlass* had dissipated itself in a spasm of jerky trembling in his cabin. The anger had returned briefly when he brought his patrol report notes up to date with an account of the exchange of signals, but not enough to affect him physically. Now *Cutlass* had gone and he was very thankful for that. That it was *Claymore* in contact with them to starboard he had no doubt at all because McIntyre had tracked both warships from the moment *Trigger* had dived.

Harding found himself wondering what sort of reception he would receive from the destroyer when he surfaced, then shrugged almost indifferently. It could hardly be worse than *Cutlass*'s and he would know soon enough.

"How long since sunset, Pilot?"

"Thirty-two minutes, sir."

Fully dark above all that water over his head, or as fully dark as it ever got on a moonless but starlit night in the Mediterranean. At least, he supposed it would be starlit. It had been such a lovely day before he had dropped down and away from it, placing his career in jeopardy.

"Where's the destroyer now, McIntyre?"

"Just crossing the bows from starboard to port, sir."

"Yarrow, I want you on the bridge with me to make the challenge or the reply depending on who starts first. They probably will because they'll hear us blowing main ballast. Come up to fifty feet, Number One."

He stood, listening to Elleston's voice from the wardroom calling out the depths from the only serviceable gauge.

At fifty feet, "What's she doing now, McIntyre?"

"Passing slowly down the port side toward our stern, sir. Bearing Red 110."

"Surface," Harding said.

The night *was* starlit and the destroyer clearly visible, a dim red light flashing from her bridge.

"Challenge and reply correct, sir."

Harding grunted, waiting, watching the red light.

"Signal, sir, 'From *Claymore* to *Trigger*. My orders are to escort you to Algiers.'"

He found that he had been holding his breath and let it out with an audible hiss.

"Make 'Thank you very much indeed,'" he said, then added, "'My gyro on the blink. Am steering west-southwest magnetic. Interrogative satisfactory.'"

"Reply is, 'Fine for now,' sir."

Yarrow stayed on the bridge for half an hour, but nothing more came from the destroyer and Harding sent him down below. Nothing more happened at all until shortly before midnight when the engine room reported overheating of the starboard propeller-shaft bearings. He decided to do his own signaling and picked up the red lamp.

"Stopping thirty minutes to cool bearings," he sent and got the reply, "Okay. Closing you for a chat I am."

"I am?" Harding whispered to himself. "What's he mean, *I am?*" and flashed the letter "R" in acknowledgment, still wondering.

The destroyer approached rapidly, then slowed and came to a stop within twenty yards, the only sounds the wash of her propellers going astern, the subdued roar of the forced-draft fans. He tensed himself against the bellow of the bullhorn and jumped when a soft voice from the direction of the dark silhouette of the bridge said, "How are you then, boyo?" Suddenly the last two brief lamp signals he had received acquired a Welsh accent as well.

"We're all right, sir," he replied. "But the ship's a bit chewed up."

"Not surprising really. Bloody fine patrol the drums are saying. The battle hymn of Llan Mawr they'll be singing for you in the valleys I shouldn't wonder."

Harding felt tension running out of him and laughter bubbling up inside, but he stiffened when the voice went on, "Come board this fine vessel and tell me what the position is precisely. We're lowering a boat now."

"I don't think I ought to do that, sir. I've never left *Trigger* at sea."

"What will you do then, when the enemy comes swarming over the horizon?" the quiet voice asked. "Crash-dive, is it, and seize your shaft bearings up solid?"

He'd forgotten how big *Trigger* seemed when viewed from near the waterline. The knife-edged stem rising high above the little boat, the dimly seen conning tower with the heads and shoulders of men showing above it surprisingly distant. But he wasn't given time to look for long. The boat turned in a fast half circle, hooked on to the destroyer's falls, and was immediately lifted clear of the surface. Before it reached deck level *Claymore* was moving purposefully ahead.

The lieutenant commander who held his hand out to him at the top of the bridge ladder was very short, very broad, and had a pair of startlingly bushy eyebrows.

"Evans. Gareth Evans. It's a Welsh name you know. There's been a Gareth in the family since the days of Owen Glendower and before. That's a barefaced lie of course, but I did have an uncle of the same name. You'll be Harding."

"Yes, sir. I'm Peter Harding."

"Then welcome aboard, Peter Harding, and come and meet Jimmy the One. Number One, meet the captain of *Trigger*. Names are Carrington and Harding respectively, mind you."

"Hello, Number One."

"Hello, sir."

At the side of the bridge somebody answered a telephone, called, "Captain, sir? Cipher room," and Evans left them.

"Enchanting chap, your skipper," Harding said. "Is he always like this?"

The other's teeth flashed whitely in the darkness. "Not all the time, sir. He's having an attack of the eisteddfods.* Usually happens when he's arguing with an admiral or some other senior type. I think he does it to confuse them."

"What brought it on tonight?"

Carrington's smile vanished. "I'd guess that he's feeling badly about the führer. Oh damn, I shouldn't have said . . . I meant Commander Fletcher. That's *Cutlass*'s captain. Look out. Here comes the skipper now."

"Right we are then, Harding," Evans said. "Let's hear it all."

It took Harding three minutes to describe conditions aboard *Trigger*, three minutes during which he was conscious of only three sounds. The rush of air created by the destroyer's speed, the steady pinging of her sonar, and his own words. When he had finished, for countable seconds there was only the wind and the sonar. Then Evans spoke and there was no trace of Welsh accent in his voice.

"Tell me, Harding, if you had no destroyer to escort you to Algiers, you would be obliged to dive by day. Is that right?"

"Yes, sir. Or at least it would be highly desirable to do so."

"I imagine it would. That being the case, perhaps you will explain to me how you would contrive that with the cat's cradle of cross-connected undamaged battery cells you have described. Surely they'd have insufficient capacity."

*A Welsh competitive festival of the arts, especially in singing.

"No, sir," Harding said. "We can hold a stopped trim for long periods."

"What's a stopped trim?"

"Well, we dive normally, balance the boat by pumping water from one end to the other, or outboard, then stop the motors and just sit there. The officers of the watch compete with each other over how long they can hold it for. Nobody's allowed to move around of course. One man moving ten feet will upset the trim. It's inconvenient, but it saves an awful lot of amps."

"There's clever," Evans said and, although he wasn't sure why, Harding was glad to hear the Welsh accent again.

"Why do you ask, sir?"

The destroyer captain turned to his first lieutenant. "Put us back close to the submarine, Number One, and have the boat's crew standing by." Then he faced Harding again. "Because, boyo, I wanted to be sure you weren't bluffing when you took off on your own for Algiers. I thought perhaps you had taken us for a ride, gambling that we'd tow you there, see. Now I know you think you could have made it on your own. I'm glad of that."

Angrily Harding said, "I'm overcome at your happiness," and saw the disapproving shake of the Welshman's head.

"No, no, say it gentle, Harding. Don't you be giving me a hard time like you did old Fletcher. I'm responsible for the safety of my own ship too you know. Not just yours."

"Yes, of course you are, sir. I'm sorry for speaking the way I did."

"Oh, don't be sorry. Nobody likes to be thought an irresponsible fool even when he's not one. Ah, we're just coming up on *Trigger*. Now, if your freshwater position gets too bad, I'll pipe some across, but I don't want to be connected to you for long."

"We needn't connect at all, sir. An open-ended pipe into the gun tower will do. That's our access to the four-inch and it's got a pressure-tight hatch top and bottom. We can drain the water off from there."

"There's clever," said Evans for the second time.

When the seawall of Algiers appeared over the world's curve, nearly five and a half days had gone by. Harding had not asked *Claymore* for water because he was stubbornly making a point. The shakes had left him alone for reasons he was not aware of, but as if to offset this blessing, his ability to sleep for more than a few minutes at a stretch had deserted him. He was dirty, bearded, close to exhaustion.

A distant pinpoint of light flickering. Yarrow's voice saying, "Message reads 'Well done *Trigger* and welcome home. Visiting VIP will board you on arrival. No formality.'"

"Oh bloody hell!" Harding said. "That's *all* we need!"

He looked around him at the flat sea, its blueness lost in the glare from a sun nearing the zenith, at *Claymore* still patiently circling them, at the hills hazy with heat framing Algiers, and the as yet formless smudges of gray which were warships lying in the harbor. His eyes began to water and his aching yawn blocked his ears for a moment.

"I'm sorry, Yarrow. What did you say?"

"Just wanted to know if there's any reply, sir."

"Oh. Make 'Thank you. We're glad to be back.'"

And that, he thought, wasn't what Yarrow or anybody else on the bridge had hoped he would say. They wanted to know who the VIP was. So did he, but he wasn't going to ask if the depot ship didn't see fit to tell him.

"I'm going below," he said to the navigating officer. "Tell me when we're a mile from the entrance."

It seemed very dark in the control room after the brightness of the day above and he stood, holding on to the ladder because he felt that he was swaying, until his vision improved. Then he made his way to the wardroom and told the first lieutenant about the visitor.

"No, I fucking well don't know who it is," he said. "I just think it's a fucking stupid trick to play on us. Ration out the rest of the fresh water to the bridge and casing parties. I want them shaved and clean."

It was midafternoon when, shaved and moderately clean himself, Harding returned to the bridge. He saw exactly what he had expected to see. The tall stone face of the harbor wall with, straight ahead, the gap in it through which he would pass. A big cruiser moving slowly, majestically out through the other entrance. The towering bulk of the depot ship. The White Ensign fluttering in the slight breeze from a variety of warships and dotted among them the Stars and Stripes. Behind them the white and pastel shades of the town with its backdrop of mountains. All very familiar and, somehow, inimical.

"Permission to hoist the Jolly Roger, sir?"

Yes, the "lads" would want that as they always did. Their tally of the death and destruction they had spread, for others to look at and admire. He pulled himself up sharply, berating himself for his cynicism. Tired. Just tired. That was all.

"Of course, Yarrow."

He watched the black flag rise to the pulley someone had wired to the top of the after-periscope standard, looked again at the distorted standard itself, jagged bright metal showing where a hurtling fragment of an exploding ship had struck it. Then he turned his back.

Two hundred yards off the port bow, *Claymore* had only enough way on to steer by. Her signal lamp flashed into life.

"From the destroyer, sir, 'You may proceed into harbor ahead of me. It's your party.'"

"Make, 'Thank you for everything. Request permission to call on you tomorrow.'"

A moment later, "Reply is, 'The gin bottle's waiting,' sir," Yarrow said.

The harbor entrance was broadening now as the angle changed at *Trigger*'s slow advance and inside Harding could see two "T"-class submarines lying off from the depot ship to give him the inside berth. They looked like sinister objects in their dark-blue paint against the pale gray of the surface warships beyond them. He was thinking that they were probably *Talon* and *Tusker* when, at his side, the first lieutenant whistled softly.

"Do you see what I think I see, sir?"

The first lieutenant's binoculars seemed to be directed at the bridge of the depot ship and he raised his own to his eyes. Immediately the magnified image of the flotilla captain's head and shoulders appeared. There were other senior officers behind him, but his attention was on someone to his left. Harding moved his line of sight fractionally, paused, then let the binoculars dangle from the strap about his neck.

His hands were aching, clamped to the front of the bridge, knuckles white with strain. He felt detached from them but grateful to them too for holding him where he was while the blood found its way back to his head. There was sweat running down his face, tickling, tasting salty when his tongue touched his lips, but he couldn't spare a hand to wipe it away because then he might fall down. How long had he been standing like this? No idea. Perhaps it would be best if he fell down anyway, claimed fatigue, let Number One handle it. Not good, but anything was better than getting the shakes in the worst possible situation he could ever envisage. Worse even than in action. No, that at least was wrong. That would be too awful to contemplate. But . . .

"The coffee you asked for, sir."

The first lieutenant's voice.

Harding lowered his eyes to the cup resting on the ledge between his hands. Its contents looked unpleasantly muddy and he didn't remember asking for coffee.

"Put your face down and drink it, damn you. It takes five or six minutes to get into the bloodstream." A fierce whisper directly into his ear.

The outrageousness of the form of address more than its urgency got through to him. He released his hold on the ledge and closed his palms around the cup. The brandy, with its tinned milk camouflage, almost choked him, but he held his breath until the need to gag was gone, then finished the drink in slow sips.

"Thank you," he said.

The great semicircular ends of the seawall seeming to slide by on either side as *Trigger* passed between them. Men looking down at them curiously. Some sailors, some dockyard workmen. Harding lifted a hand in acknowledgment of a wave from one of them. That made them all wave. His own people moving about on the casing, readying wires and fenders. Strange to see them in white tropical kit and caps again. The ensign staff being raised right at the stern because the one where the Oerlikon platform had been wasn't there anymore. The White Ensign, never flown on patrol, fluttering lazily.

"Stop starboard. Out starboard engine clutch."

The diesel note dying abruptly.

"Starboard engine clutch out, sir."

"Slow ahead starboard."

Trigger angling in toward the depot ship, propelled by electricity as the diesels were not designed to go astern. The brandy making itself felt. It would be all right now.

Row upon row of faces peering down from the big ship. Laughter and a buzz of conversation. Then individual voices calling.

"What happened, then? You surface under a battlewagon or something?"

"Been mating with a whale more likely."

"Yeah, that's it. Hear what Fred says? They've been getting amorous with a whale."

Laughter again above their heads and an officer shouting "Silence there," but his men standing rigidly to attention in two lines, one in front of the bridge, one behind it. Then, the courtesies completed, the tableau broke and everything was movement. Fenders and heaving lines dropping, steel-wire rope snaking.

"Port twenty. Half-astern starboard."

"Twenty degrees of port wheel on, sir. Starboard motor going half-astern."

The submarine trembled with the impact when she touched. It was not Harding's best piece of ship handling, but, he consoled himself, he had never had to do it with only one propeller before.

"Stop starboard. Finish off up here please, Number One, and join me on the casing as soon as you can. The pilot, the cox'n, and the chief engine-room artificer are to come too."

"Aye aye, sir."

He clambered over the side of the bridge, feeling carefully for each foothold on the way down, aware that he was a little drunk.

"My felicitations, sir. I am told that you have struck a formidable blow against prime enemy targets."

The visitor who had come aboard with the flotilla captain was holding out his hand. Harding stopped saluting and took it in his own.

"Sir," he said.

"You must all be very tired, but it would give me immense pleasure to be told a little of your achievement."

Eloquently, for him, Harding described the action against

the convoy, not too troubled by the visitor's eyes boring into his own because the flotilla captain's nodding and smiling gave him confidence. That and the brandy he had drunk.

When he had finished, "Commendable. Highly commendable, Lieutenant Harding. Again my congratulations. Now, you will have had enough of me, but I would be honored to meet whoever you wish to present me to."

"Thank you, sir. My first lieutenant, Lieutenant Gascoigne... My navigating officer, Lieutenant Walker... My gunnery and torpedo officer, Lieutenant Elleston... My coxswain, Chief Petty Officer Ryland... My acting engineer officer, Chief Engine Room Artificer Greenway."

The visitor spoke to all five of them in turn, then addressed Harding again.

"I see your comrades in arms are joining us," he said and gestured toward *Talon* nosing silently alongside. "I must talk with them in a moment, but before I do, is there any small way in which I can be of assistance to you?"

After the smallest of hesitations, "Yes," Harding told him, "there is, if you would be so good."

A few minutes later, watching a similar scene being enacted on *Talon*'s casing, seeing out of the corner of his eye *Tusker* approaching her far side, he held the punishment book back over his shoulder.

Without turning round, "Take this and get rid of him, Cox'n."

"Aye aye, sir."

Ryland took the book and went down the fore hatch into the torpedo stowage compartment. Ackroyd and Edgecombe were sitting on toolboxes at the far end.

"All right, Corporal Ackroyd, you can stop guardin' 'im. The prisoner's to be released."

Ackroyd stood up, stretched himself, and ambled away.

"Now, you my lad, get your things together and up you go to your mess in the depot ship. You're to be transferred back to general service as unfit for submarines."

Able Seaman Edgecombe sneered up at him.

"That'll be the day. You haven't got the authority to let me go, neither's the 'Old Man,' not when he's marked me for a 'court' in front of witnesses he hasn't. I'm for the bloody chop and you know it. Hazarding the lives of my shipmates with one lousy cigarette and all that crap. You've all got it in for me. Always have had."

"You quite finished?"

"Yes."

"Then listen to me, you 'orrible little twerp," Ryland said. "First, you refer to the captain as 'the Captain' in my 'earin'. Second, I won't bother explainin' the danger of one cigarette when nobody's got no air to breathe anyway because you ain't in submarines no more. Third, if it's authority that's botherin' you, the name in this book of mine dismissin' the charge against you is Winston S. Churchill. Now, if that's good enough for you, get off this ship!"

CHAPTER 13

IN WINTER IT WOULD BE A WATERCOURSE, VILLARI knew, but it was dry at this time of year and, where it turned around a spur of the hill with a big slab of fallen rock straddling it, made an excellent hiding place. Curtains of grasses and scrub screened both entrances and he had been at pains not to disturb this natural camouflage more than necessary whenever he moved in or out. For a week it had served him well and then the German soldier had come, his jackboots scrabbling and slipping on the loose debris. He was standing now, ten feet away, moving his hand in a sweeping arc above his head, signaling to someone down in the valley.

The American lay very still, listening to the thumping of his heart, feeling the feather touch of fear ghost over the surface of his skin. It had had to happen. That had been perfectly apparent from the moment the need for alcohol had driven him to break into the first of the three houses he had burgled. It was, he thought, ironic that his self-imposed drunkard's cover should contain the seeds of his destruction when the cover was no longer of use to him. Food had been a secondary consideration with fruit and nuts everywhere for the taking. The local coarse wine had been the time bomb and the woman he had killed the detonator. His mind swore at her viciously, infuriated that her whim should have resulted in the destruction of the edifice he had built and looked to be destroying him with it. There was no doubt about what the soldiers were doing. They were looking for him, not because they had any idea what he was, not because he had killed a field marshal's mistress, but because the *Gestapo* wanted vengeance for one of their own. At that time his assessment was correct, but was to remain only partially so.

With extreme caution he inched closer to the screen of vegetation, then drew his knees up under him, gauging the relative positions of the soldier and the big flat stone which he would use as a springboard when the moment came. *If* the moment came, he corrected himself.

The man's gaze had shifted slightly to the left of its original direction and Villari guessed his function to be that of a lookout watching the orchard-covered valley floor for movement which would show that his searching colleagues had flushed their quarry. Two things he found to be grateful for. The German military mentality which followed orders with a precision which seemed to exclude, in this case, a search of the immediate vicinity by the soldier near him, and his own decision never, except when he was using it, to be in the same place as his transceiver.

It was a big thing—to reach as far as Algiers it had to be—and with its batteries, it weighed a lot. That had been of little consequence when it was housed in his pedal cart, but that telltale machine was twenty miles away at the bottom of a ravine and had been there ever since his agonizing nerve-racking ride out of Spezia. From then on he had carried the set across country by night, hidden it and gone to ground himself somewhere else. Now, if he could get away from the search area at all, at least he could do it relatively unencumbered and still maintain contact with the outside world.

The soldier's head was turned farther to the left, following the slow progress of the search below him, and Villari knew that time was short. A few more degrees and peripheral vision would detect his movements. He launched himself through the curtain of greenery, landed on the flat stone, and jumped.

A knee in the back, left forearm across the throat cutting off sound, right hand knocking the coal-scuttle helmet forward before splaying across the back of the head, left hand gripping right forearm, bear down heavily just as they'd said in England. There was only a tiny click when the German's spinal cord snapped.

He could see the searchers in the valley now, the nearest

closer than he had thought, but none looked in his direction. The machine pistol was a temptation, but he didn't take it. Just conceivably they might think the man had fallen on the treacherous debris, but the real reason was that with his stolen supplies, and, when he got to it, the transceiver, he couldn't carry anything else. When he had obliterated signs of his occupancy of the hide, he crawled around the face of the hill until the soldiers were out of his line of sight. Then he stood up and ran limpingly away, his wine bottles clinking softly.

Marine intelligence was something he could no longer provide, for he could neither see the shipping nor listen to the talk of the sailors, but the *Wehrmacht* was on the move south in strength. So was the *Luftwaffe*. He wondered what was happening, but wasted little time doing it before transmitting his latest meticulous observations to Algiers that night.

Only for long enough to establish that Algiers' return transmission was again on the subject of withdrawing him from Italy did he listen to them before switching off. He was not interested in what they were saying, there was the diminishing power of his batteries to consider, and he had a long way to cover with a heavy load before dawn.

The *Abwehr* lieutenant colonel said, "My dear Engel, I don't really give a damn if the fellow's killed twenty of the *Gestapo*. In addition, I am equally unmoved by both the murder of the mistress of a field marshal and of a singularly stupid member of the Ninety-fourth Infantry. This has become a Military Intelligence matter without a shadow of doubt and it is on that basis that I'm asking for troops."

"I hear you, Kriewald," the *Wehrmacht* officer of the same rank replied, "and I haven't refused you, so before you start invoking the name of your boss, perhaps you wouldn't mind explaining how you've satisfied yourself that no shadow of doubt exists. That would help me to satisfy myself that I'm not contributing to a pointless duplication of effort."

"Oh, it *would* be a duplication of effort, but then who can work with the *Gestapo*? And if we are to uncover his organization I must get to the fish seller before they do because they don't know the right questions to ask him and they certainly wouldn't let me do it. As to my boss, Admiral Canaris knows nothing of this yet."

Engel nodded. "Thank you for your openness. Go on."

"Well, it's all very simple as such things have an irritating habit of being once you know what you're looking for, which we didn't until the field marshal's tart got greedy. Look at these. The *Gestapo* didn't know that area HQ was holding them. Fortunately I did, through Colonel Henschel who administers the place."

Engel took Villari's papers from Kriewald's hand, examined them, then dropped them onto the table.

"What about them?"

"Good, aren't they? It took Berlin to establish that they're forgeries. Probably English, they say. So what have we got? An alcoholic fish seller with forged documents, a convenient leg wound which exempts him from military service, a knowledge of unarmed combat, and a pedal cart. What would you bet me that he hasn't got a radio transmitter in that cart?"

"Nothing at all," Engel said. "He might have the führer in it for all I know, but I'd take odds against *Reichsmarshal* Goering. He's too fat. Why don't you tell me why he might have a transmitter in the thing?"

"Forgive me. I'm running ahead of myself. For approximately two years the Italians have been picking up unauthorized radio transmissions from this area. All over the country too of course, but I'm talking about Spezia. From time to time they've got a bearing on them. Sometimes a cross-bearing, but only rarely, because the transmissions have been in rapid Morse and very brief. Hardly ever have they been on the same bearing from the radio-location station. Never has anyone been apprehended." Kriewald raised his eyebrows inquiringly. "Local drunk with a pedal cart, freedom of movement to sell his wares, as everyone knows he's harmless, and a number of 'safe' houses to transmit from? How does that strike you?"

Engel stared at the table for a moment before saying, "It's conceivable, but I must admit that I'd feel more enthusiastic about committing the number of troops you are asking for to a search if I thought it was worthwhile. I mean if I knew that these broadcasts had been of value to the enemy."

"Oh, I think I can arouse your enthusiasm on that score,"

Kriewald told him. "All the evidence available to me comes from the *Kriegsmarine,* but it's pretty conclusive by itself. For a long time past there has been a suspicious connection between these transmissions and the subsequent destruction of ships from this port by submarines. You may well say that the ships would have been sunk in any event, but that cannot be proved and is definitely unlikely because the English are over-stretched."

Kriewald stood up suddenly and walked the length of the room and back before going on. "Let me give you one recent and very telling example. The week before last a convoy of six ships and six escorting vessels assembled here to load troops and armor for the Sicily front. During that period the broadcasts increased in both number and length, but again were not pinned down. That convoy never reached Sicily."

"What happened to it?"

"The English decimated it, that's what happened to it. No, that's the wrong word to use. It means to destroy one in ten, doesn't it? They did rather better than that. In a running fight their submarine wolf pack sank seven out of twelve and forced the survivors to put in to Naples. I won't bother you with the details, but please believe me when I say that our losses in men, tanks, ammunition, and fuel were alarmingly high."

"Certainly I believe you, but..."

"But here's the interesting thing," Kriewald broke in. "The English do not normally operate wolf packs because they have insufficient numbers to do so. In fact the *Kriegsmarine* tells me that there is no record of their ever having done it. Well, there's a first time for everything as that convoy found out. According to the senior surviving officer, they were attacked from all directions by a minimum of four submarines, one of which they sank. Now, for the English to have assembled such a force in the right place at the right time means that they had precise foreknowledge of the convoy and its intentions. I suggest to you that they got it from the fish seller."

"All right," Engel said. "I'll arrange for a hundred of my men to be placed at the temporary disposal of the *Abwehr.* That should be enough to enable you to work round the clock."

The sands were running out for Villari and the inaccuracy of some of Kriewald's information would not hinder the flow.

CHAPTER 14

FOR HALF AN HOUR HARDING LAY IN A DEPOT SHIP bath absently rolling dead skin from his body with his fingertips. There was less of it than usual because of the days spent on the surface, and only from waist to knee was he the typical end-of-patrol slug-white. That was where the dead skin was. When he had finished he let the scummy water drain away, refilled the bath, and scrubbed himself. Then he washed his hair twice and padded barefoot back to the cabin allotted to him with a towel around his hips. He felt better, but not as much as he usually did after that first orgiastic wallow. The sybaritic occasion to which he always looked forward had let him down and he found that annoying.

Annoyance increased when he dressed in clean white tropical kit. He was wondering if there was any point in not washing in saltwater at sea when the laundry gave one skin rash in harbor anyway by starching one's uniform.

"Oh, damn them!" he said aloud and that lightened his mood because he found enough humor in himself to laugh at his own petulance.

He thought of going to the wardroom, but abandoned the idea because he didn't want to listen to the plaudits of his friends until he had been debriefed and that was something he was not looking forward to with *Cutlass* in the forefront of his mind. Damn *Cutlass*. Damn his own inept handling of the situation. Irritability returning. "Stop it!" he told himself, looked longingly at his bunk, then sat on an upright chair to wait for the summons which the prime minister's presence had delayed.

After the fourth time he had been jerked awake by his head

dropping forward on to his chest, he stood up again. It was boring standing there with nowhere to walk to within the confines of the cabin, but he knew that if he slept now he would make little sense when he was sent for. It was a relief when the telephone on the bulkhead buzzed.

Forty minutes later the flotilla captain pushed the patrol report aside and said, "Well, Peter, everybody is very pleased about all this of course, and to put it mildly, it seems a little ungracious of me to take you to task, but that's my job when I consider it to be necessary."

Clenching his teeth to stifle a yawn made up of equal parts of tiredness and anxiety, Harding mentally rehearsed the sequence of signals exchanged with *Cutlass*.

"Your sinking of the floating dock came perilously close to hazarding your ship, you know."

Harding blinked. "The what, sir?"

"The dock, Peter. Boarding it within sight of Civitavecchia was taking a hell of a risk."

"Oh that," Harding said. "I'm sorry. I was thinking of something else. Actually there wasn't much risk involved. No sign of aircraft, and if any had been sighted I'd have been underwater in thirty seconds and at ninety feet in a minute and a half. That would have meant abandoning my boarding party of course, but I considered that the value of the target justified that."

The flotilla captain shook his head. "I think that's a very optimistic assessment. You were stopped, bows on to the dock. You'd have had to dive astern, and doing that would have taken you a lot more than thirty seconds to submerge. Nearly a minute I'd say and a fighter-bomber can cover a lot of distance in a minute. Add on your own reaction time and that of the men opening the main vents and operating the engine-room telegraphs, and you could have been in trouble."

Harding opened his mouth to speak, but closed it again at a gesture.

"Don't let's argue the toss, Peter. It was a chancy thing to do when there was a much safer alternative. What should you have done?"

"Waited for dark, sir."

"Certainly you should. All right, I won't draw attention to the matter in my covering letter to your patrol report. With any luck it will go unnoticed. God knows there's plenty more to read about in it."

"Thank you, sir," Harding said.

"Okay. Next time think a bit. It was a slowly developing situation and you had lots of time to do that instead of getting cross with yourself for having wasted four torpedoes. Bull-headedness doesn't pay."

His expression rueful, Harding nodded his agreement, depression deepening in him. His judgment had been questioned and rightly so. Add that to his behavior toward *Cutlass* and he appeared to have done quite remarkably badly. He let his eyes wander around the big day cabin, looked for a moment at Lieutenant Commander Donaldson puffing at a pipe in an armchair, then back at the flotilla captain. It would, he thought, be nice if the *Luftwaffe* were to stage one of their periodic attacks on the harbor within the next minute.

"There's one more thing you and I have to discuss, Peter."

"Yes, sir. I know."

"Do you want Ginger to push off while we're doing it?"

"No thank you, sir. If you're talking about *Cutlass*, he might as well hear it all so I can ask him to be 'prisoner's friend' at the court-martial."

The bitterness in his voice took Harding by surprise, but there was no recalling the words and the questioning look the flotilla captain gave him showed that his tone had registered there too. He sighed silently, wondering if he would ever get anything right again.

"Nobody is suggesting anything of that sort," the captain said. "Just tell us what happened."

Harding told them.

When he had finished: "So he never really gave you an order at all."

"Only one, sir. 'Carry out your orders.' As he hadn't given me any, I carried out yours, which were to return to harbor on completion of patrol by reverse of outward route. Bizerta was not on that route. The rest of his signals that day were statements, not orders."

The flotilla captain smiled faintly and turned to Donaldson.

"Do you think the C-in-C will buy that, Ginger? You've served on his staff."

"It won't fool him, sir but, yes, he'll buy it all right. It's the obvious course for him to take. Probably Fletcher of *Cutlass* will be told to shut up, and at the worst, Peter here will get some mild rebuke. The C-in-C has no time for petty squabbles that get in the way of the war effort. I'll draft the report for you if you like."

"Please do. You Peter, let Ginger have authenticated copies of all the signals you exchanged with *Cutlass* by lunch tomorrow. Now, that concluding the evening's business, who wants a gin?"

Stretched out in his comfortable chair, looking at his white-uniform shoes, Harding felt the tension running out of his muscles. The removal of the burden which had oppressed him for almost a week was, he supposed, the reason for the strange feeling of light-headedness he was experiencing. The brightness of the lamp on the captain's desk seemed to vary in intensity and he blinked his eyes until it steadied.

He took the glass handed to him, said, "Thank you, sir," sipped from it, then let his arms hang over the side of the chair, the glass dangling from one hand.

"That was a smart one you pulled on the PM today, Peter."

"Well, he did offer, sir, and I didn't want that bloody man Edgecombe court-martialed. It wouldn't have done anybody any good. Particularly Edgecombe. But it suddenly occurred to me that being let off by someone like 'Winnie' might make him think."

"I doubt it," the captain said, "but it was worth trying." He talked for a few minutes about the prime minister's visit while Harding watched the power waxing and waning in the bulb of the desk lamp.

"Said you were all such brave boys. Emotional old chap. He cried a bit when he left. Oh, that reminds me, Peter. You've done six patrols now and totted up a respectable tonnage of sinkings. It's time you made some recommendations to me for 'gongs' for your people. I'm sure Honors and Awards Branch have a couple of DSCs and half a dozen DSMs they could spare for *Trigger*—Peter?"

"I think he's asleep, sir."

"So he is," the flotilla captain said quietly. "Grab that drink of his before he drops it, Ginger. I'll get a blanket from my bunk."

"Sir? Wake up, sir. It's eleven o'clock. Captain said to wake you at eleven."

"What? Who are you?"

"Captain's steward, sir. I've got some breakfast for you here."

"Bloody hell!" Harding said. "What the devil's going on?"

"Nothing, sir. You had a bit of a nap, that's all. Captain said to bring you some breakfast at eleven. I'll put it on the table. Fruit juice, coffee, sausage and egg, toast and marmalade. Is that all right, sir?"

Harding began to laugh, then winced at the stiffness in his neck.

"Very much all right, thank you. God, my neck's seized up."

"Not surprising really, sir. You've been asleep in that chair since half-past seven last night."

"Bloody hell!" Harding said again.

He ate his breakfast quickly, scribbled a note of apology and thanks to the flotilla captain, then went to his own cabin to shave.

"'Morning, sir."

The first lieutenant was standing in the open doorway, the door curtain draped across him like a Roman toga. He brushed it aside and stepped into the cabin.

"Hello, Number One. What's the score?"

"It's a dry-dock job all right, sir. They're going to patch us up a bit and then tow us to Gib in about three days' time."

"Uhuh," Harding said and shaved carefully under the point of his chin where he often cut himself when he wasn't thinking. He cut himself anyway, muttered, "Dammit," and wiped the remains of the soap from his face.

"John?"

"Yes, sir?"

"Thank you for getting that brandy for me yesterday."

"Just taking seamanlike precautions, sir."

"Yes, well I'm afraid that's it. I'll have to turn myself over to the medicos."

"Why not leave it until we get back from Gibraltar, sir. You'll have had a rest by then. I'm sure that's all you need."

"No," Harding said, and from the sound of his voice Gascoigne knew that that was the end of the matter. He gave an almost imperceptible nod, moved toward the door, then turned back.

"Oh, by the way, sir. Able Seaman Norris is in the brig. The shore patrol brought him back aboard last night after he and an unidentified marine had beaten up five Australian soldiers in a bar. There was some doubt about who started it but, unfortunately, Norris took a swing at the naval police too. He said he couldn't see very well and thought they were Australian reinforcements. The depot ship commander let him off with ten days number eleven because he may be telling the truth. He's certainly got two splendid black eyes."

Harding grinned. "The unidentified marine wouldn't be Ackroyd by any chance, would he?"

"Sure to have been, sir. They're very chummy. But Norris isn't saying."

When Gascoigne had gone, Harding walked out onto the cabin deck and stood with his forearms on the depot ship's rail, looking down at the jetty formed by the seawall. A hundred yards away four sailors were running up and down a measured distance, encouraged by yelped commands from a petty officer. All four were holding rifles above their heads. One of the sailors was Norris. Harding grinned again and crossed to the other side of the depot ship. He was feeling curiously at peace and that, he supposed, was because he had voiced a definite decision to put himself in the hands of the surgeon commander.

Talon and *Tusker* had gone, whether on patrol or only to the submarine moorings farther down the harbor he didn't know. Only his own ship lay alongside below him, men, depot ship men, swarming all over her. Pressure tubing and electric leads crisscrossed her casing and disappeared down hatches. Oxyacetylene torches spat violet and dissolving metal threw off showers of orange sparks. Somewhere a hammer was producing a bell-like clanging. The head of Chief ERA Greenway rose out of the engine-room hatch, shouted something, and vanished again. So certain key men were still aboard. The remainder Gascoigne would have sent off to the rest camp along the coast for a short break. Except, of course, for the unfortunate Norris, now staggering back and forth on the jetty carrying a rifle which would seem to be increasing in weight by a pound a minute.

Harding turned toward the wardroom for a drink before lunch and to run the gauntlet of questions from his peers. When he got back to it an hour later, Corporal Ackroyd was standing at attention outside his cabin. He appeared to be completely unmarked.

"Do you want to see me, Ackroyd?"

"Yessir."

"Come in and shut the door."

"Thank you, sir."

Sitting on the bunk, Harding looked at the big commando. "Well?"

"Come to hand meself over to justice, sir."

Harding waited, saying nothing, and after a moment, Ackroyd began to speak.

"Able Seaman Norris and me was in this bar last night, sir, having a quiet jug or two when in come these five Aussie pongos. One of them says to me fuck off out of here you pommy* bastard and I says to him Christ it's a talking kangaroo and he swings off at me but I blocks it and clobbers him—I mean I renders him unconscious. Then the other four jumps me and it's a bit heavy for a couple of seconds until Norris piles in and flattens another and goes down hisself but he gets up and we bash another of them together before they hang one on Norris's other eye and he goes down again. Then the last two start to put the boot in which ain't right, sir, so I renders them unconscious and Norris and me helps the barman to carry them all outside. Just when we'd got them arranged on the pavement, the shore partrol arrives, sir, and Norris who can't see too good on account of his eyes are swelling up, shouts here come some more of the sods and lands a right one on one of the patrol, so they grabs him, chucks him in the paddy wagon and drives off leaving me standing there. I . . ."

A soft keening wail forced its way past the knuckles Harding had jammed into his mouth. The sound caused the commando to falter in his delivery, but he collected himself and resumed the monologue.

"It wasn't Norris's fault, sir. He only come to my assistance on perceiving that I was outnumbered, but they've got him running around on the jetty holding a rifle up in the air. He looked right beat when he finished his hour at it this morning. I'd like to do that for him, sir. It don't mean nothing to me. When I was under training they had me running up and down Scotch mountains with a hundred-pound pack. Rifles is easy, but Norris ain't used to it, sir."

All the time he had been talking, Ackroyd's eyes had never moved from some point on the bulkhead opposite him and

---

*Australian slang for "British immigrant, recently arrived."

Harding was very thankful for that. His shoulders were jerking, but he was silent now and hoped fervently that he could remain so until he had control of himself. When he was fairly certain that he could speak, he took in a long, slow breath, wiped the moisture from his eyes, and said, "Corporal?"

"Yessir?"

"Do you remember the day we surfaced with a lot of pressure inside the boat and I asked you to hang on to my legs?"

"Yessir."

"Hurts the ears when the pressure's released, doesn't it?"

"Not half, sir!"

"Well, when you've been through that as often as I have, your hearing is affected. I hardly got a word of what you were saying just now. Something about concern for Norris, wasn't it? There's nothing you can do for him, but don't worry about that. He'll survive." Harding choked, then added, "You're due to be made sergeant in a week or two, aren't you?"

"Yessir."

"Then I'd be careful about who you talk to until you are. They might not be as deaf as me. Now go away, *please!*"

Ackroyd dropped his eyes from the bulkhead to Harding's, smiled faintly, and left.

When the door closed behind him, Harding stopped holding his breath, said, "Here come some more of the sods," in a quavering voice, and hooted explosively. He did it several times, then blew his nose and wiped the tears from his eyes again. It was ages, he thought, since he had enjoyed anything so much.

CHAPTER 15

"IF," THE SURGEON COMMANDER SAID, "BY A DOC-
tor-patient relationship you mean will I respect your confidences, the answer is that it depends what they are. A confession on your part that you have been a lifelong sufferer from
hemorrhoids would be a closely guarded secret between us. I
might even treat them for you. Should you tell me that you
have contracted clap, that would be more difficult, being a
court-martial offense in the case of an officer. My fee for
dealing with the problem and keeping quiet about it would be
a double gin. But if you've come to me regarding some af-
fliction affecting your operational efficiency, then all bets are
off."

Harding smiled at the solid figure with the massive shoulders
and the almost totally bald head lounging on the other side of
the desk from him. The surgeon commander had been capped
eighteen times playing rugby for England before the war and
seemed to have lost none of his physical ability. When submarine officers half his age just returned from patrol elected
to smash up the wardroom furniture in the course of some
violent game, he was one of the few members of the depot ship
staff who could always be relied on to help them do it. He
considered it good therapy for them. Harding liked him and
that made what he had to say a little easier.

"I'm afraid it comes into your last category, sir."

"Ah! Nerves all tangled and jangling like an alarm clock,
eh? Spot of the old combat fatigue?"

Startled, Harding blinked at him. "That was a pretty swift

and accurate diagnosis, sir, although I don't go along with Americanisms like 'combat fatigue.' Does it show?"

"No, of course it doesn't show. Be better for you if it did, but they've trained that relief valve out of all of you. It's just an occupational hazard with you lot. Incidentally, whether or not you go along with Americanisms isn't relevant. Combat fatigue isn't one. We thought it up all by ourselves. Now, let's have your clothes off."

"My clothes, sir?"

"Oh Christ," the surgeon commander said. "Do your people say, 'What? Fire torpedoes, sir?' every time you tell them to poop some off? You do your job and let me do mine. Get undressed. We can play at psychoanalysis later."

At the end of an hour, "You'll probably live," the surgeon commander told Harding, then shouted, "Benson! Take these urine and blood samples away and do something clever with them. You won't find anything interesting, but the patient expects it." He turned back to Harding. "Okay, put your clothes on and tell me all about it."

The telling took much less time than the medical examination. When it was over, "Anyone else know about this?"

"Yes. My first lieutenant, sir."

"How?"

"He's observant. We've talked about it a little."

"Name?"

"John Gascoigne."

"Would you mind if I spoke to him?"

"Not in the least, sir."

"Thank you. Are you married?"

"No."

"Ever been?"

"No."

"Engaged?"

"Not really."

"Have you slept with women?"

"Yes."

"How many?"

"Two."

"That's not much for a chap of your age. How often?"

"Oh really," Harding said. "I've had exactly eleven days

leave since this war started nearly four years ago. The rest of the time I've been busy."

"Do you enjoy it?"

"Do I enjoy what? The war?"

"Don't be obstructive. Do you enjoy making love to women?"

"Look, sir," Harding said calmly, "I'm sorry to disappoint you, but the answer is 'yes, I do.' That would seem to indicate that I'm not a pansy. I liked my father rather better than my mother, so I haven't got an Oedipus complex. I..."

"Past tense?"

"Yes. They were both killed in the Blitz."

"I see. Look at your fingernails."

"What about them?"

"Nothing about them. I was just verifying your claim not to be a pansy. You looked at them the right way. Palm up, fingers folded. If you had done it palm down, fingers extended like a woman does, I might have wondered."

"How interesting."

"Are you a coward?"

"I suppose so. I'm quite often frightened. Or does that make me brave because I press on regardless?"

The questions and answers went on. The surgeon commander probing, sometimes insulting. Harding soft-spoken, a little sardonic, but no more so than was justified by the tenor of the questions.

The session ended at no logical point that Harding could see with the surgeon commander saying, "All right. That's as far as we can go today."

Lieutenant Gascoigne was hostile almost to the extent of insubordination.

"Yes, I heard you, sir."

"Then answer me."

"I prefer not to. If you want to know anything about my captain, ask him yourself."

"He can't give me your opinion of him." The surgeon commander injected sweet reason into his voice.

"How true," Gascoigne said and closed his mouth firmly.

"I have his permission to speak to you."

"So you said, sir. Speak away."

"You," the surgeon commander said, "give me the impression that you're protecting him from something."

"Very astute of you, sir. I am."

"From what?"

"Your inquisitiveness."

"Now you're being impertinent."

"And you, sir," Gascoigne told him, "are being unethical. Now, if you'll excuse me, I have work to do." He stood up before adding, "I'll make you free of this. He's a damned good skipper."

"Oh, naturally. The best in the flotilla, no doubt."

"As he's the only one I've served under here, I really couldn't say, sir," Gascoigne said and walked out.

The surgeon commander watched him go, smiled, and muttered, "And put that in your pipe and smoke it, you bald-headed old coot," but he had learned all he needed to know.

When he let himself into the day cabin, he found the flotilla captain alone, leaning against the mock mantelpiece, smoking a cigarette.

"Are you sure this is convenient, George?"

"It's fine, Freddie. Pour yourself a drink and I'll have a gin and water while you're about it in case you've come to lecture me about my ulcer."

The surgeon commander busied himself at the sideboard and said, "Your ulcer'll do for the time being. I want to talk to you about young Harding."

"Yes?"

"Yes. He came to see me today. He's got the twitch. Early stages as yet with mild agoraphobia. Funny how everybody expects them to be claustrophobic and they hardly ever are. Quite happy in a steel tube which would drive most people round the bend, but ask them to do something ordinary in public, particularly out of doors and they..."

"Freddie."

"Yes?"

"I know all that. Just give me that gin you're gesticulating with and get on with it."

"Sorry. Here you are." The surgeon commander handed over the gin, poured himself a glass of sherry and went on. "He tells me that he has been getting these bouts of trembling at unpredictable times, they don't last long and do not occur when approaching or during action or any other marine crisis. In his words, a different circuit seems to take over then, but he's afraid that that could fail too and he's right of course. Physically there's nothing the matter with him except for muscle tenseness which is all part of the same problem."

As though he hadn't been listening, the captain said in a preoccupied voice, "I've put him in for the big one as a result of the destruction of that convoy coupled with his earlier successes."

"Are you talking about the Victoria Cross?"

"Yes."

"Will he get it?"

"Lord no. Rarer than hens' teeth. Still it'll be something to have been recommended for it. They'll give him a DSO. I'm sorry, Freddie, that's got nothing to do with anything. Keep it to yourself and go on with what you were saying."

"Very well. The only other person who knows anything about this is *Trigger*'s first lieutenant, Gascoigne. Harding told me that Gascoigne had bowled him out and gave me permission to speak to the chap." The surgeon commander smiled reminiscently. "I did, and got the biggest flea in my ear I've ever had from a junior officer. Gascoigne was fiercely protective and refused to tell me anything except that Harding was a damned good skipper. His other officers support that view. Naturally, I haven't spoken to them, but I've done a little eavesdropping in the wardroom and they're shooting quite a line about him."

The captain looked at him somberly and asked, "Is that supposed to make everything all right?"

Returning his gaze, the surgeon commander realized that he was talking to a tired man, a man much more tired than the one he had spoken to the day before.

"No," he said. "It isn't. I've been trying to build up a picture of Harding so that I can recommend to you either that you release him from submarines or send him home on long leave to which he is certainly entitled. The undoubted support he has from his officers is a plus. Nobody will shield another out of sentiment when his own life is at stake, but I'm very much afraid that . . ."

"In your opinion is he salvageable, Freddie?" The interruption was abrupt.

There was a long pause before the reply came.

"I can't reverse the condition, George. We don't fully understand it yet, but it's possible to suspend its progress as you know, if the reactions are right and if there was enough time, which there isn't."

The captain put his untasted gin carefully down on the mantelpiece before saying, "There's time. *Trigger* is going to Gib for docking. Gascoigne can take her. That'll give us about five weeks."

"I see, but I must warn you, George, that there is no guarantee of success. He might even come out of it worse. It really *would* be better if you were to send him home. Get him right out of it for a few months. You've got a perfectly good spare commanding officer in Williamson. Why don't you give him *Trigger?*"

"Because Harding has six patrols in command behind him, all of them in a tough theater of war. Williamson did one off North Cape, Norway, when nothing happened. That means Harding has fifty times the experience. Look, Freddie, try giving Harding the treatment Candlish got. If it works, and we know it can, he'll be good for another patrol and possibly two. If it doesn't, I'll give *Trigger* to Williamson as you suggest. All right?"

"Not from where I'm standing," the surgeon commander said. "When we used Candlish as a guinea pig there was an emergency. As I remember it the flotilla was down to three experienced commanding officers. You had to keep Candlish going. I've got to think about Harding's future."

"And I've got to think about minimizing the *Wehrmacht*'s ability to repel the Allied armies when they land in Italy!" The captain's words came out with a savage intensity which made the other narrow his eyes in speculation.

"So you're giving me an order."

"If that's what it takes to stop you arguing and get the job done—yes I am."

The surgeon commander shrugged helplessly and moved toward the door.

"Freddie."

"Yes, George?"

"There's something else for you to keep to yourself until I release the news. *Tarantula* is overdue and *Tusker* stopped acknowledging signals twenty-six hours after she left here yesterday."

"No hope?"

"None at all."

"I see," the surgeon commander said. "That does put rather a different complexion on things, doesn't it?"

When the door closed, the flotilla captain sat down and wrote out a signal to flag officer (submarines) advising him of his intentions. He coded it himself.

The jeep had waited until Algiers was nine miles behind it before it decided to overheat. After that, progress had been slow with frequent stops for it to cool down while the driver prodded unenthusiastically around under the hood. Harding didn't mind. It was a lovely day, the coastal strip of Algeria, with the mountains to his left and the Mediterranean to his right, was pleasant to look at and he had nothing to do for the next couple of days other than talk to a Commander Mainwaring. Commander Mainwaring was a specialist in nervous disorders, the surgeon commander had told him. Two and a half cheers for Commander Mainwaring, who preferred to interview patients a long way from their familiar surroundings.

A small flotilla of harbor craft had pulled and pushed *Trigger* into a position where the big ocean-going tug could take her in tow. Harding had watched from the depot ship, returned Gascoigne's wave, waved again in response to a shouted message he didn't hear, then turned away when the submarine began to follow the tug obediently out of harbor. He experienced a sense of loss, but no stronger than the anticipation of it which he had lived with for long enough to deaden its impact. It felt as though *Trigger* and the war no longer had anything to do with him. Sitting in the shade of a rock at the side of the dusty road, there was only the presence of the gently steaming navy jeep and its disgruntled seaman driver to remind him that there was a war at all.

It was a pity about *Tusker* and *Tarantula* he thought, but he thought about it more as loss of striking power than the death of friends. Long ago it had been tacitly established in the "Trade" that you did not mourn friends because that saved them the embarrassment of mourning you if you went first.

He was wondering why the Submarine Service referred to itself as the "Trade" when the driver said, "I think we can push on now, sir."

When the jeep topped a spur in the coastline and they saw the villa set in a semicircular stand of trees fringing a tiny bay, it was early evening with the sun only a few diameters above the horizon.

"That's it, sir," the driver told Harding, turned off the main road onto a dirt track leading downward, and immediately switched off the engine. A minute later the jeep coasted almost silently into a clearing and stopped in front of the villa.

"Do you think you can make it back to Algiers in this thing?"

"Yes, sir. It seems to be curing itself and it'll be cooler now with the sun going down."

"Okay. Thanks very much."

Harding took his bag from the back and walked into the villa. It was single-storied, marble floors precisely level with the surrounding ground so that a fine film of sand had drifted some distance into the first room he entered. Archways without doors led to other rooms. The furnishings were simple and brightly colored. It was cool and very quiet.

"Anybody here?" he called, but there was no reply except the hiss of the sea on the beach and the sound of the jeep grinding back up the dirt track to the road. The engine noise faded and then there was only the sea whispering to itself, but that was enough to cover footsteps in sand and he jumped when a voice said, "You're very late."

He turned and looked at her framed in the entrance. Red hair, water-darkened, hanging in tangled strands to her shoulders and plastered across her face. One very long leg, sand-covered except where tiny rivulets of seawater meandering downward had washed it clean, protruding from her white beach robe. The robe itself sand stained. Crazy-looking girl.

"Yes. The jeep kept overheating."

"Never mind. You're here now." Quiet voice. Calm. Pretty to listen to.

She moved then and there was nothing crazy about her walk.

It was graceful, effortless, as though gravitation didn't exist for her. Water from her hair spattered him when she shook her head passing on her way toward one of the archways.

"I'm going to have a shower. Come and have one too. You can desand me. Or, if you'd rather, there are drinks in the room to your right."

Stunned, he stood staring toward the archway she had disappeared through, then breathed in deeply and raised his voice.

"I'm supposed to report to a Commander Mainwaring."

"I know," her voice came back to him. "You just have."

For long minutes Harding stood where he was, the bag hanging from his left hand forgotten, listening again to the surgeon commander's words. "Commander Mainwaring is a specialist in nervous disorders.... You'll like Commander Mainwaring. Everybody does.... You'll find Commander Mainwaring the sort of person you can tell things to, and that helps a lot when..." He searched his memory, but found no record at all of he/she, his/hers, him/her. Just Commander Mainwaring.

"Oh bloody hell. Now what do I do?" he whispered and frightened himself both because there was a tremor in his voice and because the question which had forced itself out of him was a real one. He didn't know what to do, had no idea at all, and that was alien to him. His training had taught him always to do something, but it had also taught him what those somethings should be. They covered all foreseeable contingencies. All? Not this one, they didn't!

The thought of flight occurred to him, but he discarded it almost at once. Walking fifty miles to Algiers at night in an occupied Arab country wouldn't be very wise. That conclusion reached, he put his bag down against a wall. A shower running. "Come and have one too. You can desand me." It was unbelievable to him that a strange woman could make such a suggestion.

"Oh bloody hell," he whispered again and moved slowly toward the room where she had said the drinks were. Bottles, glasses, an ice bucket glinting in the dusk on a corner table. He turned his back on them and sat down. She isn't Winston Churchill, he told himself and waited for the statement to make him feel better. It did not, so he waited for her instead, wondering why he was frightened. Half an hour later he was still doing it when the clicking of heels on marble brought him to his feet.

"You could at least have got a drink for yourself instead of standing in the dark," she said. "I'll get you one as soon as I've lit this lamp. There's no electricity here."

A match flaring. The wick of an oil lamp burning smokily, then growing into brightness when its glass funnel was placed over it. The red hair still damp, but curling tentatively away from her head and neck as though preparing to frame them. A mouth too wide for beauty and eyes too slanting, seeming about to slide inward toward a short straight nose. He couldn't tell their color, but knew that they were laughing at him although the mouth was not. No, it wasn't a beautiful face because he knew from his drawing skill that the proportions were wrong. It was simply the most strikingly provocative face he could ever have imagined and that made everything a great deal worse.

Time, too much time, had passed since she had lit the lamp. "I beg your pardon. I was staring," he said.

She nodded once. "That's what the war paint's for, to make you do that. Don't apologize." The mouth joining the eyes in the laugh, showing a lot of very white teeth, predatory teeth, he thought. When he said nothing more she turned away from him and began to make their drinks. He was glad about that because her regard had been disturbing and her black dress, so demurely cut except for the missing panel in front showing her flat stomach and the undercurve of her breasts, had shocked him. His mind groped for something to say before she should turn back again. It found it.

"How do you make ice without power?"

For a moment her shoulders shook, then, "I'll say one thing for you, Harding, you have the makings of a marvelous conversationalist. I get it from a restaurant about five miles away. We'll be dining there this evening."

Spirit stirred somewhere within him. "Not with you in that dress we won't!"

She pivoted slowly on heel and toe toward him, a drink in either hand. The light caught the slanting eyes and he saw that they were amber flecked with green.

"It's my instant seduction number. Don't you like it?"

The skin on the quarter spheres was almost translucent in its mauve-blushed whiteness. It seemed ridiculous to say no, so he didn't say anything.

"Here."

Harding looked at the brimming glass, moved his hand, let it drop to his side again, and shook his head. Then the glass was against his lips, tilting.

"Drink it—more—that's better. Now you can hold it, shaky paws. It's only half-full."

He took it from her and it was all right.

"I think . . ." Harding said and stopped.

The woman watched him over the top of her own glass.

"I think," he finished steadily, "that I'm falling apart."

She nodded her head in enthusiastic agreement. "So do other people. That's why you're here. *I'm* here to catch the pieces, so disintegrate anytime you want to."

"That wasn't what I meant," he told her. "I was more or less all right until . . . until . . ."

"Yes, I do rather have that effect on men," she said. "But don't let it worry you. It's pretty painless when you get used to it."

Harding sighed in bewilderment and drained his glass.

By the time they reached the restaurant, the warm night air flowing past the open car had dried her hair so that it floated about her head like a corona. He hadn't mentioned her dress again, but was relieved to find the place run by Frenchmen, not Arabs. It was a small bungalow set, like the villa, in trees, some sort of pine he supposed they were. Colored lights hung from the branches, five tables were grouped around a dance floor of hard-packed earth, and the candles on them burned without a tremor in the stillness.

He touched her for the first time when she took his hand and led him onto the floor to dance to the music of a gramophone operated by the man serving behind the bar against the bungalow wall. The record was playing "Room Five Hundred and Four." He touched a great deal more of her when she slid inside his arms, moving her body against his. The contact was more sexually arousing than anything he had ever experienced before and, embarrassed, he drew away from her.

"Oh, Harding," she said. "Just relax."

Trying to do as she said, his feelings lurched between contentment and surging excitement, each fluctuation taking him unawares, making him feel light-headed. When the record ended and they walked back to their table, he did it carefully because he was dizzy, but not too dizzy to be aware of the eyes of the other diners on the redheaded girl. A proprietary sense of pride touched him and even his awareness of its unjustifiability did nothing to lessen it.

"No, you order, please. You know the place."

"All right," she said and gave her attention so completely to the waiter that she made him stammer.

"And a beetroot salad to go with it."

Almost joyously Harding laughed.

She looked at him, smiling. "That was nice. You haven't done it before. But what's funny?"

"We have beetroot all the time at sea. It's supposed to be good for us. Beetroot with meat. Beetroot soup. Beetroot and sardines. Even beetroot in sandwiches."

"No beetroot salad," she said to the waiter and placed her hand over Harding's. Why, he didn't know, but the gentle caress was as exciting as the touch of her body had been.

Harding really tasted the food and the wine, each mouthful, every sip, enjoying them. He couldn't remember when he had last done that. Night sounds from the trees came to him as distinctly as the murmur of conversation from the other diners and the scratchy music of the old gramophone. His awakened sense of perception delighted him for itself, but also because he realized that the radiant figure on the other side of the small table, her leg resting against his, was the catalyst which had brought it about. Neither talked much, but she more than he in her gently calm voice. They danced five more times and he no longer tried to maintain space between them. The inevitability of what was to come rested on him like a blessing, blunting the edges of urgency.

Inside the entrance to the villa she lit two lamps, handed one of them to Harding, and said, "Your room's through there. Breakfast is at nine. Sleep well."

* * *

Drearily Harding tried to calculate how many miles he had walked on the basis that it took him four seconds to cover the seven paces from wall to wall of the room, another second to turn, and that he had been doing it for five hours and eleven minutes. His bare feet were sore and his pyjama trousers, the only piece of clothing he was wearing, soaked with sweat. He didn't mind that as much as the periodic racing of his heart, hammering as though it were running loose, relieved of the necessity of pumping blood around the system. It was doing it now and he paused in his aimless shambling to put his head under the tap and let the tepid water run until the back of his neck felt cool. That, he had learned, seemed to put his heart back into gear.

Light was beginning to show through the thin material of the curtains, dimming the already feeble glow of the oil lamp. He glanced at his watch, then resumed his restless journey without registering the message of its hands, no longer interested in the distance he had covered. But he had also learned that night that it was impossible to walk without thinking. Movement called on some part of the brain to control it and that part, he had concluded, alerted the rest out of spite. As if to prove his private theory, it did so now and his mind settled automatically, as it had done innumerable times, despite his feeble attempts to set it on some other course, on the evening before, an evening which had begun with shock, grown into enchantment, and ended with a greater shock for which he had been totally unprepared.

Her final words might as well have been her hand slashing across his face and he had stood, blinking, watching her retreating back until it vanished through an archway. Then, obediently, he had gone to his room, undressed, and put on his pyjama trousers. For half an hour he had sat on the side of his bed, confused by the shifting kaleidoscope of his emotions. Frustration coupled with a deeper feeling of the loss of something he had never owned. Anger at the woman jostling contempt at himself for believing that so exotic a creature would ever sleep with him. Puzzlement at what she had been trying to do, vying with the certainty that she had simply enjoyed walking all over him. Bewilderment about why he was at this place at all.

He had stood up finally and gone to her room, grimly de-

termined at least to settle that final point, but she was not there
and the bed had not been slept in, nor was she in any of the
other rooms. When he went to look for it at the back of the
villa, the car had gone. After that he had returned to his room
and begun to walk as he was doing now, hoping for an exhaustion which would let him attempt sleep, achieving only a
nervous tiredness which would not.

The day outside much brighter. One end wall approaching,
then the other, as they had been doing for so long. Legs rubbery.
Path growing erratic. Sensation of light-headedness.

"I think you must be about cooked now, Harding," she said.

Harding turned slowly and squinted at her. She was leaning
in the archway, naked except for a piece of green-and-white-
striped material around her waist, knotted above one hip.

"Good morning, Commander Mainwaring." He had tried
to inject a sneer into his voice, but all he achieved was a croak
as though he had been shouting all night.

She made no reply other than to lever herself clear of the
wall and move slowly toward him. As slowly, he backed away.
When he stopped, he stopped too and stared at her staring
balefully at him.

Her hand felt cool against the bare skin of his chest. She
let it rest there for a moment in a motionless caress, holding
his eyes with her own, then he fell backward at her sharp push,
the bed catching him behind the knees.

In seconds it was all over, and when his vision cleared, he
met the same brooding regard, except that she was looking
down at him now.

"It must have been a very long time," she said and he nodded
a wordless reply. Only then did she begin to make calculated
love to him.

Harding, who had little experience of the process, was both
appalled and enthralled at her expertise. She dealt with him
clinically, precisely, and without tenderness, as if she were
dissecting his soul while she ravished his body. In a haze of
undreamed-of sensations, he wondered if she had been trained
since childhood for such work.

An hour later and after the third time, he began to cry and
immediately everything changed. Immovable bonds of per-

fectly formed arms and legs, unbreakable in their gentleness, cream-slick breasts a prison for his head.

"Thank God," she whispered to him, "I was beginning to think I'd have to tie you up and beat you to make you do that."

Harding cried for a long time before his jerky breathing slowed and he spiraled downward into darkness.

Breakfast was at four-fifteen in the afternoon that day.

"Would you please get this number for me?"

The owner of the bungalow restaurant in the woods looked up from his desk in the little foyer, smiled at the redheaded girl in the long green dress, and took the piece of paper from her hand. He liked the dress which, although it covered all of her, was hardly less suggestive than the black creation she had worn the previous evening. The way it clung and her slanting eyes reminded him strongly of the stylized drawings of showgirls outside *les Folies Bergère*.

"At once, *mademoiselle*. Or perhaps it is best to say as soon as the system permits. It is sometimes not easy with the war. Please to sit."

He watched her from the corner of his eyes while he was waiting for the call to come through. A strange one this, he thought. Some months before she had come often to his establishment with a blond Englishman whose right eyelid fluttered continuously to begin with and then it had stopped doing it. For a while after that he had seen her no more, but now she was back with another Englishman of unremarkable appearance. As she could obviously have any man she wanted, he concluded that the two he had seen in her company were very rich.

"Aha! Wait please." He held the telephone toward her. "Your number speaks, *mademoiselle*."

"Thank you," she said. "Surgeon Commander Gilmore, please."

Suddenly aware that he was being looked at with questioning arrogance, the owner murmured, "Excuse please. I have much to attend to," and walked away.

"Hello, Freddie. I'm just reporting in as requested. . . . Yes, he did. . . . No. . . . What? . . . Oh, Freddie, don't be silly. How can I possibly say how it's going when I've only just started?

The poor sweet's punch-drunk at the moment if that's of any interest to you.... Yes, of course I'll phone.... Have they? I'm so glad. I'll tell him straight away.... You too. 'Bye."

She left money on the desk and went out into the warm North African night, conscious of Harding's regard on her as soon as she passed through the doorway, pretending not to be. Knowing, as well, that he was at the hour-counting stage, resenting even the few minutes she had spent apart from him because they had told him he would be away from Algiers for only two days and that made the next day the last. That was good as it would keep him off balance and she had decided to let him fret about it until the morning. But it was Harding who brought the matter to a head.

Sinking onto a chair at their table, she said, "I've just been told that they've awarded you a DSO and a bar to your DSC. Isn't that fun?"

"Hurrah for me."

"Oh, Peter, do be pleased about it. I am. *Awfully.*"

His face went so rigid that she guessed he was stopping himself from crying. She wanted him to cry, often, but from relief and release, not unhappiness. Encircling his wrist with her fingers, she dug her nails in deep.

"What's the matter?"

He glanced at her, then dropped his eyes. It was half a minute before he spoke.

"Gail?"

"I'm here."

"I'd like to go back to Algiers tonight. I know I'm not due to go until tomorrow, but I've been thinking while you were inside there and—well—if I leave it until then, I don't believe I could stand it."

"Oh my God," she said. "He's gone and got all sentimental. That wasn't in the script." She released his wrist, then went on. "Now you listen to me, Peter Harding. You are overtired, overstretched, and close to a nervous breakdown. Those are facts about which I was informed and which I have now seen for myself. From what you have just said and from one terribly obvious point you've completely missed, you're closer to the brink than I thought you were. As it happens, that makes my job easier. I want you over that brink, but by a course of my choosing so that I can pull you up the other side."

She fluttered her hands as though seeking words in the air before continuing. "Something like that can't be done in two days. They only said that to prevent your being suspicious, but I had imagined that as soon as I walked in on you, you would realize what the situation was."

Knowing perfectly well the force of the impact she had had on him, she had imagined nothing of the kind and his inability to think was no surprise to her. But it all had to be said now because, after her steamroller tactics, the last thing she had expected was the type of emotion implicit in his words. Emotion yes, but not that kind.

"They," she told him, "don't give a damn about you as a person, only as a factor in this war. Quite an important one in a minor way or they wouldn't be going to all this trouble over you. So the alternatives are for you to run back to Algiers like a frightened little boy and wreck everything for yourself, or to play mummies and daddies with me for the next few weeks and see what happens. Which is it to be?"

Hating herself for the hardness in her voice, she waited for him to say something. When he did not, she hated herself more for having to add, "I wouldn't have thought the average male would find the latter an unattractive proposition."

"It's the most attractive proposition I could dream of."

She sighed silently, agonizing for him. Agonizing a little for herself too. That wrong emotion, the nice one, was still there. Not like Clive Candlish. Not like Clive Candlish at all. This was going to be a difficult one.

"So?"

"It means I'm so weak."

"Then accept a prop when it's offered you."

"And how about that prop? You, Gail."

"That's my business."

He looked woebegone when, more in surrender than acceptance, he nodded his head. She felt her heart lurch and turned quickly to fumble in her handbag, find the car keys, drop them in front of him.

"Please take me home to bed now, darling," she said.

CHAPTER 16

THE FLOTILLA CAPTAIN STOOD UP WHEN THE civilian with graying hair and the RAF squadron leader were shown into his day cabin. He nodded dismissal at the officer of the watch who had conducted them there and said, "Come in, gentlemen." When the door behind them closed he added, "Perhaps you would give me your names."

"I'm Vibart," the civilian told him, "and this is Hunt. You're Captain Anderson I take it."

"Yes, I'm Anderson. I've had a signal about you from FOS/M. I mean Flag Officer (Submarines), my admiral. He mentioned a means of identification."

"Quite so. We've come to talk to you about Conrad."

"In that case, sit down and talk to me about him."

The civilian perched himself on the arm of a chair, but the RAF officer walked to the door of the sleeping cabin, peered inside, then went to the steward's pantry.

"It's empty and the outer door is locked," Anderson said and received a wink in reply. The wink irritated him, but he kept his face expressionless, waiting for the civilian to speak. After a pause he did so with a question.

"Did the PM mention that name to you when he was here?"

"No, he did not."

"Ah. In that case I'll start from scratch. Conrad is the code name for an American called John Villar who, for the last couple of years or so, has been working for us in northern Italy, mainly in the Spezia area. He's been using the Italian form of his name, Giovanni Villari. Do you mind if I smoke my pipe?"

"Not a bit."

"Thanks," the civilian said, took an already filled pipe from his pocket, and talked on without lighting it. "Conrad has been one of the most accurate and prolific agents we have. In fact most of the intelligence you yourself have been given about shipping movements in and out of Spezia originated with him."

"And now you want to pull him out."

"Well, that does rather follow, doesn't it? Otherwise we wouldn't be here telling you about him."

"Is one permitted to ask why? Now just a minute. Before you answer that, let me make my position quite clear. I have been ordered to give you my fullest cooperation, but I am not going to do that blindly. I have to balance the risk of losing an extremely valuable submarine and its crew of more than seventy against the problematical removal of your agent who, if he's as good as you say, one could be forgiven for wondering why he isn't left where he is. No matter what you people in civvie street may think, we in the services don't necessarily treat every order as coming from God."

The civilian smiled, lit his pipe, and said, "I know. Don't spread it around, but I commanded my division not so long ago."

Captain Anderson looked at him curiously.

"Are you Major General Vibart?"

"That's me."

"Quite a job you did on the Mareth Line, sir."

"Oh, don't start calling me sir. It embarrasses my snoopy friend masquerading as an aviator here. He's my boss."

"Is that so? Well, let me tell you something else. I find confidences from your fraternity suspect. You have some reason for revealing who you are."

"Correct," Vibart told him. "I thought you would be more likely to believe an astonishing admission I have to make if you knew that it came from a fellow professional. You asked a moment ago if you were permitted to ask why we want to pull Conrad out of Italy. By all means do so, but I'm afraid the unsatisfactory answer is that, at local level, we haven't got the remotest idea. As you point out, it would appear to be logical to leave him where he is, but he's urgently wanted in the States."

He gave an apologetic shrug and went on, "If it's of any help to you in balancing the risk factors, it was put to me in London that the man is worth an armored division to the Allies. Translate that into your own terms. An aircraft carrier? Two aircraft carriers? I wouldn't know, but I would suggest to you that his value, for whatever the purpose may be, is in excess of one submarine."

Speaking for the first time, the man in RAF uniform said, "That assessment is shared by the prime minister."

Captain Anderson glanced at him and away again before addressing Vibart.

"As it's pointless to conjecture about what his value consists of, I'll have to take your word for it that it exists. The strong wording of my admiral's uninformative signal seems to bear out what you say. Apparently I have no choice in the matter."

"We'd both feel happier," Vibart told him, "if you didn't look at it in quite that light. Our object in coming to see you was to enlist your help, not point a gun at your head."

"All right. Thank you for the soft soap. When do you want it done?"

Vibart moved his shoulders apologetically again. "That's something else we don't know, but it will be vital to move as soon as humanly possible when we do and that is why we are forewarning you."

"This," Anderson said angrily, "is getting beyond all reason. Placing a submarine at your disposal between specified dates is one thing. To dislocate the deployment of the entire flotilla for the sake of an operation which appears to be approaching the hypothetical is another. Would you, General, hold back one of the brigades in your division from an assault because you had been told that it might conceivably be required elsewhere at some unspecified time?"

"I think he might," the squadron leader broke in, "if to do so was worth an armored division. Or two aircraft carriers. Tell him the rest, Harry."

"Very well. This is the situation, Anderson. Conrad came into the war long before most of the rest of his countrymen because he felt that he had a personal ax to grind. That's why he's working for us and not the Americans. Well, that ax is his contribution to the downfall of the Fascist regime in Italy and he's still grinding it to the extent of refusing to be pulled out. It has proved fruitless telling him that his services are urgently required at home for the simple reason that not knowing what it is he is required to do, we cannot convince him by radio of its importance. To his way of thinking, what he is already doing is the most important thing there is. Clear so far?"

"Not really. Can't you send in a courier to persuade him forcibly?"

"No. His cover's been blown and he's gone underground."

"I see. Go on."

"Sicily is about to fall. There's no possibility of their stopping us now. When it does, it is virtually certain that Italy will surrender. When Italy surrenders, Conrad's personal crusade will be at an end. He'll agree to come out then."

For some seconds Anderson whistled softly to himself, then he said, "Give me as much warning as you can. I'll try to lift your armored division off the beaches for you."

"Tell me about Gascoigne and Ryland and Elleston and Norris and all your people."

Harding blinked and lifted his head off her stomach to look at her, but a lock of his hair wound around her finger stopped the movement and subsided again. He liked lying like that, but not so much as usual this day because she was as covered with sand as the first time he had seen her.

"You feel like an emery board," he said.

"Poor darling, how you must be suffering. Tell me about them."

"You'll be suffering too if you don't move your right arm out of the sun. Have I been talking in my sleep?"

Gail said, "Damn!" and squirmed a yard further into the shadow of a tree, drawing him with her by the hair. "No, you haven't been talking in your sleep. All you do is make uninteresting woofling noises."

"Then how do you know those names?"

"From your patrol reports of course."

"But they're secret documents."

"And I'm your secret mistress, so that's all right. Well, almost secret anyway."

That they should show the reports to her was, he decided, logical. She would need to know what had happened. That he accepted, but the acceptance only increased the feeling of defenselessness she inspired in him. It was very far from unpleasant, but he wasn't sure that he liked being a completely open book to her when her background was closed to him. Of herself she gave him everything, of her past nothing at all, and he knew only that she was Senior Commander Gail Mainwaring ATS, a year younger and a lot older than he. Commander Mainwaring, the doctor had called her, because the prefix to her rank would have revealed her branch of the service and, therefore, her sex. The fact that she outranked him on top of everything else was really neither here nor there but . . .

"Don't just nod off on my tummy," she said. "Talk to me."

Harding told her about Gascoigne and Ryland and Elleston and Norris and all his people just as she had asked him to, but only the funny things for the reason that it didn't occur to him to tell her anything else. That he was doing it well he knew from the frequent quivering of her stomach under his ear. That he was doing it very much better than would have been possible for him a week earlier, only a recording would have shown. There was no such recording and he remained unaware of the beginnings of change in him and knew only that it was a happy thing to make her laugh. The surgeon commander would have been pleased with the slackening of tension in the muscles too, but Harding was not aware of that either.

She wailed softly throughout the telling of Corporal Ackroyd's submission to justice, then pulled herself from under his head and ran into the sea. More slowly he followed, anxious because she swam so fast and so far, wishing that Ackroyd was with him now to give her the help he could not should she need it. She didn't need it and he watched thankfully as she left the water to throw herself facedown at full length before turning on to her back.

For the walk to the villa she wore her beach robe and a hat almost as large as an umbrella to protect her pale skin from the evening sun. Harding went beside her, wondering how she managed to look both absurd and elegant at the same time.

It was very sweet, the desanding process in the shower.

When she was sure that Harding was completely asleep, Gail Mainwaring turned up the wick of the oil lamp beside the bed a little and took the letter she had been writing to Surgeon Commander Gilmore from her handbag. She took out her pen too and put it between her teeth, then began to read, skimming the first page, concentrating on the second.

"... so don't try to pin me down, Freddie, and don't send any more letters here by messenger. I know I said I'd telephone and I will when there's something you need to know. You can't expect me to call you every time we go to the restaurant—how on earth do you think he'd feel, knowing who I was talking to?—and there isn't another telephone for miles."

She tilted the paper under the light to see what she had written next and then crossed out heavily, could not distinguish the words, and read on.

"I'm certainly not going to give you a blow-by-blow account, now would you want me to, but I'll tell you what I believe to be relevant and it's this. You were right in thinking that Peter was in a much worse state than he had given you to understand. I don't think he knew himself, or wouldn't admit it to himself.

"I induced a crying jag which went on intermittently for six days and gradually it all came tumbling out. Fear for his sailors' lives, fear for his own life too, but that largely obscured by the fear of being seen to be afraid. There's the fear of professional inadequacy as well and a deeply ingrained belief that he isn't experienced enough to be doing what he does. Apparently he does practically nothing in harbor except set himself imaginary problems of attacks on enemy ships and analyze other people's reports on how they did it.

"I don't know how typical this is, but I should think it was a jolly good recipe for mental exhaustion. Anyway, by the time he was cried out, he was physically and emotionally exhausted too, but relaxed enough to sleep naturally for long periods. The relaxation is visible now. Neither the look in his eyes nor the set of his shoulders is defensive anymore. That's a definite gain as is the fact that he has begun to be more outgoing, telling me funny things that his people have said and done. There was no humor in him at all when he first arrived here.

"To be thoroughly cynical, and this is a pretty cynical sort of situation, there's another gain. The poor chap fell in love with me almost at once. Quite genuinely. I don't know why I'm surprised, but after Clive Candlish I hadn't seriously considered the possibility. Never mind. It'll keep him going through at least one of those stinking patrols."

Frowning, she took her pen from her mouth, uncapped it and inked out the whole paragraph.

That done, "He's going through an embarrassed stage now," she read. "Embarrassment for himself, but more for me. I'll get him over that and start work on building up his self-confidence."

Apart from some more obliterated words, the letter ended there. She remembered that she had been going on to point out that whatever magic spell she succeeded in weaving, it would not last under the bludgeoning of Harding's kind of warfare. But Freddie Gilmore knew that perfectly well, so she had deleted it.

Having read the untidy pages through once more, she glanced down at Harding, bit her lip, and began to write.

"Peter's lying beside me now looking awfully sweet. He's quite safe, sound asleep, and I love him very much. Isn't that the funniest thing you ever heard?"

Then she slid off the bed, padded into the living room, and burned the letter in the open fireplace there.

Two days later Surgeon Commander Gilmore received an envelope addressed in Gail Mainwaring's hand. He opened it and read, "Leave me alone. I'll tell you when it's time." The note wasn't even signed.

It was four and a half weeks since Harding had arrived at the villa and their last evening together. As he had done once before, he was waiting at the restaurant table they had made their own for her to come back from the telephone. That he was going away in a few hours saddened him, but less than he had feared because of the book of the future she had opened for him, quite the prettiest book he had ever seen.

He picked up his wineglass, then put it down again as the book's main illustration appeared in the doorway and moved quickly toward him, long legs striding, red hair floating up and down, up and down.

"All arranged. A driver will collect you at eleven in the morning. Come and dance."

Laughing, animated, so that he should not see that she wanted to die. He didn't see. Her dancing light, companionable, not seductive now.

"I take it that the stockings I found when I repacked your bag *are* mine."

"Oh, you haven't taken them back have you?"

Swallowing the lump forming in her throat at the anxiety in his voice, "No, I haven't taken them back."

"You see, you won't let me have a photograph. I had to have something."

"You're a fool, Peter."

"Yes," he said, a little puzzled at the sudden gravity of her tone, but he had forgotten about it by the time the music stopped and they returned to their table.

Predictably: "Will you marry me, Gail?"

She smiled at him. "That was sweet of you, darling, but no, I won't marry you."

"Any particular reason? I believe you do love me."

"Yes, there's a particular reason."

"Will you tell me what it is?"

The smile came again, but the corners of the wide mouth were turned down.

"Isn't it obvious?"

"Not to me."

The brooding look he remembered so well from the time when she had first taken him was back in the slanting eyes.

"Your sort of people, Harding," she said, "don't marry the local whore. But, if they try to, they should be prevented from doing it."

He laughed softly, the shake of his head a total disavowal of her claim.

"Is that it? All right, I'll ask you again another day."

Gail nodded, a slow, almost imperceptible nod, but didn't say anything.

She was back at the restaurant as soon as it opened for the prelunch trade the next morning, talking to Surgeon Commander Gilmore on the telephone.

"Yes, a jeep came for him half an hour ago. . . . Well, that's difficult to say. You had better read my report. It'll be delivered to you shortly after I get back to Algiers this afternoon. I had meant to send you an interim one, but it didn't work out.... No, I don't want to meet you and tell you about it. Just read it.... Listen, Freddie, I haven't actually been able to give him any 'field' trials on naval warfare, for heaven's sake, or public speaking, or anything, but you probably have ways of putting him through the hoop. You'll find he'll be all right. That is until you people have had time to get him in a muddle again.... I sound what?... Oh, bitter. No, I'm not that. Certainly not that. I'm sorry if I sounded it.... What?... Oh, yes, there is something else you should know, Freddie. Damn the war effort! I've finished and you are never to send me any of your lame ducks again. Never!"

The restaurant owner found her standing, staring straight in front of her. Apart from the tears running down it, her face held no expression.

"Can I bring you anything, *mademoiselle?* A cognac perhaps?"

He was rewarded by a flashing smile and a negative swirling of the red hair, then watched while she walked away through the dappled sunlight under the trees.

Surprisingly to him, there was no embarrassment in rejoining the depot ship for Harding. "London, to tell FOS/M about that convoy," he said to those who asked him where he had been. The surgeon commander greeted him cheerfully and took him to the sick bay for a check, but talked only generalities. It was pleasant when Captain Anderson at least acknowledged her existence.

"Come in, Peter. Nice to have you back. How's your pretty lady?"

He was ridiculously pleased at the use of the word "your," wondered, as he had done repeatedly of late, if he should try to express his thanks in some way, but decided against it. There was nothing adequate he could say.

Believing it to be so, "She's fine, sir," Harding said.

"Good. I had a signal from Gascoigne this morning. *Trigger* will be ready for sea in five days. You'll want to get along to Gib. Ask Ginger to book a passage with the RAF for you and let me know as soon as you've resumed command. I'll send you your orders through Flag Officer Gibraltar. Okay?"

"Yes, sir. I'd like to have one full day for diving and high-speed trials though. A gunnery shoot too."

"So you shall. Any qualms, Peter?"

"Qualms, sir? Oh, I see." Harding shook his head emphatically. "None at all. That's past. I'm sorry to have been a nuisance."

"Right, carry on, Peter."

"Aye aye, sir."

Harding found Able Seaman Norris waiting, as Ackroyd had, outside his cabin.

"What the devil are you doing here, Norris?"

"Missed the ship, sir. They gave me this ten day's number eleven for a brawl in a pub, and as we weren't going on patrol I had to stay here and finish it."

"I see. Come in."

He took the telephone from the bulkhead and talked into it while Norris stood, fidgeting with his cap.

"Thank you, Ginger," he said, replaced the telephone, and turned to the sailor. "What did you want to see me about, Norris?"

"What you just done, sir. I heard you was back and I thought you might take me to Gib with you. Cor! This is really living! I've never done it before."

"Done what before?"

"Flown, sir. In a plane, sir."

"In that case," Harding said, "you had better get your gear together and meet me at the quarterdeck gangway in fifty minutes."

Listening to the sound of running footsteps receding, he was grateful, however unwitting the source, for another vote of confidence. There seemed to be a lot of people still prepared to trust him and he was as certain now as it was possible to be that he wouldn't let them down.

When he had finished packing, he sat at the desk making a sketch of Gail Mainwaring from memory. It was difficult and he still hadn't got it right when he was told that the car for the airport was waiting.

CHAPTER 17

"ITALY HAS SURRENDERED...ITALY HAS SUR-rendered...Italy has surrendered."

It took some seconds for Villari to realize that Algiers was transmitting in plain language, so accustomed was his brain to receiving code and simultaneously deciphering it. Several more times the message was repeated while he digested it and its implications, then, in code, he broke into the transmission.

"Tell me about it."

Those words were the first indication in weeks that Major General Vibart had had that Conrad was prepared to listen to anything. He sent a messenger to find his colleague and superior, the bogus squadron leader, then told the radio operator to send the signal he had prepared. From it Villari learned of the fall of Sicily and knew why the *Wehrmacht* and the *Luft-waffe* had been and still were on the move. He learned too of the downfall of Mussolini and the formation of the Badoglio government and was content. Of the not unimportant part he had played in bringing these events about, he had little idea. It was enough for him that they had happened and that his self-inflicted task was over.

"Hold," Algiers said.

He held, lying on the roof of the last house he had broken into. It seemed the best place to stay because the troops had already searched it without looking up there and he could see them now, peering into storm culverts under the road two hundred yards to his front. They were never far from him these days, the Germans.

Algiers began transmitting again. He listened carefully, then signed off and massaged the shoulder he had strained lifting the heavy transceiver with him onto the roof. All he had to do was make his way to a point on the coast nearest to him, reconnoiter, and inform Algiers of a suitable location for a submarine pick up.

The voices of the people inside the house and of the soldiers on the road reached him with roughly equal clarity. Turning his head to the left where, twenty miles off, the coastline lay, he thought that the British really were an extremely humorous race. He began to swear at them with quiet venom.

In Algiers Squadron Leader Hunt said, "If anybody can do it Conrad can. He's bloody good. I'll get on to Thayer Street. Would you go and tell Anderson that we're going to need one of his submersible craft at very short notice? Like today for example?"

Major General Vibart nodded and walked out of the room.

"Hello, sir. Welcome to Gib. You're looking very brown. Hello, Norris. Bummed a lift off the captain, did you? Good show. Grab the captain's bag and put it in that truck over there. Sir, if you're not too tired we thought we'd take you out on the town tonight. The pilot wants to celebrate his DSC. Oh, and thanks for mine too, sir, and congratulations on your lot. We thought we'd wait until you rejoined and . . ."

It was good to see Gascoigne again. Tall, grinning, obviously tanned himself with, apart from his white uniform, reflected light from teeth and eyes the most prominent thing about him on the darkened airfield. Not as dark as it had been though and with far fewer planes than the last time he had stood on it just before the North African landings. The war had moved on.

"I'm not tired, Number One. We'll get quietly pissed. Half the bill's mine."

They hadn't been particularly quiet about it, he and Gascoigne, Walker and Elleston, and the new engineer officer called Sykes. They had talked animatedly, sung loudly, and Elleston had walked out of the last bar on his hands. No mention was made of the late engineer officer and nobody asked Harding where he had been. Correctly he credited Gascoigne with that.

From below, *Trigger* looked enormous to Harding as he walked the next morning from the banked torpedo tubes in the bow under the bulging curve of the ballast tanks to the twin bronze propellers at the stern. The noise of the pneumatic riveters was appalling and he didn't stay long before clambering up the stepped side of the dry dock, smiling ruefully at the memory of the medal celebration party. "Oh, Peter, do be pleased about it. I am. *Awfully*," she had said. He had been pleased about it the previous night and now his head ached abominably.

"Sir?"

He turned and looked at the sailor pulling a motorcycle onto its stand.

"Yes?"

"Are you the captain of *Trigger,* sir?"

"I am."

"Signal for you, sir."

He read the contents of the envelope the man gave him, said, "Thank you," and walked rapidly away, his head pounding at each step.

"There's some flap on, Number One. We've got to leave for Algiers at the first possible moment. When's that?"

Gascoigne pulled at his lower lip before saying, "I'll have to check with the chief, but I'd guess the day after tomorrow. Not before then, certainly."

"All right. Target for that, please."

"Aye aye, sir."

No headache now. That had been seven hours of intense activity ago. Not tired, but suddenly very hungry.

"Can someone find me a sandwich?"

"Bacon, omelet, and peas in two minutes if you'll stay where you are that long, sir. 'Ad to throw the last two lots away because you kept dashin' off somewhere."

"Did I? Oh yes, I believe I did. Sorry about that, Cox'n. I'll stay put."

He *had* been dashing about. The captain of the dockyard to ask for more men to be assigned to work on *Trigger*.

"Sorry, Harding. I've got an aircraft carrier, two cruisers, and two frigates on my hands apart from you. If you'd taken the trouble to look you'd have seen that for yourself."

"I saw, sir. Would you mind reading this signal?"

"Yes, I would. Get out, Harding. I'm extremely busy."

Pig-eyed little bastard!

Up to see the admiral's Chief of Staff with a request to put pressure on the dockyard.

"Tricky. Been better if you'd come to me first. Still, you weren't to know that. Okay, Harding. Leave it with me."

Additional men had arrived within the hour.

To an office somewhere with a helpful lieutenant commander in it.

"Advance your fueling by about three days? No, that's no problem, chum. Give me an hour's notice when you're ready."

The torpedo store.

"Yes, my seventeen Mark VIII-two star, with warheads. Eight magnetic, nine contact. Can you make it first light Thursday? You can? Thanks very much."

Always better to see them than telephone.

Four-inch ammunition, Oerlikon twenty-millimeter ammunition, .303 gas-operated Vickers ammunition, water, food, and more food for seventy-seven men for eight weeks. Arrangements for swinging the magnetic compass, then for sea trials.

"Thank you, sir. Could you have somebody warn all ships and aircraft that a friendly submarine will be carrying out high-speed and diving trials off Europa Point on Thursday morning?"

"Wouldn't you like me to tell the shore batteries too, Harding?"

"Christ, I'd forgotten about them, sir."

Back to the shed which was serving them as an office and a message from the captain of the dockyard. "ICU 1600."

"Shit!" Harding had said. "Pilot, how're you getting on with your chart corrections?"

"No problem, sir. I gave the charts and the notices to mariners to the dames at the store. They're doing them."

"How did you persuade them to do that?"

"Promised them kisses on completion, sir. They're crazy about me. Handsome war hero, sir."

"In that case you can stand in for me. I've had an 'I'll see you' summons from the captain of the dockyard for 1600. He's angry with me. You think the first lieutenant and I are with the admiral so you've come along to have your arse chewed instead. Okay? Right. Cox'n, I think—no, never mind. I've got to see the captain of *Cleaver* about his escort plans. I'll be there if I'm wanted."

It had gone on like that all day and Harding had slept in the shed, but he wasn't the first down at the dry dock in the morning. He thought he was probably the last.

Most of his men and all his officers, stripped to the waist, formed a line between the ship and a railway wagon in a siding. They were supporting the long shapes of four-inch shells joined to brass cartridge cases in the crooks of their elbows, passing them from man to man down the line.

Gascoigne saw him and left the chain.

"Bit irregular, sir, but it's something we won't have to do tomorrow."

"Damned good idea. Did you break into the ammunition truck?"

"'Fraid so, but it *is* ours."

"Ah well. Any idea what happened to the pilot yesterday afternoon?"

"Yes, he took a drubbing from the captain of the dockyard for you. Apparently we've been causing labor problems by having the chaps help the dockyard workmen paint the ship's bottom."

"What did he do about it?"

"Nothing, sir. Couldn't find you and he wasn't prepared to countermand your orders in your absence. The painting's finished now."

"Anything else untoward occurred?"

"Two of our people arrested for drunkenness, but I got them back on my promise that they won't leave the yard again before we sail. Oh and there was a prick of an army lieutenant from the provost marshal's office asking about an officer who had disgraced his uniform by walking on his hands in the street. You wouldn't know anything about that, would you, sir?"

"Not a thing, Number One. Can't have been any of us."

"That's what I thought. Damn. Look out, sir. Here comes trouble."

The man in the uniform of a commander seemed too astonished to be fully angry.

"What the flaming hell's going on here?"

"We're cutting corners, sir," Harding said.

"But you can't ammunition ship in dry dock! All these oxyacetylene torches and..." Words deserted him.

"I know it's against regulations, sir, but there aren't any torches yet. It's too early for the workmen and the trouble is..."

Instead of explaining what the trouble was, Harding held out the now much-handled signal ordering utmost dispatch.

The commander took it, read it, and handed it back. He looked at Harding, at Gascoigne, then back at Harding.

"Well, as I can't possibly be seeing what I think I'm seeing, I can't have walked this way this morning. Good day to you."

"Good day, sir, and thank you."

Harding watched the retreating figure for a moment, then glanced up at the Rock looming over him. So busy had he been since his arrival he had scarcely noticed it. He supposed it wasn't much as rock formations went, really little more than a long hill, but it seemed to possess the loweringly watchful power of some prehistoric leviathan with igneous stone for armor and the tunnels honeycombing it for veins. Once he had seen it awaken when its guns and rocket batteries had turned a cubic mile of night sky into a raging inferno of shell bursts of such intensity that it shocked the senses. Until then he had had not the slightest notion that firepower of that magnitude existed. The monster was quiescent now under the growing warmth of the early sun, but the latent force within it was a tangible thing.

He was touched by a zephyr of superstitious fear that the element of farce which had obtruded itself into his and Gascoigne's hurried arrangements would offend the Rock, then reminded himself that farce was a part of war and that the Rock had seen it all before.

Trigger lay in the dry dock, patiently swallowing the endless stream of shells the long line of men fed to her. Harding turned away and walked toward the office shed. There was still a great deal to be done.

* * *

Captain Anderson signed his report to flag officer (submarines), then picked it up and read through the final section again.

"I have practically decided, despite recent trouble, to give Operation Conrad to Harding. He appears to be fully stabilized (for want of a better word) at this time. There is, of course, no guarantee that he will remain so, but a short 'in and out' operation of this nature should impose much less strain on him than a full war patrol. In addition to that, with three boats already on patrol and one detached to Beirut, he is simply the most suitable commanding officer available to me for this task.

"Of the other two, Marsh is methodical to the point of slowness, and although his record is good, he is temperamentally unsuited to 'smash and grab' work. Kennaway, on the other hand, from inexperience and anxiety to prove himself, is too far toward the other end of the scale (see remarks under *Talon* above).

"*Trigger* is expected here from Gibraltar within forty-eight hours and I shall make my final decision then."

He folded the report in three, slid it into an envelope and sealed the flap. The action moved a young British submarine captain and a not so young American professor of advanced mathematics a square nearer to each other on the chessboard of life and death.

Fuel tanks, water tanks, and batteries full, every torpedo, every shell, every loaf of bread in its place, *Trigger* lay stopped in the center of Gibraltar harbor, her bows pointing toward the entrance. The destroyer *Cleaver*, sister to *Cutlass* and *Claymore*, was moving slowly seaward through the gap.

"From the tower, sir, 'Commanding officer *Trigger* to report to captain of dockyard forthwith.'"

"Half-ahead together, steady as you go," Harding said, then added, "I don't agree with you, Yarrow. The Golden Gate, for one, is much bigger than the Forth Bridge."

The chief yeoman of signals smiled and rested his Aldis lamp on its bracket.

"What do you suppose he wants now?" Gascoigne asked.

"I dunno, Number One. Perhaps he's heard about the lorry we commandeered for victualing ship, or about the pilot and Guns riding that bedstead down Scud Hill. I'd like to have seen that. According to the chief they'd got up to thirty mph before it started shedding its castors."

"Yes. You know, sir, I think it might be wise if we stayed away from Gibraltar for a bit."

"I agree. Take her out through the entrance and follow *Cleaver*, Number One. Yarrow, make to *Cleaver*, 'Due panic departure unable arrange gunnery practice. When we have sea room could you chuck some boxes over the side for us to shoot at?'"

"From *Cleaver*, sir," Yarrow said a few moments later, "'I can do better than that. We'll stream a buoy and you can bang away at it to your heart's content. Try not to hit us.'"

Within days Harding was to be glad that he had grasped the opportunity of exercising his gun crews and their weapons.

CHAPTER 18

WHEN THE DOOR CLOSED BEHIND HARDING, Captain Anderson looked at his staff officer and raised his eyebrows.

"What did you make of him, Ginger?"

"Cool, calm, and collected as far as I could tell, sir. Do I take it that the flak you gave him over the complaint from Gibraltar was deliberately harsh? I haven't heard you lay it on with a trowel like that before."

"Yes. I wanted to see if I could rattle him. I didn't succeed to any noticeable degree and that was one of the reasons why I finally decided to let him do the Conrad pickup."

Lieutenant Commander Donaldson nodded. "I had no idea he was a nerve case. What on earth did the medicos do to him to straighten him out?"

"Put him through some sedation process they've thought up," Anderson said and waved a hand in a vague, meaningless gesture. "It appears to have worked. He was very tired, of course. Remember him falling asleep in that chair?"

"I do indeed. You know, sir, one's inclined to forget how young they all are. Almost still in their needing-their-sleep stage." Donaldson laughed before adding, "I loved the indignation in his voice when you got to the bit about a couple of his officers riding down the hill on a bed. You must remember that they're *only* twenty-two, sir! How old is Harding? Twenty-four?"

"Twenty-five I believe. You're right though. Frightening, isn't it? I was a commander with two years seniority when I did my first war patrol in 1939. Nowadays about half our submarine captains are lieutenants and not particularly senior ones either. Still, never mind. They're doing the job and Harding as well as most." Anderson's voice suddenly became brisk. "Look, Ginger, I know it isn't a staff function, but would you mind looking after his requirements yourself? It'll save time if I don't have to go over them with someone else."

Donaldson began to read aloud from a pad on his knee. "One Royal Marine commando, a certain Sergeant Ackroyd, to be loaned to *Trigger* again, plus one other commando to be selected by the aforesaid Ackroyd. Twenty-five four-inch-caliber smoke shells. Three two-seater canvas canoes. Three army field-radio sets. So on and so forth. Yes, can do, sir. I imagine you'll arrange for the extra officer he wants."

"Yes, I will."

"Right. Then I'll—Oh, incidentally, a couple of minutes ago you asked me what I made of Harding. Shore operations can't be his main preoccupation by a long way and I thought the way he trotted this lot out off the top of his head without hesitation was rather impressive."

"So did I," Anderson said. "It was another factor in my decision to send him."

Villari had covered eighteen of the miles separating him from the coast before they shot him. He lay in the shallow ditch beside the lane he had just crossed listening to the fear rasp of air in his windpipe, watching the German soldiers running across the sloping field toward him, feeling blood oozing between his fingers where they gripped his thigh.

He had never seriously thought that he would make it. There were so many of them and they seemed to be operating in two groups, so that in avoiding one he sometimes found himself in the area patrolled by the other. Twice they had passed within feet of him when he had thought them far away. On both occasions their trucks had appeared within a few minutes of the completion of a transmission and it was that which convinced him that they were employing mobile radio-location units. After that he had resolved to transmit no more until he was ready to tell the submarine where to come for him.

The decision had proved to be the right one, and after it, he had covered a great deal of ground without interference from the searchers. So good had been his progress that he had just conceded to himself that a chance of reaching the coast existed when the rifle bullet tore through his leg and snatched the possibility from him.

The four soldiers were close now, their outlines blurred by the sweat running from his temple into his left eye. He closed the eye, but could then see only the bank of the ditch inches in front of the other, so he opened it again and saw one of the running figures raise an automatic weapon chest high. The gun bucked repeatedly and he tightened his muscles against the slamming impact of the bullets.

"Jesus! Quit that, will you?" he said in English, but only a croak came from a throat suddenly dry and no more bullets touched him. Flustered, frightened, he watched four pairs of legs spread almost in unison like those of hurdlers to clear the ditch he was lying in, the nearest ten yards from his head, then they were out of his field of view. The machine pistol kept up a sporadic fire, the sound of it diminishing in strength.

Shock and effort combined to set up convulsive trembling along the length of his body when he levered himself onto his right elbow and peered cautiously over the other bank of the ditch. Five figures running now, the one ahead of the four following a zigzag course toward a belt of trees. Just like the movies, Villari thought, when the leading figure threw up its arms in an extravagant gesture and fell.

While, by a shorter route, the soldiers carried the body by its wrists and ankles to the lane, he wondered what peasant, with what on his conscience, had been panicked and flushed by the gunfire to be mistaken for the original quarry and die in his place.

Alone again, Villari lowered his trousers and examined the wound in his thigh. The bone was untouched, the bleeding had almost stopped, and that was good. But the entry hole had strands of dirty cloth driven into it and that was bad. He used a stolen cigarette, lit with stolen matches, to cauterize both apertures and fainted both times. There seemed to be nothing else wrong with the leg except that he wanted to scream every time he moved it.

There were two additional officers aboard *Trigger*. Lieutenant Wallace, who had taken over gunnery control from Elleston, and Surgeon Lieutenant Cass. It had annoyed Harding that the suggestion that he should take a doctor with him had had to come from Captain Anderson because it hadn't occurred to him that a man who had been working in enemy territory as a spy for over two years might be in need of medical help. Very silly and, he supposed, Captain Anderson must regard him as an unimaginative fool. The small worry had nagged at him periodically for twenty-four hours after leaving Algiers and then been forgotten thanks entirely to Cass.

Without being asked, the doctor had quietly taken over the encoding and decoding of all signals, the censorship of the crew's letters, the supervision of the daily rum issue, and the typing of Harding's not particularly legible patrol report notes. He spent the rest of his day taking samples of air from different compartments for analysis on return to harbor and let it be known that surgery hour was whenever someone dropped a wrench on his foot. It was good to have him aboard.

Lieutenant Wallace had a record of calm efficiency during gun actions. He was good-looking, self-confident, and witty. Harding couldn't stand him.

With Corsica below the horizon to the south, *Trigger* lay near-motionless under the surface of the blue Ligurian Sea. Occasionally she sank down to where the sunlight could not reach until some approaching plane had gone by. Once an hour she turned lethargically to point her bows and aerials toward the massive transmitter at Rugby, England, to listen to the long-wave signals which penetrated water. Rapid Morse poured into the earphones of the telegraphists, but throughout the whole of the first day, Rugby spoke only to others and nothing prefixed by *Trigger*'s call-sign was received. She idled silently up and down a set course, waiting for a man named Villari to summon her.

In his cabin Harding sat working on his seventeenth sketch of Gail Mainwaring. It still wasn't right and he held it out at arm's length, a tiny puzzled frown on his forehead, knowing that he should be able to get it right. Given his ability with a pencil, his knowledge of the proportions of the human frame, and with her image on call by simply closing his eyes, there ought to be no problem. What, therefore, was wrong? He covered different parts of the drawing with his hand, carefully examining those still exposed. Nothing.

Grunting impatiently, he got up, took his sixteen earlier attempts from a drawer, and spread them out on his bunk. Her stockings had been in the drawer too and he pulled them absently through his fingers while he stood looking down at the sketches. Gail standing, sitting, lying, running, walking. Gail dressed, undressed, half-dressed. Gail smiling, laughing, grave, brooding. But not quite Gail. Something about the action of the body. Yes, getting closer. But closer to what?

The stockings were hanging from his right hand, their tops held between his finger and thumb. He looked down at the toes resting on the deck, at the heels not far from it.

"Can't be," Harding said aloud. "She's shorter than I am."

When he had put everything except one of the pages back in the drawer, he sat down and worked on the sketch, shortening the trunk, lengthening the legs, making the lower leg disproportionately long in comparison to the thigh. It was right and Gail Mainwaring, standing legs astride, hands on hips, laughed up at him from the paper.

"You're deformed," he said softly and laughed back at her. He decided that he liked her deformity very much.

"It's good of you to see me, ma'am."

The older woman looked at Gail Mainwaring curiously, a little enviously, thinking how beautiful she was, for unlike Harding, she was not handicapped by thoughts of the stereotype of classical proportions.

"Why do you call me ma'am? We hold the same rank."

Gail glanced sideways at the major's insignia on the shoulder of her khaki shirt, then shook her head.

"Not really. Not at all, in fact. They just let me put on whatever uniform at whatever rank suits the situation and allows me to come and go without too many people asking why. My actual rank is second officer in the Wrens. I'm on your establishment list for convenience. Mine, I'm afraid. Not yours."

The ATS officer nodded. "I thought you were much too young to be a senior commander, and as I'd had orders to leave you to yourself I assumed you were Intelligence."

"That's right. I am. But now I've done something very stupid and I'd be grateful if you would arrange a passage home for me."

"Are you permitted to tell me what this stupid thing is you say you've done?"

"Oh yes. I've fallen in love and that makes me quite useless," Gail Mainwaring said and waited for the motherly, understanding smile to form on the other's face. When it did she sighed inwardly.

"Surely that can't be too serious. It happens to all of us, you know."

"Not to me, ma'am. Never before. Well, once a long time ago, but not like this. I've tried to think myself out of it for over a week, but it's no good."

"I see, but we can't move people from one theater of war to another just because they're in love." The compassionate smile was still there. "All you've proved to me is that you aren't very experienced in men and love, or you wouldn't think that a week was long enough to get over anything."

For several seconds Gail sat motionless, staring at her hands, thinking about how she could put it to this pleasant, rather stupid woman who hadn't the sense to recognize the possible existence of a dilemma not susceptible to platitudes. When she began to speak it was slowly, apologetically, as though she were a small girl admitting transgression of a nursery rule.

"I'm afraid I'm horribly experienced in men. The only difference between me and a tart is that I'm paid by the government." Her delivery quickened then and bitterness grew progressively clearer in her words. "They give me enemy agents to confuse so that they can be interrogated more effectively. Then, if I haven't done my job properly and they can't turn them, they kill them. They give me our own agents with their nerves in shreds for me to stitch together before they send them back for the Germans to kill. Recently the emphasis has shifted to submarine captains. It seems they're at a premium. I suppose I should be grateful that one of them enabled me to experience love too before I had trussed him up for the sacrificial stone. Anyway, it's over now. I couldn't possibly do any of it again, so I might as well go home."

She continued to look at her hands, feeling the woman's eyes on her, waiting for her to say something. When she did not, Gail, her voice brittle, said, "If you're at a loss for words, try, 'How utterly revolting!'"

"I don't think I'm revolted, but I'm certainly appalled."

"I didn't ask you to be pleased. I asked you to arrange a passage home for me."

"Don't, my dear," the ATS officer said and Gail's head jerked up to look at her.

"Don't what? Don't ask you to send me home?"

"No. Don't be so hard. Particularly on yourself. And there's no sense in your picking a fight with me. In fact it would be downright unkind of you to do so. I had not the slightest idea that your

sort of world existed, so give me a little time to catch my breath."
The superior smile of ignorance had gone from her.

"I'm sorry, ma'am. Truly," Gail told her and was touched
by the sight of hands fluttering a confused denial of the need
for apology. She had to wait for nearly a minute before anything
else was said, then her eyes narrowed defensively when the
older woman finally spoke.

"I hope you won't think that I'm interfering in something
that is none of my business, but you having told me so much,
I think I'm required to try to think responsibly about this."

"Yes?"

"Yes. What about the chap?"

"He's gone back to sea, ma'am."

"I didn't mean that. I meant is he in love with you?"

"Hopelessly." The single word carried some pride, more
sorrow and total certainty.

"Is he married?"

"No."

"Does he want to marry you?"

"Yes."

"Then, forgive me, but I don't see your problem."

"My problem," Gail said, "is that I may have sold myself
to the government, but I'm damned if I'll sell *him* tenth-hand
goods. He's too nice for that." She lowered her regard to the
desk between them and added almost to herself, "Well, eighth-
hand actually." Harding would have recognized the brooding
look in her eyes.

"How much does he know about you?"

"I told him I was a whore, but he brushed it aside. When
he comes out of his daze, he'll start to wonder just what sort
of woman could be pulled out of a hat for him to spend four
weeks in bed with."

The ATS officer sat, blinking rapidly, turning her head from
side to side as though searching for something. Her hands
fluttered again.

"Really," she said, "this is the most unbelievable conversation
I've ever had in my life. I should be shocked, outraged, but in-
credibly, I find myself wanting to ask if you're not being a
little too noble about all this. It's all very well being high-
minded, but if you love each other..." She let the rest of
the sentence go.

Gail smiled for the first time. "You're really being very

kind to me, but it isn't a question of nobility. In time, as I've said, he'd begin to wonder what had made me so available and how many others I'd been available to. Even if he didn't ask me, the worry would always be there. If he did ask me, well, how much could I water it down by? Not enough to be both convincing and acceptable. Promiscuity he might accept, but not the cold-bloodedness of what I've done. So forget high-mindedness. It's a question of plain common sense."

There was another silence, then the questions came again and Gail decided that she had been wrong to believe the woman stupid.

"As you are anxious to get away I assume that the man is coming back to Algiers. Is that right?"

"Yes. If he makes it."

"And will he think of looking for you at these offices?"

"I'm sure of it."

"Very well. Now, you told me that you had stitched him together, or his nerves together, or something like that."

"I did."

"That sounds like a very delicate operation to me. Wouldn't you think that there is a grave risk of the threads parting again when he finds that you've gone?"

Gail Mainwaring nodded her head emphatically as though the movement could reinforce her prayer.

"I would, and please God let them part. They're far too fragile to last for long anyway. He *must* crack again, then they'll have to send him back to England. He'll hate me for it, but I'd rather that than have him die loving me."

She took an envelope from her bag and put it on the desk before adding, "I would be awfully grateful if you'd tell him that I never want to see him again. There's no chance of his accepting your word for that, so if you would also give him this letter, perhaps rather reluctantly, as though you knew what it said and were embarrassed for me, that should..."

Her throat closed then and there were no more words. Sitting, looking at the envelope, listening while the silence lengthened, she began to think that the ATS officer would refuse to help her.

When the woman said, "I'll do it but, oh my dear, how heartbreakingly sad for both of you," she experienced simultaneous relief and the anguish of finality.

CHAPTER 19

FIFTY-NINE HOURS AFTER HE HAD BEEN SHOT, Villari sent his last signal to Algiers. In little more than the same number of minutes later, Algiers had told London, London had told Rugby, and Rugby had told *Trigger*. Aboard *Trigger* Harding opened his sealed orders, read for the first time the names "John Villar alias Giovanni Villari," and ordered a course alteration to the east. In London Professor Morris telephoned the American Embassy and spoke to Harkness about the signal. In Lisbon, where an Imperial Airways flying boat on its way to Poole, Dorset, was on stopover for the night, Gail Mainwaring slapped the face of a *Lufthansa* pilot who was trying to pick her up. In Italy Villari sat in cover on the side of a hill above the coastal village of Forte dei Marmi examining his leg.

It was hurting him less than it had, but the fact gave him no comfort. The flesh was swollen, the skin hot to the touch with a madman's rainbow of colors around the entry wound. Fear churned in his stomach and the bitter taste of bile came to the back of his throat. Angrily he washed the taste away with a mouthful of wine from his next to last bottle, but it did nothing for the fear. He sighed tiredly, his breath making a faint whistling sound as it passed between his clenched teeth. Then he pulled his trousers up and resumed his vigil.

There were a few soldiers to be seen in the village, but they didn't appear to be doing anything in particular. Military traffic on the coast road carried more of them, but there was no urgency in its movement. It didn't surprise him. For a time at least he expected the searchers to concentrate on the hilly country to the north of Carrara where he had made his long transmission from and then abandoned the set. The transceiver had been with or near him for so long, his link with the outside world, and he felt oddly naked without it. But it had become a magnet for German troops, and relieved of its weight, he could travel three times as fast. The thought of traveling reminded him of his leg and he shuddered. Not that walking was all that important now. The leg had done all that could be asked of it in bringing him where he was, some two miles from the rendezvous he had selected between Forte dei Marmi and Poveruomo. He could crawl the rest of the way if he had to. It was the thought of part of him festering, spreading poison through his system, that made him cringe. That and the knowledge that the fever had for some time past reduced his ability to think coherently. There was something he had done with the radio set which had seemed right at the time, but he now knew to have been ill-advised although he couldn't recall what it was. Shaking his head to disperse the fog inside it, he looked along the coast toward his destination.

It was an unremarkable stretch of shore, straight and virtually featureless. An expanse of sand from the water's edge to the road, a narrower strip of sand between the road and an area of mixed pine wood and dried swamp. Small villas were dotted among the trees. The ground sloped upward after that, merging with the foothills. It was the same right to the point where visibility lost itself in distance. No outcrops of rocky headlands, no indentations, no harbors. Villari hoped that the coast's very openness would protect the submarine from surprise attack, but was unsure whether he was rationalizing or had thought it out carefully before sending his signal.

After a frowning interval of concentration, he abandoned the attempt to think and lay down to sleep until the sun had set.

"I beg your pardon, sir," Surgeon Lieutenant Cass said. "Didn't know you were in here."

He was backing through the gap in the wardroom curtains when Harding looked up from a heap of charts.

"Come in, doc. It's your mess. I'm just using it because the pilot is busy at the chart table."

"Not secret, sir?"

"Not any longer. We're all in this together now. I'm just trying to work out what the devil we are going to do."

"Problems?"

"Yes, this bloke we're supposed to pull out has selected what is probably the worst bit of water for a submerged approach along the entire western seaboard of Italy. Look at these soundings. A depth of less than a hundred and fifty feet for over twelve miles out from the coast. There's hardly anywhere as bad as this between here and the northern Adriatic. Still, he probably didn't have any choice, or didn't know."

"Will it be mined?"

"Oh, it's mined all right," Harding said. "Spezia is a large naval base and we're not far from it. There are underwater defenses covering it and what we have to try to do is find out how far they extend."

"When do we get there, sir?"

"We *are* there, doc. On the edge of it that is. Come and look."

Cass walked after Harding into the control room, saw him gesture for the periscope to be raised, turn it through a full circle, and stop.

"Here you are."

The doctor hadn't liked to bother the officers of the watch during the passage from Algiers and this was his first view. He was surprised by the large size and extreme clarity of the image. With the upper lens of the periscope only a foot above the surface, the sea horizon was very close, but beyond it towered the peaks of the Apennines tinged pink by the sun.

"Remarkable optical instrument," he said and folded the periscope handles upward to show that he had finished with it as he had seen the others do. The gleaming brass tube had sunk down into the well at his feet before he added thoughtfully, "There's a trawler between us and the coast, sir."

"Yes, several of them."

"Couldn't you follow their track through the mine field?"

Harding shook his head. "Nice thinking, but they only draw about four or five feet, which means that they could sail straight

over the top of the mines. Tidal rise and fall in the Med is
negligible, so there'd be no danger."

"And our draft on the surface is too great?"

"Hell, yes. Three times theirs. This is quite a big vessel you
know."

"I see your problem. Is there an answer to it?"

"We'll probably think of something," Harding said and returned to the wardroom. He picked up the charts he had left
there and took them to his cabin to think of that something.

Colonel Kriewald of the *Abwehr* said, "How many killed?"

"Two, *Herr Oberst*. A *Leutnant* and a *Feldwebel* Hans Clau-
sen."

"What *Leutnant?*"

The infantry captain shrugged. "I have no idea. I knew the
Feldwebel by name, but the *Leutnant* only by sight. The radio
set blew up the moment he touched it and I came straight to
you without waiting for an identification. When we know who
he is, I'll see that you are informed."

"It isn't important," Kriewald said, then repeated the statement to himself because something else was important and he
couldn't put his finger on it. There was an incomplete line of
thought twisting about in his head and he grasped the end of
it with words before it could elude him entirely.

"It would be interesting to know whether the radio was
carefully hidden or left . . ." The words ceased there, his mind
jumping ahead of what he had been going to say.

"Left for us to find, *Herr Oberst?*"

"Exactly. But no, that doesn't make sense. Let us assume
for a moment that the spy recognized that the pressure we have
been putting on him had become too great to permit him to
function any longer. If that were the case, would he advertise
his departure from the area for the sole satisfaction of killing
a German or two? No, it's too ridiculous. Continue with the
routine search."

The infantry captain was closing the door behind him when
Kriewald called him back and said, "On the other hand, suppose
it was a mistake, something he never intended to happen, he
might panic now and try to make a break for it."

"With respect, *Herr Oberst*, he has given no indication of

being a man who panics in all the time I've been following up these radio fixes. In fact he's made me look like a damned fool on several occasions and I wouldn't put it past him to do it again."

"You've done your job as well as anyone could and better than the *Gestapo* party," Kriewald told him. "I withdraw the word panic, but look at it this way. His set has gone, and as I can't bring myself to believe that he has another, his reason for staying here has gone with it. What will he do? He could move inland back to his home if that's where it is, but without papers he must be picked up eventually, even if that means years from now. Might he not think of stealing a fishing boat and going to ground in Corsica? It's only sixty miles away and a very good place to lose oneself in."

The other nodded slowly and the colonel went on, "So, we're agreed that the idea is worth considering. Good. Take a small combat unit with you to impress the natives and put the fear of God in all the fishing communities between here and Viareggio. Anyone unable to explain the whereabouts of his boat on any given day..." He leveled a finger like a gun pointing at the infantry captain and clicked his tongue.

"But for the fact that losing your ship would defeat the whole object of the exercise, this would be classed as an 'at all costs' mission, Peter."

For a moment Harding was back in the big cabin aboard the depot ship listening again to the sound of Captain Anderson's voice. The message it carried was plain enough despite its apparent contradiction, a message repeated in the written orders and the long executive signal lying on the combined washbasin and desk in front of him now. He found the repetition mildly irritating. "At all costs" was a phrase so rarely included in a submarine's orders that he doubted that it had been used more than twice in the entire war. It didn't need to be said more than once, even when qualified.

The signal was three pages long, and although he knew it by heart, he began to read sections at random. "Conrad wounded in leg but mobile... in position approximately three thousand yards north Forte dei Marmi village by 2000 tonight... will flash Morse letters QF repeat QF three times on different bearings to seaward at 0015, 0110, 0205, and 0300 repeating nightly until pickup effected. Morse letters RB repeat RB at same times as above indicate Conrad in position but landing not to be attempted until QF . . . reminded possible mine hazard both offshore and on . . . desirability of extreme . . ."

"Blah, blah, blah," Harding said, then wished he had not because he had done it only to bolster himself and he didn't want to be reminded that he needed bolstering. He left his cabin abruptly, walked into the control room, took the tannoy microphone from its clip, and began to talk into it.

"This is the captain speaking. As you probably all know by now, we have been given the job of taking a chap off the beach. I don't know what entitles him to this personal taxi service. Perhaps he has the plans for the German invasion of Paraguay in his pocket or something, but anyway . . ."

Two people in the control room laughed dutifully, someone else groaned and Harding went on. "Anyway, in about three hours from now we shall close the land so that Lieutenant Elleston and his merry men can do their stuff. To do that we have to pass through a mine field. Petty Officer McIntyre, who all of us have reason to dislike from time to time, assures me that it is there and we have been cruising along its edge today trying to find a way round it. There isn't one so we're going through. McIntyre, who isn't always that bad, also tells me that the mines are thinly sown and we know that the field isn't wide because we've watched a two-thousand-ton ship pass up the coast on the other side of it."

He paused, scratched the stubble on his chin with the microphone, then said, "If this sounds like a dicey procedure to you, I would remind you that *Torbay* managed it without trouble when she attacked shipping in Corfu harbor last year. We have better sonar than she had then and I don't anticipate any difficulty. That's all."

With the microphone back in place, he stood looking absently at the depth gauges, wishing he felt as lighthearted as he'd tried to sound, listening to the distant upsurge of conversation at both ends of the ship which his words had produced. Gradually it subsided and he turned to the officer of the watch.

"Anything going on up top, Guns?"

"Just fishing boats stooging around, sir, and the odd aircraft or two, but nothing close."

"All right. Get someone to relieve you and bring your landing party along to the wardroom, please."

"Aye aye, sir," Elleston said.

Sergeant Ackroyd sat massively at one end of the wardroom table, looking faintly embarrassed at finding himself in the officers' mess. On his right Marine Cooper pared his nails with a commando knife. He had been Ackroyd's choice as his companion and it was known throughout *Trigger* that he had only two interests at sea. One was dismantling and reassembling a Luger automatic taken from a German officer he had killed. The other was paring his nails with his dagger. It was assumed that he was good at his job because Ackroyd had picked him, but nobody knew for certain. Ackroyd wasn't telling and it was rumored that Cooper's longest recorded utterance was "Pass the ketchup." The story had reached Harding who, remembering that he had known Ackroyd for days before hearing him say anything other than "Yessir," concluded that the two were well matched. Elleston sat beside Cooper, opposite Able Seaman Norris. To Harding, facing them from the other end of the table, Norris had the air, half-deferential, half-smug, of a clerk invited to join the board of directors.

He said, "Thanks for coming along, chaps," realized that that must be the most fatuous remark he had ever made, and hurried on with, "Is this the whole party, Guns?"

"Yes, if you agree, sir," Elleston replied. "We've talked it over and as nobody has been able to detect any barbed wire on the beach, we've sort of decided that there isn't any. It's hard to be certain at this range, but Number One *did* plane up to twenty feet for us which gave us a pretty good periscope view."

"All right. I agree that there appears to be no wire. So you're leaving out the two people who were to have cut it. In that case how about canoes?"

"Two only. When we've collected this bod, Sergeant Ackroyd will swim back. Or we'll tow him back. It means less chance of confusion. Detection too for that matter."

Harding looked at the back of his hands, then turned them over and looked at the palms.

"I don't like it," he said. "It's very shallow in there and I may have to put you over the side anywhere up to three-quarters of a mile offshore. That's a hell of a long swim back and even Ackroyd isn't as fast as a canoe in the water. Take all three. The commandos one each. They're trained to use the things. You and Norris in the third. With luck you and he will cancel out each other's errors."

"Aye aye, sir."

"Okay. Now, about the reference point. I want you to use the left hand one of the two white villas visible from here. It's bigger and whiter than the other. You'll be able to see it easily in the darkness and I'll have Chivers on the bridge with me to try to be sure that we can see it too. Take only one field radio as you're fewer now. Who's going to operate it?"

"Norris, sir."

"Happy about that, Norris?"

"Yes, sir. Easy, sir. On—off—send—receive. It's got a throat mike so your hands are free. Ackers showed—I mean Sergeant Ackroyd showed me how. Call signs are 'Gin' for you and 'Rum' for me. Like Mr. Elleston says, I can't forget that, sir."

Harding smiled and turned back to Elleston. "Tell me the procedure after you reach shore."

"Well, we had thought of swamping the canoes to hide them, sir, but I'm afraid they could still be sucked out to sea, and if they weren't they might be difficult to empty. We'll pull them above the waterline and proceed toward the road in single file ten yards apart, treading in each other's footprints in case of land mines. I shall be in the lead, followed by . . ."

"Nah."

All eyes turned toward the speaker and all but Ackroyd's had surprise in them. He nodded his head in benevolent approval before saying, "What Marine Cooper means, sir, is that he should take the lead on the beach hisself on account of he has done it before and knows what to look for in respect of locating antipersonnel mines and similar devices whereas with all due respect, sir, Mr. Elleston is only a sailor. Sir."

For a moment Harding experienced a near-tactile memory of Gail Mainwaring's flat stomach quivering beneath his cheek while he told her about Ackroyd, but this time he had no inclination to laugh.

Coldly he said, "Thank you for clarifying Cooper's point, Ackroyd, but I don't think Mr. Elleston is likely to appreciate being wet-nursed by you."

"I didn't mean that, sir."

"Then what did you mean? We haven't got a mine detector and in sand there will be nothing to show Cooper or anybody else what's underneath."

Ackroyd's face reddened and he rolled his shoulders as though straining to give birth to an idea. The delivery was a difficult one, but he achieved it.

"Thing is, sir, Cooper and me has been landed on enemy territory together four times. We lost our officer once. That was a firefight, sir, and couldn't be helped, but to lose your officer going up the beach before you've rightly started is just bloody silly if you'll excuse me, sir."

It touched Harding that these two highly trained professional killers should need Elleston or rather, he supposed, the protection of the authority vested in him by the two gold stripes on the shoulders of his shirt. Being so inured to accepting total responsibility himself, it took him a second or two to recognize the need for what it was. When he had done so he looked at Elleston.

"I don't imagine that you'll want to argue against that, Guns."

Recognizing not the need but the order behind Harding's words, Elleston shook his head before saying, "Cooper will lead, followed by me, Norris and Ackroyd, in that order. What we do at the road depends on what we find when we get there, but we shall cross, separately if we can, and regroup in the trees. Sergeant Ackroyd and Norris will take up position there and inform the ship that that stage has been reached by sending the single word 'Concrete.' Cooper and I will then move up the hill on the original compass bearing on which the light was seen, corrected for any deviation in our course, either in the canoes or on shore, which I have noticed. A hundred yards up the slope we split left and right to search along that contour. The bod's identification is 'Panhandle.' Ours is 'Bulwark.' Total permitted elapsed time from sending 'Concrete' is thirty minutes, then we return to the ship, having signaled 'positive' or 'negative' as the case may be."

He stopped talking, breathed in, said, "Pause for gathering thoughts," then went on. "If you can see us, sir, but we obviously can't see you because we're paddling the wrong way, you'll talk us in on the field set. If, after one hour, no contact has been made, we are to assume that you have been forced to dive, go back ashore, hide the canoes, and lie low until 0100 tomorrow. I mean the day after tomorrow. Then we paddle seaward, keeping the larger white villa due east astern of us. Same one-hour routine and repeat as necessary for following nights until we get ourselves sorted out."

And that, Harding decided, was another reason why the commandos wanted Elleston with them.

"Well done, Guns," he said. "You've got it down pat, but I've thought of one more thing. We'll rig a dim yellow light to look as much like one of the fishing boat's acetylene flares as possible. You know the way they appear to flash on and off with the wave motion? Right, ours will too, but it will be making the word 'gin' in very slow Morse during the last fifteen minutes of the hourly period. Teach your party those three letters if they don't know them. Incidentally, the forecast is for continued calm weather. No moon of course for the first three nights. Any questions?"

"What do we call this bod, sir?"

"Call him 'Panhandle,' Guns. He's got a code name, but he doesn't know what it is, so use the identification words he gave us. I'll keep his actual name to myself until you're all back on board. Anyone else?"

"Yes, sir," Norris said. "Which way's Switzerland?"

Villari was in bed with three women and he wished they would go away because it was stiflingly hot. Sometimes they did leave, but others replaced them as though working on a rotation system. Who they were he was uncertain, although he thought he recognized one of the girls whose home he had used as a temporary "safe" house all that long time ago when he had been sending reports to someone or other by radio. He suspected that another of them was the mistress of some senior German officer. That made him angry, as her presence could lead to trouble with the authorities for him, and he pushed the bodies violently from the bed.

The women vanished and he was immediately bitterly cold, with pain pulsing behind his eyes. He put his hands to his face to stifle the pain and the chattering of his teeth. When both had lessened a little, he began trying to remember who he was.

Slowly, in bits and pieces, it came back to him. His leg. The hillside near the coast. A man from the *Gestapo* lying dead in an alley. Other dead people. Something to do with the British. What the hell had the British to do with anything? Start again. "Can any of you suggest a method of establishing if the non-Euclidean geometries of Lobachevsky and Riemann are consistent?" Who had said that? He had of course, during his lecture on Riemann's theory on the functions of complex variables. Hold on to that. Riemann. German mathematician. *Gestapo?* Oh, don't be stupid. The man died in 1866. "Great lecture of yours, John..."

Then he had it.

"Holy God!" John Villar said and jerked himself into a sitting position. His head yelped at him reproachfully, but he ignored it, fumbled a flashlight clear of a pocket and looked at his watch. Carefully, grimly, wobbling almost but not quite out of control, he got himself to his feet, cursing wordlessly for having overslept. When he was reasonably sure of his balance, he gripped his injured leg with both hands just above the knee and helped it toward his rendezvous with the submarine. He didn't think he could make it.

The sea calm and velvet-black under the stars, the swell idling landward from the west too lethargic to induce more than the gentlest rolling motion, the diesels throbbing out their song of power to the batteries. Harding experienced a growing sense of unreality as though he were watching the ship and himself from somewhere above. It had happened to him before under similar conditions and he recognized it as the form of self-hypnosis which put men on watch at sea to sleep where they stood. Pulling himself sharply back from wherever he had been, he straightened up from his comfortable slouching position against the side of the bridge and looked around him, wishing that the hour ahead was not part of reality.

"I think I can hear aircraft engines, sir."

"Diving stations," Harding said into the voice pipe.

The diesels fell silent, their rumble replaced by another high overhead, a persistent bass thrumming that seemed to fill the sky.

"So you can, Number One. Hundreds of 'em by the sound of it. Spezia in for a dirty night probably."

As if in confirmation, the tiny fireflies of distant anti-aircraft bursts began to dance over the northern horizon and searchlight beams touched fleetingly on the bellies of clouds.

"Well, if you're satisfied with the state of the battery, Number One, we might as well take that as our cue and get on with it."

"It's just about fully charged, sir."

"Okay, I'm going below," Harding said. "Dive when you're ready."

He stood in the control room watching the lookouts scrambling down the ladder from the bridge and saw them walk wordlessly away to their messes. Their silence was very unusual, but it didn't surprise him. The klaxon snarled twice.

"Upper lid shut." Gascoigne's voice from the tower, then his legs appearing through the lower hatch.

"Go straight down to one hundred feet, Number One."

"Aye aye, sir."

Gascoigne standing behind the seated figure of Chief Petty Officer Ryland, tapping him on the shoulder.

"Right, Cox'n. Let's see how good you are. As we don't want any mine cables snagging in the for'ard hydroplanes, I'm going to turn them in."

"Just as long as you done your sums right on the trim I can 'old 'er on the after-planes, sir," the coxswain told him. It was said lightly, but with none of his usual cheerful acceptance. Harding noted the fact, just as he had noted the tenseness in the face, or posture, or both, of every man he had glanced at since diving, just as he was aware of fear tugging at his own nerve ends. Beside him he could hear the monotonous sibilance of air drawn in and expelled between someone's teeth. He wanted to order the man to stop doing it, but did not.

"One hundred feet, sir. Fore planes turned in."

"Thank you, Number One."

"The plot estimates a thousand yards to go, sir."

"Thank you, Pilot."

No more words in the control room and no sound of voices from any other part of the ship. The breath of the man beside Harding continued to hiss softly. Somebody cleared his throat and swallowed. One minute. Two minutes. Harding searched for something to say, but couldn't find it. Three minutes.

"SST indicates object bearing Green 2, range four hundred and fifty yards, probable mine, sir."

"Thank you, McIntyre. Chivers, steer ten degrees to port. Number One, you may shut all watertight doors." Voice tone just right. Keep it that way.

Acknowledgments and the thud of heavy steel doors closing. Some of them in some of the compartments should survive if there was a mine explosion. The depth from seabed to surface was already shallow enough for the use of escape apparatus. Palms damp. Throat dry. Don't swallow.

"McIntyre, I'm going to run the echo sounder for a few seconds."

"Right, sir—no, wait! Object bearing dead ahead, four hundred yards, probable mine."

"Very well. What's the bearing of the first one?"

"Green 11, sir. Range three-fifty."

"Chivers, are you steady on 075 yet?"

"Coming on to it now, sir."

"Three probable mine contacts bearing Red 7, Red 15, and Red 21, sir. Ranges are four hundred, three hundred, and—hang on—four hundred again respectively."

"Thank you."

Harding walked to the chart table and the navigating officer moved aside for him.

"Carry on plotting them, Pilot. I can see over your shoulder."

Situation. Present submerged speed, necessary to maintain trim with only one set of hydroplanes, two knots or four thousand yards an hour, making four hundred yards in six minutes or one hundred yards in a minute and a half. Plenty of time. Try not to think about the possibility of undetectable magnetic mines lying on the bottom. If the neutralization of the ship's magnetic field they carried out in Scotland is still holding, they

should be harmless. *If?* Forget it. There's not a thing to be
done about them. Think instead about the horned spheres, bar-
nacle-covered, trailing fronds of weed, swaying to the movement of the sea at the end of the wires anchoring them to the
bottom. For years only the water-filtered light of the sun has
reached them but one nudge from *Trigger* and for a fraction
of a second they'll turn into a tiny sun of their own. Careful!
Think about them, but not that way. Only how to avoid them.

"McIntyre, give me the range of the mine ahead and the
range and bearing of the first one you detected."

"The one ahead is two-fifty, sir, and the other two hundred
on Green 26."

Two hundred and fifty yards and closing. Little more than
twice *Trigger*'s length. Time to turn toward the one twenty-six
degrees on the starboard bow.

"Chivers, come to starboard onto 085."

"085. Aye aye, sir."

"McIntyre, I've got to take that sounding before..."

Trigger touched bottom with a jolt and the grinding rasp of
steel running across sand. The hull set up a slow oscillation
which made people grasp for handholds. Then it began to rise.

"Can't 'old 'er down, sir," Chief Petty Officer Ryland
sounded apathetic.

Gascoigne took down the tannoy microphone. "It's all right,
everybody. That was only the bottom." He put the microphone
back in place. For a few seconds more he watched the depth
gauges and the inclinometer, but the ship continued to rise
quickly and the bow-up angle stayed at five degrees.

"Flood 'Q'" he said.

Tons of water rushing into the emergency quick-diving tank.
The ship leveling. The rate of ascent slowing, stopping. Nobody at all making the time-honored whispered response to the
last order of "Fuck you too." Just a taut silence, the bitter tang
of fright-sweat, then someone yawning shudderingly.

"Stop flooding. Blow 'Q'"

McIntyre, voice raised, "There's another of the bastards
three degrees to starboard of this new course!"

"All right," Harding said. "All right." Gently like a concerned parent. "What range?"

"About the same as the other, sir. Say a hundred and fifty yards."

"Then we'll have to go between them. Steer 081, Chivers."

Feel of a droplet trickling down the side of the nose onto the mouth. Keep hands in pocket and don't dab at it.

"Ship level at eighty feet, sir. Better not go deeper or we'll bounce again."

"No, eighty's fine. Well done, Number One."

Question—what is the distance between two mines twelve degrees apart at one hundred and fifty yards? Answer—very little. Strangely calm now because there is absolutely no point in being anything else and at least the ship hadn't broken surface in the middle of a mine field. That would have done it. Marvelous time to find out that the soundings on the chart are wrong. How far apart are those mines? Makes no difference. Couldn't have turned without fouling one or other. Couldn't have stopped with the one to starboard so close. Might have drifted onto it. Couldn't have gone astern because that would have meant starting all over again and the nervous system would have balked at that. Better to trust the jumping wire and the after-hydroplane guards to deflect the mine cables and . . .

"I think we're through, sir. I'm getting strong contacts astern but only slushy echoes from the shore on forward bearings."

"Thank you, McIntyre," Harding said. It sounded the same as his normal automatic politeness, but this time he had spoken for all of them.

CHAPTER 20

"CORKSCREW PORT, SKIPPER! NIGHT FIGHTER!"
were the last words the rear gunner of the Lancaster ever spoke.
Whether or not the captain of the bomber heard him was unimportant because the same burst of cannon fire killed him too
and splintered the legs of the flight engineer beside him. The
Lancaster flew on as though heedless of the smashing of nearly
half its human cargo.

The pilot of the Ju88 dropped the fighter's nose, gathered
speed, then pulled it up again under the bomber. He fired his
second burst and saw flame spread along a wing, engulfing
both engines there. At first hesitantly, then bowing to the inevitable, the Lancaster dipped the wing and turned tiredly toward the Italian coast thirty miles away. Anybody alive on
board could have admired the fires he had helped to start in
Spezia.

Slightly under six minutes later, the bomber struck shallow
water with a towering splash four miles to the north of the
village of Forte dei Marmi. The sea tore off the plane's tail
section, but did not slow the rest of it enough to prevent it
grating across the strip of beach to explode in a violent frenzy
of colors on the coast road.

The German fighter pilot who had followed the dying
bomber part of the way down, eased the Ju88 in a climbing
turn back toward the main stream of bombing planes, pleased
at having destroyed a big *Tommi*, unaware that he had also
taken part in the end game on someone else's chessboard.

* * *

"Well," the infantry captain said, "nobody will get past that on the road for an hour or two. Try the sand on either side."

The driver nodded, clambered from the cab of the truck, and stepped on to the beach, his form brilliantly illuminated by the blazing plane. He was back quickly.

"Hopeless, sir. It's too hot to walk past even right down at the water's edge and the trees are smoldering on the other side. If the wheels got stuck in the sand, we'd lose the truck."

The infantry captain shrugged. "So we wait until it's cooled. Tell them in the back they may get out and make coffee if they want to."

He got out himself and lit a cigarette, then stood watching the fire.

John Villar watched the fire too, but did not associate it with the sound of aircraft engines because he thought that that was in his head. He supposed that a fuel tanker had been in a collision and hoped that it would burn itself out soon because the light would be dangerous for the submarine. The image of a submarine was clear in his mind and he was fairly certain that it had something to do with taking him home, wherever that was. There were two letters he had to flash to it at fifteen minutes after midnight. What they were he couldn't remember, but that didn't matter because he had written down the letter preceding the first and succeeding the second. Smiling at his own cleverness he took a scrap of cardboard from a pocket and shone his torch on it, shielding the beam carefully. PG. It took him a minute and several false conclusions to arrive at QF from that. There were two other letters written there and he began to search his memory for their meaning.

From his seat by the sonar, "Quiet all around, sir," McIntyre said.

"Thank you. Periscope depth, Number One."

Harding ordered the periscope raised when *Trigger* reached forty feet and stood staring into the binocular eyepieces seeing nothing until the upper lens broke surface.

"Oh, no!"

"Trouble, sir?"

"Of a sort, Number One. There's a bloody great fire ashore.

Hell and damnation! I wonder if the bloody RAF can have found something to bomb this far south of Spezia. What's the time?"

"Ten to midnight, sir."

"Twenty-five minutes to go. It's pretty fierce so it may have burned itself out by then. I certainly hope so. There's no chance of our seeing a torch in this. It's like daylight."

Harding muttered something else and Gascoigne said, "I didn't hear that, sir."

"Just reminding myself that what Guns refers to as 'the bod' can see the fire too. He won't be flashing any torch until it dies down."

It was a new experience for Harding to have such visibility through a periscope at night. The source of the fire was hidden from him by the earth's curvature, but the tops of vehicles could be clearly seen to either side of it and farther away its light played on a belt of trees. That seemed to place the fire on or near the road. Traffic accident?

"Bring her up to thirty feet, Number One. I want to take a good look at this."

With an additional four feet of periscope showing, he could see the road and the vehicles on it. There were two farm carts, a small bus, two cars, and what appeared to be an army truck. People, some of them soldiers, were moving aimlessly about on both sides of the blaze. They looked to be close enough to hail, but when he clicked the periscope handle to low power, the scene leaped away to its real distance from him.

"All right," Harding said. "Go back to thirty-four feet. There's been some sort of pileup on the road."

"It's burning itself out fast, sir."

"Yes, it is," the infantry captain agreed, "but look at the road surface."

He and the driver slouched against the hood of the truck watching the contorted remains of what had been a heavy bomber. The flames were less bright and lower now and the large blocks of metal which were engines glowed more red than white. The alloy which made up the bulk of the aircraft had itself burned in the intense heat and was turning from rose to black. Over a wide area the road seethed, bubbled, and occasionally flickered with fire like marsh gas igniting above some fetid swamp.

"There's another fishing boat coming into the beach," one of the soldiers said.

Without bothering to look, the infantry captain nodded. "Take two men and scare the shit out of the owner. Wear your helmets and look menacing. You know what to say."

Three uniformed figures marching in unison down the beach, machine pistols held across their chests, the flames dying quickly as the last of the rubber and high-octane fuel were consumed.

"Should I try the sand again, sir?" the driver asked.

The officer thought for a moment before saying, "No, it isn't worth it. We've a lot of stops to make between here and Viareggio, and as we're late already I'd rather make sure of getting there than have this big cow break down." He banged the side of the heavy truck with the palm of his hand and added, "We'll wait for the road to cool."

From the after-periscope Elleston said, "I think I just caught the Morse letter 'R,' sir, but..."

"Somebody put me on the same bearing as Mr. Elleston. Quickly now."

Hands on top of Harding's pushing the forward periscope a few degrees to the left, Harding never moving his gaze from the eyepieces.

"That's the bearing, sir. Green 89."

"Thank you, Smith."

"'R' is the last part of 'F,' sir. You know, dot-dash-dot instead of dot-dot-dash-dot."

Patiently, "Yes, Guns. I did know."

"Sorry, sir. There he goes again! It's 'QF,' sir."

"Pilot, plot that bearing," Harding said. "Chivers, come ninety degrees to starboard. Number One, have Chivers relieved at the wheel. I shall be surfacing as soon as we're on our new course and I'll want him on the bridge then. Guns, you join the landing party. We're going to collect your 'bod.'"

It was dark when *Trigger* surfaced, darker than Harding had expected, with a light overcast obscuring the stars, and he was grateful for that. The fire was nothing more than a dull glow two miles to the north which required binoculars to see it at all. The swell was a little more pronounced this close to the shore, producing a slow pitching motion. He didn't think it was enough to cause the canoes any trouble, and although he could hear the surf sighing on the beach there was nothing formidable about the line glowing faintly white a mile ahead.

Harding bent to the voice pipe. "First lieutenant, please."

"Here, sir."

"Number One, I'm going to trim down for'ard. That'll make it easier to launch the canoes, and if we run aground on the way in we can lift off again by blowing main ballast. When the fore hatch is open, you had better have a strong man standing by all the time to close it quickly if she decides to dip under."

"Aye aye, sir."

"Right. Open one and two main vents," Harding said.

He heard the metallic click of the valves opening and the off-shore breeze sprinkled the bridge with droplets of water thrown up from the vents. The submarine's bow sank a foot, two feet, paused.

"Open number-three main vent."

Spray soaring close to the bridge now, the bow dropping further.

"Shut main vents."

Trigger, propelled by electric motors, moved silently in toward the coast, water lapping almost to the top of her pressure hull, the constant stream of echo soundings reported to the bridge telling Harding of the rapidly shelving bottom.

"Eighteen feet, sir. Fifteen feet..."

"Stop starboard."

"Twelve feet, sir."

"Stop port."

Gliding forward without power, losing speed.

"Eight feet, sir. Six. No reading, sir."

A lurch not much stronger than when torpedoes were fired. Aground.

"Open the fore hatch and get the canoes onto the casing," Harding said. "And ask Lieutenant Elleston to report to me on the bridge."

He looked around him at the dim figures of the four bridge

lookouts and the officer of the watch, wanting to ask if they could see anything except the lights of a few fishing boats and the dark backdrop of Italy. Not doing it because if they could, they would have said so. Above their heads Chivers was perched on top of the forward periscope standard, binoculars trained on the shore.

"Any sign of wire, Chivers?"

"No, sir, and the fishing boats seem to beach themselves more or less anywhere, so maybe there's no mines either."

"Good. Anything else?"

"Nothing special, sir. Occasional truck or bicycle. Pretty quiet really."

Harding turned away and found Elleston standing beside him.

"Hello, Guns. Did you hear what Chivers said?"

"Yes, sir."

"Okay, look. There's the larger white villa. The light came from roughly a hundred yards this side of it, a little to the left of that break in the trees. Approach with caution. There's always the chance that those recognition letters have been compromised. If there *is* an ambush, try to get off that Very light before they nab you."

"Yes, sir."

"All right. The for'ard hydroplanes are being turned out now. Man the canoes from them as soon as you're ready and good luck. You've got about seven hundred yards still to go."

"Yes, sir. Thank you, sir."

A flash of teeth and Elleston clambered over the side of the bridge. Harding watched him walk forward to join the group standing where the prime minister had once stood, saw the canoes lowered to the hydroplanes, saw them placed in the water and paddled away. At first their course was erratic, then it steadied as they began to fade into the darkness.

Inevitably someone said, "Come in, Number Five. Your time's up," and Harding experienced an irrational spurt of anger. He suppressed it and spoke into the voice pipe.

"Bring the ship to full buoyancy please, Number One, and I'll have that yellow lamp rigged. When that's done you may go to gun action stations."

Elleston's arms were aching, but he forced himself to continue paddling strongly because with most of the distance to the beach covered, the two canoes with the commandos in them were about fifty yards ahead of him and Norris.

"Come on, Norris. Let's show them!"

"Cor! Fuck this!" Norris said.

Ackroyd and Cooper standing, knee-deep in water, prevented Elleston's boat from broaching to in the light surf and dragged it onto the sand.

"All clear as far as that fishing boat, sir. We just follow the keel mark. See?"

Elleston heard himself whisper, "Thank you, Ackroyd," and supposed he'd caught that from Harding. Then he added, "Anyone around?"

"Only the bloke in the boat, sir. Cooper done him in."

"An Italian?"

"'E didn't say," Cooper said.

Outrage flooded over Elleston, but he shook it off him angrily. He had asked a stupid question and Cooper had done the only thing he could do.

"No, I don't suppose he did. Right, let's hide the canoes under that boat. Move!"

It was only a few yards and they carried the three canoes in a single line between them, then pushed them under the curve of the beached fishing boat's hull. There was enough light to show the gaping wound in the throat of the man lying under the boat's tiller. Elleston wished there had not been and gestured for Cooper to lead the way to the road. Thirty seconds later they crossed it and ran for the belt of trees.

"Gin," Norris said, "this is Rum. Concrete, repeat Concrete." He nodded to himself, then called softly to Elleston crouching three trees away. "They've acknowledged, sir."

A .303 Lee-Enfield rifle in his hand, Elleston swung wordlessly around, snapped finger and thumb at Cooper, and jogged away toward the rising ground behind the strip of woodland. The commando picked up his Bren machine gun and loped after him.

At the foot of the slope: "Wait here, Cooper. If they open up on me, fire this Very pistol in the air and get back to Sergeant Ackroyd at the double."

"Nah, I'll..."

Spacing the words for emphasis, "Shut up," Elleston said, then went on, "Don't make one of your long speeches, Cooper. You haven't got Ackroyd here to interpret for you. Just do as you're told. If they haven't shot at me within two minutes, they probably aren't there. Follow me then. If they do something cagey like knocking me on the head, you'll be able to see that because I'm only going a hundred yards or so."

Without waiting for a reply, he thrust the Very pistol at Cooper, turned and began to climb the hill, placing his feet carefully for fear of twisting an ankle in the dark. He felt terribly exposed and the skin all over the front of his body seemed to be moving fractionally as though each individual square centimeter was anxious not to be a point of impact when the bullets came. At his seventy-ninth step he fell over John Villar's legs.

Villar was aware that suddenly renewed pain in his thigh had awoken him, but couldn't place the pressure of something hard under his chin forcing his head back, or the English voice saying, "Panhandle?" as though it were a question.

He thought about it and said, "West Virginia or Texas, I guess. Goddammit, will you quit shoving that thing into me?"

Elleston withdrew the muzzle of his rifle half an inch.

"Are you Panhandle?"

"Panhandle? Oh yeah, I think maybe I am, but it's kinda foggy."

"Then who am I?"

"You? Reckon you're QF. No. No, you're a bullock or something like that. Goddammit, I can't remember!"

Cooper's approach had been silent and Elleston jumped at the sound of his whispered question.

"That 'im, sir?"

"Yes. He can't remember Bulwark, but he got close to it. He's the bod all right and I think he's pretty sick."

As if in agreement with an exchange he hadn't heard, Villar said, "Goddammit!" for the third time and fainted.

Elleston and Cooper, each with one of Villar's arms across his shoulders, had almost reached the trees when they heard the fast savage yapping of Ackroyd's Bren gun.

* * *

"The road's cool enough now, sir."

"Good," the infantry captain said. "Tell them to climb in and let's get on."

The truck moved forward, passing a bus and a collection of cars and carts, its big tires lifting gobs of semimolten tar from the road. Some of it splattered the sides of the stationary vehicles. Then it was rolling south on a hard surface, its dipped headlights fanning just ahead of it like a cowcatcher on a locomotive.

"There's another group, sir."

"Pull over. It's time I earned my pay, so I'll do this one with Schmidt. Gruenther to interpret, of course."

The driver stopped the truck, angled it so that it was pointing at the two boats being dragged from the water onto the sand, and switched the headlights to full beam. The men around the boats stood looking toward the truck, shielding their eyes against the sudden brightness, watching the silhouettes of the peak-capped officer and the two helmeted soldiers marching toward them. Several of them moved their feet nervously in the shifting sand under the shallow water.

"Who's in charge of this boat?"

"I am."

"And that one?"

"Me."

"I see. Now listen carefully all of you."

Gruenther launched into his speech about escaping spies and the grim prospect facing anyone who made escape possible for them by failing to guard his boat day and night. He had made it eleven times between Spezia and wherever they now were and was enjoying polishing his Italian on a succession of captive audiences. On this occasion he was interrupted and that made him angry until he began to understand what was being said to him and his anger was replaced by puzzlement.

"Say that again."

The fisherman said it again, stabbing the air with a forefinger, then Gruenther turned to the officer.

"Sir, this man says he doesn't know anything about anybody getting out of the country, but he's seen some men coming in

tonight. They landed from canoes along the beach there and
hid . . ."

"Tell me as we go!" the infantry captain snapped and began
to run along the beach, fumbling with the flap of his holster.
Gruenther started after him and was about to finish what he
had been saying when the officer turned sharply left and threw
himself facedown into the sea. Surprise at this eccentric behavior was growing in the interpreter's mind when four Bren
gun bullets tore through his chest from back to front. The
soldier called Schmidt, and the observant Italian fisherman who
had followed them, died with him. The infantry captain was
already dead.

"Didn't have no choice, sir," Ackroyd told Elleston. "This
bloody truck comes along full up with Jerry pongos and lights
up this stretch of beach while three of them goes to talk with
the fishermen. First there's a lot of chat in wop which I doesn't
understand, then one of the fishermen starts pointing at where
we hid the canoes and the Jerries take off toward them like it
was three minutes to closing time. I didn't fancy that too much,
sir, so I done them."

"Quite right too," Elleston said. "Norris, tell the ship 'Positive, but in action with German patrol.' What happened then,
Sergeant?"

"The truck reversed back down the road a bit sharpish, sir,
but Norris and me thinks we got its front tires, so they won't
be charging about in it. Five, maybe six pongos got out and
legged it into this wood. They'll be coming at us through it,
or they'll work along the side of the hill to take us from behind.
Or both."

"Then it's about time we got out of here."

"Yessir. Cooper, take a saunter toward the road and see
what the weather's like."

In the dim wash of light from the headlights of the distant
truck, Elleston watched Cooper, elbows and knees working,
squirm rapidly away from the shelter of the trees. Almost immediately he heard the ripping sound of fast automatic fire like
the gas-operated Vickers machine guns aboard *Trigger* and
vicious spurts of sand stitched across the ground toward the
crawling figure. Cooper turned and squirmed his way back.

"Rainin'," he said.

Ackroyd nodded. "Schmeisser, and much closer than the truck. They're not wasting any time. What I..."

The first blast was close and stunning. So were the second and third. The fourth was more distant and the fifth farther away still. Bits of several branches fell on and around them and the air was heavy with the stench of explosives. Nobody was hurt.

"By the truck, Sarge. I seen the flashes. Fuckin' mortar."

"Right, Cooper," Ackroyd said. "You go and do the bloke with the Schmeisser and make it nice and quiet or they'll put another man there." He turned to Elleston. "They'll be ranging back again with that mortar in a minute, sir, trying to flush us for the machine gun on the beach one way, or the blokes on the hill the other. Permission to bring the ship in on this, sir?"

Harding had known tenseness before often enough, but his present personal uselessness and the impotence of his ship in such circumstances were a new experience. He hated it. The sound of the initial bursts of automatic fire had dismayed him. Speed and silence had been the essence of the entire operation and the silence had been broken. That that in turn would remove any possibility of speed he knew before Norris's voice had told of action with a German patrol. Then it had been necessary to stamp out the urge to ask questions and that he had done, but it had dug deeply into his reserves of control.

When the distant crump of mortar bombs reached him, he winced and began to toy with the idea of putting down smoke, but gave no order because its effect could be the opposite of what was needed. First he had to know where the enemy was.

"Chivers, can you make anything of that vehicle almost directly in line with the white villa? Is it the same one that was lighting up the beach just now?"

"Could be, sir, if they backed up with the headlights off, then switched them on again. Might be using them as a pointer."

"So they might," Harding said and was wishing illogically that he still had the visibility the big fire had provided when Chivers added, "Can't be sure, but I may have seen some flashes near it a moment ago."

"May you, by God? Then..."

Both the second and third army-type field-radio sets were in use aboard *Trigger,* one on the bridge, the other on the four-inch gun platform below it where Lieutenant Wallace and the gun's crew waited. They crackled experimentally and a metallic voice, hardly recognizable as Norris's began to speak.

"Gin, this is Rum. We are pinned down and under fire from a mortar—er—a mortar located by lighted truck approximately six o'clock white villa from your bearing—what, Ackers? Oh yes—request artillery stonk. Did you read that? Over."

"Roger," Harding said and took the one pace separating him from the front of the bridge in time to hear Wallace say, *"Artillery stonk?"*

Harding flared at him. "Don't stand there twittering like an old woman, Wallace! Lighted road target bearing Red 15 range one thousand yards. Open fire!"

The violent slamming of the big gun wiped his anger away and eased the tenseness of his muscles. He was back in business and he watched calmly as round after round burst among the trees or inside the white villa. The truck had doused its lights and was only visible at all because the villa behind it was burning. It was not an easy target to hit at a thousand yards from a rocking platform and he thought no less of Leading Seaman Peters, the gun layer, for missing with seven rounds before the truck erupted into flame.

"Cease firing."

The gun fell silent, but the hills continued to rumble with the diminishing echoes of its voice.

"Well," Harding said to nobody in particular, "now they know where *we* are." Then abruptly, "I'll have smoke now, Wallace. All we've got. Spread it from Green 15 to Red 25. Aim at the base of the hill."

The gun began to thunder again.

"How about it, Sergeant?" Elleston whispered. "We should be able to make it to the canoes now the lights are out. Whoops! There goes the truck."

"Dunno, sir. I don't think that machine gunner was relying on the truck lights. They were too far off. Just pointing the direction for the mortar shouldn't wonder. That Schmeisser's very close. Best to wait 'til Cooper's done his stuff."

"You seem very confident that he'll succeed."

"What? Who, Cooper? Oh, he'll do him all right. Good lad is Cooper. That's why I brung him."

John Villar stirred in his sleep, spoke several words in loud, rapid Italian, and subsided again.

Elleston said, "For God's sake keep that man quiet, Norris." On the side of the hill three German soldiers changed direction at the sounds and ran down toward the wood.

The blade of Cooper's fighting knife was tacky with German as well as Italian blood now and he drove it into the sandy soil several times to clean it, then crawled away from the dead machine gunner. Oily-white chemical smoke from the submarine's shells began to roll soundlessly through the trees. He paused to check his bearings, then in quick succession the crack of a grenade, a scream, a single rifle shot, and a prolonged stutter of automatic fire reached his ears. Cooper got to his feet and ran silently forward, not hurrying.

A prone figure in German uniform delayed him for a moment. The man was unconscious, with a deep bullet graze along one side of his head. Cooper killed him with his knife. The second soldier, eight yards farther on, had died by the same means, the hilt of Ackroyd's dagger protruding from his diaphragm.

"Nice throwing, Sarge," Cooper said, but he said it to himself.

The third soldier stood crouching forward, peering about him, a machine pistol held at the ready. Drifting smoke gave him the appearance of an actor in a pantomime. Cooper shot him through the head.

It took him a moment to find Elleston and Ackroyd in the thickening smoke. Both had been hit several times by automatic fire and he noticed that Elleston's right foot was missing. The man they had come to fetch was sleeping quietly nearby. There was no sign of Norris.

"Looks like it's you and me, cock," Cooper said, picked Villar up, and carried him toward the beach.

CHAPTER 21

THE INSISTENT HAMMERING OF KNUCKLES ON HIS door brought Colonel Kriewald slowly out of sleep. He turned on his side, switched on the lamp beside the bed, and shouted, "Come in if you must and stop that damned racket!" Then more quietly, "Oh, it's you, Engel. What the devil are you doing here?"

"Trying to wake you up," Colonel Engel told him. "Now I've succeeded, I suggest you get into some clothes. There's something odd happening."

Engel's tone and facial expression were enough. Kriewald was on his feet and stripping off his pyjamas before he asked, "What odd thing's happening?"

"There's a battle of some sort in progress down the coast toward Forte dei Marmi. Machine-gun fire, a lot of smoke, and a naval bombardment. It's very small-scale, but I find it curious."

Kriewald paused in his dressing, half in and half out of his trousers. "So do I, but why come here to tell me about it?"

"Because the English flyers have messed up the telephone system again. I tried to call you, but I couldn't get through."

"I didn't mean that. Naturally the *Abwehr* is interested, but at this stage, I'd have thought that the fighting services were more immediately concerned."

"That's as may be," Engel said, "but it was you who talked me into lending you troops to search for this fish seller and after exploding radio sets and other incidents, it strikes me as a strange coincidence that . . ."

"God in heaven!" Kriewald broke in. "I hadn't even made

the connection. I must be half-asleep still. But can he be *that* important?"

"You tell me, Kriewald. He's your fish seller, not mine."

"You're a good officer and a good friend," the *Abwehr* colonel told him. "To save time I'll finish dressing in your car if I may."

The thickness of the smoke made it hard for Cooper to identify the figure crouching under the fishing boat beside the canoes, but he thought he knew who it was. Carefully he lowered Villar to the sand, drew his knife, and held it by the point between the forefinger and thumb of his right hand, its hilt resting on his shoulder.

"Norris?" A sibilant penetrating whisper.

"Oh Jesus! My face!" Norris said. His voice was slurred as if he had been drinking heavily.

Cooper put his knife away, pulled apart the hands Norris had pressed to either cheek, and peered closely at him. A bullet had gone in one side, passed through the mouth and left by the other. The size of the exit wound seemed to indicate that teeth had accompanied the bullet.

"You'll live. Bring a canoe."

Norris gave no sign of having heard. Cooper left him, picked Villar up, and walked toward the sea. Norris, a canoe held over his head, joined him before he reached it.

"They shot me!" Shock and incredulity in the voice.

"I seen. Where's your wireless?"

"Dunno."

"Lost your gun too?"

"Yes."

"Marvelous," Cooper said. "Take this one and don't fuckin' shoot me."

Kneeling between the unconscious man and the flimsy contraption of wood and canvas, Norris waited for Cooper to return with another canoe. His face was throbbing and each beat sent bright shafts of pain lancing through his upper and lower jaws. He scarcely noticed them or the adventurous surge of a small wave which soaked his legs, swirled around Villar, and carried the canoe a foot up the beach. "Don't fuckin' shoot me," Cooper had said and the remark blended with shame and terror to create an idea. He looked down at the dark shape of the Bren lying across his thighs.

The weapon was already cocked and he moved the safety catch to the "fire" position. Cooper might be tough, he thought, but he couldn't fight a machine gun. Not even old Ackers, who was much bigger than Cooper, could do that. The memory of the storm of bullets fired by three dimly seen figures came back to him with such clarity that he gasped, feeling once more the savage wind of their passing and the hot breath of the grenade which had exploded by Mr. Elleston. He heard again the officer's scream, saw him whirl, fire his rifle, and two of the figures fall. The recollection only added to his confusion as it didn't seem possible to hit two widely spaced men with one shot. Perhaps Ackers had done something too. All he was clear about was that he had done nothing but sit frozen, with the light Thompson submachine gun they had given him lying untouched at his side.

That had been bad enough. What had been very much worse was that with the third man continuing to advance, the ranting ripping sound of his gun growing louder and closer, he had run. That was when metal had torn through his face.

Worst of all was that Cooper, who had been somewhere else, knew what had happened and would report what he knew. That was insupportable. Norris took the Bren in both hands, pointed it in the direction of the beached fishing boat where the canoes had been hidden, and waited with his finger on the trigger.

"I'll 'ave me gun back now," Cooper said.

Total defeat settled on Norris like some otherworldly increase in atmospheric pressure. Slowly he turned his head until he could see the dark figure of the commando standing behind him, a knife dangling from one hand, a second canoe resting on the water at his side. Clicking the catch to "safe," he handed the Bren to him.

"Right. Get in and paddle."

Wordlessly Norris did as he was told.

It was eerie out on the gently heaving black sea with the ceiling of chemical smoke just above his head blanking out the sky. Voices shouting in German reaching him from the invisible shore, the sound of paddles dipping, splashing softly, and water bubbling past canvas. Nothing else except the beating of his own heart.

"Twenty degrees to your left, Norris." Cooper calling from the second canoe.

"Turn right, Norris. More. More. Okay. Keep the wind on the back of your neck." It seemed to be just as well that his insane idea of killing Cooper had come to nothing.

Back and arms aching, blood pulsing, shepherding pain, driving it to the assembly point of his face. Head beginning to swim and vision erratic. How far had they come? Half a mile? A mile? Two? He had no idea. A distant rumbling sound, unidentified and immediately forgotten in a gust of panic when he thought that the sea had fallen away beneath him and he grabbed at the sides of the canoe to prevent it turning over.

"Get fuckin' on with it, Norris!" Cooper's voice close behind.

The rumbling sound growing, growing fast, roaring overhead. The smoke suddenly incandescent like the mantle of a gas lamp, glowing all around him. Superstitious fear shaking his body until reason had persuaded him that the aircraft had dropped flares. The glow brightening as they fell, showing him a long, ghostly something to starboard.

Cooper shouting, "If you bastards ain't doin' nothin' special, 'ow about pickin' us up?"

Clipped orders clear across the water and the submarine beginning to move. Turning toward them and gathering speed, shouldering the smoke aside like a train emerging from a tunnel. Oh careful, you fool! Don't capsize the canoe at this stage! Sit still and wait for them. Moments of blankness, then a vast shape looming over him. Hands reaching down.

"Up you come, Norris boy. Easy with him. He's taken a smack in the kisser. There we are, old son. No, face the other way and let's get you down this ladder."

Crushing sadness because in a few minutes they won't be friendly anymore. The heavy thump of a hatch closing and the raucous sound of the diving klaxon. An officer's voice saying, "Well done, Norris."

That was insupportable too and Norris let himself sink into unconsciousness.

The ten dead Germans, an officer and nine men, lay in a neat line by the side of the road, with two Italian civilians near them. It was thought that there were more dead Italians in the burning villa, but the flames were still too fierce to allow anyone near.

"Where are the enemy dead?"

"We left them in the wood, *Herr Oberst*," the lieutenant said. "Follow me, please."

A minute later Kriewald stood looking down at the bodies of

the young naval officer and the big sergeant with the green beret still jammed pugnaciously on his head. The insignia on the sergeant's upper sleeve appeared to interest him particularly and he stooped, moving his flashlight closer, seeing the words "Royal Marines" with "Commando" below them and the number "2" above. All were in red on a navy-blue field. Underneath was a triangular patch showing a vertical fighting knife, then the initials SBS.

Kriewald glanced up as Engel joined him.

"I've never seen one of these before," he said.

"They're dangerous men."

"Who? The Special Boat Section?"

"I don't know anything about a Special Boat Section," Engel told him. "I mean the commandos."

"Oh, I've seen them before. I was talking about this particular branch. They often operate from English U-boats. I think it might be worth telling the *Kriegsmarine* that that's probably what they should be looking for rather than a fast patrol vessel or anything like that. The fairly heavy-caliber shell bursts fit the submarine theory too."

Engel nodded and walked away to relay the information. Kriewald straightened, nodded to the lieutenant, and followed him.

He had taken five paces when the lieutenant shouted, "Schechter! Bring three men with shovels and bury these murdering swine!"

Rolling his eyes upward, he grimaced with distaste but continued to stride on. It was the *Wehrmacht*'s affair now, not the *Abwehr*'s. Then he saw that Engel had stopped and heard him call, *"Leutnant!"*

"Herr Oberst?"

"Come here."

Engel stood rigidly, facing the way he had been going, waiting until the lieutenant stood in front of him.

"Your name?"

"Braun, *Herr Oberst*. Heinrich Braun."

"Braun, you will give my compliments to your commanding officer with the request that the enemy dead be buried in Spezia with full military honors. You will add my further request that you yourself act as officer of the guard for the occasion. That just might teach you a lesson in humility."

"*Jawohl, Herr Oberst.*" The hesitation had been little more than two seconds.

Engel looked at him for considerably longer, then said, "I'm so glad you agree with me," and brushed past without acknowledging the salute he was given.

Kriewald waited until they were both in Engel's car before saying, "Thank you for that, Engel. It's bad enough losing the fish seller without being left with a foul taste in the mouth as well."

Engel grunted. "I detest the type of German officer who models himself on the enemy's caricatures of him. Too many seem fated to do it and—oh, never mind. Are you sure you've lost your fish seller?"

"I'm afraid so," Kriewald said. "Three canoes landed and four men were seen to get out of them. Two of those men died. Why would the survivors leave in two twin-seat canoes instead of one unless they had a passenger?"

"Difficult to fault that," Engel told him. "I suggest that as they are now in *Kriegsmarine* territory, you and I might as well get some sleep." He settled himself into a corner of the backseat of the big army car and closed his eyes.

The intense air activity helped Harding. A gentle offshore breeze had carried the smoke from his shells where he wanted it while he needed it. Now it was pushing the white cloud farther out to sea, thinning it to no more than a haze of mist, leaving the night clear but too dark for periscope observation. Then the bombers had come again, annihilating the darkness for miles around with their brilliant parachute flares and he could see everything with extreme clarity, even the two destroyers approaching from the direction of Spezia on the far side of the coastal belt of mines.

That they were safe from the flares he knew perfectly well. The flyers would see no more of *Trigger* underwater than they had under the cloud of smoke. There was no shipping in the mine-free channel close to the shore and he increased speed along it past Forte dei Marmi and on to Viareggio beyond. For a long time the bombers continued to light his way.

"Can you spare me a few minutes, sir," Surgeon Lieutenant Cass said.

"What? Oh, hello, doc. Yes, of course. How are your patients?"

"Norris'll be all right, sir. He's more shocked than anything. But it's the other one I'm worried about. I may have to amputate his leg."

Harding blew out his cheeks, then said, "Oh dear. Gangrene?"

"Not yet."

"I see. It's like that, is it? What can I do?"

"Well, I hardly like to ask, sir, but could I have your cabin to put him in? It's very important that he's disturbed as little as possible and there's nowhere else private."

The embarrassment Harding felt that it had been necessary for the question to be asked, that he hadn't thought to make the offer, untypically transformed itself into anger. That, until then, he had no knowledge of the man's condition didn't occur to him.

Crossly he said, "What do you mean, 'I hardly like to ask'? Apart from the prime minister that man's the most important person ever to come aboard this ship!"

Cass regarded him levelly for a moment before saying, "I'm not interested in his importance, only his life. If he was the king or Able Seaman Norris it would make no difference."

Harding's sudden anger died. "Forgive me. I was completely out of order there. Have the cabin by all means and ask the first lieutenant to give you whatever help you need to prepare it."

"Thank you, sir," Cass said and smiled. "There's one more thing. He's delirious at the moment, but when he starts to come around I'd like to make contact with him quickly. May I know who he is?"

"Certainly," Harding told him. "He's an American called John Villar, but it might be better to call him Giovanni Villari. That's the name he's been going under for the last couple of years or so and he might react to it more readily. Let me know as soon as he's conscious."

The surgeon lieutenant nodded, smiled again, and walked away. Harding gestured for the periscope to be raised. There were no more flares dropping and very little moonlight, but the mountains to the east had begun to absorb substance from the dawn growing behind them. He stepped back from the periscope, watched absently while it hissed down into its well, then glanced around him at the people in the control room. They were all silent, their faces a study in expressionlessness, each man staring straight in front of him at depth gauge, compass repeater, sonar dial, or nothing. Guessing their thoughts, he took the tannoy microphone from its clip.

"This is the captain speaking. We are now proceeding south along the Italian coast, searching for a gap in the mine defenses we came through last night. I think we'll find one before too long. Anyway, I don't intend to penetrate the mine field itself again unless there is no choice. That is all."

Rigid spines flexed and settled themselves into natural curves, shoulders were worked, someone broke wind loudly, said, "Beg pardon I'm sure," and giggled. Harding felt no surprise that men who could stand up to many hours of depth charging, without suffering more than the normal tensions associated with the experience, should so readily become mesmerized by fear in proximity to mines. It didn't surprise him because he felt the same way himself. There was something malignant in their passivity and it was thought that they had claimed a number of submarines whose disappearance had never been explained in any other way.

"Hydrophone effect dead ahead, sir," Petty Officer McIntyre said.

"Up periscope."

The light was growing, but was still not enough to let him see more than a mile.

"Nothing in sight yet, McIntyre. What does it sound like?"

"Not sure, sir. It's a long way off."

"All right."

He stood at the periscope for several minutes, staring ahead, occasionally turning in a circle. Nothing except land all along the port side, lighter patches against the black hills showing the location of buildings. The hills themselves standing out in silhouette against the sky.

"Sounds like a slow steam reciprocating engine, sir."

"Thank you, McIntyre."

It was another three minutes before Harding saw it. The tall masts and thin funnel of an old-fashioned freighter. Almost from the first sighting he had the feeling that he had seen her before. He looked up at the azimuth ring encircling the periscope just above his head.

"Exactly where you said it was, McIntyre."

"Yes, sir. Sir, can you see anything bearing about Green 30 to Green 40?"

As Harding swung the periscope to starboard, the day spilled over the tops of the mountains behind him and flowed out across the sea.

"Yes," he said. "A destroyer. Make that two destroyers. Possibly the ones we saw by the light of the flares earlier. I think they're stationary."

"They are, sir," McIntyre told him. "No propeller sound at all, but I thought I heard sonar transmissions a moment ago. They've stopped now. No they bloody haven't! Two sets of transmissions. Hang on a minute, sir."

He was silent for only half that time before he went on, "They're not sweeping. I think they're both transmitting on a fixed bearing, but not at us."

Only the gray upper works of the two warships were visible to Harding, but that was enough to show him that they were lying stopped with their bows pointing at the coast. The lazy swell of the night before had increased considerably and occasionally the heaving water hid them from his sight altogether. It didn't matter. He knew what they were doing.

"Ask the first lieutenant to come here, please," he said and yawned shudderingly. It had been a long night and it seemed as though the period of greatest danger was yet to come. He turned the periscope to look at the freighter again. It was appreciably closer, still bows on to them, still dead ahead, converging on a collision course.

Gascoigne came into the control room, wiping his hands on a bloodstained towel.

"How is he, Number One?"

"The doctor thinks he's pretty bad, sir. He's still working on the bullet wound. It doesn't look very nice."

"Hmm. Now listen. This is the situation. There's a freighter coming along the swept-channel toward us from ahead. I think she's the same one they used as a decoy for that convoy we attacked last patrol. Range is about two miles and there's just enough water for us to pass underneath her, so no headache there. But there is here."

He turned the periscope toward the starboard bow as if the action was an explanation and paused before adding, "It's the passage through the mine field and they've corked it with a couple of destroyers. They're lying more or less stopped about a mile off at the far end, transmitting toward the shore."

The warships disappeared, reappeared, disappeared again

with monotonous regularity as the long waves rose and fell between them and the periscope lens. They were very close.

"What are you going to do, sir?"

Before replying Harding looked again at the old freighter ploughing steadily toward them, a plume of black smoke from its funnel streaming horizontally toward the land in the increasing wind.

"I'm going to try to torpedo them," he said, "after the merchantman's gone by. You'd better send the crew to their stations."

It shouldn't be difficult, Harding told himself while men jostled each other to take up their appointed positions in the confined space, to torpedo two stationary targets, and telling himself knew that he lied. Their draft was shallow and only half his torpedoes had magnetically operated detonators; he would have only their width to fire at, not their length, and if they didn't detect him at once with their sonar impulses, they would, still and silent as they were, almost certainly hear the scream of the three-hundred-horsepower motors driving the torpedoes toward them.

If that would give them enough time to take evasive action he was unsure, but could not disregard the possibility, and if it did give them time . . . He shook his head to break the trail his imagination was following toward the retribution that would result and to enable him to think once more of the other courses open to him.

To continue south down the narrow channel between mines and shores was out of the question because they would detect him by sonar as soon as he crossed the bearing they were transmitting on. To turn back was impossible. The ship's submerged turning circle was so large that it would carry them into the mines or onto the shore. To back away was too risky. Depth control going astern was far trickier and they might give themselves away by breaking surface.

Harding frowned in concentration, his gaze directed at the sailor standing at the diving panel. The man stared back, then dropped his eyes, and shuffled his feet nervously, not knowing that he was unseen.

Lie on the bottom and wait for dark? Then what? The destroyers might go away. Then again they might not. Almost certainly would not. Not soon enough.

"Number One," Harding said, "did the doctor say anything to you about Villar's chances if he has to amputate?"

"Yes, sir," Gascoigne told him. "They're not good. He's running a very high temperature. He's starving and seems to have let himself get progressively more run-down over a long period of time. In the doctor's words he's in poor shape for major surgery under primitive conditions."

Gascoigne hesitated, then, as though he had read Harding's mind, added, "We can't afford to hang about, sir."

Without comment Harding flicked his fingers and the periscope rose in obedience to the gesture. The freighter was less than half a mile away now, almost level with the destroyers. Nearly time to go deep and pass underneath her. He swung in a full circle again. The land, the freighter, the destroyers. Nothing else. The thought came to him that he should have gone out the way he had come in, through the mine field, but he brushed it aside. It was too late to bother about that and he doubted if he could have done it.

"Fifty feet, Number One. Stand by all tubes, fore and aft."

Voices relaying his words, the upper lens of the periscope almost level with the surface of the water, dipping under now. Had he seen sky opening between the freighter's masts and funnel just before the sea deprived him of vision? Was she turning?

Urgently, "Belay the last orders! Bring her back to periscope depth! Quickly, Number One!"

Fruitless pressure on the periscope handles from his hands as though he would lift the submarine by the strength of his arms. Come on! Come on! Must see! Grave danger of being rammed and sunk if wrong. Light tracing shifting filigree designs in silver and gold on the underside of waves. The patterns breaking. Water clearing from the lens. The freighter close, beam on to him, heading out to sea.

"Group up! Emergency full ahead together! Starboard thirty! Fifty feet!" Said that too loudly. Keep voice down, damn it!

"Flood 'Q,' sir?"

"No, it's all right, Number One. The freighter's altered course to the west. She's going out through the gap and we're going with her. I don't think the destroyers' sonar will be able to distinguish between us."

Trigger vibrating, boring through the water, the illuminated red figures of the gyrocompass repeater tape clicking fast, faster, as the submarine curves around into the freighter's wake, overtaking the old merchantman.

"Steer 270, Chivers."

"Two-seventy. Aye aye, sir."

The feeling that the ship is running across cobblestones, the sound of crockery clinking frenziedly somewhere, and the rush of water past the hull.

"Steady on 270, sir."

"Very good. Group down. Stop starboard. Slow ahead port. As soon as you can hear, McIntyre, let me know who's doing what."

When the turbulence had subsided, "Hydrophone effect all around, sir," McIntyre said. "It's swamping out everything. I reckon we must be about underneath her."

Harding nodded and ordered the speed increased again. Several times over the next half hour he slowed to enable McIntyre to listen, then ordered the ship brought up to periscope depth.

The rusty freighter, belching smoke and butting into the increasing swell, was a mile away to starboard. Far astern the destroyers lay guarding the gap in the mine defenses.

"All right, Number One," Harding said. "You may go to patrol routine now and tell the crew that we're back on the high seas."

CHAPTER 22

FREE TO MOVE ABOUT AGAIN WITH THE SHIP AT patrol routine, Cooper went in search of Norris. He found him lying in a bunk a petty officer had relinquished to him. He squatted on his heels in the passageway beside the bunk and began to pare his nails with his knife.

"'Ow you doin', Norris?"

"All right." Norris's jaw had stiffened and his voice sounded even more slurred than it had.

"Looks like you got mumps with that bandage wrapped round your mug."

"Yeah."

Cooper searched for something else to say. Found it.

"Slipped out of that little mess neatly, didn't we?"

Norris watched the rhythmic movement of the long-bladed fighting knife in the other's hand. The blade was clean, glinting in the electric light, but the underside of the hilt was stained a reddish brown. He shivered, then met the commando's eyes.

"Listen, Cooper," he said. "The skipper's been busy. I'll go and talk to him when he's free."

"Why? You got some tips for 'im?"

"Lay off, will you?"

"What, then?"

"I'm going to tell him," Norris said steadily, "about what you call me slipping out of that little mess. You needn't bother. I'll do it."

The knife paused, then resumed its featherlike caress of Cooper's nails. "Oh, I see. Matter of fact I was thinkin' of us

235

thumbin' our noses at them two destroyers. If you was thinkin'
of somethin' else, I'd keep me fuckin' face shut if I was you."

"I can't do that. Ackers was my friend and Mr. Elleston
was always nice to me. I let them down."

Cooper stood up and peered behind the curtains of the bunks
above and to either side of Norris's. They were empty and he
squatted down again.

"So now they're dead you wanna spread it around they
picked the wrong team, right?"

Norris scowled and the facial contortion nudged at the pain
which had become quiescent in his cheeks.

Hands pressed against his bandages, "Stop confusing me,"
he said. "It was all quite plain before. Anyway, I've got to turn
myself in. I was going to kill you to stop you telling on me."

"I know," Cooper told him. "That's why I circled back
through the smoke to come up be'ind you."

"Well?"

"Well what?"

"We can't just pretend none of it happened."

Cooper looked down at his knife as though surprised to find
it in his hand. He spun it, caught it by the handle, and slid it
into the sheath strapped to his ankle. Then he looked back at
Norris.

"Funny old war this is," he said. "There's a marine in our
section who panicked so bad on 'is first landin' 'e tried to shoot
'is corporal to get away. The corporal took 'is gun off 'im,
smashed 'im somethin' rotten, give 'im 'is gun back, and never
said no more about it. The marine never done it again."

"Go on. That's just one of those stories that gets passed
around."

"Well, don't you go passin' it around, sonny. Could be
embarrassin'. I was the marine and Ackroyd was the corporal."
Cooper stood up, added "See yer, Norris," and walked off.

Harding found himself with too little to do, and what was worse
for him, no cabin he could retire to. It had grown to be a
sanctuary, the cabin, a place where he could compose himself
when he came down off the high plateau of intense endeavor,
or let the trembling of his body drain the poisons from muscles
too long held rigid.

Since Gail Mainwaring there had been no trembling, but then, until the past night, nothing had occurred to cause it. Even now the symptoms were distant flickers, not quite part of him, signs to be watched with suspicion rather than fought. He hoped very much, for all the obvious reasons, that they would remain distant, but the sudden cessation of the need for mental activity, the loss of the privacy normally his, and the fear of letting Gail Mainwaring down brought them edging closer.

Unnecessarily, because the navigating officer had already done it, he fixed the position of the ship by taking bearings of points on the Italian mainland through the periscope, transferring them to the chart and ordering a southwesterly course to carry them north of Corsica. That occupied him for nearly a minute. He talked to Gascoigne about the state of the main battery following the heavy discharge resulting from his rapid maneuvering under the freighter. It was satisfactory and would permit slow but steady submerged progress until dark. That took twenty seconds.

Half an hour passed while he stood in the wardroom asking questions while Surgeon Lieutenant Cass trimmed the long hair and shaved the flushed face of the blanket-covered figure lying on the table. An extraordinarily handsome man emerged as the gray-black beard fell away to reveal a strong mouth and chin, but the skin was too taut and the cheekbones painted with the flush of fever. Occasionally the man said something in Italian. When he did that, his thick, almost girlish lashes fluttered, but the eyes did not open.

When the doctor had finished, Harding watched Villar carried to the cabin, then went to talk to a morose, monosyllabic Norris. He left him after a moment and found Cooper.

"Would you let me have a written report on what happened ashore last night, Cooper?"

"Reckon I could, sir, but I'm not much in the way of spellin'."

"Oh, don't worry about that. By the way, what's the matter with Norris? Apart from getting shot I mean."

"Well, 'e's probably a bit shook up. There was a fair amount of shit flyin' what with automatic fire, grenades, and a mortar stonk. Takes it out of you when you're new at it."

Stonk. That word again which he had never heard until the night before.

"Nothing else?"

"Ackroyd was 'is pal, sir. They used to get pissed together."

"Yes, that's right," Harding said. "They did, didn't they?"

Encoding a signal for transmission to Algiers when the ship surfaced for the night, a night still nine hours away, occupied another few minutes. When it was done, Harding tore it up because Villar's condition might have changed radically by then. Realizing that he was behaving irrationally, he went to the bunk Gascoigne had vacated for him outside the wardroom, got into it, and drew the curtains shut.

In the near darkness he lay listening to the quiet sounds of the ship beyond the curtains, the hum of conversation forward, and the half-heard orders from the control room in the opposite direction. After a little he allowed himself to think about Elleston and Ackroyd for the first time, then tried to force them out of his mind when he found that their deaths had saddened him more than those which had occurred on the previous patrol. Why that should be he was uncertain, but thought it might have something to do with their having died in enemy territory. He hoped that the Germans would treat them with respect and that they had not died uselessly. The first hope came, he decided, more from the sense of rightness that the navy had taught him than any religious conviction. The second brought him out of his bunk.

Cass's voice reached him softly when he tapped on the door of his own cabin.

"Who is it?"

"The captain."

"Oh. Come in, sir."

He slid the door aside, went in, and stood beside the doctor, looking down at Villar's leg. The sight of the gaping hole in the thigh made him wince.

"I suppose that's the exit wound," he said.

"No. It's the entry wound. The bullet drove material from his trousers into him and set up infection. I've cut away the detritus. That's why the hole's so big now."

"Detritus? I thought that meant debris."

"So it does and that's exactly what was in there. Very dangerous debris. Poisoned flesh."

"I see. What's this?" Harding pointed to the tube taped to the thigh and connected to a bottle suspended above the bunk.

"It's a Eusol drip, sir. A chlorinated solution I'm using to irrigate the infected area. It was developed in Edinburgh. In fact that's what it stands for—Edinburgh University Solution. That, four-hourly injections of sulfanilamide, keeping him cool, and getting some soup down him is about all I can do. The rest's up to him."

While he talked, Cass's hands moved ceaselessly, sponging Villar's face and neck, swabbing excess solution delicately away from the craterlike wound.

"I'll do that for you when you're tired," Harding said.

"It's all right, sir. Gascoigne's already offered. So has the pilot."

"They've got watches to stand," Harding told him. "I haven't, so I'll double for you."

"Right-oh, sir, but I suggest you go and get some sleep now. You look wiped out to me. Not surprising after last night."

Harding nodded noncommittally.

"Doc?"

"Sir?"

"If he does get gangrene and you have to amputate . . . ?"

"I think he'll die, sir," Cass said.

Back in his bunk Harding let his mind drift. It settled, as it so often did, on Gail Mainwaring, and with nothing else he could usefully think about, he was content to leave it there. By no means for the first time he wondered who she was, what sort of background could produce such a tangle of contradictions. Ineffable gentleness and thrusting arrogance. An ability to entertain amusingly and a refusal to inform at all. An attachment to him which he was sure went beyond affection and a claim to be an unrepentant professional wanton. It was all very puzzling.

He thought of her calm, beautifully modulated voice and of her passion which occasionally amounted to frenzy, of an appealing demureness which, without warning, could turn into a blatant exhibitionism which both excited and alarmed him, of her gaiety and her brooding moodiness.

Too inexperienced to recognize the sophisticated attack on his inhibitions for what it had been, he remained in a state of happily bemused imbalance, neither accepting completely nor delving deep. Any reservations he might have harbored about her all too obvious experience were rationalized out of existence by an acknowledgment of innate priggishness in himself. The only two things Harding was quite certain about were that she was wonderful beyond belief and that he loved her very much.

"Excuse me, sir, but the first lieutenant says to tell you that there's a big sea running and it's blowing hard."

Angry at having his redheaded enchantress snatched from inside his head, Harding rolled over and scowled at the face of the messenger peering at him past the raised end of the bunk's curtain.

"Well, what does he want me to do about it? Take in a reef or something? If he can't maintain periscope depth ask him to go deep."

"Er—Aye aye, sir."

The curtain fell back into place and he lay on his side, aware now of the ship's faint uneasy movement, a trembling and a tiny rolling motion. He knew that it had to be very rough on the surface to cause that.

Again the curtain was lifted and Gascoigne was grinning down at him.

"Hello, sir. It's time to surface."

"Time to *surface*?"

"Yes, sir. I somehow felt my message hadn't made any sense to you. You've been asleep for nearly eight hours."

"Good God!" Harding said and swung his feet to the deck. "How's Villar?"

"The same, sir, but he's no worse and the doctor says that's a good sign. The immediate worry now is the weather. He mustn't be thrown about, so when it really started to blow about noon I altered course a bit to the south to close Gorgona Island. It'll be easier to ride this out in the lee while we're charging the battery. I hope you don't mind, sir. It's more or less on the way home anyway and I didn't like to wake you."

Harding shook his head, smiling, thinking how well served he was by Gascoigne.

"Well done, Number One. How far is the island?"

"About sixteen miles, sir, but we're approaching it from the opposite direction to the storm so we'll be in the lee before we've gone as far as that—I hope."

"And how's the battery?"

"Very low, sir. We really should surface and start charging it right away."

Harding glanced at the lights. There was no sign of dimming yet.

"We'll stay dived for as long as we can keep a propeller turning," he said.

Trigger clawed her slow way two miles closer to the island before Harding ordered her taken up into the howling night. He stood on the swaying, bucking bridge watching white water race past on either side, picturing the havoc it would have brought to the landing of the night before.

Almost directly below his feet, a hammock had been slung outside his cabin and the unconscious Villar transferred to it. Two men, their backs braced against the sides of the narrow passageway, supported it in their arms, cushioning it from the worst of the shock when the hull smashed down onto the crest of waves or fell into the troughs between them. Other men stood near to take their places when they tired. They tired quickly and changed places often until the submarine reached calmer waters in the lee of Gorgona Island and lay almost stationary, rocking gently, thundering diesels forcing life back into the battery cells.

In Algiers harbor, "Thank you for coming aboard at this unearthly hour," Captain Anderson said. "Sit down, General. I expect your RAF friend would like to poke about in the cupboards before I say anything."

The bogus squadron leader shook his head. "This is outside my union hours. Say on."

"All right. The news is good and bad. *Trigger* has picked up Conrad, but he may die of his wound."

His visitors looked at each other, then back at Anderson. Neither spoke.

Anderson handed the major general a flimsy sheet of pink paper. "That's an extract from the signal I've received. It describes his physical condition."

The two read it together, then the squadron leader said, "Time is obviously of the essence. I'll arrange for a destroyer to rendezvous with the submarine and take him off. Come to think of it, one of those fast mine-laying cruisers would be better. They do about forty-five knots, don't they?"

"No. You can't do that," Anderson told him. "It would . . ."

"What the hell do you mean I can't do that? I've got the prime minister's authority to do anything necessary."

"Do you mind if I finish what I was saying?"

"Not at all."

"Thank you. To transfer a fit man from one ship to another in storm conditions is virtually impossible. To attempt it with somebody in Villar's state would certainly kill him. Oh, I hope you don't mind my referring to him as Villar. We all know what his name is now."

The others shrugged their agreement and Anderson went on. "Additionally, in the unexpectedly heavy seas which are now forecast for the next couple of days or so, he's far better off in a submarine than a surface ship. *Trigger* can dive for about twenty out of the twenty-four hours and keep him perfectly still. On the surface he'd be shaken about like a set of poker dice. I am informed by the captain of *Trigger* that absolute quiet is considered by the ship's doctor to hold out greater hope for Villar than any attempt to rush him ashore. Do I make myself clear?"

"Yes, you do, Captain Anderson, and I apologize for snapping at you."

Anderson looked at the man in RAF uniform and said, "That's okay. Nobody's at his best at quarter to four in the morning. Now, you were talking about destroyers. What I suggest you ask the C-in-C for is a couple of them to be stationed on *Trigger*'s homeward route. Then if the weather moderates she can make a fast surface run to Algiers with them as escort. I'll act as the wireless link between her and the destroyers."

"Come on, chum," the bogus squadron leader said to Major General Vibart. "You heard. Let's get on with it and I promise never to interfere in naval affairs again."

He winked at the depot ship's captain and Anderson, to his own surprise, winked back.

* * *

Fifty miles to the west of Ajaccio in Corsica, *Trigger* moved slowly south. Big waves, tossing their plumed heads like chargers, marched endlessly from horizon to horizon, but ninety feet down in the still darkness the submarine felt nothing of their passing.

Equally oblivious, Villar lay supine on Harding's bunk, but he no longer muttered in Italian and the flush of fever had faded from his cheeks.

"I'm rather superstitious about answering questions like that," Surgeon Lieutenant Cass said, "but yes, I think he's made it, sir."

"Very modest of you, doc. You make it sound as though you had nothing to do with it."

"Apart from gouging out some rotten meat I didn't really. There's a strong subconscious will to live in this chap."

"What makes you say that?"

"I don't know. There just is. I can't explain it."

Harding glanced sideways at the red-rimmed eyes in the doctor's tired face and said, "Two days ago when you started nursing him you told me that I looked wiped out. My diagnosis is the same in your case now. I don't want to give you an order because you have skills nobody else on board can duplicate, but I would be very pleased if you'd go to bed. I'll watch him."

Cass smiled. "I'd like to turn in for a bit, but please let me know . . ."

"At once," Harding promised him. "Push off and get your head down."

The drip had been disconnected and there was no sweat on Villar's face to be sponged away. Harding sat down, unlocked a drawer, and took out his pile of drawings of Gail Mainwaring. He had missed having them near him, missed too his freedom to draw more, and now, after a break of three days, seeing them with fresh eyes, he felt astonishment at how good they were. As he studied each one he also felt a growing shyness at his intimate portrayal of her. Exotic? Erotic? Both of those words and neither of them.

Harding was still searching for the right one when John Villar said, "She's lovely. She's *really* lovely."

Replacing the papers in the drawer, closing it, locking it,

Harding experienced a shortness of breath as though he had been struck in the stomach. Without looking at the man beside him, he jerked the cabin door open and beckoned to the sailor standing nearest to him in the control room.

"Tell the doctor his patient's awake."

"Aye aye, sir."

He turned to Villar then.

"Welcome aboard." His voice sounded cold to his ears and he knew that his face must look the same. He knew too that there was nothing that he could do about it, the relief he had anticipated at Villar's recovery, the long-hoped-for satisfaction at the successful completion of the mission, swept aside by what he saw as a desecration of his personal shrine.

"It's great to be aboard," Villar said.

Cass's hands pushing him unceremoniously aside Harding accepted gratefully as his cue to leave. He stood for a moment in the passageway outside the cabin, listening, but when after hearing Cass's "Lie back please, Mr. Villar, and don't talk," there was only silence, he went away.

His examination finished, Cass asked, "How are you feeling, Mr. Villar?"

"Weak, doctor, but a whole heap better than before you guys snatched me off the beach. I guess it was you, wasn't it? I remember I was waiting for a submarine and I know this is a submarine because I was put into Italy from one way back."

"Yes, it was us. You're on your way to Algiers now. Are you warm enough?"

"Sure. Just right."

"Then I wonder why you're trembling."

"Oh that," Villar said, extended an arm, and frowned at his quivering fingers. "How long have I been unconscious?"

"I don't know exactly. It depends on when you originally lost consciousness. You were flat out when our people found you, but it's been days, not hours."

"Then that explains it. My system's run out of juice. You see, I'm an alcoholic."

Cass regarded him curiously for a moment before saying, "That's a strange thing to be in what I take to have been your profession."

Villar shook his head. "No. It was half of my cover. Nobody pays much attention to the town drunk."

"Well, well. In that case we'd better put a little juice back into you after you've had some soup. This is no time to be drying you out."

"I could use a lot more than soup, doc."

"Soup," Cass said. "Just soup."

The American's hands were shaking badly now and the doctor spooned broth into his mouth, followed it with a glass of watered gin.

"My stomach won't notice that drink, doc."

"Perhaps not, but let me write my own prescriptions, will you? I don't want you shaking the teeth out of your head, but I don't want your pulse racing either. Leave the balance to me."

"Sorry. Who was the kid in here when I woke up? Your pharmacist's mate?"

Cass smiled. "We don't have pharmacists' mates in the Royal Navy. We call them sick-berth attendants. But he wasn't one."

"No?"

"No. That was the captain. This is his cabin you're in."

"Oh-oh," Villar said and Cass smiled again, then began to change his patient's dressing.

The size of the hole in his thigh made Villar whistle and say, "I'm glad you left some of me in place. You British really have it in for that leg of mine."

"It wasn't us that shot you, Mr. Villar."

"It was too," Villar said. "That other hole below the knee. That was the second half of my cover."

When Cass reported to him, Harding listened gravely, but without apparent interest, saying only that he would signal Algiers when the ship surfaced that night and telling the doctor to go to bed. Cass did what he had been told to do gladly enough but, tired as he was, lay awake for a long time thinking about his final exchange with the surgeon commander before *Trigger* sailed from Algiers.

"One other thing, Cass. Keep an eye open for any signs of stress and tell me about them when you get back."

"Stress in whom, sir?"

"You'll know that if it happens," Gilmore had said.

He was wondering now if he had just witnessed the symptoms in Harding. Admitting to himself that he had virtually nothing to go on and wishing he knew more about the subject, he found the abrupt change from quietly methodical aggression to indifference at the very moment of assured success difficult to accept as a normal reaction. Would it not, he mused, be reasonable to expect relief from anxiety to produce at least a trace of enthusiasm? Could it be that Harding felt none of the satisfaction that he as a doctor experienced at the recovery of the patient? No. Harding might be totally devoid of humanity, although Cass believed that not at all, but he would certainly feel professional gratification. There had been that brief outburst of irritation from him in the control room when Villar had first been brought aboard. *What do you mean, 'I hardly like to ask'? Apart from the prime minister that man's the most important person ever to come aboard this ship.* So . . .

The doctor was still trying to pinpoint the exact source of his mild concern when sleep rolled over him. Five hours later he rose slowly upward out of deep slumber to the sound of Wallace telling one of his extensive fund of stories. The voice was coming from about four feet away on the other side of the curtain screening his bunk.

Cass's mind turned at once toward Villar and he tensed his muscles to lever his head off the pillow, then relaxed. The others were watching the convalescent man now and they would have woken him if there had been any change for the worse. He could allow himself a few more minutes.

"Then there were these two commanders at the Admiralty," Wallace was saying. "Smith and Brown. Smith was on the circulation list for Brown's memoranda and he read one which he thought was balls, so he drew two circles on it and returned it. Next morning, it was back on his desk with a penciled note on it saying, 'Commander Smith's comments not understood,' so to make it quite clear Smith wrote 'Round objects' and dropped it in his 'out' basket. When it came back to him again Brown had written, 'Who is Round and to what does he object?'"

The mixture of laughter and polite murmurs told Cass who

had and who had not heard it before, then he was listening to the voice of the seaman who acted as wardroom steward.

"Excuse me, sirs. Supper is beef braised with peas and spuds, but if any officer wants anything else with it, he can have it if I've got it, this being a sport patrol."

Various requests were made. Wallace wanted canned tomatoes.

Harding said, "Would you gentlemen mind leaving me alone with Wallace for a few minutes? I'm sorry to inconvenience you, but my cabin is occupied as you know."

Cass listened to the sound of feet shuffling, chairs squeaking on the deck, then silence until Harding spoke again.

"Wallace."

"Sir?"

"You're a very amusing chap."

"Sir."

"Yes, but if I had to choose between having amusing chaps or efficient bores in my ship, I'd take the latter every time."

Wallace said nothing and Harding went on. "I should have spoken to you about this before and I blame myself for not having done so, but we'll get it over with now. When our landing party was ashore in Italy, they radioed a request for an 'artillery stonk' on that truck and you wasted seconds running around like a blasted headless chicken because you hadn't heard the expression before. All right, it isn't in the book so I don't blame you too much for that, or I wouldn't if you didn't give such bloody silly orders yourself."

Harding had not raised his voice, but Cass was aware of his anger from the slow, deep sound of his breathing.

"I don't think I understand, sir," Wallace said.

"Don't worry," Harding told him. "I'm going to explain it to you. When you are on watch on the surface and you want to increase the ship's buoyancy, kindly do so by giving the correct sequence of orders. They are very simple, but they do not include instructing the control-room watch to pump up the tires! Similarly, diving is not best achieved by shouting, *plongez pour la gloire de France!* You may think you're being hysterically funny, Wallace, but think instead of the poor bloody sailor at the other end of the voice pipe and what could happen to all of us if he does the wrong thing because he doesn't know what the hell you're talking about."

"I'm sorry, sir. It won't happen again. Is that all, sir?"

"Except for one thing," Harding said. "If I hear you refer to canned tomatoes just one more time as madwoman's afterbirth, I think I'll *scream!*"

The last word, spoken loudly, was followed by the hiss of rings as the wardroom curtains were jerked aside. Cass supposed that Harding had left and the impression was confirmed by Wallace's long sigh. He decided that it would be diplomatic to feign sleep for another half hour at least and he spent it considering what he had just heard. That it amounted to virtually nothing in navy terms he knew very well. Often he had heard seniors abusing their juniors, raving, cursing, hectoring, in a way which made Harding's words scarcely a rebuke at all if, that was, one ignored the underlying viciousness with which they had been spoken. The little outburst worried Cass only because it was unlike what he knew and had heard of Harding.

Later he recalled hearing that, due to the crowded conditions and the long periods spent at sea, men had been removed from a submarine for little more than the irritation caused to others by the way they used their knife and fork. They went without a stain on their characters, but they went, because harmony on board was of prime importance. Cass concluded that he had been a witness to just such a case of petty animosity and pushed the matter to the back of his mind.

Not so with Harding. He lay in his bunk sweating after the first attack of the shakes he had experienced during the mission, an attack set off by his own uncharacteristic behavior, although he knew it to be far deeper rooted than that. Emotions assailed him from all sides, entwining him until he felt like Laocoön struggling with the sea serpents. His inept handling of a situation, which should have required no more than a quiet caution to an officer who was only unthinkingly stupid, infuriated him, his subsequent loss of composure over something so petty filled him with dismay, and despair gripped him at this sudden proof of the fragility of his newly found equilibrium. Worst of all was the conviction that he had let Gail down.

Other worries seeded themselves in the fertile soil his mind had prepared for them, sprouted, and bloosomed. First his

churlish attitude toward a wounded American who had done
him no wrong, unless to look at something staring him in the
face was a wrong. To have thought of it as the desecration of
a shrine had been childish in the extreme and that piece of self-
knowledge depressed him the more. He would make amends
in that direction, Harding thought, but when the time for that
came, his shyness or embarrassment was to form a barrier
between them.

Half-sitting in the cramped bunk, a pad on his updrawn
knees, he tried to find distraction in bringing his patrol report
notes up to date, but it proved to be a mistake when he saw
that he had reached the part where he had to record the casualties
suffered by the landing party. They brought the fatalities in his
crew to six in two patrols and he wondered if he was a Jonah
because such a figure was simply not typical of submarine
operations. Occasionally a gun action might claim a life, or a
man could be lost overboard, but much more frequently either
nobody was badly hurt or everybody died together. The facts
that he had almost completed his seventh war mission in command without having caused everybody to die together and that
the casualties he had inflicted on the enemy were out of all
proportion to his own did not occur to him.

The hour it took Harding to reach a state of precarious
balance was a bad one, but after it only the pilot noticed anything peculiar in his behavior. He became mildly incensed at
the frequency with which his captain seemed to find it necessary
to check on the navigation. The explanation, that Harding's
repeated visits to the chart table were for the purpose of measuring the constantly decreasing distance he thought separated
him from a girl named Gail Mainwaring, was not available to
the navigating officer.

Across the night sky *Trigger* spoke to Algiers and Algiers spoke
to London. Over land lines the Admiralty spoke to Thayer
Street and Thayer Street spoke to the United States Embassy.
In each case the message was the same. "Conrad is out of
danger."

Ninety minutes after dawn Petty Officer McIntyre picked
up the sound of fast turbines on his sonar and eleven minutes
later Harding made a periscope sighting of the two destroyers

sent to escort them home. When he was certain who they were, he ordered *Trigger* brought to the surface and the small force of warships raced over a flattening sea toward Algiers three hundred miles away.

Illuminated only by the dim gangway lamp, *Trigger* looked darkly sinister as she lay motionless on the night-black water alongside the depot ship. No sound came from her and there was no sign of life on deck. Harding leaned on the depot ship rail staring down at her, waiting for Cass, feeling vaguely disturbed because there had been no message for him from Gail. He was seeking consolation in the thought that she would not have expected him back so soon when Cass joined him.

"Sorry to keep you waiting, sir."

"Hello, doc. You didn't. Got your patient safely stowed in the sick bay?"

"Yes. All's well. They were slightly startled at the thought of giving him alcohol, but they've got the message now. Oh, I've put Norris in there too. Just for the night and a checkup."

Harding nodded. "You did awfully well, you know."

Cass's teeth flashed in the darkness. "That sort of remark could lead to the formation of a mutual admiration society."

"All right," Harding said. "Let's go and report to the 'brass.'"

When they walked into the big cabin, Captain Anderson said, "This is the captain, Lieutenant Harding, and behind him is Surgeon Lieutenant Cass, the ship's temporary medical officer. They're about equally responsible for bringing you Villar alive."

The civilian smiled. The squadron leader winked. Neither volunteered his name. Harding and Cass murmured conventional nothings in unison.

Anderson went on. "Ask your questions, gentlemen. I'd like my chaps to spend as much as possible of what's left of the night in bed."

The squadron leader looked at Cass. "How soon can we have Villar, doctor?"

"Ask me again in three days."

"Why then?"

"Because I may have an answer for you."

"Okay. Now you, Harding. The Americans want to give you a medal. 'The Legion of Merit,' or whatever they call it. Do you accept?"

"No," Harding said. "Ask them to dredge up two and send them to the next of kin of Elleston and Ackroyd. Captain Anderson will tell you who they were."

"Not being very gracious, are you Harding?"

Harding turned away from him and faced his flotilla commander.

"May Cass and I have a word with you, sir?"

There was a frown on Anderson's face, but humor moved behind it. He jerked his head toward the lobby at the entrance to his cabin and they followed him there.

"I'm sorry, sir. I thought we'd better beat a retreat. We're not at our diplomatic best and they don't seem to have anything sensible to ask us."

The humor broke through the frown.

"It's all right, Peter. That RAF type's been getting on my nerves too. The first question was the only important one and they've had their answer to that. Push off, both of you."

"Thank you, sir. Will you need me tomorrow? Well, it's today now. Ginger Donaldson's got my patrol report."

"No. You put your feet up," Captain Anderson said.

CHAPTER 23

HARDING GESTURED TOWARD A BIG PALM. "WAIT
in the shade there. I'll walk the rest of the way."

"Thank you, sir," the driver said and let the jeep coast to
a halt in the shadow of the tree. Harding got out and strode
purposefully toward the building diagonally across the street.
He didn't feel purposeful at all. Shyness had hold of him and
a *frisson* of anticipation selected nerves at random to run along.
Neither sensation was entirely unpleasant.

An army corporal emerged from a temporary wooden gate
house and saluted.

"Can I help you, sir?"

"Yes, please, I'd like to see a Miss Mainwaring."

"Ah. Would you be Lieutenant Harding by any chance?"

"Yes, I would," Harding said and blinked. "Have you got
a message for me?"

"No, sir, but the chief chick—beg pardon, sir—I mean
Senior Commander Shannon wanted to be informed if you
came here. Shall I call her?"

"Yes, please do," Harding told him and watched thoughtfully while the man went into the hut and picked up a telephone.
Women in ATS uniform moved in and out of the big main
door. Most of them glanced curiously at him, some smiled,
and he turned his head self-consciously away from them so that
he was looking down the length of a road heavy with heat. The
Mediterranean summer was growing old, but the North African
sun had lost none of its power. He wondered why he felt
shivery.

"Mrs. Shannon will see you right away, sir. Through the door there, up the stairs facing you, turn left, last room on your right."

The commandeered house was a French colonial mansion with a broad staircase rising gracefully from the great hall to a gallery serving the upper floor. Harding, preoccupied, was nearing the top before he realized that the small figure, bustling to match the rate of his climb, was addressing him.

"I beg your pardon?"

"I asked you, young man, if you were looking for someone."

Absently, "Yes, I am."

Two steps higher up he stopped in obedience to a tugging at his white tropical shirt, looked down at the angry face of the ATS officer beside him, and added, "I'm sorry. That wasn't very informative, was it? I'm going to see Senior Commander Shannon."

The statement seemed to mollify the woman, but she still regarded him suspiciously.

"Oh. Well, I suppose that's all right then, but we can't have just anyone wandering about in here you know."

"No," Harding agreed. "I'm sure we can't."

He went on up the stairs, amused now, wondering what the ejection procedure was, picturing himself marched to the door by enormous black eunuchs, or submerged by a wave of khaki-clad bosoms and hurled down the stairs. The amusement lasted all the way to the threshold of Mrs. Shannon's office and died there.

She was standing on the far side of her desk, the knuckles of the right hand gripping the left, showing white through her tan, a pleasant-looking middle-aged woman who appeared to Harding to be frightened. He paused in the doorway, staring anxiously at her.

"Come in and close the door, Lieutenant Harding."

He did as he was told, noting the tremor in her voice.

"You're looking for Gail Mainwaring, aren't you?"

The fear which seemed to have hold of her reached out and touched him.

"Yes, as I told the sentry. He referred me to you." The words grated in his throat as he uttered them.

"I've been dreading this day," she said.

The probing tentacle of fear encircled him. Gripped.

"What's the matter, Mrs. Shannon? Are you trying to tell me that something's happened to her? Has she been killed?"

She shook her head wordlessly. Harding waited for her to speak, then, when she did not, crossed the room with long strides, rounded the desk, and stood over her.

"Then what *are* you trying to tell me?"

There was a savage intensity in the question which would have astonished anybody aboard *Trigger,* which would have astonished anybody anywhere who knew Harding, but its effect on the woman was to steady her.

"Don't bully me!" she said. "I'm very sorry about this, but shouting at me isn't going to make it any better. It's really nothing to do with me at all and I *won't* be knocked about like a hockey ball between the pair of you. Is that clear?"

The urge to shake her was almost irresistible, but he subdued it and moved a pace back from her.

"Perfectly clear, and I apologize for shouting at you. Now will you please say whatever it is you have to?" Harding's voice no longer had any tone to it and his face was gray.

"All right. She never wants to see you again, but I don't suppose you would settle for just that, would you?"

For a moment he considered the question, then jerked his head in an abrupt negative.

"I can't. Not if there's more. Wondering why and spending the rest of my life arriving at a series of wrong answers wouldn't be much fun. I'm sorry if that makes it hard for you."

"Not hard for me," she told him. "It's only that she rather hoped that you wouldn't have to know why. I can't explain that. You'll have to see for yourself."

She took an envelope from a drawer and handed it to him before adding, "I'm sorry, Peter Harding. I was supposed to have tried harder before giving you whatever that is, but I'm no use at this sort of thing and you wouldn't have believed— Oh *please* don't open it in here!"

Harding nodded and put the torn envelope into a trouser pocket.

"I suppose it's no use asking where she is."

"I only know that she's no longer here," Mrs. Shannon said.

He nodded again, smiled bleakly, and walked out of the room.

At the bottom of the big staircase he stood reading the letter, heedless of the women moving past him because he was unaware of their existence. When he had finished he tore the pages into small pieces and left the building with the morsels of paper clenched in his fist.

"Back to the ship, sir?"

"Yes."

The jeep swung out from under the shade of the palm tree and turned toward the harbor, the driver threading his way cautiously through the throngs of wandering Arabs and small donkeys almost invisible under their improbable loads. Beside him Harding sat with an arm dangling over the side of the vehicle. Every few yards another piece of confetti was released by his fingers to dance for a moment on the warm air before fluttering down on to the dusty road. Then they were all gone.

Harding said, "Pull over and stop."

"Aye aye, sir."

"Right. Walk back to the ship, will you? It's less than half a mile."

"Can't do that, sir. I'm responsible for this jeep."

"Get out." The words were widely spaced giving them an emphasis which Harding's soft voice lacked.

"I'll have to report this, sir."

"Do what you must," Harding said. "No trouble will come to you."

Afterward he had no very clear recollection of the drive to the villa, his mind mercilessly holding up to his eyes the letter his fingers had destroyed so that its words repeated their bitter message over and over again. They drew a vivid picture of Gail and her sister growing up together in a London orphanage, growing defensively closer as their increasing desirability attracted male attention they neither wanted nor could protect themselves against. The clarity lessened not at all when his brain projected the images of the two women's final complete absorption in each other and their relegation of men to sources of income readily available on any West End street. The war had changed the venue but not the source and separation had served only to forge the attachment between the sisters into a permanent bond.

She was sorry, the letter had said, that she had caused him to fall in love with her. That had never been her intention, but he would see now that there could never be any place for him in her life. He saw and in seeing doubted if any door could have been more effectively slammed in his face.

The villa was locked, deserted, and Harding couldn't decide whether or not he was relieved about that. He had half expected to find her there with somebody else, perhaps another woman, and it surprised him a little that he could contemplate either possibility with such cold detachment. For a little while he stood, looking at the building, wondering what he would have done if she had been there, wondering too what he was doing there himself. No answer came and he walked down to the water's edge, taking her stockings from his pocket.

There weren't many pebbles, but he found enough to fill the toes, knotted the gossamer things together and swung them around his head like a bola. Far out to sea they made only the tiniest of splashes and he turned his back, absently brushing sand from his fingers on his white shorts.

"Tell me about Gascoigne and Ryland and Elleston and Norris and all your people."

The tree they had used to shade her delicate skin was four paces away and he could see the indentations made by their bodies under it. There were no indentations.

"Don't just nod off on my tummy. Talk to me."

Suddenly he was running fast toward the villa, taking the line she had followed so often in her beach robe and ridiculous hat, his shoes spraying sand behind him. The door threw him back when he charged it with his shoulder and he stood wincing with the pain, looking about him for the rock they had used to hold the door open when the sea breeze was strong. It was by his feet and he picked it up and carried it around the corner of the building.

Glass exploded and part of the frame was torn away when he hurled it at the window of the room in which he had spent that first long, lonely night. Scrambling through the jagged gap he had made, he leaned against a wall, panting shallowly, unaware of the blood running down his legs.

"I think you must be about cooked now, Harding."

When he had smashed the bed she had toppled him onto, he took his rock into the room they had afterwards shared and broke up the big bed there.

He was wrenching the fittings off the wall in the shower stall when Surgeon Commander Gilmore said, "Hello, Peter. How about coming back aboard for a drink?"

Harding turned slowly and extended an arm at full length, finger pointing at the doctor.

"Don't you fucking well humor me! The bitch is having an incestuous Lesbian affair! With her own sister! It's been going on for years! Bloody funny people you pimp for!"

The outburst was so forthright, so filled with rage, sadness, and accusation, that Gilmore set aside his assumption that he was dealing with a case of complete mental breakdown. The genuine conviction in Harding's voice obliged him to do so.

"Is that what the letter said?" he asked.

"What letter?"

"I telephoned the queen bee at the ATS headquarters when your driver told us you'd been there. She said she had given you a letter from Gail Mainwaring. That's how I knew you would probably be here."

"Oh," Harding said. "I see. Yes, that's what was in the letter."

The strong emotions seemed to have run out of him and he pushed experimentally at the bent piping, but it gave no sign of straightening and he stepped out of the shower.

"That's what was in the letter," he repeated and nodded as if in confirmation of the statement.

"In effect, what you are telling me," Captain Anderson said, "is that La Mainwaring has conned the lot of us."

Gilmore ran his fingers over his pink scalp, unconsciously smoothing the hair which hadn't been there for a decade, frowned thoughtfully, and said, "Hmm."

"What do you mean, 'Hmm'?"

"I don't believe she's conned anybody, George. The word implies misleading others for personal gain, and from what Mrs. Shannon told me about her this morning, she has gained nothing but unhappiness for herself. Having said that, I grant you that she has manipulated us, or Harding anyway. In her report to me all she claimed to have done for him was blot out the memory of strain and give him back his pride for a period of time. Well, it's pretty obvious now that she had her own views on how far we could be trusted to follow her recommendations on the time factor. Not very flattering views either, so she planted her time bomb to make sure we got the message and then went home."

"Conceited baggage," Anderson said.

"More of a tiger mother, I think."

"All right, Freddie, I know you carry a torch for the girl, but the fact remains that she has seen fit to place herself above authority and that could land her in a great deal of trouble if I decide to report this."

"Which you won't," Surgeon Commander Gilmore said. "Even if you did, I bet you'd find that she'd forestalled you by reporting the whole thing herself. Gail Mainwaring doesn't do things by halves."

The other didn't reply and both men sat staring at their feet until Gilmore asked, "What happens to Harding now?"

"I'm sending him home as soon as he's handed *Trigger* over to Williamson. That's what you recommended in the first place if you remember."

"Of course I remember."

"The pity of it is that I was going to send him home anyway after Operation Conrad. None of this pressure was necessary."

"She didn't know that, George."

"Ah, that must have been where I went wrong," Captain Anderson said ponderously. "Remind me in future, Freddie, always to consult wives and sweethearts before I make any decisions regarding their men." For a few seconds he appeared to contemplate what he had just said with satisfaction, then shook his head irritably and added, "What fatuous nonsense I do talk. It was I who involved her in this."

It had been a good farewell party as such things go. Gascoigne had reserved a room over one of the less disreputable bars in Algiers big enough to accommodate all of *Trigger*'s people. Harding had asked Williamson to attend, but the invitation had been smilingly refused.

"No thanks, Peter. I'll take the duty on board and protect my new command with a few chaps from the spare crew. I can't think of anything worse for my morale than spending an evening listening to seventy men say to you 'You're the besht fucking shkipper we ever sherved with.'"

Only nineteen of them had said that, the majority during the last hour, fights, rapidly quelled, had been limited to three and a mere handful of men were sick. When the giggling mob weaved its way aboard the depot ship, the officer of the watch had been tactfully engaged in a close inspection of nothing at the furthest point of the quarterdeck.

Gascoigne, rather pale, woke Harding at nine in the morning.

"Good morning, sir. Permission to die, sir?"

"Granted, John, but do it quietly, will you?"

"Yes, sir. Brought you a cup of coffee. Sorry about this dawn awakening, but you're leaving at noon and Norris wants to see you."

Harding levered himself upright in his bunk, took the coffee, and sipped it.

"Norris? He's nothing to do with me now. He'd better talk to you, or his new captain."

"I told him that, sir, but it's you he wants to see. Something very personal, I gather."

"Oh, very well. Tell him to be here in half an hour. If it's okay by you that is."

"Of course it's okay by me, sir," Gascoigne said, smiled, and left the cabin.

Shaved, dressed, and with aspirin inside him, Harding felt a little better. He tried to calculate how much he had drunk the night before, but abandoned the exercise. It was impossible even to guess when partly finished drinks had repeatedly been taken from him and fresh ones thrust into his hands.

Sitting on the edge of his bunk, he picked up the scale model of *Trigger* he had been presented with. Eighteen inches long, it had been machined from a solid bar of metal by the engine-room artificers in less than twenty-four hours. They must, he thought, have worked in relays to complete it in that time. Every detail was perfect, including the imperfections. The periscope standards bent out of true, the four-inch gun slightly canted and pointing over the side, and the Oerlikon cannon and its platform missing altogether, a tiny area of jagged metal marking where they had been. The little plaque set into the polished wooden base which supported the model bore the legend: "To the Skipper from the crew of Harding's Convoy Killer." He was still playing with the thing like a small boy when Norris arrived.

Norris was growing a beard because he couldn't shave with a plaster on one cheek and a wad of gauze taped to the other. Harding listened gravely to a confession which included the twice-repeated phrase "cowardice in the face of the enemy," nodding his head at intervals when the narrative showed signs of faltering. When it was over he gestured toward the only chair and, when Norris was seated, lay back on the bunk with his hands behind his head.

His first reaction was one of resentment that this new problem should be thrust upon him when the eleventh hour of his command of *Trigger* had already run its course, but it was extinguished beneath a flood of self-contempt. Norris had had to live with his failure just as he himself was living with what he saw as his own, and he owed him at least the consideration of a fellow sufferer.

"Norris."

"Sir?"

"Mr. Elleston and Sergeant Ackroyd were already dead when you left them, weren't they?"

"Yes, sir, but the Yank wasn't. Marine Cooper had to bring him off." Norris not meeting his eyes, but his voice calmly stubborn.

"Cooper mentioned nothing of this to me."

"He didn't know I'd run, sir."

And that, Harding knew, had been said much too quickly, but he didn't pursue the matter. Instead he asked, "Are you frightened at sea? During depth charging and times like that?"

"Scared shitless, sir, but not frightened, if you know what I mean."

Harding knew what he meant. Despite the apparent contradiction of the strange lower-deck terminology, the fine distinction was not lost on him. To be scared shitless was acceptable, even natural. To be frightened was neither of those things.

"In that case," he said, "I suggest you stick to submarining and stop volunteering for things you're no good at."

Norris looked at him then, his face puzzled.

"Is that all, sir? Aren't you going to turn me in? They shoot people like me, don't they?"

"Everybody has his breaking point, Norris. When that point is reached, it only makes sense to shoot whoever has broken if it persuades others to postpone breaking too. It doesn't do the man himself much good."

It seemed to take Norris a long time to consider the statement, but finally he shook his head.

"Nice of you to put it like that, sir, but it's not all true, is it? Not everybody has that breaking point. You don't, for a start. We all know that. You just keep chasing the buggers no matter what they do and that's what I should have done."

What flimsy evidence a reputation could be built on, Harding thought and remembered Gascoigne saying, "They think you're a sort of amiable icicle." It didn't matter. Norris had given him the opening he needed.

"Then you are all very much mistaken," he said. "I'm not being sent home to learn about new technical developments as you've been told. I'm being sent home because I can't take it anymore. That I consider to be letting the side down much worse than you losing your head for a minute at a job I should never have sent you on in the first place. I should have asked for more commandos."

Harding swung his legs over the side of the bunk and stood up before adding, "Anyway, I no longer consider myself a fit person to judge another's conduct, but I will express the opinion that there's nothing much wrong with you, Norris, so stop eating your heart out. None of our people died because of *you*."

Later he wondered if he had accented the last word for Norris's benefit or if it had been a reflection of his own emotional state, but there was no time to think about it then because Norris had begun to speak.

"Wasn't your fault . . ."

"Norris!"

"Sir?"

"We know each other's secret now. Shall we just keep it that way?"

"I think I'd like that, sir."

"Right," Harding said. "Go away and help your new captain to sink some bastard."

His head was aching again, but he didn't move from the spot he had been occupying when the sailor had left. He was thinking about his approach to naval discipline, an unorthodox approach for which he had occasionally been criticized on the grounds that his punishment book had virtually nothing in it. There had been no reason to put much in it. The rules had been designed to counter the thoughtless or rebellious acts of men of a vast, largely conscript navy, not really for the cream, the volunteers who manned ninety percent of the Submarine Service. It was rarely necessary to treat them as dangerous delinquents because each knew that he mattered as an individual and that as an individual, his own stupidity or carelessness could destroy both him and all his shipmates. There was very little stupidity or carelessness and consequently, little need for punishment or the outward trappings of authority.

Harding was aware that he was laxer than most in his treatment of offenders, but was satisfied that he was right to be so when dealing with intelligent men, particularly those who demonstrated genuine regret, because they repaid him with devotion to the ship. That a degree of rationalization could have existed in his handling of Norris he knew, but was certain that neither Norris nor the war effort would have benefited from official action resulting, at least, in a prison sentence.

He sighed, threw a battered suitcase on to the bunk, and began to pack. When he had finished he was left with the big folder of drawings, drawings he had not looked at since he had read the letter, drawings he did not look at now. There was no string, so he pulled the cord from his pyjama trousers, rolled the folder into a tube, and tied it tightly. Then he went out on deck.

The tube floated when he dropped it over the side, drifting slowly along the depot ship's waterline. Harding followed it anxiously until it began to sink, fading gradually from his sight, leaving only an immense sadness.

When Gascoigne drove him away from the harbor toward

the airport, *Trigger* was lying at her moorings, waiting patiently
for someone else to steer her into battle. He didn't look at her.
He was trying unsuccessfully to view with sympathy the plight
of two underprivileged sisters driven into each other's arms by
social forces over which they had had no control.

Gibraltar was a howling desolation peopled by ghosts. Gascoigne grinning a welcome at him. Norris carrying his bag. A
crew to greet. Officers waiting for him so that they could start
their celebration party. A ship to be made ready for sea. The
wonder that was Gail Mainwaring in his mind. Not so many
days before, when he had stood on this very spot, all that had
been his. Loneliness settled around Harding like a damp mist.

"Want a lift into town, chum?"

He turned his head toward the pilot of the Hudson bomber
in which he had flown from Algiers. The plane was going no
farther and he had to make other arrangements for his onward
passage to England.

"Yes please. I'd be very grateful."

Picking up his suitcase, he followed the aircrew across the
tarmac to an RAF truck.

"What are your orders exactly, Harding?"

It had taken him some time to locate the lieutenant whose
duties included looking after officers in transit who had nothing
sufficiently important to do at the other end to warrant priority,
but he had succeeded just before the office closed.

"To return to England and report to my admiral on arrival."

"And he is?"

"Flag officer (Submarines). Look, Algiers must have told
you I was coming. In fact I know they did."

"Oh, you're that bloke, are you? Sorry. I'd locked the file
away for the night a couple of seconds before you walked in.
Can't do anything for you immediately, I'm afraid, but there's
a cruiser coming through here on her way home in a day or
two. You could go in her."

Harding knew better than to ask the name of the cruiser or
where she was coming from and confined himself to the question "When?"

"Not allowed to say, old boy. You're not in a hurry, are
you?"

"No," Harding said. "I'm not in a hurry."

The day or two stretched to five, then Harding awoke on the sixth morning and saw the heavy cruiser *Sutherland* lying against the mole. He went aboard an hour later, almost at the precise instant that the keel of the flying boat carrying John Villar cut a lengthening V of white water across the surface of Poole Harbor in England.

Villar was very tired after the long flight which had taken him from Algiers to Casablanca, to Lisbon in neutral Portugal, then far out over the Atlantic to avoid German fighter planes based in western France, before turning in toward the English coast. A still slightly surprised Surgeon Lieutenant Cass, dressed in a civilian suit and carrying a passport to avoid internment by the Portuguese, was with him. Villar liked Cass, not only for saving his life, but for being likable, a quality with which he found it difficult to credit the British.

An ambulance with its crew and a car with three men standing by it were waiting for them on the jetty.

"Jesus! Look at the reception committee, will you?" Villar said. His voice sounded strained. "That's all I need. What the hell's going on, Christopher? Limey heavyweights sitting outside my door every place we stop. Now this lot. What do they think I am? The second coming or something?"

Cass smiled, shrugging his shoulders. "I've no idea, but I'd guess from his clothes that the man heading this way now is one of yours, not ours. Your leg's hurting, isn't it?"

"Some."

"All right. Leave the talking to me and don't get yourself steamed up."

Villar nodded, but when the man said, "Welcome back, Professor Villar," he snapped, "Who the hell are you?"

"My name's Harkness, Professor. I'm with the OSS."

"Well, bully for the OSS. I've been away a long time, so I'm not familiar with all these initials people have taken to throwing around in this war, but if those stand for the Obstetric Surgeons' Society, I'm not in need of that kind of attention. Anyway, my own doctor is right here beside . . ."

"Shut up, John," Cass said, and to the other American,

"Let's get him into the ambulance. He's been tetchy ever since he started to get better. I'd like to ride with him myself and nobody else, please."

"You're the boss, doctor," Harkness told him and waved for the ambulance crew.

Villar was growing sleepy from the effect of the pill Cass had made him swallow.

"What's the OSS, Christopher?"

"Not sure. I believe it's some new organization your people have. Something like our MI6. You know about them, don't you?"

"Shit, yes!" Villar said. "I know about those bastards. So it's out of the frying pan into the fire for me, is it?"

"I don't know, John."

"Well, try to find out what they want of me, will you buddy? It's worrying me sick."

"I'll try. Incidentally, you never told me you were a professor."

"You know something?" Villar said. "I'd genuinely forgotten."

He fell asleep then and was still sleeping when they carried him into St. George's Hospital in London.

As a matter of courtesy, and to give himself something to do, Harding offered his services as a watch-keeping officer during the voyage home to the first lieutenant of *Sutherland*. The man was an aging lieutenant commander unlikely to progress beyond that rank.

"Nice of you, Harding. Gratefully accepted. I'll fit you into the roster after we sail tomorrow morning."

The Straits of Gibraltar might have been the dividing line between summer and autumn. *Sutherland* was burying her bows into the long Atlantic rollers before Cape Trafalgar was abeam and dawn revealed a heaving gray sea indistinguishable in color from the overcast above it. The tannoy public-address system instructed the ship's company to change from white uniforms to blue.

At breakfast Harding sat at the long wardroom table eating cornflakes and powdered milk. His thoughts were far away and he didn't notice the curious glances of the people sitting opposite him until another officer joined them.

"Dear God!" the newcomer said. "We've got a bloody hero on board!"

He looked up at that to meet the gaze of half a dozen pairs of eyes and wonder why they were staring at him. Then the answer came. He had joined the ship the previous day in white tropical kit with which medal ribbons were never worn, but they were fixed permanently to the blue uniform jacket he was wearing now. Without speaking, Harding returned his attention to his cornflakes.

The first lieutenant summoned him to his cabin an hour later.

"Are you a submariner by any chance, Harding?"

"Yes, sir."

"Ah, we guessed you might be from your medals. Why don't you wear dolphins on your chest like the Americans so we could tell at once?"

"I don't know, sir. We just don't."

"Well, never mind. By the way, the captain sends his compliments and thanks you for your offer, but thinks it might be best if you didn't keep watch. I expect he's afraid you might pull the plug on us, or whatever it is you chaps do when you dive. You'll understand, I'm sure."

"No, not really," Harding said. "But have it your own way."

Most of the following days he spent in his cabin, feeling at a lower ebb than he would have believed possible, wondering if there was anyone else left to reject him.

CHAPTER 24

JOHN VILLAR DECIDED TO WALK TO THAYER STREET
for his debriefing. He wanted to see something of London and
to test the strength of his injured leg. London was a mess.
Sandbags, millions of them, forming antiblast walls around
doorways, great beams of timber supporting damaged buildings, scaffolding and hoardings against others, gaps where
buildings had been. And this area, he had been told, had suffered only slightly. Barrage balloons like cartoon elephants
floating above were glinting in the sunshine, antiaircraft guns
pointed skyward everywhere, and there were uniforms, uniforms, uniforms. He had never seen so many, but nobody
seemed to mind that he wasn't wearing one. People smiled at
him, made way for him, and steel-helmeted police held up the
traffic for him while he crossed streets. He supposed it was
because of his limp and his two canes.

He got to the Department's building sooner than he had
expected, more than half an hour before his appointment, and
decided to walk on, then changed his mind because his leg was
aching. They would, he thought, probably find him somewhere
to sit down until he was wanted. As he turned toward the
sandbagged entrance a girl in what he now knew to be the
uniform of an officer in the British Women's Royal Naval
Service came out of it.

Her tricorn hat was tilted over her nose at what he guessed
was a nonregulation angle, the hair under it wound into a neat
roll around the back of her neck was red, and she was very
beautiful. Villar stood, propped on his sticks, watching her as

269

she passed him, aware from the faint smile on her lips that his stare had been noted and was accepted as her due rather than resented.

"Hey!" he said.

She faltered in her stride, stopped, and turned around.

"Are you shouting at me?"

Slanting hazel eyes. Or were they green? A cool, very self-possessed British voice.

"I didn't mean to shout. It's just that you're even better-looking than he made you."

Yes, the eyes were green, green and watchful. Or were they hazel?

"We all know about Americans over here now," she said, "but you're something new. You must be the fastest pass maker east of the Rockies. I've never been told that I had improved on the Lord's work before."

He blinked, then grinned at her. "Yes, I suppose that was a pretty ambiguous statement of mine. I wasn't referring to the Creator. Just Peter Harding. You *are* his girl, aren't you?"

A look he couldn't identify on her face and a small voice saying, "Am I?"

"Well, if you have a twin sister maybe you're not. The sister I have in mind has a mole, or a birthmark, or something on her left hip."

The eyes were green, green and blazing.

"What *fun* you must have had discussing me!"

She had whirled and was ten yards away, walking fast, before he jerked himself into motion, stumbling after her, suddenly unable to coordinate the movement of his legs and sticks.

"Don't go!" he called. "Don't go! You don't understand. Let me set the record straight!"

For several seconds she went on her way, then halted abruptly as though she were on parade, looking straight ahead of her. When he reached her side, her face was as expressionless and as tearstained as a French restaurateur outside Algiers had once seen it. She began to speak before he had recovered his breath.

"You're an extremely good-looking man, Mr. American. Let's go to bed. Now! I'm just in the mood for some really torrid sex. Would you like that?"

"Yes, I would, but I have to decline."

"Why? Nobody ever declined before. I'll show you my birthmark, and when you see Peter Harding again you can compare notes on my performance. Come to bed!"

Villar looked at her averted face, then around him at the buildings.

"Is that place with 'The Red Lion' written on it a pub?"

"Yes."

"Then that's where we're going," he said. "Not to bed. You are going to sit down, have a drink, and listen to me even if I have to drive you there with these sticks. March!"

She shrugged disinterestedly, but walked beside him, adjusting her pace to his clumsy progress.

"What happened to your leg?"

"That's part of the story," he told her. "What do you want to drink?"

"That depends on what they've got. There's a war on."

"Yeah. I heard."

They sat at a small round table, its dark brown top disfigured by the circular marks left by glasses and scarred with cigarette burns. Both had a tankard of watery beer in front of them.

"I was in Italy for a while, working for you people," Villar said. "Then it got to be time for me to be pulled out and they sent this submarine for me. This is getting to sound like dangerous talk, so although it's over now I won't tell you the sub's name. It . . ."

"It was called *Trigger* and the second in command is John Gascoigne who's rather special to Peter and the coxswain's name is Ryland and there's a nice boy called Elleston and a sailor named Norris who gets into trouble and Ackroyd who's a huge marine who makes Peter laugh and—and—oh, damn you!"

Her face was raised toward the ceiling and the slanting eyes were closed. She had stopped crying, but hadn't bothered to wipe the tearstains from her cheeks.

He watched her for a moment before saying, "Yes, you should damn me. Elleston and Ackroyd were killed getting me away."

She nodded without either lowering her head or opening her eyes. "That's right. Pile it on. Overcome with remorse, our two heroes sob on each other's shoulders. You tell Peter that war is hell and that your nerves are all shot to bits and he tells you that that's funny because so are his but that there's this hot piece Gail Mainwaring who can make it stop hurting and being with Intelligence you find out where she works and..."

"Shut up, you stupid cow." It was said softly, but it penetrated. Gail Mainwaring opened her eyes, looked briefly at the ceiling, then down at Villar.

"That's another first," she said. "I've never been called a cow before either."

"Pretty name."

"What? Stupid cow?"

"Gail Mainwaring."

"You make it sound as though it's the first time you've heard it."

"It *is* the first time I've heard it."

"You said that as if it were true, but..."

"Listen, Miss Mainwaring," Villar said, "why don't you hear what I brought you to this place to tell you, instead of yapping at me?"

He found himself meeting the brooding regard so familiar to Harding, waited for her to say something, then when she did not, began to speak himself.

He talked for several minutes before saying, "When I recovered consciousness, the first thing I saw was the back of this guy's head. He was sitting in this cabin beside the bunk I was in, looking at a whole raft of drawings of a girl—of you. There were maybe twenty of them. He just looked at them one after the other, then looked at them again. I did too and got to know you pretty well by sight. They were very well done. They were more than well done, they were done—hell, I dunno—I guess they were done with love."

Gail interrupted his story for the first time. "You're a romantic, Mr. American." She might not have spoken.

"Then," Villar said, "I have to go and open my big yap and say how great you look or somesuch and that finished a beautiful friendship before it had gotten started. He sort of froze, locked his drawings away, yelled for the doctor, said I was welcome aboard, and beat it. I scarcely saw him after that except once a day when he came and looked at me like I was a piece of freight he was thinking of jettisoning."

"But didn't you talk at all?"

"Not so that you'd notice. The next day I asked him if he'd drawn the pictures and he tells me yes and wants to know if I have any objection, so I shut up. After that we didn't push it beyond 'good morning.'"

"How very nasty of him. I hope somebody talked to you."

"Oh sure. The whole darned crew would have come visiting if the doctor had let them. I was a curiosity. As it was, I got to know a number of them quite well."

Villar drank some of his beer, then went on. "Harding nasty? I don't think so. I think he's a mixed-up kid who isn't liking himself too well right now. The exec, or whatever they call him in the British navy, the man Gascoigne you mentioned, he talked with me often. Very careful to protect his skipper, but I learned a bit from what he didn't say. My guess would be that Harding's blaming himself for the death of two men he liked and isn't exactly crazy with delight about the Yank he got in exchange for them. Add to that the Yank taking a long look at his dreamworld and it doesn't surprise me that I lost his vote as man of the year. Make sense to you?"

"Oh yes," Gail said. "Now that I know about his dreamworld. I didn't realize that he could draw like that. In fact I didn't know that he could draw at all. And there was me refusing to give him a photograph. How silly."

She sat, elbows on the table, stirring her untasted beer with the tip of a forefinger until Villar asked, "Does that mean that you never intended it to be permanent?"

Gail frowned, still stirring the beer. "I don't see that it's any business of yours, but no, it was not intended to be permanent. It was a—well, never mind what it was. I left Algiers to make it a clean break and left a message for him so he wouldn't want to try to find me again. I suppose you people would call it a Dear John letter, except it wasn't quite as straightforward as that."

The circular action of her finger seemed to absorb her for a moment, then she flicked it dry, sat back, and put her hands in her lap. The American was staring at her intently.

He said, "That almost certainly explains why he cracked up

after we got to Algiers. I heard the doctors talking about it when they thought I was asleep."

"He did, did he? That's good."

Villar wondered if he had ever heard a more glacial voice, thought for a moment about the field marshal's mistress he had killed, then forgot her. She had never achieved as icy a tone as this woman.

"Seems he smashed up some beach house or other."

For a second the beautiful face in front of him contorted until it was almost ugly before relaxing into a mask.

"That's even better," she said.

He raised his eyebrows questioningly and lowered them again, sighing as though he were tired.

"So they took his submarine away from him and are sending him back to this dump. I suppose that's just great!"

"It'll do very well," she said.

There was something hypnotic about the slanting eyes. He broke the visual contact angrily, looked in turn at the six other people in the dreary bar, then back at her.

"Miss Mainwaring?"

"Yes?"

"I apologize to all cows. You're not even in the same grade. I don't care much for Peter Harding, but God protect him from a bitch like you!"

She nodded. "Now we're back on familiar ground. That I *have* been called before." A further emphatic nod as if to confirm the accuracy of the statement, then Gail Mainwaring stood up.

"You're a nice man, Mr. American," she said. "Oh, and thank you for not taking me to bed." Stooping, she kissed him hard on the mouth and walked out of the bar.

Confused, and angry because he was confused, John Villar levered himself to his feet. The barman had once worked in the dock area and could read trouble in men's eyes. It took him only a moment to recall that there *was* a bottle of Scotch somewhere that he kept for special customers. He didn't even object when the American raised his glass and said, "To hell with the goddam British." It seemed unwise.

Gail Mainwaring sat in the bed-sitting-room the Department had found for her and cried with quiet determination for twenty minutes. Then she washed her face and wrote a letter. The reply reached her three days later.

For a long time she stared at the envelope with the familiar writing on it before ripping it open with a nervous jerk. She skimmed the preamble, then read carefully.

"Yes, my old beetroot top," the second paragraph began, "I did know what you have been doing for the last three years. Couldn't help it really because, in an indirect sort of way, I've been one of your superiors during that period, but keep that to yourself. Anyway, it was kind and courageous of you to tell me. I am not shattered, appalled, revolted, ashamed, or any of the other expressions dotted about in your letter. On the other hand I won't pretend that I'm overcome with delight, but that doesn't stop me being proud of you. In war one uses the best means available for destruction and healing and you have had an astonishing capacity for both in you ever since you stopped being a nauseatingly conceited schoolgirl. My prayer is that your very special attributes don't turn you into another of this war's casualties and leads me to the question you ask, although why you bother to ask it is beyond me.

"You marry the poor bastard of course. If you love him, as you say you do, I don't follow the logic of punishing him for things you have done. But perhaps I'm being naive and if that's the case you can put it down to the fact that the only woman I ever half understood was your mum. If he loves you, and I can't imagine that he would not after so much exposure to you, he won't give a tinker's damn about your past. Somebody has got to make an honest woman of you sometime. Why not him?

"I dote unashamedly,

"Your fond parent.

"P.S. For a scarlet woman you have the damndest puritanical code of ethics.

"P.P.S. I know his boss, if you need help in making contact."

Gail Mainwaring smiled sunnily and burst into tears.

When he reached the top of the ladder, John Villar took his sticks back from the American sergeant, propped himself on them, and twisted round in the doorway of the converted Lib-

erator bomber which was to carry him to Iceland on the first
stage of his flight home to the States. Surgeon Lieutenant Cass,
the wind whipping his raincoat about his legs, stood beside the
control tower near the end of the Scottish airstrip, waving an
arm. Villar raised one of his sticks, swung it back and forth
above his head like a metronome, then turned away and hobbled
to the seat next to Harkness. The door of the plane slammed
shut.

Ten miles out over the Atlantic, he inclined his head toward
Harkness and shouted to make himself heard above the thunder
of the four big Pratt and Whitney engines.

"Okay. You've stalled long enough. What in hell is all this
about?"

Harkness said something he didn't catch.

"What?"

"You'll be told when you're told, Professor, and that won't
be until you're back in the U.S. of A. under tight security
wraps. Just lay off the questions, will you? They're getting
rather boring."

"Getting *rather* boring, are they? Now you're making noises
like the goddam British."

"How was that again?"

"Oh, skip it," Villar said.

Villar took a pint flask from his coat pocket, poured brandy
into its cap, drank it, not offering the flask to Harkness. He
wondered without much interest what his nerves would be like
when the doctors began to dry him out. The thought brought
back a memory of Harding's closed-in face and his subsequent
breakdown in Algiers, then, as if through divine revelation, he
understood with absolute certainty what Gail Mainwaring had
been trying to do. Realizing that among the strange people he
had left behind there were two he positively liked pleased him.

Filling the cap of his flask again, "Good luck Christopher
Cass, and good luck pretty girl," he said.

Nobody heard him over the roar of the engines.

He drank the brandy.

The admiral, hands in his jacket pockets, thumbs outside, stood
gazing downward through a window of the building named
Northways, the London headquarters of the Submarine Service.

He stayed like that until the red-haired girl had disappeared from his sight.

Then, "I think I've just been seduced," he said.

"You could be forgiven for that, sir. From what I saw, you didn't stand much of a chance."

He chuckled. "I mean seduced away from those matters which should be receiving my undivided attention."

"Of course. What else?"

Slowly he turned away from the window and toward the blond Wren officer with the calm eyes who was his confidential secretary, chauffeuse, or flag lieutenant as the situation demanded. Over some things she was also his counselor.

Grave-faced now he asked, "Do you think he's strong enough, Susan?"

She shrugged her shoulders. "In character? I only know from his file, but it's a little late to worry about that, isn't it? We got him into this position for reasons of our own, so we owe him the chance of finding out the answer to your question himself."

"We? It was hardly your responsibility."

"Mine as much as yours," she told him. "You asked my advice and acted on it when you gave Captain Anderson your authority to proceed."

He appeared to consider the statement for a moment, then nodded his head.

"Coming home in *Sutherland*, isn't he?"

"Yes, sir. ETA Portsmouth first light tomorrow."

"Good," the admiral said. "And there's a 'do' at the palace the following day. That gives us just enough time. Now, this is what I want done."

CHAPTER 25

"HARDING," HARDING SAID. "I MADE AN APPOINT-
ment by telephone yesterday to see the admiral at 0830 this
morning."

The cool blond Wren officer in the immaculately cut uniform
glanced at the clock, Harding's face, his medal ribbons, and
the two gold stripes on his sleeve. Somewhere in her survey
she found something that made her smile a small private smile.

"Would you wait over there please, Lieutenant Harding?"

He sat on one of a group of chairs, watching her, but she
neither looked at nor spoke to him again until the minute hand
of the clock pointed precisely to the half hour.

Then: "You may go in now, Lieutenant Harding."

Supercilious bitch, he thought, stood up, straightened his
jacket, and walked into the room of Flag officer (Submarines).

"Hello, Harding."

"Good morning, sir."

"I suppose you've come to ask me to give you *Trigger*
back."

"Well no, sir. I know you can't do that when I've just
handed her over to Williamson, but I was thinking during the
trip home that you might consider me for one of the new
construction jobs going to the Far East. I'll be all right again
by the time she's ready to sail."

The man sitting on the far side of the big desk was small
and the gold bands on his sleeves reached almost to his elbows.
He shook his head.

"It's not on. Not for the foreseeable future. I think you know
that."

"But, sir, I . . ."

"Harding!"

"Sir?"

"The doctors say no, your immediate superiors say no, and I say no. Can you give me any reason why I should reverse their and my decision?"

Harding didn't speak and the admiral said, "Oh for God's sake, boy, stop standing there looking surly. You've had a good inning and made a very reasonable score. Go off on leave and report back here six weeks from today. I'll have arranged an appointment for you by then."

"I don't know anything about surface ships, sir. I'd be useless in one."

"That's an excellent reason for making you find out about them, but perhaps you have some other suggestion."

The idea came to Harding unbidden and out of nowhere. He certainly hadn't considered it before.

"Would there be any room for me as an instructor on the officers' submarine initiation course, sir?"

A faint smile appeared on the older man's face.

"You don't rate yourself very highly, do you Harding? Never mind the new entries. What I want you to do is take over Franklin's half of the Commanding Officers' Qualifying Course. It's time he went back to sea, and as you seem to have some knowledge of how to destroy the enemy you can try your hand at passing it on to the young hopefuls. All right?"

To have half of the trainee submarine commanders in his care and under his instruction was, Harding knew, more of a sacred trust than a simple vote of confidence in him. He was pleased, or as pleased as he seemed capable of being about anything nowadays.

"Thank you very much indeed, sir," he said.

"Good. That's that. You're due to collect your medals this morning, I believe."

"That's right, sir."

"Good show. Carry on, Harding."

"Aye aye, sir."

"One moment."

Harding turned back from the door and approached the big desk again. The admiral was holding a small buff-colored ticket in his right hand, an envelope in his left. He looked from one to the other as though comparing them. There was a long silence before he said, "This is none of my business, but I took the liberty of getting you a guest ticket. You're entitled to two, but one seemed enough."

"That was kind of you, sir, but there's nobody I want to take."

"Well, there's someone who wants to be taken. The Marquis of Trent's only child. Of course what you do about it is entirely up to you."

"I don't understand, sir. I don't know any marquises. Or their children."

The ticket was lying on the desk now and Harding read it upside down. "Buckingham Palace. Admit one to witness the Investiture (at 10:15 A.M.) Clarendon, Lord Chamberlain."

He looked questioningly at the admiral, heard him say, "I think you do, my boy," and watched while he placed the envelope beside the ticket. He did it slowly as though it was a card he doubted the wisdom of playing.

The inscription, "The Lady Abigail Mainwaring," stared up at him and Harding felt himself sway. Touching the desk with his fingertips steadied him and he stood very still, unable to speak, not yet believing, but wanting desperately to believe. Unknown to him, his face registered doubt, hope, confusion, and elation in rippling succession. The admiral read the expressions and sighed thankfully.

"It's a relief to me that you think so visibly, Harding. I was getting into where-angels-fear-to-tread territory there, but she's a very persuasive young woman. Before you collect her downstairs she has two messages for you. You are never, on pain of death, to call her Abigail, and the letter she left for you in Algiers was a tissue of lies. What these messages mean I have no idea, but no doubt you can interpret them. Now, if it's not asking too much, I'd like to be allowed to carry on with the war."

The book of the future which had been snatched from Harding was back with him and the frontispiece glowed in his mind. Long-striding legs, red hair floating, crazy, wonderful eyes.

"Carry on, sir. Carry on by all means," he said and laughed for the first time since Elleston and Ackroyd had died.